CHOCOLATE FOR THE POOR

A STORY OF RAPE IN 1805

by David Beasley

Prejudices in politics insert themselves into the human mind in the same manner as they are seen in matters of religion and morals. - James Sullivan.

DAVUS PUBLISHING

My thanks to Angela Ariss, David Adams, Charles Jambor and Christopher Lee for reading and commenting on the ms. and in particular to Edward Greenspan, Q.C. for suggesting valuable editorial changes.

Beasley, David, 1931-
    Chocolate for the poor: a story of rape in 1805

ISBN   0-915317-04-4

    I. Title.

PS8553.E14C46 1995   C813'.54   C95-900367-3
PR9199.3.B3765C46   1995

DAVUS PUBLISHING
DAVUS SUM/ NON OEDIPUS

AMERICAN ORDERS: CANADIAN ORDERS:
P O BOX 1101   150 NORFOLK ST. S.
BUFFALO, N.Y.14213-7101   SIMCOE, ON N3Y2W2

ONE

It was the eighth of June 1805 in Windsor, Massachusetts.

Ephraim Wheeler twisted convulsively onto his side and stared out the open window at the white streaks of dawn across the black. His tormented sleep left a dull pain throughout his body. He had no work again this day.

Betsy and young Ephraim were asleep in the next room; the baby slept near the bed on the mother's side. Ephraim had moved his family between villages in these Berkshire hills until William Martin took them in.

He lifted himself on one elbow to look round at his wife sleeping beside him. He resisted an impulse to strike her. She was the reason for his unhappiness. The law bound them together fourteen years ago. He felt chained to a wheel that carried him through cycles of argument, violence, separation, and unhappiness. He could not control his destiny. His situation controlled him, leading him into ways that he feared.

Harriette sat up suddenly. She brushed her hand tightly over her face and stepped onto the floor.

It was William Martin's sick wife who was worrying her. Ephraim watched her leave the room in her night shawl. He despised having to be beholden to the Martins. They had taken in their furniture while he and Harriette went their separate ways to earn enough to bring the family together again. They had to be humble in other people's homes.

Harriette reappeared at the doorway and stared at him. Her fair-skinned beauty had dissolved over the years into worried lines and nervous twitches. He thought she concealed her disgust for him in her matter-of-fact tone.

"Ephraim, go for the doctor. Will says she's worse."

He grunted and fell back onto the pillow. "Tell him to go himself."

"Please, Ephraim! She could be dyin'."

CHOCOLATE

A cool breeze carrying the fresh smell of early summer stirred a longing of pain and desire within him. He swung out of bed, threw off his nightshirt, and, stretching, felt the litheness of his muscles and the reassurance that comes from the athletic physique of a forty-four year old. Harriette's eyes traveled over him disinterestedly. He glared at her and watched her turn and disappear into the Martins' side of the house.

The jagged scar on his upper arm suddenly took him back to his childhood and to the hatred he saw in the face of his master. It disturbed him that he should remember it now. He washed himself with the water in the basin and enjoyed the cold tingling in his skin. Harriette was right that he should fetch the doctor. It was smart to show good neighborliness. He pulled on his breeches and put on the silk shirt with the fancy ruffles that he got in France.

He stepped quietly into the next room where Harriette had heated the water for him and went close to Betsy's bed. Her eyes were open. She was watching him. He nodded and took the water back to his room where he shaved. Betsy had a good full figure for a thirteen-year-old. She was prettier than her mother.

When he finished dressing, he went through the door on the other side of the room and encountered Martin sitting and brooding in the semi-light. He was a hefty farmer, strong-jawed, and serious. Ephraim, who had been to sea and knew the world, despised him as a dullard--but not openly.

"Hear she's doin' poorly," he said. "I'll get the doctor."

Martin looked up sadly. "Thankyee, Ephraim. I can't leave 'case she needs me." He looked sharply, suddenly mistrustful. "You won't delay?"

"I'm off!" Ephraim smiled and buttoned his frock coat as he pushed open the front door with his shoulder.

By the time he saddled his horse, the sun edged into the sky, and the trees cast off their heavy shadows.

Betsy watched her father ride by the window. Her fear went away with him. She listened until the sound of hoof beats died away in the distance, and then got up to wash and dress herself.

Little Ephraim slept peacefully in the straw matting. He looked so small and helpless, like the baby, that she felt protective towards him. Since she knew her mother was caring for Mrs. Martin, she had the responsibility of fixing the breakfast, after which she'd wake up her brother.

Betsy had two dresses that she washed and wore alternately. Both needed some mending, but she had no time for her own clothes. She spent her time on household chores while her mother went out to work. She had barely put on her petticoat when the baby began to cry, and she had to rush to put on her dress and run barefoot into the bedroom only to see that her mother was already bending over the crib. Betsy, like her mother, reacted immediately to a child's call ever since her youngest brother tipped a cauldron of boiling water off the stove and was scalded to death. There was the painful memory of that in the look that passed between them. The baby was sucking contentedly at Harriette's breast.

"I'll fix the coffee, Ma. Shall I toast us corn fritters?"

Harriette nodded. "Your Daddy's takin' the day off. It'd be nice for him."

As Betsy returned to finish dressing, Harriette called to her to help her move her Daddy's bed after she had put on the coffee.

A chilling fear swept over Betsy. Ephraim would not want his bed moved. Betsy foresaw the shouting, the threats, and the anger that would blight the day. But she had learned to suffer the quarreling of her parents in silence and to shut out the hatred as if it were a foreign element that was passing through the household.

By the time she had the coffee heating and the fritters toasting, her mother had dragged the bed to the doorway. Young Ephie woke up and scrambled to help his mother. Betsy helped them to tip the bed and drag it through the doorway. They found space for it along the wall.

3

"Now, I've got to dress," Harriette said, but she sat on the bed to catch her breath.

"Ma." Ephie sat beside her and put his arm as far as he could reach about her waist. "Are you goin' away again?"

"Just for a few hours, dear," she smiled at him and cuddled him to her. "No different today than every day. How strange you are today!" She kissed his forehead. "Ma won't leave you. Never again."

Betsy felt tears come to her eyes, and she turned away to mind the coffee. She heard a horse snort at the window and her father entering the house. She took the fritters off the fire and readied the cups for the coffee, almost dropping them in her nervousness.

"What the Sam Hell's goin' on?" Ephraim demanded, his face stretched in disbelief.

"Get dressed," Harriette said to Ephie and pushed him away. She stood up and tried to pass Ephraim, who blocked the doorway.

"Why'd you move our bed, woman?" Ephraim gripped her shoulder tightly.

Harriette tried to pull away. "Mrs. Martin needs the room. She can't climb the stairs."

"So you got me out of the house by trickery so you could move my bed?" Ephraim snarled.

"Be reasonable, Ephraim."

Betsy saw that her mother was frightened. Ephraim had been sniping at her ever since they had been back together. But the fury in his eyes indicated that this was different.

"You must be stupid, woman! Trick me!" He struck her hard across the face with the flat of his hand.

Harriette stood silently glaring at him.

"You can move it back then," he shouted. "Now move!" He shoved her hard toward the bed.

"It's not our house!" Harriette cried. "Please be reasonable."

"Nobody's makin' a fool out of me. Least of all, you!" Ephraim punched her on the shoulder and watched her cringe away in pain. Suddenly, he lashed at her again and again, striking her everywhere on her body as she twisted and turned with the blows.

Ephie began to cry. Betsy was frozen still in shock. Ephraim's fury filled the room with terror. Harriette was sobbing and pleading with him to stop. As if his rage had peaked and was temporarily subsiding before rising again, Ephraim stepped to the window and pulled a bayonet from its sheath hanging on the wall.

"Put my bed back or I'll kill you!" There was a desperation in his voice. Betsy had heard that tone before and witnessed her mother's suffering and nursed her through days of agony.

Harriette retreated into the corner of the room as Ephraim advanced with the bayonet raised to strike her.

"Don't Daddy!" Betsy ran to him, but he pushed her sprawling onto the floor and continued to advance on her mother.

Betsy got to her feet, gripped Ephie by the arm, and whispered, "Get Mr. Martin, quickly!"

Ephie ran through the rooms into the Martins' side of the house and saw William Martin coming down the stairs.

"Come quick! Daddy's going to kill Mommy!"

William Martin looked with alarm at the frightened little boy. The family was under his roof so that he could watch out for Harriette. He strode angrily through the rooms and found Harriette and Betsy pleading with Ephraim.

"Put that down!" he commanded.

"Go back where you belong!" Ephraim turned to shout at him. His rage was out of control.

"Don't you touch her!" Martin warned and stepped toward him.

Harriette made a sudden move to pass by Ephraim, but he pushed her back with one arm and brought the bayonet down hard on her back. She screamed and fell to the floor.

5

Martin jumped on Ephraim, encircling one arm tightly about his neck and wrestling the bayonet out of his grip with the other. They struggled briefly until the bayonet clattered to the floor and Martin was able to kick it away. Ephraim broke away to go after it. Martin brought his right fist hard into Ephraim's face and stunned him. Then he pushed him through the next room and out the front door.

"Don't set foot in here till you cool off!" Martin said between his teeth. He had given Ephraim a good thrashing some years ago, so he knew Ephraim was afraid of him.

"You won't get away with this!" Ephraim cursed. "God-damn you, Martin. I'll make you pay."

Martin watched with disdain as Ephraim went to his horse and mounted.

"Where's the doctor you went for?" Martin asked.

"Go to hell!" Ephraim dug his heels hard into his mount and galloped away.

Martin returned to the Wheelers' room where Betsy was pouring coffee for Harriette and Ephie, who were sitting at the table.

"Oh Will!" Harriette said. "I don't know what I'm going to do." She winced with pain. "There'll be no end to this. But least, we got the room free for your Mary." She smiled slightly.

"At what price!" Martin snorted. "You almost dead and your young'uns scared out of their wits. Harriette, you just can't go on with him. It's never going to work."

"Ssh!" Harriette warned and looked at her children.

Martin composed himself, patted her on the shoulder, and returned to his part of the house.

Betsy was not hungry. She gave her corn fritter to Ephie who had finished his and was looking for more.

"Has Daddy gone away?" Ephie asked.

"He's comin' back," Betsy warned.

"You children pretend that nothing happened," Harriette said softly. "Everythin'll be fine again." She stood up stiffly and went to the next room to get dressed.

"Will Daddy beat me?" Ephie asked.

"No!" Betsy said crossly. "Drink your coffee."

"Daddy hates Ma again," Ephie said.

"Daddy's just not feelin' right," Betsy said. "Everythin' is goin' to be all right. You'll see, honey."

Betsy cleared the dishes. She sensed that things were out of control. She saw the anger building up in her father, and she knew she was as much to blame for it as her mother. The day was so fresh and bright yet her heart was so heavy with dread. School was out for summer. Ephie would be at home with her. She was glad he would be with her when her father returned, but in another sense she wanted him safely out of the way. As she washed the dishes, she began to cry quietly. Ephie was still eating and could not see her crying.

Harriette appeared at the doorway in her work dress. She held her black shawl tightly about her shoulders with one hand and carried the baby wrapped in a blanket in her other arm.

"I'm taking her with me today, Betsy. Now, be a good girl and do what Daddy tells you."

"Don't go, Ma!" Betsy cried. "Stay home today."

"Daddy's not going to hurt you," Harriette said reassuringly. "It's me he wants to hurt."

"Ma, stay with us, please, Ma." Ephie ran to her and threw his arms about her legs.

"You'll be nine years old soon," Harriette said playfully. "You'll be the man in the house before long." She motioned with her head for Betsy to come and take Ephie away from her.

"Come here, honey. Ma's late for work."

"If I don't work, we don't eat," Harriette said.

As Ephie dropped his arms, Harriette patted him softly on the cheek and backed away. Betsy took Ephie by one arm, pointed him towards the broom by the stove, and told him to start sweeping. He was a good boy and always did what she told him.

Betsy heard William Martin putting a bed into the next room. Her family was all in one room now. She felt guilty, confused, and fearful. Ephraim's anger and his powerful arms seemed to hold her heart in a vice as she made the beds and tried to think what she should work on next.

She heard a woman's voice. It was Eunice Hart looking in on Mrs. Martin. Betsy went to get her parents' toilet articles in the room that Martin was preparing for his wife.

"Hallo Betsy!" Eunice said cheerfully, but there was an edge to her voice that indicated that she knew there had been trouble.

Betsy, embarrassed, mumbled a greeting and gathered up her father's razor and shaving dish.

"Dr. Wright wants me to stay the day," Eunice informed her as much as to say that she would be near-by if needed.

Betsy pretended to take no notice, but she was glad. Eunice Hart's plain face and heavy figure brought a solid feeling to the house. Eunice was a practical nurse, who, because she went from house to house in Windsor and neighboring communities, knew all the gossip, and would inhibit Ephraim Wheeler from causing more gossip.

By the time Betsy was clearing away the last of her mother's belongings, William Martin was carrying his wife in his arms into the room, and Eunice was holding back the covers to receive the sick woman into the bed she had just finished making.

Betsy felt safer with the Martins and Eunice Hart in the next room. She began to think she could get through the day until her mother returned. She looked in the mirror by the stove. Her face was tear-stained. She took a wet cloth and wiped her face. People said she had her father's jutting chin and full-lipped mouth. She had his dark hair.

Ephraim Wheeler was back. She heard him entering the house with another man. Ephie was just getting ready to sweep the dust into the dustpan, but he was awkward. She rushed over, seized the broom and pan, quickly swept up the dirt, and carried it to the dustbin by the stove just as Ephraim walked into the room with Justice Walker.

"We can talk here," Ephraim said, "since you pushed me out of my room. Do you hear me, Martin? We'll talk in here." Ephraim gestured to Justice Walker to take a chair and be seated.

Justice Robert Walker stood by the chair until Martin entered the room. Calm, dignified, a man of few words, Justice Walker gave Betsy the feeling of divine authority, not just because he was considered wise, but because her father was very deferential to him.

"You two sit there and listen," Ephraim said to his children and pointed to the far end of the table.

William Martin, looking resentful, walked heavily into the room, sat down, and folded his arms across his chest. "I got enough worryin' me," he said to Justice Walker.

"Well, Ephraim," Walker said. "Your charge."

Ephraim remained standing. "I accuse William Martin of interfering in the rightful relationship of a man to his wife, and without provocation, of assaulting me in my living quarters."

"William?" Justice Walker asked, staring straight ahead as if he feared that by looking at either party he would show favoritism.

"He struck his wife with a bayonet. He would have killed her if I hadn't stopped him," Martin said quietly.

"You're a liar!" Ephraim shouted.

"The young'un there," Martin nodded at Ephie, sitting wide-eyed at the table and watching the proceedings, "came fetched me."

"Why did you ask Mr. Martin to come?" Justice Walker asked young Ephraim in a kind tone.

"Betsy told me to," Ephie blurted and looked at Betsy.

"Daddy was beatin' Ma," Betsy said, without waiting to be asked. "With that bayonet." She pointed to the bayonet hanging in its sheath on the wall.

Justice Walker glanced behind him at the bayonet.

"No man!" Ephraim's angry voice began to rise in frustration, "no man should be interfered with when dealing with family problems. I'm master in my own home. William Martin ain't going to run my family."

"Is Mrs. Wheeler available?" Justice Walker asked drily.

"My ma's at work," Betsy volunteered since neither of the men responded.

"A man's home is his castle," Justice Walker said. "That's the law."

Ephraim heaved a sigh of relief and sat down.

"But no man has the right to abuse his trust," Justice Walker said, continuing to look straight ahead of him. "Therefore, I fine you, William Martin, one dollar, and you, Ephraim Wheeler, one dollar." Justice Walker stood up and waited.

Martin looked at Ephraim with disgust and pity. He fished in his pocket for a dollar and gave it to Justice Walker. "I was savin' that for the doctor," he said grimly and strode from the room.

"Ain't got a dollar," Ephraim said between his teeth. "I'll pay later today." He glared at Walker as if he were an enemy.

Justice Walker nodded, glanced at the children, and mumbled as he turned away that he would be waiting.

Left alone with his children, Ephraim brooded in silence. Betsy and Ephie dared not move or speak--not until Ephraim gave them an order.

Ephraim felt that the community had turned against him. He could get no justice here. He had to leave his wife for good because she was at the bottom of his troubles. She tricked him so his bed could be moved, and Martin was her accomplice against him. Ephraim looked at Betsy. It was best that he and his children got away now. That would show Harriette. Where would she be without her family? He stood up suddenly.

"Get your things," he ordered fiercely.

Betsy was alarmed. "I don't want to go."

10

"We're going," Ephraim said angrily.

"Ma wants me to clean the house," Betsy pleaded.

"We're not living here any more," Ephraim said derisively. "You got all you need?" he asked Ephie.

Ephie, although upset by his sister's fear, wanted to please Ephraim. "I got nothing to bring, Daddy. Where are we going?"

"To Uncle's," Ephraim said sharply and looked at Betsy. "Hurry up!"

"My other dress is in the wash," Betsy said. "I can't go without it."

"We'll send for it." Ephraim strode to her and pulled her by the arm. "Get moving. We got a long road."

"Please Daddy!" Betsy broke into tears. "I don't want to go." She began to sob convulsively. All the pent-up emotions she had concealed for months now came out in a tearful wail of fear and misery.

Ephraim slapped her across the head. "Get outside. Both of you." He shoved Betsy ahead of him.

Ephie ran outside into the sunshine and looked at the low rounded hills in the distance where they would be going. Betsy was still crying and pleading to be left in the house.

William Martin watched from the window as Ephraim helped the boy sit on the horse, and then made Betsy mount behind him. Taking the reins, Ephraim led the horse away in the direction of Cummington, and Betsy's low sobs drifted back on the cool fresh air.

TWO

Betsy desperately wanted to cry for help to Mr. Martin. But she could not. She felt Martin's eyes watching them go, and she felt ashamed. Her Daddy was in a temper tantrum. He would brook interference from no one. She knew that she had to submit to him to keep from provoking him further. But she was frightened. She felt that there was danger with him this morning. There was an unpredictable side to him that terrified the family. Betsy had learned to stay clear of him when he was in one of his moods. For months now she had sensed him contemplating her in a sexually suggestive way, but she had avoided his approaches which were few and inhibited because of the closeness of their living quarters. Her Ma had said nothing, and Betsy did not know if she had divined Ephraim's altered attitude toward her, although on occasion she had seen her Ma frown as if preoccupied with unpleasant thoughts. Oh! she thought, if only Ma could come upon them now, be returning to retrieve something, or because she was not needed at her workplace. But the road sloped down empty of human traffic straight by the farmlands to the woods at Partridgefield, which she saw with apprehension in the distance. There she would be hidden from view.

The day was beautiful and the sun was climbing in the sky winking through the clouds. A breeze bent the long grass. She held Ephie firmly about the waist. She had to protect him, which added to her sense of hopelessness and uncertainty. From the moment her mother had moved her father's bed, Betsy sensed her descent into unfathomable depths. She was still falling, falling. She would not stop until Ephraim did something to bring them out of the fatal spiral and restored them to an even equilibrium.

Ephraim's angry glances back at them as he walked, leading the horse, warned her that he was thinking of them. She had a premonition that he intended to hurt them, to pay them back for his frustrations this morning. She watched with dread as they approached the woods at the hamlet of Partridgefield. Across the fields in the distance she could see the cabin they had lived in years ago. Ephraim pointed it out to them, his harsh voice smashing the happy thought of those other days when her Daddy was a very different person.

"Built that house with my two hands," Ephraim called back to them in angry justification. He dropped his head as if the memory was grievous to him, and Betsy heard him cursing to himself.

Betsy knew how much her Daddy loved these valley roads and rolling hills. He had told her that they calmed him when he was restless and unhappy, which was why, whenever he had to move, it was to one of the villages in the area. He said that when he was at sea, he would slide the images of farms, hills and forest across his mind. She began to hope that his thoughts of the past were calming him now, and that he would lead them round the bend in the road beyond the woods toward the hills and Cummington. She began to relax slightly and sensed the pain of apprehension as her nerves released the tautness strung throughout her body. The copse was very close now. It was thick and ran far back from the roadside. She saw gloom and danger in it and held her breath as they began to pass it by. But, suddenly, Ephraim brought the horse to the side of the road and tethered the reins to a tree. Betsy glanced up and down the road but saw no one. Her heart sank.

"We'll stop here," Ephraim said sharply. "Get down."

Betsy burst into tears.

Ephraim reached up, put his hands about her waist, and dragged her off the horse.

"Get down, son."

"Why are we stoppin' here, Daddy?" Ephie asked, jumping to the ground.

"Betsy and me are going to look for avensroot," Ephraim said impatiently. "You wait here with Daniel."

Betsy thought of running, but she knew Ephraim would catch her and drag her into the woods in front of Ephie. She could not bear to be shamed in front of her brother.

"Please, Daddy, I don't like avensroot," she cried. "I don't want to go." She pulled against the firm grip he had on her arm.

"Your Ma likes it," Ephraim's eyes glinted with meaning. "You're goin' to like it."

"I don't want any," Betsy said, tears coursing down her cheeks.

"I'll go with you, Daddy," Ephie cried. "Let Betsy watch Daniel."

"No," Ephraim said. "You watch Daniel. We won't be long." He half-lifted Betsy off the ground and pushed her in front of him.

"If you help me get avensroot," he said. "I'll let you take it back to your Ma."

Betsy heard his offer as if it were a reprieve. If she could see her mother again, she thought, she could be saved from Ephraim. She stopped crying, walked through the shrubbery and trees ahead of Ephraim, and stumbled disconsolately over tufts of grass all the while sensing Ephraim's growing desire for her.

"Keep goin'," Ephraim said, pushing her by the shoulders. "You do what I tell you, and I'll let you see your Ma again."

Betsy knew that she could not plead or argue with Ephraim. He had his mind set on her submission. She wanted only to get far enough away from Ephie so that he would not hear them. She felt mortally ashamed as if it was her fault that her Daddy wanted to make love to her. She was helpless to know what to say or do. As they stepped into a small clearing, Ephraim seized her from behind and moved his hands over her body. She felt him trembling as he caressed her breasts.

"Daddy," she pleaded, "you said we were picking avensroot." She felt weak with fear.

"Don't play dumb," he said sharply. "Lie down here. It's private enough."

Suddenly twisting, she spun away from him and began to run, but in three paces Ephraim had her by the shoulders, turned her to face him, and slid his hands about her neck. "Do as I say or I'll kill you," he said and began to choke her.

"Daddy, don't, it's sinnin'."

"Get down," he forced her onto the ground.

Betsy gasped for breath and tried to pull Ephraim's hands from her throat. His intensity frightened her into believing that he was going to kill her.

When he took away his hands to pull off his trousers, she rolled away and sprang to her feet, but immediately he seized her leg and brought her heavily down onto her back. She sat up pleading with her hands and tearful voice, but he hit her across the jaw, stunning her, and, when she struggled, he seized a rock, pushed her flat and threatened to crush her skull.

"I mean it," he hissed. "I'll smash you if you don't."

She went limp then. She could think only of placating him. She turned her face aside as Ephraim pulled off her skirt and panties. She did not care what happened to her. She felt worthless. A sense of guilt overwhelmed her. She felt Ephraim's penis thrust against her vagina, and she cried with fear and pain as he entered her. Ephraim clamped his hand over her mouth. She sucked in air through her nostrils. She felt her body responding to Ephraim's urgency and soon she could no longer think as she succumbed to a mixture of his pleasure and her remorse. Her mind spun away from the present into a nether world dominated by a sense of maleness. Ephraim seemed to explode within her. She felt him pull away from her, and she lay still with her eyes closed. She thought that he might kill her now.

Ephraim lay on his back beside her and gazed up at the trees like a canopy overhead. Slowly he brought his nerves under control. He felt triumphant, powerful. He smiled. He had taken his revenge on Harriette. His frustrations had gone. He felt positive about starting a new life of which Betsy was a part, for she belonged to him completely now.

"You tell anyone, anyone at all," he warned, "and I'll kill you."

Betsy opened her eyes and smelt the earth and the grass as she realized that he was not going to kill her.

15

"Do you hear me?" he demanded angrily.

"Yes, Daddy." She began to hope again that she could get away from him. She heard him stand up and looked over to see him pulling on his trousers. A feeling of revulsion for herself came over her. She sat up and slowly began to put her clothes on. She thought of Ephie and blushed; if he had heard them, she could never face him again.

"Stay here," Ephraim said. "I know where there's avensroot."

Betsy watched him disappear into the trees and heard branches crack in the distance. She thought of running away then, but she knew that she would be caught and maybe Ephraim would kill her. The only way she could survive was to obey him. She feared him more than she thought it was possible to fear any person. Her neck hurt, and her jaw felt as if it had been kicked. The intercourse had frightened her at first, but, when she saw the pleasure it gave Ephraim, she felt guilty and confused. Above all, she felt his sense of ownership over her. He had become a part of her, inexplicably, carnally, a part of her. Such an admission came suddenly, involuntarily, with a sense of shame, a sense of being abandoned and unloved. It terrified her. She thought of her mother betrayed. She could never tell her mother. She began to cry quietly.

Just then, out of the silence, Ephraim stood in front of her with avensroot in one hand. He motioned for her to walk ahead of him.

"Don't look so sad," he said with a wicked smile. "It weren't so bad."

Still frightened that he might throw her down again, she hung her head, stood up, and stepped obediently through the underbrush.

Ephie was nervous after the beating of his mother, and he had watched with helplessness and fear as his sister disappeared into the trees with Ephraim. He was frightened for her, but, at the same time, relieved that she stood between him and his father. At times he loved his father--when he went fishing with him or watched the birds migrating over the wilderness--but his father had become a threatening figure. After they disappeared from view, he heard their muffled voices followed by a deep silence. He listened with all his body but heard nothing as if his mind refused to record sound. He went to Daniel and stroked the old horse's snout and looked into its brown eyes to find solace there. The steady, reliable look of the farm animal reassured him. Ephie passed the time patting Daniel's neck and gazing over the fields, which were a part of his earliest memories. He connected certain people with this land and imagined them, farmers and their wives working in the fields. He wished that he was back in those days when his Dad and Ma got on better. He remembered his Ma crying when his Dad told them he was selling the house and moving them to Uncle Odel's in Cummington. He felt her hurt at leaving her own place to live in someone else's house again. Since then, he was always expecting to be moving along sooner or later. They were moving again now, and his Ma was going to be hurt. He resented his Dad. Everything had to be done because his Dad wanted it. He closed his eyes and concentrated his resentment on Ephraim for as long as he could, and, then, sensing the passage of time, he thought of Betsy and wondered if Ephraim was beating her in the woods. He thought of riding Daniel back to find his Ma and get help and looked up and down the road wishing for someone to be coming along, someone like Mr. Martin who would not be afraid of his Dad, but the stones reflected the hot midday sun in a glare that stunned his eyes. At the cracking of underbrush he turned as Ephraim and Betsy came out of the woods.

"Did you get avensroot?" he shouted nervously but with expectation because it was like candy.

Ephraim looked at him accusingly. "Did you fall asleep?"

"No, Dad," Ephie said. He sensed a strange mood about his father--subdued and defensive at the same time--but he did not try to understand it.

Betsy gave Ephie the avensroot to carry but could not look at him.

"Stop your sulkin', God damn you!" Ephraim shouted at Betsy.

He had a distaste for his children then. They were a nuisance, slowed him down. He had to get his affairs in order before he went to sea. He had to collect the money owed him.

"Go home to Ma for tonight. It's startin' to cloud over. I'm takin' Daniel for private business." He looked severely at Betsy. "If it ain't rainin' tomorrow, you bring Ephie to Cummington. If it's rainin', come the next day. Bring the baby."

"What shall I tell Mama?"

"I told her I'm leavin'. We're goin' to the seaside and I'm puttin' you out in some nice place."

The words "putting out" stirred a deep-seated fear in Betsy. Throughout her childhood she had heard of the beatings and deprivations that Ephraim had suffered when he was put out to a shoemaker as a child.

"Ephie and me are goin' to sea," Ephraim added with a look at Ephie and mounted Daniel.

"Don't do it, Daddy," Betsy cried, tears coursing down her cheeks anew. "Please, Daddy, please don't."

"You do as I say," Ephraim barked sharply, and, heeling Daniel, moved away in the direction of Cummington.

Betsy stifled her sobs when he was gone. She took Ephie by the hand and tried to conceal her tension and fear as they returned to Windsor. The sudden darkness in the sky had saved her for the moment, but only her mother could save her from Ephraim and the life of a servant girl in a sea front hotel. She began to feel the hopelessness of her situation and the worthlessness of her life.

"Did Daddy beat you?" Ephie asked sympathetically.

Betsy nodded. "Did anyone pass by?"

"No," Ephie said. "Why is Daddy takin' us away from Ma?"

Betsy put her arm about Ephie as they walked.

"Daddy hates Ma," Ephie said. "I'm afraid. He's going to take me away in a ship."

Betsy brushed her tears with her sleeves. "We won't go to Daddy."

Ephie stepped away from her. "But Daddy will make us."

"I'd as soon die as go back to him," Betsy said firmly.

Ephie, sensing her sadness and her determination, walked worriedly at her side. If Daddy killed Betsy, Daddy would kill him too.

"One way or t'other I'd be killed," Betsy said.

They walked in silence as the sky grew darker and menacing. When they reached home, it was late in the afternoon. Harriette was not back from work. Eunice Hart welcomed them, her large face beaming with good cheer and curiosity.

"Where's your father?"

"Gone to Uncle's," Betsy said morosely.

Eunice could tell that she had been crying and was very unhappy.

"I've made tea," Eunice said. "And there's biscuits. Help yourself."

Betsy sat in a chair and looked glumly out the window. Ephie poured them tea and brought her a biscuit. Betsy felt hopelessly condemned. If Eunice Hart or William Martin knew what she had done, she would be barred from the house, she would be barred from Windsor. Her face was so raw and swollen she could hardly swallow the biscuit for the pain. Although she knew her mother had to obey her father as they all did, at least her mother loved her and might find a way to save her. She wondered how to tell her mother that Ephraim wanted to take the baby away from her.

At that moment Harriette returned with the baby. She was famished for tea and directly poured herself a cup. Dark bruises had appeared on her face and neck as a result of the thrashing she had received, and she favored her left leg when she walked. She was cheerful, however, and, after settling the baby in the crib, remarked on the somber look of her children.

"Your husband took them away this morning," Eunice informed her. "They came back alone a little while past. You best take a look at Betsy. She's lookin' poorly."

Harriette, alarmed, went directly to Betsy. "Where's Daddy?"

"Gone to Uncle's," Betsy said. "He wants us to bring the baby to him tomorrow." She put down her head and cried, "Oh, Ma!"

"He's gonna take me on a ship," Ephie said. "I don't want to go."

Harriette reached for him and kissed his forehead. "Go out and play, dear." She looked at Eunice. "Will you leave us to talk."

Eunice nodded, and, taking Ephie by the hand, led him out of the room.

"My dear daughter, what happened? Your face is all swollen." Harriette knelt beside Betsy. "Did Daddy do that?" she asked accusingly. "Oh, my poor darling."

Betsy flung her arms about her mother and sobbed on her shoulder.

Harriette divined that something was troubling her more profoundly than a thrashing. Betsy was level-headed with strong control over her emotions. This uncontrolled crying was unusual for her. But Harriette said nothing until Betsy spoke.

"Oh, Ma, I'll never see you again. He's goin' to put me out."

Harriette started back in anger. "He wants to take you away from me?"

Betsy nodded glumly.

"I knew it," Harriette said. "I took the baby with me today."

"He's puttin' me in a seaside hotel," Betsy said. "Ma, what can I do?"

"I don't know what we can do," Harriette said desperately. "He may be bluffin'."

"Mama, please help us!"

"You're not goin' to any seaside hotel," Harriette said, holding Betsy more tightly as she thought of her daughter being forced into prostitution. Her mind whirled with indecision as she tried to think of someone she could turn to for help. She knew Ephraim was determined to hurt her, but taking away her baby was just too cruel. "We have to think of something."

Betsy pitied her mother then. She felt her helplessness yet at the same time she sensed her inner strength aroused by her maternal instinct to protect her young.

"There's something else you want to tell me, isn't there, Betsy?" Harriette said calmly. "Tell me, whatever it is. I have to know if we are to save ourselves."

Betsy looked painfully into her eyes and realized that she could no longer keep her secret regardless how hurt her mother would be.

"I don't want to tell," Betsy said, staring at the floor. "I feel unclean." She paused and then blurted, "Daddy made me sin with him."

Harriette was stunned, but, the moment she heard it, she knew it was true. She had endured hell on earth with Ephraim because despite the arguments and the beatings she persuaded herself that he loved her. Now, as if struck by revelation, she knew it was false. Ephraim had violated their love. She repressed her need to cry out with the hurt, and her heart went out to her daughter. She hugged Betsy tightly.

"He made me go into the woods. He said he'd kill me if I didn't."

Harriette lightly touched Betsy's bruised neck and face. "He forced you?"

Betsy nodded. "I tried to stop him. I thought he was goin' to strangle me to death." Her eyes rounded with apprehension. "Ma," she said in warning, "he said he'd kill me if I told anyone."

"My poor Betsy," Harriette kissed her. "You did right by telling me." A fury began to mount inside her.

"I'm afraid, Ma. I don't want to see him again."

Harriette got to her feet. Her own pain had disappeared in the greater agony of her daughters, but she sensed a hysteria threatening to erupt under her calm. She hesitated to confide her troubles in anyone, but she had to do something. Otherwise Ephraim would destroy them all.

But the disgust she felt seemed to paralyze her. Would it not be better to say nothing and avoid the disgrace that would follow, as she had done often in the past? By keeping their troubles within the family, she had managed to keep it together. Yet this time his betrayal went beyond redemption. Ephraim had replaced her with her daughter. The thought hurt her unbearably. She wanted to keep it secret to save herself from humiliation, but, she knew that for Betsy's sake, she could not keep silent. It occurred to her that Ephraim threatened to take the children away to force Betsy to give into him. The thought sickened her. If he allowed the children to stay with her, he would want to continue with Betsy. All the shame in the world would be less painful than that unspeakable situation. She groaned aloud and became aware of Betsy's worried stare at her.

On impulse in a wild hope that Betsy was mistaken or even lying, because she did not want to be taken away by Ephraim, Harriette brought her to a chair by the window and made her draw up her skirt, take down her drawers, and sit with her legs open. She knelt to examine her. Neither of them said a word until Harriette drew back and looked at Betsy in commiseration and despair.

"Oh Ma!" Betsy said in anguish. "I've done this to us. I'm sorry, Ma! Oh, what can I do? Can I go away before Daddy finds out?"

"He'll find us," Harriette said glumly.

"And he'll kill me, "Betsy said. "And he'll kill you too, Ma."

"I think Daddy means what he says," Harriette said. "He'll take you all away from me. I won't let it happen."

Betsy sensed the strength of her mother then. The long-suffering woman, whose constant deference to her father brought Betsy to pity her at times, had become transformed. The attack on her daughter seemed to harden her.

"We have to get help," she said worriedly. "We have to ask Mr. Martin."

Betsy nodded, relieved that she had told her mother. She watched Harriette go into the next room. Already she felt the reassuring strength of William Martin. But she was apprehensive. Would he condemn her? Would he persuade her mother to send her back to her father? Betsy sensed that an alien force had interposed itself between her and her father.

William Martin strode into the room. He bent his tall frame to look closely into her eyes and take her hand. "Your mother told me what happened to you, Betsy. Tell us the truth. If you tell a lie or try to conceal something, it could hurt us and you."

"Yes, Mr. Martin," Betsy nodded.

"What time did it happen?"

Betsy paused to consider. "We reached Partridgefield about half an hour after leaving the house."

"Did young Ephraim see you?"

Betsy shook her head. "Daddy made him stay with Daniel. But he might've heard."

"Did you tell him?"

She shook her head vigorously. "He's too young to understand. Besides, if I did, Daddy might kill him too."

Martin patted the top of her head affectionately. "You're a clever girl." He took a deep breath, drew up a chair, and sat facing her. "We come now, my girl, to the important part. Did your father ever try it before?"

Betsy hesitated, looked worriedly up at her mother, who entered the room, and replied in a whisper. "Yes."

William Martin waited.

"Twice before," Betsy admitted. "Last fall. First time he told me to get off the horse and take the stick. I wouldn't do it."

"Did he try to persuade you?"

"He said he'd give me a gown and petticoat."

"And the second time?" Martin frowned.

"We were gathering wood out where there's brush about a couple 'a miles from here."

"Oh, do we have to hear all this!" Harriette cried, twisting her hands nervously.

"Just to be sure," Martin said evenly. "If you inform the magistrate, you have to be sure there's no little thing that can spring up and condemn you 'stead of Ephraim. Go on, Betsy."

She bowed her head. "He made me lie down in the bush."

"Did he go into you?" Martin asked.

"Partially."

"Partially?" Martin frowned. "What do you mean, girl?"

"I wouldn't let him. Then someone came as he was goin' to. And he stopped."

"That's not good," Martin said to Harriette. "Betsy never told you?"

As Harriette was staring at Betsy in a trance of horror and misgiving, Martin asked Betsy sharply, "Why didn't you tell your mother?"

"I was afraid," Betsy said. "I thought if I could stay away from Daddy, he might change his mind."

Martin stood up. "There's nothing else but to send for Justice Walker and Dr. Wright. But be prepared for the worst from Ephraim. I'll stand with you, Mrs. Wheeler." He turned his long serious face on Betsy and broke into a warm smile. "You're alone no longer, girl."

Betsy seized his hand and kissed it.

"I'd better fetch Justice Walker," Harriette sighed with resignation. "Oh, Mr. Martin, and Mrs. Martin so sick!"

"I'll look after it all." Martin strode to the door, paused, and said in warning, "Don't waver in your story and be brave."

THREE

When Justice Walker arrived, he dismissed everyone from the room, save Betsy, whom he questioned intently. His line of questioning followed that of William Martin but was a more thorough examination. He was interested in the possibility of witnesses and corroborating evidence. Sitting stiffly and speaking tersely, he intimidated Betsy, so that she could barely find words to reply, until he lightly tapped her on the arm and said kindly, "Take your time, young lady." The words "young lady" coming from Justice Walker brought her miraculously out of the depths of her despair.

"I didn't tell no one till now," she said, "'cause I thought that as long as Mama was in the same house, Daddy would leave me alone."

Justice Walker patted Betsy on the arm again. "Not a word more till I ask you." He went to the door and opened it for the white-mustached, roly-poly doctor, who went with an air of professional despatch to examine Betsy.

Justice Walker gathered Harriette, William Martin and Eunice Hart in the hallway. "She's a brave young lady," he said. "I believe her. I shall apprehend your husband, M'am. If you wish Betsy well, say no word of this to anyone." He looked at Eunice Hart with a meaningful eye. "No word to anyone."

"You'd best lock Wheeler up," Martin said. "If you don't, he'll be here in a rage, and Lord knows what he'll do. I can't guarantee I can stop him."

"Rest assured," Justice Walker said firmly.

"What penalty will Ephraim get?" Harriette asked nervously.

"If convicted, he could hang," Justice Walker said softly. "It's difficult to convict."

"Hang!" Harriette suddenly felt very weak and turned to find a chair.

Eunice Hart supported her until she was seated on the hall chair. At that moment Dr. Wright joined them, and, taking Justice Walker aside, told him that Betsy had been violated. Nodding grimly, Justice Walker went over to Harriette, encouraged her to be as courageous as her daughter, and went quickly out of the house.

"Well then, now that I'm here, Martin, let me see your missus," Dr. Wright smiled cheerfully. "How is she Eunice?" He took Eunice by the arm, and they were followed by Martin to the sick woman's bed.

Harriette sat in the stillness wondering how she could survive with three children to feed and one just a baby. She went over again, as she had thousands of times, the major events, the turning-points in her life with Ephraim. They had had happy days. Why did he hate her who was so capable of love? The questions seemed to pile up as if against a wall.

Justice Walker rode home convinced that Ephraim Wheeler had brought evil into the community. It was his duty to keep it from spreading and corrupting them. Since it was supper-time, he instructed his son to notify half a dozen men in the community to meet him with their mounts in one hour. Then he sat down to supper, and, clearing a space on the table beside him, he wrote out a warrant for Ephraim Wheeler's arrest.

There was still daylight when the Justice left his house to find five mounted men waiting his command. His son had readied his horse. As the Justice mounted, he said to him, "Ride to forewarn Sheriff Larned in Lenox." Spurring his horse, he called out to the men, "I hope you've all got arms 'cause I ain't." The men laughed and followed him.

Hugh Culpepper, a young-looking, handsome, brown-haired man of forty-two, who took the lead of posses in matters such as these, came to ride alongside the Justice.

"It's Wheeler we're after then?"

"Yep," said the Justice.

"What'd he do? Kill his wife?"

"Nope," the Justice spat. "Raped his daughter."

26

Hugh sat back in the saddle as if a sudden burst of wind had knocked him off-balance. He drifted back to tell the others. Their good-humored banter ceased. The men rode the five miles to Cummington in silence.

Cummington was set on the side of a slope in a shallow valley among beautiful hills. The sun was setting on the scene as the men rode into the village. They all felt the beauty of the place.

"Odel's home," Justice Walker said, and led them down to the river and along its banks to a large, white-painted farmhouse.

Justice Walker and Hugh Culpepper dismounted and walked together to the door. Isaac Odel, a stern-faced man, was working in the barn, and, seeing the posse approach, he ran across the yard to encounter the Justice at the door.

"What is it?" Odel asked, surprised.

"I have a warrant for the arrest of your brother-in-law," Justice Walker said sternly. "Is he with you?"

"Oh Lord no!" Odel said angrily. "What for?"

"I'll tell him," the Justice said sharply.

Odel nodded and went inside. Walker and Culpepper heard a commotion and looked meaningfully at each other. Hugh went back to the posse and instructed one of the men to ride to the other side of the house. Odel appeared in the doorway. He looked upset.

"He says he's done nothing wrong. You'll have to come in to talk to him."

The Justice turned to wait for Hugh to walk back to him.

"Is it my sister?" Odel asked. "Did he beat up on her again? Is that it?"

"Worse," the Justice said, and, nodding for Hugh to follow, pushed into the house.

Odel led them to Ephraim who was lighting an oil lamp in the sitting room. Ephraim smiled at them and shook his head.

"You got nothing better to do than tail after me? Did my wife make up something against me?"

"You've been charged with raping your daughter, Betsy," Justice Walker said quietly.

Ephraim frowned. "Did Betsy say that?"

Walker nodded.

In the ensuing seconds of silence, Odel's face registered alarm, disbelief, and anger, but he said nothing, and simply stared at Ephraim, who was looking calmly at the Justice.

"I didn't rape Betsy," Ephraim said with disgust. He looked at Odel. "This is Harriette's doin'. She don't want me to leave."

"My sister's a crafty one," Odel said to Walker. "I wouldn't believe her further than I could throw her."

"Let me talk to my daughter," Ephraim said with an easy grin.

"She's been examined by Dr. Wright and her story confirmed," Justice Walker said.

"That old man! He don't like me 'cause I woke him up early this mornin' to attend to Mrs. Martin," Ephraim smiled in complaint. "Get me a jury of physicians and matrons to examine Betsy, and you'll find she's lying."

"She's telling the truth," Justice Walker replied sternly. "There's nothing more to say. You're keepin' the men waitin'."

"Be fair to me," Ephraim looked to Odel for support. "Get me a jury." He frowned. "You'll find she's lying."

"Come along with us now, Ephraim," Culpepper spoke up with a strain of impatience in his voice. "It's dark now. We're taking you to Lenox."

Ephraim looked around him with resignation. "Guess I'm set. I never owned more than I'm wearin'." He went ahead of them out of the house.

One of the men had taken Ephraim's horse from the barn and saddled it. There was a sense of both curiosity and disgust in the night air.

Ephraim turned to Isaac Odel before he mounted. "Will you come get Daniel back for me?" He saw the serious look in Isaac's face. "I didn't rape my daughter," he said loud enough for all to hear. He mounted and rode forward. Immediately the posse closed about him with Culpepper riding by his side and Justice Walker riding in front.

Ephraim reproached himself for not seeing that he was taking a risk in sending Betsy back to her mother. But no one could prove anything. He was master of his household and the law was on his side. Now that he was arrested, he felt strangely complacent. He felt as if the emotional strain he had been under for the past weeks had suddenly dissipated on this silent ride with the posse.

The road to Lenox, the county seat, went diagonally south to the west. The night was dark because clouds concealed the stars and the half-moon appeared only occasionally. It would take the posse about three and a half hours at a fast pace. And then there was the long ride back to Windsor. Justice Walker and the men in the posse hoped that they would not have to ride the full distance.

To Ephraim, his arrest seemed to be just another burden with which people wished to punish him. He had taken so much punishment and survived, he could overcome this one, he thought. But rape! Betsy charged him with rape! His own flesh and blood was doing this to him! He thought back with resentment to when he was not yet nine, Ephie's age, and as an orphan was bound over with his older brother and sister to that brute, Jedudiah Hammond, shoemaker.

Hammond's heavy calloused hand crashed against the back of his head. He could feel his ears ring.

"Is that what you call nailin'?" Hammond demanded. "Get those nails straight, damn you!"

Ephraim tried to hit the nail on the side to straighten it in the shoe leather. Hammond cracked him again.

"Pull it out, you damn fool!" Hammond seized the shoe, and with a deft tip of the hammer took out the nail. "For not getting it right, you work till nine tonight."

"He's been workin' hard, master," Ephraim heard his brother say.

"You work to nine with him then," Hammond laughed. "Keep the lazy bones company."

The shoemaker hitched his breeches up over his thick girth and moved heavily out of the room. The boys looked at each other somberly.

His brother shrugged. "Let's work hard and the time will pass."

"But I'm hungry," Ephraim said. "I'm going to get somethin' to eat." He tip-toed to the door, opened it cautiously, and glided along the hall to the kitchen.

There was no sign of Hammond. Ephraim opened the bread box, grasped two large buns, and tip-toed stealthily back down the hall. He was mortally afraid of Hammond, but his hunger overcame all fear. He entered the workroom jubilantly and had just run over to his brother and waved the buns in front of his brother's smiling face when Hammond looked through the door at the other end of the workroom.

The cutting slash of leather against flesh and the heavy wallop of each blow stinging deep inside him throughout the years caused Ephraim to wrench his body with sudden anger in his saddle. Hugh Culpepper reached over to seize his arm and to steady him.

"I'm all right," Ephraim said impatiently and drew his arm away.

The night air was turning cold. A stiff breeze blew across a long level stretch of road and made the blackness of the night ahead of them seem the more inhospitable.

"Justice," Ephraim called out to Walker riding ahead of him. "You put me in jail, and who feeds my family?"

"Should have thought of that before," Justice Walker said. He slowed his horse to allow Ephraim to come alongside. Culpepper still rode on the other side.

"You take them to Odel's," Ephraim said. "I don't want them in the house of William Martin."

"They can go where they please," Culpepper said amiably. "Your missus is in charge now."

Ephraim glared at him, but Hugh could not make out his expression in the dark. Ephraim felt thwarted in everything. But he felt his wife thwarted him most. She had made his unlucky life unluckier.

"Hold it, men," Justice Walker shouted. "Slow down."

The posse slowed to a walk. The sound of galloping horses came from ahead of them. In a few seconds several horsemen loomed out of the blackness, and, at a cry from the posse, brought their horses to a halt.

"Sheriff?" the Justice demanded.

"You're right, Mr. Walker," one of the horsemen said and rode up to him.

Walker recognized the slim, wiry-like man in his fifties as Sheriff Larned. "Glad you saved us some traveling," he said.

"Your boy's a quick one," Larned said. "He's been worrying me like crazy to get a move on. So I'll exchange him for the prisoner, if you don't mind."

Justice Walker laughed with his son and motioned Ephraim to move up level with the Sheriff. "Here's the warrant." He handed the paper to the Sheriff, who put it carefully into his breast pocket, took out handcuffs, and, leaning over to Ephraim, cuffed his hands together in front of him, so that he was still able to hold the reins.

"We'll be seeing you in court," Sheriff Larned said. "Let's go men."

Justice Walker and the posse turned round with some pleasure and satisfaction in that they had done their duty and faced a return journey of only just over an hour.

Ephraim, on the other hand, began to feel depressed. The handcuffs were an affront.

"You're making a mistake doin' this to me," he said angrily to Sheriff Larned. "I'm an innocent man."

Larned stared straight ahead. "That's not for me to decide," he said in a tone that discouraged further conversation.

They rode in silence to Lenox. The several horsemen broke off to go their own ways when they reached the town, until the Sheriff was left alone with Ephraim before the prison looming malevolently in the darkness.

FOUR

In the late morning of the next day, which was sunny and fine and not rainy as people had feared, Isaac Odel stopped by at William Martin's house in Windsor. Untying Daniel's lead from the back of the saddle of his own horse, he turned both horses free to graze, and, stepping toward the door, caught a glimpse of Betsy watching him from one of the windows.

Harriette met him in the hallway and looked at him with such helplessness that he had to feel sorry for her despite his annoyance at the situation. But neither said a word. She led him into her part of the house where Betsy sat crocheting and looking very subdued, very down.

Isaac Odel was fair like his sister, but his expression was stern whereas her face was open and youthful. He was five years older and had counseled her throughout her life. Whenever her marriage was in trouble, she would bring the family to live with him in Cummington. He was always obliging, but he was concerned about the family's reputation. The constant trouble in his sister's marriage was a worry to him. This latest family business was a tragedy because it had not been contained within the family. Already it was being talked about throughout Berkshire County and soon it would be known all over Massachusetts.

"I've brought you Daniel from Lenox," Isaac said with a note of impatience. "Tried to see Ephraim but they wouldn't let me."

"Is he coming out on bail?" Harriette asked.

32

CHOCOLATE

"Not likely on a capital offense," Isaac looked glumly at her. "He'll be tried in September."

"Oh Isaac, I don't care anymore. I just can't afford to care anymore." Harriette buried her face in her hands.

"You should have thought of the family," he said.

"I did think of the family. What sort of man rapes his own daughter? No!" She shuddered. "That I could have wasted so many years of my life with that man is God's mockery."

Isaac raised an eyebrow. "We'll leave God out of it. I'm asking you, how are you going to live?"

"I don't know. I suspect I'll not be wanted in some houses around here."

"Yep. Well, you'd best move back to Cummington," he said and looked over at Betsy. "And bring your daughter. She's going to be famous, but it's not going to bring her any money."

Harriette nodded, her gratefulness evident in the look she gave him.

"What about your knitting," he said to Betsy, "does it sell?"

"Some," Betsy said.

"They'd better do," he said sternly. "We'll need the income." He turned abruptly on Harriette. "Lord, woman, why did you call in Justice Walker? You could've spoke to me."

"Ephraim was leaving me for good, final!" Harriette cried in exasperation. "He was taking my children, my baby."

"So he said," Isaac interrupted.

"So he said, and I think that's what he was going to do. He was leaving me for good."

"Ah, but you made a mistake the way you handled it."

"Isaac, you act as if Betsy wasn't touched. You think we concocted that story just to stop Ephraim from leaving, is that right?"

"You can't stop people from thinking that."

"There's one thing you got to understand as my brother." Harriette went to Betsy and put her arm about her shoulders. "Whatever we have to do to get the truth out we'll do gladly,

33

rather than the alternative which was to leave our lives in the hands of a brute."

"I had to tell," Betsy said, "and he said he'd kill me if I did."

Odel nodded as if agreeing. "You still made us a heap of trouble," he said. "I'll be going. They'll need me at the tannery. The wagon will be by tomorrow to pick up your furniture."

Harriette accompanied him to the door. Betsy heard her talking to him as if trying to reason with him. They went outside and out of earshot.

Some of her mother's anger had passed into Betsy. It helped her feel less guilty if she got angry with Ephraim. Moreover, her mother's anger made her feel justified in telling what happened. It was her uncle who made her feel guilty. She did not want to have her father in gaol. A nauseous feeling of aversion for Ephraim came over her, a feeling of being the flesh of his flesh that was corrupted through sensuous familiarity. The first pleasure from coition spiced her thoughts when she remembered the act in the woods, but it was like a faint undercurrent in an overwhelming sense of remorse.

Harriette returned looking dispirited. "He thinks we're going to get a lot of blame and Ephraim's not going to be convicted."

Betsy looked at her in fear.

"Do right. That's all I know," Harriette said firmly. "If we do right, we'll be all right. The Lord will watch over us."

Betsy realized for the first time that her mother was frightened. Harriette identified with Betsy. That was evident from her voice. Furthermore, Harriette seemed to regard her differently, as if she were a woman, or almost a woman. Harriette's fear was for their vulnerability as women. But at the same time, her identification with her daughter gave her courage. Betsy felt this courage as well. It was a resolve to face whatever happened with determination. Alone, Harriette would have crumbled, weeping and distraught, as Betsy had seen her do countless times. But now Betsy sensed her strength.

As Harriette settled into spinning at the wheel and Betsy bent over her crocheting, they heard a man and woman arguing. The argument continued for some time, during which mother and daughter glanced apprehensively at each other, as if they sensed they were the subject. Finally it stopped. They heard a man clear his throat at the doorway and looked up to see William Martin step into the room.

Martin looked about uneasily and tried to make an off-hand remark, but Harriette cut him short.

"We're leaving tomorrow, Will. My brother's sending a wagon."

Martin winced. "I'm sòrry, Harriette."

"It's better that we live at my brother's," Harriette said with a smile.

Martin looked at Betsy. "Right. I'll be here to help you load." He turned to go and then stopped himself. "We been friends many a long year and that still goes with me," he said, looking directly at Harriette. "If there's a trial, you count on me."

She smiled broadly and looked away quickly because she felt tears come to her eyes.

Martin nodded at Betsy and left the room.

Betsy sensed the prejudice building toward them and thought of her school friends spurning her. If it were not for her mother, she would perish.

FIVE

Attorney-General John Sullivan was a solid man of sixty. He was solid in build, in reputation, and in intelligence. When he opened the door of his office in Lenox to Justice Walker, he was courteous and warm. Walker liked him, but, at the same time, the Justice feared his analytical mind. This interview was to discover if Justice Walker had made a mistake in arresting Ephraim Wheeler.

"I haven't had an opportunity to get over your way in some time, Justice," Sullivan said. "I used to love to see the wild flowers in the hills out the Windsor way."

"They were all out this spring," Walker said emphatically.

"Beautiful! Here, please use this table to arrange your papers." Sullivan cleared a space for him and waited for him to sit, before he sat behind his desk.

"Wheeler has been in our gaol for a week," Justice Walker introduced the subject abruptly. "He's complaining about no legal representation."

Sullivan nodded. "I've read the arrest warrant. It seems satisfactory as far as it goes. How are you sure that rape took place? Dr. Wright isn't willing to say that she was actually raped."

"The mother examined Betsy Wheeler," Walker said drily.

"The mother?" Sullivan raised an eyebrow.

"She's an honest woman."

"Honest is beside the point. Wheeler was taking the children away from her. She could have seized on the issue of rape to strike back at him. I understand they often quarreled."

"True," Walker admitted.

"What made you believe her?"

"I've known her a long time," Walker began, "and...."

"You've had a lot of sympathy for her," Sullivan added with a wry smile. "Perhaps you didn't want her to be separated from her family? Perhaps you were angry with Wheeler because he beat his family and generally caused much difficulty in the community?"

Walker sat very stiffly. Sullivan picked up a paper in front of him and studied it.

"I believe Ephraim Wheeler is a nasty fellow," he said. "But I would have to doubt that he raped his daughter.

However, if his daughter said he did, then we have her word against his. If it were simple intercourse, the issue would be incest and not so serious. Unfortunately for Wheeler, his reputation for violence leads us to assume that if he is not convicted on the serious charge, he could very well kill his daughter and his wife."

"Exactly so, sir," Walker nodded emphatically.

"Ah!" Sullivan regarded Walker shrewdly. "It was your sense of this which caused you to believe Mrs. Wheeler so readily."

"Exactly." Walker allowed a touch of humor about his eyes in his otherwise sombre face.

"You've committed the Government to a course of action which we have no choice but to pursue, Justice Walker," Sullivan said gravely, and, noticing Walker's uneasiness, added, "I might haved done the same."

"Thank you, sir," Walker said, his sense of relief evident in the relaxing of his stiff posture.

"But I fear that the success of our case depends on the nature of Wheeler's response. Now!" Sullivan stood up abruptly and rubbed his hands in an expression of energy. "You brought the mother and daughter with you. Let us meet them."

Walker went to the door, which he opened wide and, from the threshold of which, he signaled to someone in the next room. Harriette Wheeler and Betsy stepped into view. Sullivan noticed that their homespun dresses were well-tailored and neat-looking. Both women were pretty: the mother fair and the daughter dark. The hard physical work of their class had stamped them with its burden. The slight stoop of shoulder of Harriette Wheeler spoke of long hours at the spinning wheel.

Sullivan saw their anxiety and tried to put them at ease. "Sorry to have to bring you to Lenox, Mrs. Wheeler and Miss Wheeler. Please sit down. I was just mentioning to Mr. Walker that the press of business has kept me from visiting in your area for some time."

"T'weren't no trouble, sir," Harriette said respectfully, and, indicating to Betsy where to sit, she took the chair that Walker had vacated.

"Betsy enjoyed the ride," Walker volunteered from where he was sitting behind them.

"Did you Betsy?" Sullivan smiled. "Was this your first trip to Lenox?"

"Yes, Mr. Sullivan," Betsy said pleasantly. She felt at ease.

Sullivan was pleased. Betsy spoke out well and forthrightly. She was smart.

"I suppose Justice Walker has explained my role to you. I shall prosecute Ephraim Wheeler in the name of the State for the crime of rape. There is, therefore, the need on my part to understand every incident rather thoroughly." He flipped papers on his desk as if trying to remember where he had left a notation. "Therefore," he cleared his throat, "I would like to hear your version, Betsy, of what happened when you left your brother on the roadside and went into the woods with your father." He looked at Harriette. "You understand that she will be obliged to repeat the story in court before three judges, a jury, and spectators."

"She told me and Justice Walker what happened," Harriette said nervously. "We just want the truth to be known."

"The truth, God's truth is what we all want, Mrs. Wheeler," Sullivan affirmed. "I admire Betsy for the service she is doing us all. Now, Betsy, don't spare us any detail. Tell it as you remember it."

Betsy lowered her face as she began to talk. Her voice shook slightly as she remembered her tearful protestations against accompanying Ephraim into the woods.

"When we went a little distance...."

"How far?" Sullivan asked.

Betsy hesitated and then said firmly, "Twelve rods about."

Sullivan thought that her mother had gone over every detail with her.

She described how she tried to run but Ephraim, seizing a rock, threatened to crush her head. Ephraim slapped her head hard, and when she would not lie on the ground, he hit her twice again. Then, he seized her by the throat and threatened to choke her unless she agreed to lie on her back.

"Were you shouting, both of you?" Sullivan asked.

"No." Betsy shook her head. "We spoke low. I didn't want Ephie to hear, but I think he must have heard some."

She described with growing embarrassment how Ephraim forced her onto her back and struggled to undo her clothes. At first she struggled to keep him from pulling off her underclothes, but the powerful pressure of his hand on her throat almost paralyzed her with pain. She held her legs tightly together and showed him how strong was her resistance, but Ephraim struck her when she resisted his hand. Ephraim forced her to separate her legs. She felt the pine needles against her skin and then her father's member probing against her. He clamped his large hand over her mouth to prevent her from screaming, and she felt her father's strength inside her.

Sullivan put up his hand signaling her to stop when he saw that what she was saying was consistent with her written statement.

"When did you tell your mother?" he asked gently.

"I just came out with it," Betsy said. "I didn't know I was going to tell, but when Daddy sent me home, I was thinking of telling her, because I didn't want to go away from Mama."

"Did you know what your father was planning for you?"

"We were just going to Uncle Isaac's." Tears came to Betsy's eyes, and she turned her head away.

"Are you comfortable there, Mrs. Wheeler?" Sullivan asked pleasantly. "Is Mr. Odel kind to you?"

"We'll be all right for a while," Harriette said.

"Good," Sullivan said. "You'll need a stable home for a time. Thank you for coming to see me."

As Sullivan walked to the door with them, he patted Betsy on the shoulder. "Cheer up, dear girl. Be happy in the knowledge that you did the right thing."

Betsy gave him a slight smile of thanks.

Justice Walker asked the women to wait for him, and, closing the door, returned to speak with Sullivan.

"Did you believe her, Mr. Sullivan?" Walker asked.

"She's telling the truth," Sullivan said pensively, "up to a point. The weakness for our argument lies in what we call 'intention.' Did she consent to intercourse because they had had what she calls partial intercourse some months before? Did she confess the rape only because she saw that her father was taking her away to victimize her more easily? And perhaps she has had intercourse on other occasions."

Walker shifted uneasily on his feet.

"You see, Mr. Walker, the case of Betsy Wheeler is not so simple. A good deal depends on the posture taken by the defense. Aside from being hot-headed and violent, what kind of man is Wheeler?"

"Stubborn," Walker said.

"That's fortunate for us," Sullivan smiled. "He is a simple laborer, is he not?"

"Was a sailor, too, I believe," Walker said.

"Was he? Traveled a bit, then. Not so simple." Sullivan tapped his desktop with his forefinger. "Has his counsel been chosen yet?"

Walker nodded. "Mr. John Hulbert."

Sullivan remembered that Hulbert was an ardent Federalist. "I'll give permission for Mr. Hulbert to see his client. And oh! Mr. Walker, before you escort your charges back to Windsor, allow the Courthouse doctor to examine the girl, will you, please. Surely we can find stronger evidence of rape. There are people who don't like to see evil where it exists."

SIX

John W. Hulbert was assigned by the state of Massachusetts to the most difficult case he had encountered in a ten-year career. Having to rescue a client from a charge of committing the original sin had always been a difficult task in Massachusetts, but to have a client who compounded it with rape on the one hand and incest on the other was to ask for disaster. "Oh Lord!" he cried and slapped his forehead as he paced his law office and sought inspiration. The law in Massachusetts, when the state was formed, altered the colonial law on the subject. Before the Revolution, the penalty for rape was incarceration or death so long as the victim was over ten years of age. Since the Revolution the penalty was certain death. Hulbert dare not refer to the colonial law for guidance, although it had guided the people for two centuries and was particularly applicable to Wheeler's case. He could try to refer to it privately with the judges--that is, if the judges were of the right understanding. He seized his briefcase and headed for the prison for his first meeting with Wheeler.

Ephraim was in the common room and talking with two other prisoners. Hulbert walked jauntily into the room with a guard.

"Wheeler!" shouted the guard above the din of chatter.

Ephraim, breaking away quickly, came up to Hulbert with a broad smile. His manner was ingratiating, Hulbert thought. He distrusted him. Wheeler, he could tell at once, belonged to that underclass of petty thievery and drunken rowdiness. The guard directed them to a small conference-room which was actually a cell converted for this purpose.

"As your lawyer, I must know everything as it really happened," Hulbert began, intending to make a brief speech about cooperation.

"I wouldn't be here," Ephraim broke in, "if it weren't for my wife."

"She reported the rape, you mean?" Hulbert frowned with annoyance.

"No! She said she'd serve me out someday." Ephraim gritted his teeth.

"You didn't rape your daughter?" Hulbert asked with a look of distaste.

"I never did rape Betsy. I did never think of that sort of thing with Betsy," Wheeler said emphatically.

"Mr. Wheeler, look here," Hulbert said uncomfortably. His somewhat superior, self-composed look gave way to one of concern. "If you had intercourse with your daughter, please tell me truthfully, and we can arrange a suitable defense."

Wheeler shook his head. "I had no such thought about Betsy. I wanted my children away from my wife."

"And did you not take Betsy into the woods at Partridgefield?" Hulbert asked.

"Yes, I did. To gather avensroot. We went two or three rods and were gone about as many minutes." Ephraim sat back in his chair and regarded Hulbert steadfastly.

Hulbert scribbled notes to himself.

"My wife is particular sweet on avensroot. I wanted the children to take some back to her," Ephraim explained.

Hulbert thought for a moment. "I suppose the question which everyone would ask at this point is why would you want to give your wife a gift after you quarreled violently with her that morning and after you made up your mind to leave her for good?"

Ephraim looked away, but not before Hulbert saw the sad expression in his face. Hulbert waited, but Ephraim did not reply.

"I understand then," Hulbert said. "You wish to base your defense on the fact that your wife plotted against you."

"She's done it before," Ephraim said fiercely. "And she's always been hampering me."

"Done it before? How?"

"Well," Ephraim seemed to struggle with himself. "We had separated for a year and a half, and she returned to me for only a short while when she left me again. She laid a plot with Samuel Peters and William Martin to injure me. They had a frolic at Odel's, and, while I was peaceably passing the road, they dragged me from my horse and beat me severely. I complained to the authority, and they were both fined for the assault; but they swore that if I did not pay the money back to them, they would obtain satisfaction by abusing me; but in what way they never told me."

Hulbert felt himself beginning to believe Ephraim, and he checked his sympathies. He had to remain objective. "Has your wife ever threatened you?"

"Oh yes," Ephraim admitted. "She often told me that if it were not wicked, she'd poison me or bind me when I was asleep and whip me to death."

"But surely that was said only in the heat of argument," Hulbert smiled.

"She was in the daily habit of wishing me dead," Ephraim said adamantly, "so she could put the children out and be in as good a situation as she was before I saw her."

"Wait a moment!" Hulbert said sharply, glancing at his notes. "Did you not tell me that she accused you of rape to prevent you from taking the children away?"

"Yes, sir," Ephraim said, looking Hulbert directly in the eyes. "I'd have kept from her the money she'd have made."

"Hm," Hulbert rubbed his chin thoughtfully. "If your wife wished you such evil, why did you stay with her; why did you keep taking her back when she left you?"

"For the sake of the children," Ephraim said sadly. "If I left them with her, she'd put them out. At the same time, they needed their mother. So I had no choice but to take her back."

"Well, Ephraim, you sound like a compassionate man."

Ephraim looked at the floor. "I been passionate and many times to blame. But I love my children. I'd do nothing to hurt them, Mr. Hulbert. And I know the evil of being put out because that happened to me when I was eight." Tears came to Ephraim's eyes, and Hulbert watched in dismay as they ran down his cheeks, until Ephraim roughly brushed them away.

"That's enough for today," Hulbert said, getting to his feet.

"That's all I want to say for any day," Ephraim said gruffly. "I said too much as it is."

"Not if you want to save yourself," Hulbert warned.

Ephraim grimaced. "Sorry to make your job difficult, Mr. Hulbert. But I did not rape Betsy, and there's an end to it."

Hulbert noted the resentment in Ephraim's voice and, fearing to provoke him with further comment, put out his hand and shook Ephraim's hand with firmness and without another word.

As soon as he was back in the street, Hulbert was beset by contradictory thought. Was Ephraim lying, or an honest man victimized by a cruel wife, a compassionate person who bore his hardships stoically, or nothing but a rough-necked villain. He decided to talk with Ephraim's brother-in-law, Isaac Odel, to see if he could discover the truth about Ephraim. There was something strange in Ephraim's blaming his wife for the whole nasty business. After all, Betsy was his accuser. But he would say nothing against his daughter. Hulbert saw a tangle of emotions and arguments developing in this case and wondered if he could keep from being overwhelmed. In the meantime, he had other legal business to attend to.

Ephraim's interview with Hulbert made Ephraim think of his children's future. He sensed the great gulf that had opened between him and his family. He was truly a wretched man, doomed to suffer from birth, it seemed, and doomed to be misunderstood. He retreated to his cell and lay on his cot in a mood of despair.

His mistake was to marry Harriette Odel. If he had stayed a bachelor, none of this trouble would have happened.

"Don't take the lawyers so serious-like," a voice said.

He recognized the speaker and kept his eyes closed.

"Don't believe them, and you won't get depressed. I learned that early in the game."

Ephraim sat up and, leaning on one elbow, regarded the tall slim man whom he knew as Gentle Adams. His real name had been lost shortly after he was born over fifty years ago. His strong, lean, unshaven face had seen life from all angles. Ephraim had seen it first as his Captain during Shays' Rebellion.

"The law only wants your money," Gentle Adams said sarcastically and took a seat on the end of Ephraim's cot.

"It's not the lawyer; it's my family," Ephraim sighed. "They want to do me in. I don't mean nothing to them."

"Aw, it'll blow over, Ephraim," Gentle said with a wave of his hand. "They're not gonna see you hung. They'll withdraw the charges."

Ephraim felt relieved at those words. He respected Gentle Adams as a wise and experienced man who could read and write yet lived and suffered with the common folk.

"I hope so, but you don't know how vicious Harriette can be," Ephraim said.

The turnkey appeared at the cell door and bellowed, "Every man to his own cell!"

"Cheer up, my friend," Gentle clapped him on the shoulder as he stood up. "We'll get you out of it."

Gentle moved swiftly out the door with an amused look at the rotund turnkey. The door slammed shut. Ephraim fell back on his cot while his mind seized upon Gentle's last words as a promise of hope.

SEVEN

The summer weather had come. The long sunny days were beautiful. Betsy remembered the joy from previous years of walking in the hills, drinking from the streams, and lying in the warm sun. She turned away from the window. All that seemed far in the past. She dared not show herself outside the house. Her friends snubbed her, the townspeople stared at her, and the shopkeepers waited on her with hostility in their eyes. Her mother did the shopping. She was shown some sympathy. The Congregational Minister had said a few words in praise of wives who protect their daughters, and everyone thought he was referring to Harriette Wheeler.

Betsy was still terrified of her father. She thought that he was not going to be kept in gaol, and he would come to the house in the night and murder her. For several weeks after the rape, she had hardly slept, but, through sheer exhaustion, she did begin to sleep, and, in time, her nerves became less raw. There was the possibility that Ephraim would escape confinement and arrive in the house to force her to lie with him. She had nightmares about such an event and awakened screaming in the night.

Harriette tried to comfort her daughter whenever she could, but she had little time. She worked long hours in other people's houses while Betsy plied the spinning wheel at home and prepared the meals for the family. Isaac Odel gave them room in his home and nothing more. His family treated them as strangers, and Isaac was barely civil. They were tolerated only because they were relatives.

The terrible sin was in everyone's mind. Betsy did not have to go into the village to feel it. Like a ghostly presence, it lived with her in the house. She had come to terms with it. She acknowledged its existence but refused to relate to it. Moreover, her anxiety over the possibility of Ephraim taking revenge against her and her mother far outweighed her concern about the sin for the moment. The many beatings Harriette suffered at Ephraim's hands were closeted in Betsy's memories of growing up. When she saw her mother kneeling and weeping inconsolably, Betsy was overwhelmed with a sense of helplessness. This sense came over her when she allowed her mind to dwell on the past. She threw down her stitching work and picked up a pail to fetch water from the well for the noonday meal. All the family would be returning from the fields soon. The Odels were a hungry lot, and her aunt was a demanding woman.

As she approached the door, she saw the shadow of a man against the glass. She froze with fear. The knocking on the door frame seemed like the rap of doom. She prepared to die, and, unable to move, waited for her father to push the door open and come up to her.

The knocking recommenced, louder. Still she did not move. Then the man moved away. She waited for what seemed several minutes before she went to the window and peered out stealthily from the side. There was a man standing outside the barn and patting the head of his horse. He was not Ephraim. He appeared to be waiting. Betsy could not stay in hiding. She had a meal to prepare. Summoning her courage, she walked briskly out the door and crossed the field to the well.

As she raised the bucket and prepared to carry it back to the house, the stranger came up from behind.

"Is this the Odel farm?" he asked.

"Yes sir," Betsy glanced at him and started to walk with her heavy load.

"I came to see Isaac Odel," he said.

He was sort of stuck-up, she thought.

"He's comin'," she said. "Wait a little."

He stood by the well and watched her carry the water into the house. John W. Hulbert guessed that he had spoken to Betsy Wheeler. She had the dark coloring of her father and his independent attitude.

Hulbert lowered a cup into the well and drew up the cool water for a long drink as he reflected on Betsy's full figure. At thirteen she looked like a woman. Could her father have been attracted to her? The thought was disconcerting.

He caught sight of a man astride a horse and a horse and wagon carrying people emerging from behind a line of trees. The man, when he saw Hulbert, galloped ahead of the wagon and presently dismounted at the barn and approached in a long-legged farmer's stride.

Odel nodded and regarded him curiously.

Hulbert introduced himself as Ephraim's lawyer. "I won't keep you long, Mr. Odel. I know you're hungry."

Odel nodded, his expression stony as usual.

"Your brother-in-law will get himself hanged if he's not careful. If I'm to help him, I'll need to know more about him than he's willing to tell me."

"I'll help," Odel said.

"Well then, I'll be straight with you. What kind of relationship did Ephraim have with his wife, your sister, I believe?"

"Not good," Odel spat.

The wagon stopped near them. Two women and two boys lifted out burlap sacks, bulging presumably with food, and carried them hurriedly into the house.

"He's violent with her, but he provided for them best he could," Odel said. "If things got too stormy between them, they'd move in with me. Then they'd be all right and move out again."

"Would she do anything to hurt Ephraim deliberately?"

"She would," Odel said. "She can't forgive him for wanting to take away her children, 'specially the baby."

Hulbert smiled slightly. "Do you mean she's not so much worried about the rape?"

Odel shifted uneasily. "Hard to tell. Rape, if such it was," Odel paused, "is her weapon against Ephraim."

A woman called him from the doorway of the house.

48

"Excuse me, Mr. Hulbert," Odel said, indicating that he had to go.

"When you're in Lenox, stop in to see me," Hulbert said hurriedly as Odel moved away.

"Will do," Odel called back.

Hulbert went to his horse and led it to a trough of water before mounting for the journey back to Lenox.

When his wife called, Odel was always quick to respond. Mrs. Odel hated him to be late for meals, and, quite early in their marriage, she scolded him unrelentingly such that he became anxious about being on time for meals, for bedtime, for appointments involving his wife. He did not argue. He remained silent in the stream of abuse, which, unchecked, swelled to a torrent at times.

Today Mrs. Odel seemed satisfied with Isaac's quick response. "Who was that person?" she asked suspiciously and followed Odel to the meal table in the kitchen. When he told her, she laughed derisively. "Ephraim's gonna need more than lawyers. I hope you didn't tell him anything."

As she did not expect a reply, Isaac bowed his head in prayer, waited until the others did the same, and said a brief grace.

Betsy who was standing at the stove, ate her soup there in between watching the main course cook. Only when she took away the soup plates and set down the main course did she join the others at table. They ate hungrily in silence.

Betsy gathered that her father was to be defended in court. This whole new world of courts and lawyers seemed vaguely menacing. A trial date had been set in September. It seemed far enough away not to cause her great anxiety as if the beautiful summer days reflected a contentment of simple living before the reckoning.

Finally, she broke the silence, timorously. "Is Daddy coming home?"

Odel looked sternly at her and shook his head.

Ephie glanced quickly at Betsy, a pang of regret in his look, and, resuming eating, he banned further thoughts of his father by reflecting on his happy companionship with his cousin who was sitting beside him.

Betsy did not believe Odel. Ephraim always came back. But she did expect him to be different. The trial would change him.

"One thing is sure," Mrs. Odel said sternly. "Ephraim is not coming back to this house."

Odel did not reply.

"He's hurt our reputation enough as it is," she said.

Betsy left off eating. She felt nauseous. She excused herself and went to her bed in the next room where she stretched out and pushed the pillow hard against her face.

The Odels and Ephie continued to eat in silence.

In the meantime, John W. Hulbert had reached Partridgefield in his round-about way back to Lenox. He had decided to take a look at the scene of the alleged crime since he was in the neighborhood. The copse at the bend in the road lay just ahead of him in the bright noonday sunshine. To his surprise, he found a horse tethered at the side of the road. He dismounted and tethered his horse close by, and, feeling for his dagger inside his coat, he undid the strap on its holster so as to be able to pull it out quickly. Then he proceeded cautiously into the woods.

EIGHT

Hulbert walked about sixty yards through the underbrush when he caught sight of a man sitting on a stump with his back to him. He stood for a moment trying to decide whether to retreat or continue, when it occurred to him that the man may have been investigating the scene of the crime as well. Curious now, he stepped forward quickly and trod on a twig which snapped. The seated man looked round. His elegant dress and powdered hair marked him as a gentleman. He seemed familiar, but the trees prevented Hulbert from getting a good look until he was almost upon him.

Sullivan got up from the log he had been sitting on and, smiling broadly, stretched his hand out to Hulbert. "The coincidence can be explained somewhat by the fact that this is the best day we've had for prowling the woods."

"I had business near-by," Hulbert explained, "so I...."

"Nice to see you take an interest in your client's welfare," Sullivan said, and turned to survey the small clear area in front of him.

Tall oak stood about them. The underbrush thinned out at this spot. Pine needles and tufts of long grass covered the ground.

"An ideal place for a romantic tryst, wouldn't you say, Hulbert?" Sullivan said. "One can imagine the naughty thoughts of a would-be lover who had arranged to take the object of his fascination into these woods."

Hulbert smiled warily. "I can't imagine it, Attorney-General."

"This is the spot where Wheeler took Betsy to gather avensroot," Sullivan said. "Do you see any avensroot, Hulbert?"

"I wouldn't know it if I saw it," Hulbert said. "I don't eat it, and I don't know any one who does."

"True, it is a delicacy only for those who cannot afford chocolate," Sullivan said quietly with a slight hint of reproach. "But even gentlemen know that roots come from the ground, and, therefore, we should see the signs of digging, shouldn't we?"

Hulbert blushed.

Sullivan moved forward into the small clearing. "Instead, we see some marks of a struggle--grass clumps torn up from the ground, small sprouts of trees crushed and broken, and scratchings on the ground evident even several weeks after the rape."

"That's just it, Mr. Sullivan," Hulbert said quickly. "They could have been made a few days ago."

"Ah yes, but we know only of the Wheelers who came to this place," Sullivan smiled. "That is our frame of context."

"If other lovers were here," Hulbert said, "we could hardly expect them to inform the Attorney-General of Massachusetts."

Sullivan threw back his head and laughed. 'Touché, mon ami. But I am making the point that all signs point to a struggle rather than, shall we say, a snuggle in the woods?"

Hulbert gazed up at the treetops swaying gently in the wind and tinted with sunlight. He acknowledged that the desires hidden in the caverns of men's minds could rush out to express themselves in idyllic hideaways such as this. "We don't even know if the Wheelers stopped here or perhaps twenty yards over there?"

Sullivan walked about inspecting the ground for some clue, a button, a piece of cloth. One leg had been badly broken in childhood and the knee of the other was stiffened by disease.

"If we suppose that Wheeler took his daughter on this piece of ground," Hulbert said thoughtfully, "those marks could be from passion as much as from resistance."

"Ah! you concede that the act of coition took place," Sullivan said, still watching the ground.

"For the purpose of conjecture," Hulbert warned. "Remember, Wheeler claims he did not rape the girl. For the purpose of conjecture, then, we think of it as an act of passion. On the way back to her mother, Betsy begins to feel guilty. She confesses her crime to her mother and makes it appear that Wheeler forced her to lie with him."

"My dear Hulbert, what child is going to disobey her father's commands unless he forces her to do something which is repulsive to her? Going into the woods was a command to be obeyed. But having intercourse? well, her bruises and swollen jaw were evidence that she fought against it."

Hulbert looked questioningly at Sullivan. "Betsy might have cried out in passion, and Ephraim clamped his hand over her mouth to prevent the boy from hearing them. The bruises and the swelling may have been inadvertent."

"It is an argument I hope you will make in court," Sullivan said giving up on his search. "You cannot draw me out, Hulbert. I keep my own counsel."

"And part of it is, I hope, not to send an innocent man to the gallows."

"That is for the jury to decide, mon ami." Sullivan started back for the road. "I have my duty to represent the State which accuses Wheeler of rape."

They walked through the woods in silence. Hulbert had come to understand that Ephraim's only defense was to deny there was a rape.

When they reached the road, Sullivan wished him good luck on the long road to the trial in September, and mounting his horse, headed north-east to Cummington. Hulbert decided to walk for a while, and, leading his horse, he followed the road through the hamlet of Partridgefield.

The man in Hulbert's thoughts was at that moment talking with Gentle Adams in the Lenox gaol. Ephraim had no thoughts for his defense. Rather he was reminiscing with Gentle about an incident in the Rebellion, which they had fought for the sake of the men who lived on the land against the class in the halls of government.

"We were a messy lot, messy!" Gentle said. "Lincoln's boys picked us off like flies at Petersham. We should never have met 'em head on. Never!"

"They didn't meet my head," Ephraim said. "They saw my behind."

"Never mind," Gentle laughed. "From the hindsight of twenty years, we know we lost the battle but won the war. We got paper money and no one's being evicted."

"Yes," Ephraim said sarcastically, "and you're still locked up and the same old River Gods are governin' us."

"I've stayed clear of 'em," Gentle smiled at Ephraim's reference to the Federalists, who made fortunes in banking out of the misfortunes of the farmers. "This charge is like the others. They'll have to let me go."

Ephraim shook his head slowly. "They'll get you like they got me."

"They ain't got you, Ephraim, if you don't let 'em."

"I should've taken a blast at Petersham," Ephraim said. "It would have spared me the miseries since then."

"I'm worried about you, lad. You're lettin' yourself get ripe for the executioner." Gentle regarded him intently. "You're sick in the soul. I see the symptoms. Look!" Gentle seized Ephraim by the shoulder. "In our time together every afternoon, tell me about yourself."

"Ah'" Ephraim shrugged off his hand. "Don't be daft!"

"There's a reason for it," Gentle insisted. "You don't know it, but you're makin' yourself a martyr. But for what? There has to be a cause. The answer to that is in your life."

Ephraim looked at him skeptically. "What good would it do?"

"It'll help you to defend yourself. How do you think I could have survived these years in and out of gaols if I had not examined myself?"

Ephraim had great respect for superior intelligence, the kind he saw in Gentle Adams. The pressure and turmoil within him seemed to want to seek relief in that intelligence, to be guided by it, assuaged by it.

"Just before I was twenty-one and got my freedom," Ephraim confessed hesitantly, as if the memory were causing him pain, "I fell in love with a beautiful woman named Susanna Randal. We were going to be married."

Adams knew something of Ephraim's youth bound to a shoemaker after his parents died. "Her love for you must have been very meaningful," he said.

Ephraim nodded. "You see, I had never known affection. My older brother was put out to a sea captain years before, and my sister married young and lived in a distant place. My master's wife feared to show me affection. After my master struck me on the head with a hand-spike injuring me so much that I almost lost my life, I knew he cared nothing for me, and I resolved to leave him. I went to Easton, about forty miles distant, and looked for a laboring job. But my master pursued me," Ephraim began to speak with the passion of remembrance. "I had just found refuge at a farm where I could work when I recognized my master's harsh voice shouting at the front of the house. I ran out the back door, but I had gone only twenty yards before he ran me down with his horse. He took me to the barn and tied me for the night. He kicked me awake early in the morning. 'We'll learn you to shirk your obligations,' he said. Tying me to his horse's tail with a rope around my neck, he pulled or rather dragged me back the forty miles in one day. At those settlements along the way where I was known, he would call the people out and inform them that he had caught the runaway. I was mortified to the point where I no longer cared if I lived or died. Despite my exhaustion, as soon as he released me into the house, I walked through it and out the back door. I escaped and traveled as speedily as I could to Providence to find a ship bound for a foreign country. But before I got aboard, my master's brother and another man, who pursued me, caught me, and took me back bound hand and foot. This final failure completely broke my spirit. I fell into a deep depression and determined to serve the rest of my time, which was short."

"So it was Susanna Randal who made you want to live again," Adams suggested, impressed by Ephraim's eloquence.

"Her and Elder Hunt in Middleborough," Ephraim said softly.

Adams concealed his surprise. He knew enough about Asa Hunt, the Baptist preacher, to imagine the magnetic charm that such a dynamic, welcoming soul could have for this lonely and much-abused boy. After the meeting house was erected in Middleborough, Massachusetts about 1780, there was an extraordinary mass conversion to Hunt's Church. He remembered thinking at the time that if he was ever traveling in the direction of Middleborough, he would go round the town rather than through it. Tom Paine's writings were his gospel, but even common sense might momentarily succumb to the unpredictable powers of the supernatural.

"My master became a different man when I attained twenty-one," Ephraim continued after a pause. "He treated me well, and I forgot my hatred. Susanna seemed agreeable to marry me. But just as I engaged to work another year for my master, I ruptured myself lifting a stone. I was confined for a year, and it took all the property I had in the world to pay my physicians and nurses during my confinement. In the meanwhile, friends of Susanna Randal persuaded her to refuse me, because I was destitute of property."

Adams listened for a false note and wondered if there were other reasons for her to lose faith in Ephraim's ability to provide for them.

"Despairing and desolate," Ephraim continued disconsolately, "unable to find comfort for my loss, I shipped myself on board a brig which sailed to Brazil. How many times did I think of casting myself over the rail into those waters, as my father did before me. The voyage lasted a year, and, with the anxiety in my mind, it was a painful period.

"Shays' War was underway when I returned. You know my story then." He looked sadly into Adams' eyes. "When released from detention, I blew and struck for blacksmiths for a year at a time moving from town to town. Then, hearing that Susanna Randal was in Saratoga, I went to see her. She told me she was soon to be married to another man. My wounds, which had almost healed, were opened again and bled anew by my foolish action."

"People heal over time," Adams said. "But you're still suffering. Why did you marry?"

Ephraim shook his head. "I should never have taken that foolish step had it not been for the distracted state of my mind and my lonesome and despised condition. But after I married Harriette, I considered it my duty to live with her, and treat her as a wife." He was about to add something, but the prison guard came between them.

"You," he said gruffly to Adams. "The sheriff wants to see you." He pointed toward the anteroom.

"The sheriff!" Adams exclaimed. "This means either very bad or very good news." He nodded to Ephraim. "Won't be long."

In the anteroom where visitors encountered prisoners, Colonel Larned, High Sheriff of Berkshire County, stood inside the metal grating, his hands on his hips and an impish smile on his strong intelligent face.

"What's the news, Colonel?" Adams smiled broadly. He was cheered by the sight of this man, one of the few true democrats who held an authoritative post in the governments of Massachusetts.

"You're free," Larned said, showing him a document.

Adams, elated, just glanced over the words. "Now! This minute! How did you do it?"

"I'm running for Congress as representative from Pittsfield," Larned said softly.

Adams laughed. "So now the locals are listening to you."

"There's a condition," Larned said.

"That they set or you set?"

"I set. You work for me."

'That's not a condition," Adams smiled. "That's a pleasure. What do I do?"

"Travel." The sheriff looked round to make sure they were not being overheard. "Throughout the State."

CHOCOLATE

"Aha," Adams said. "You need eyes and ears."

"Exactly," the sheriff emphasized sharply. "And political savvy."

"Will it be an official position? I mean, representing you?" Adams asked, puzzled.

"Nope," Larned smiled mischievously. "Officially, as soon as you get your things and leave this prison, you are going to the West Indies. Let's get out."

Adams sensed the sheriff's sudden impatience, and, still puzzling over the nature of his political role, he retrieved his small bag, threw in his few personal belongings, and called by at Ephraim's cell.

Ephraim was lying on his bed. His face was buried in his pillow.

"I'm going on the outside," Gentle said. "We'll get you there too," he added compassionately, "then we can finish your story."

Ephraim looked at him with puzzled surprise.

"It's secret business," Gentle said. "But I'll be back for you."

"You got the luck, my good friend," Ephraim said and fell back onto his pillow.

Gentle Adams regretted leaving the man before he had been able to do anything for him. He sensed the gloom he was leaving behind in contrast to the colorful adventure awaiting him.

Sheriff Simon Larned epitomized adventure. A heroic Colonel in the Revolutionary War, he was a true democrat, who supported the farmers and used his office to mitigate the rulings of the courts against them. He had the respect of the community, so his election to Congress would help the cause beyond what he could actually do as a Congressman. The Federalists feared him because they could not disparage him with the people. Moreover, they never knew what he was thinking because he was taciturn, and he was circumspect in his actions.

Gentle Adams passed out of the anteroom behind Colonel Larned and into the great outdoors. He sighed, closed his eyes, and took a deep breath. "It was ten months this time," he said to the Colonel who stood regarding him.

"We're giving you a new identity to keep you out of those places," the sheriff said as they began walking.

Gentle marveled at the dark greenery of the trees along the street, and looked with love at the hills in the distance; such soft and gentle shapes were soothing to the eyes.

"The Berkshire Inn is three miles out of Lenox," Larned continued. "We have a room for you there." He stopped to frown at Gentle who seemed not to be listening. "We'll meet there privately for dinner tonight."

"How do I pay for it?" Gentle smiled.

"You don't, we do" the Colonel said, "at least, for the first three nights." He fished some coins from his pocket and gave them to Adams. "We'll arrange it all tonight."

Larned recognized John W. Hulbert approaching them. He fell silent, nodded at Hulbert as he passed, and gave a questioning look at Adams.

"That man won't save Wheeler's life," Adams said as if in answer. "Wheeler is ready-made for our leaders to remind people of the original sin," he added sarcastically.

The sheriff said, touching the broad brim of his hat, departed from Adams.

John W. Hulbert looked back to see Colonel Larned separate from Gentle Adams. Instead of sheriff and prisoner they looked like old friends. Probably they had been through the wars together, he thought. Moreover, the sheriff was a Republican and seemed to relish mixing with the low life. The low life held no attraction for Hulbert. It was all Hulbert could do to stay fifteen minutes with Ephraim Wheeler in the gaolhouse. Without refinements, life was not worth living, he thought, yet he sympathized with Wheeler for wanting to continue to live despite his poverty. It was this sympathy which caused him to put some effort into defending Wheeler--

aside from advancing his professional reputation. At bottom he suspected that Wheeler raped his daughter. The obscene seemed a part of the low life; it was to be expected.

Hulbert was conducted through the anteroom to Wheeler's cell where the guard left them together. Ephraim was still lying on his bed, but he sat up when Hulbert sat on the chair.

"Have you changed your mind about our line of defense?" Hulbert asked.

Ephraim shook his head.

"Look," Hulbert sighed in exasperation. "We are not interested in the truth. We are interested in saving your life."

"That's the truth, what I said."

"Just to deny something happened isn't positive enough," Hulbert argued. "Our best defense is to attack Betsy's testimony. Make her appear to be lying."

Ephraim shook his head vigorously. "Leave my daughter be. You want to know who's lying? It's my wife. Attack her. She's behind it all."

"But," Hulbert protested, "don't you see she is not on trial. She will not be called on as a witness. To the jury she is going to be an abstract entity."

"What's that?"

"She won't exist for them because they won't see her or hear her," Hulbert said calmly, although he felt like shouting it in Wheeler's ear.

"I don't care about that," Ephraim said firmly. "She's done this to me, so if you attack anybody, attack her. She's always been against me so you'll be doing me a favor if you bring that fact out."

"Let me be clear." Hulbert stood up and took a step away. "You want me to build a case against your wife on the facts that she had always hated you and took every opportunity to hurt you? That is why she cooked up this story about rape and persuaded Betsy to testify against you?"

Ephraim nodded.

Hulbert made a grimace. "Very well, I'll do my best, but I am warning you, it is not your best defense."

"I refuse to use Betsy," Ephraim said sternly. "She has been used enough."

"Do you love her?" Hulbert asked suddenly.

Ephraim looked taken aback. "I love my daughter," he said so quietly that Hulbert barely heard him.

"And your wife?"

Ephraim groaned and brought his hands over his face.

Hulbert winced at the remorse he saw there. He thought of simply ending the conversation, but he pursued it. "How are they going to survive if you are taken from them? Have you thought of that?"

"Many times." Ephraim took away his hands and looked at Hulbert with misery in his eyes.

"I spoke with Betsy," Hulbert smiled. "She's a nice girl, a pretty girl. Ought to make some lucky man a fine wife some day."

Ephraim followed his words with interest. "How is her uncle looking after her?"

"We didn't observe that, except that he's a responsible man," Hulbert said.

"Yes." Ephraim looked at the floor. "Just as long as she gets no disrespect."

"I'll see her again," Hulbert said. "We have to try to get her to withdraw her accusation. Enough time has gone by for that to be possible, I think."

"It's not Betsy, it's my wife. She wants me out of the way."

"I can't believe she can be that vindictive." Hulbert shook his head.

"Things between us have been getting worse over the years. We lived separate all last winter and got together for only a month before this happened." Ephraim fell back onto his bed and closed his eyes. "She'd like to see me in my grave."

Hulbert caught a glimpse of the tangled relationship of Ephraim's marriage and realized that Ephraim was right; it was his wife who was prosecuting him. But was it willful? Hulbert guessed that she was doing her duty as a mother-- carrying out the social imperative--doing what society expected.

"I'll speak with her," Hulbert said. "But it is Betsy who will decide whether you live or die."

"I told you what to do," Ephraim said angrily. He opened his eyes and glared at Hulbert as the lawyer left the cell.

Hulbert was perturbed. He disliked taking orders from his client, and he felt uneasy about Ephraim's stubbornness. There was something the man was hiding from him. But perhaps he would find the answer through the wife.

NINE

From what he had learned, Hulbert knew that the Wheelers had a stormy marriage. First of all, the clergyman of the Congregational Church refused to marry them because Ephraim was a Baptist. They went to Rhode Island to be married and returned to live for two years in her father's house in Worthington. Ephraim fell into debt. When his only possessions, a horse and cow, were taken, she left him for a year and a half. This became a pattern throughout their married life. Debt, separation, reunion.

Hulbert encountered some reluctance on James Sullivan's part to allow him to confer with Harriette Wheeler. He sensed that Sullivan wanted the trial as a vehicle to keep him before the public. He had been the gubernatorial candidate for the Republican Party in the last election and remained its leader. After some arguing carried out by correspondence, Sullivan relented. Since he lived in Boston and was occupied with political matters, Sullivan took a good two weeks to come to Lenox.

Sullivan and Mrs. Wheeler were in Sullivan's office when Hulbert arrived. Harriette was trying to look composed, but Hulbert sensed she was nervous. She clasped her hands tightly, and she darted glances between Sullivan and Hulbert as if she mistrusted them.

After shaking hands with Harriette, Hulbert took a chair near her by Sullivan's desk, behind which Sullivan sat.

"You are most kind to see me," Hulbert began. He noticed that she held herself in a rigid posture. She nodded stiffly and slightly, as if she were determined not to commit herself in any way.

"We recognize that you have a duty to your client," Sullivan said affably, "and we welcome an opportunity to make our position clear to you."

"Your husband, if you don't mind my saying it," Hulbert smiled slightly at Harriette, "is a man of strong opinions."

Harriette nodded. "Yes, he's stubborn, right enough."

"He appears to me to be dedicated to the welfare of his family."

Harriette made no reply.

"He cares very much for Betsy, and he denies adamantly that he abused her," Hulbert said.

Harriette sat in silence.

"Now, I know that relations between you have not been good. But you have always made your peace with one another and held your family together."

Harriette looked at Sullivan.

"This was unlike any other time," Sullivan said.

"I know, the charge is heinous. The people of this county are revolted by it," Hulbert continued speaking to Harriette. "And if Ephraim goes to trial, the State and even the country will hear of it and be revolted in turn."

Harriette gripped her hands so that the whites of her knuckle began to show.

"This is an awful thing to happen to a family."

"But I can't go back to him," Harriette said hoarsely. "I just can't do it. He won't change. I've tried, oh God, I've tried!"

Hulbert, taken aback, looked worriedly at Sullivan."But you need not live with him," Hulbert argued, half-admitting that she was right. "We'll arrange it so that you can live separately with the children. Ephraim won't be able to harm you or the children again."

"No one can guarantee that," Harriette said sadly.

"There's the issue of the crime itself," Sullivan broke in. "A grand jury has seen the evidence and ordered a trial. I must say, Mr. Hulbert, that matters have gone too far in the public eye for us to withdraw now. Because, after all, the higher issue is what counts. Does he pose a threat to the morality of the people of Massachusetts? The people must pass judgment on Wheeler's guilt. If Mrs. Wheeler and Betsy withdrew the charge now, it would appear that they had fabricated it. What unholy terror would descend upon them? Instead of being criticized by the uninformed few who suspect their motives today, they would be vilified by everyone."

Hulbert could find no reply to Sullivan. The Attorney-General's long experience in state government, and his distinction as the close political ally of the famous John Hancock during the Revolution gave him a reputation for sagacity in public affairs.

"He *did* rape Betsy," Harriette emphasized firmly, breaking the silence. "She *is* telling the truth."

"Then our course is clear," Sullivan said, getting up and coming round his desk. "In good conscience we must prosecute the case."

Hulbert stood, took Mrs. Wheeler's hand, mumbled his thanks, and followed Sullivan to the door. Dazed by the swiftness of the termination of the interview, it was not until he was in the street that he became despondent. He felt trapped as if he himself were headed for the gallows. Less than a month remained before the trial. His mind began to race in a panic as he tried to think of a defensive argument for

Ephraim Wheeler. Whatever thoughts came to him, he rejected as absurd and infantile when confronted with the dignity of the court and the gravity of the crime. Nauseous, he turned off the walkway onto the grass and stood beside a large elm where he put his forehead against the bark and closed his eyes to try to restore some calm to his soul. Within a few minutes he felt better. He walked toward the courthouse where, as it was late afternoon, he expected to find the Chief Justice in his chambers.

Judge Simeon Strong signaled to his clerk that he would see Hulbert. He was a large man with a sour expression. Lawyers, it was said, found it hard to ask him for small favors.

"Yes, young man?" Strong said as he finished reading a paper.

Hulbert stood waiting until the Judge looked up at him with an impatient frown.

"About the Ephraim Wheeler case, your honor," Hulbert began hesitantly. "I was assigned to defend him, but I fear that I am not the right man."

The Judge stared at him sourly in silence.

"It is not fair to the prisoner," Hulbert continued. "I cannot give him adequate defense. I've tried, but every move I make leads to a blind alley."

Strong reached a large hand across his desk to a calendar and turned the leaf to regard the month of September.

"I'm sorry," Hulbert said meekly.

"Your distress is evident, however." Strong allowed a note of sympathy to enter his voice. "What's troubling you?"

"I can't get a handle on it. Wheeler could be innocent, but he seems to think that his innocence before God is sufficient to defend him in a court of law. I'm afraid, very afraid, that I cannot do right by him. I'm just not the right man." Hulbert's eyes pleaded with Strong.

The Judge raised his large frame from his chair, and, coming slowly round to the front of his desk, he put his hand on Hulbert's upper arm. "There are two reasons why I cannot take you off the case. First, it will hurt your reputation, and, second, it will be truly unfair to Wheeler. Do you realize that you are his support? Suddenly deprived of you, the fatalism you tell me he has will be all he had. Now, I can't discuss the case and will allow you to say no more." He began to walk Hulbert to the door.

Crestfallen and ashamed, Hulbert walked like a man on a gangplank.

"On the other hand," Strong said, "the court recognizes the difficulties you are encountering and the formidable opposition which the Attorney-General and his staff represent. Therefore, I am assigning a competent lawyer to assist you--Mr. Daniel Dewey."

"Thank you, your honor," Hulbert choked with relief.

"Don't take it all so seriously," Simeon Strong frowned and spat into the cuspidor beside the door. He patted Hulbert on the shoulder and turned back into his chambers.

The clerk smiled at Hulbert and accompanied him to the street with a few pleasantries about the fine weather.

Hulbert knew Daniel Dewey slightly. He was inexperienced but socially well-connected and with a reputation for cleverness. Dewey practiced law out of Boston. Hulbert decided to write to him about the case that evening; already he was beginning to feel that some of the burden was shifted off his shoulders.

At that moment, he caught sight of Isaac Odel driving a wagon in the street towards him, and he hailed him. Odel pulled his horse to a standstill and came down from the wagon.

"Are you in Lenox for Mrs. Wheeler?" Hulbert asked pleasantly.

"Yep," Odel said. "We're leaving shortly."

"She won't call the trial off," Hulbert said. "I'd hoped she would."

"My sister's got a stubborn streak," Odel said. "And Betsy's no better. 'Course they're scared of Ephraim, scared he'll kill them when he gets out."

"He's not a murderer, surely," Hulbert said.

"No, he's not," Odel said. "I just been to see him. He tells me he holds nothing against them one way or t'other."

"I wish he did," Hulbert snorted. "He won't accuse Betsy of lying."

"Oh, Ephraim's a good man. I've known him many years and I've not heard him talk anyone down. You won't get him to accuse his own daughter. Listen, Mr. Hulbert," Odel stuck out his finger for emphasis. "There's bad blood between Ephraim and my sister, and I'm not saying who's to blame, but there's where the answer to your problem lies. Well," he started to mount the wagon, "we've to get back before night."

"You'll be at the trial?" Hulbert asked anxiously.

Odel nodded and drove away.

Far down the street Hulbert could make out Harriette Wheeler waiting.

TEN

Gentle Adams rode into Lenox on the twelfth day of September, 1805, looking very different from the thin and ailing prisoner who had left it barely a month before. He had grown a mustache and allowed his sideburns to grow long. His breeches and coat were a fine brown leather, and he wore a silk shirt. He left his horse at the Inn and walked directly to the Court House where the Supreme Court of Massachusetts had commenced the proceedings against Ephraim Wheeler.

As he stepped into the courtroom, the jurymen had just been sworn and the foreman was reading their charge: "that Ephraim Wheeler, of Windsor, in the County of Berkshire, laborer, not having the fear of God before his eyes, but being moved and reduced by the instigation of the devil, on the eighth day of June now last past, with face and arms, at Partridgefield, in the County of Berkshire aforesaid and in and upon one Betsy Wheeler, single woman and spinster in the peace of God...violently and feloniously did make an assault and her, the said Betsy Wheeler, then and there did ravish and carnally know, against the law in such case made and provided, against the peace and dignity of the Commonwealth aforesaid."

Adams sat quietly at the back of the room. He had been traveling incognito and wished to remain so. He watched keenly as the three judges agreed to add Daniel Dewey as counsel for the defense with Hulbert and as the jurors came forward one by one to take their place in the jury box. He shook his head in exasperation when he heard Dewey's name.

Suddenly, Ephraim Wheeler's voice rose in challenge. "I said, your honors, I don't trust Mr. Churchill, the Second. He'd sooner see me hanged as not."

Justice Simeon Strong glowered at the prisoner. "Your reason, Mr. Wheeler."

"We had business dealings, and he cheated me," Ephraim said.

Strong raised his thick eyebrows at John Churchill II.

"I have had nothing but good will for him, your honors," Churchill said with a broad smile.

Justice Theodore Sedgewick, a thin man with a long jaw, cleared his throat. "What business is he referring to, Mr. Churchill?"

"He borrowed from me to invest in his land," Churchill explained. "There was a downturn, so I had to reclaim. He could pay only part of the amount, but I cleared the debt."

"He took my horse and cow and left my family starving," Ephraim said angrily.

"Over-ruled," Strong said, looking with disdain at Hulbert and Dewey for failing to control their client.

Daniel Dewey nervously leafed through papers in front of him. He was socially well-connected and exhibited confidence wherever he went in Boston society. In a courtroom, however, he seemed ill at ease, as if he feared being unable to come up with an answer.

Ephraim sat back to watch the next juror being interviewed. "I object to that man on the grounds of his Federalist politics," he said suddenly. "He hates my kind."

"Is that true, Zacharaiah Fairchilds?" Justice Strong asked indifferently.

"Certainly not!" Fairchilds said indignantly.

"Mr. Wheeler," Strong said patiently, "the Governor of this Commonwealth is a Federalist. Does that make him an enemy of yours?"

"I know Fairchilds," Ephraim replied. "He was with General Lincoln at Petersham when they caught us sleeping, and he showed us great cruelty."

Zacharaiah Fairchilds raised his hands in exasperation.

"Did Mr. Fairchilds show great cruelty to you?" asked Justice Sewell, his small eyes boring down at Ephraim as if pinpointing the issue.

"I heard tell what he did to others," Ephraim said quietly.

"This is not a court to tolerate hear-say," Strong thundered. "Your objection is over-ruled."

Ephraim let the next two jurors pass without comment, but at the appearance of Edmund Hinckley, he again demanded the court's attention.

"He took away my house at Partridgefield," Ephraim cried. "I couldn't raise the money on the mortgage and he wouldn't give me time."

"Will you please explain what the prisoner is saying," Justice Sedgewick asked Hinckley.

Edmund Hinckley related how he had lent money to Wheeler to buy land on which Wheeler built a house, but after a couple of years Wheeler fell behind in payments, and, to his great regret, Hinckley was forced to claim the house.

Ephraim raged inwardly as he listened. The memory of his humiliation of being turned out in winter with his family pained him again as it had on many lonely nights when he lay awake thinking of his past. He felt now the same helplessness before the court as he had felt then before Hinckley and the men of the law who accompanied him.

"You did nothing illegal?" Judge Sedgewick asked.

"Not at all, your Honor," Hinckley said.

"Because you entered into an agreement with a man and failed to keep it," Justice Sedgewick explained to Ephraim, "you have no right to blame him for your misfortune."

Ephraim's voice came out of him like a groan. "I built it with my own hands."

Daniel Dewey began to whisper excitedly to Ephraim, but Ephraim shoved him away with both hands and listened keenly to the questioning of Roswell Barber.

"He's always shown me enmity," Ephraim interrupted.

"Explain yourself," Justice Strong demanded impatiently.

"He always took the side of my wife when we lived in Windsor--always interfered in our marriage," Ephraim said petulantly. "I knew him years before I got married; he was never friendly."

"Mr. Roswell Barber," Justice Strong said, "how long have you lived in Windsor?"

"Fifteen years, sir. I knew Ephraim Wheeler when he worked for the Westcot brothers," Barber spoke quickly, his small thin body perched forward like a bird on a tree limb. "I never interfered in his marriage. We used to hear her screaming."

"How did you intervene?" Justice Sewell asked.

"Passing his home I heard the bedlam."

"You saved Mrs. Wheeler from the consequences of his actions," Judge Sewell said.

"Next juror," Justice Strong barked.

Ephraim folded his arms and sat back expressionless to watch the remainder of the proceedings without another word.

Gentle Adams watched with thoughts of all he had been through in the past--revolution, rebellion, imprisonment--and still an oligarchy ran Massachusetts. With Thomas Jefferson, a Republican as President of the nation, he hoped that democracy could be brought to the State where the Federalists held all the power as these three judges demonstrated. Yet here the issue was clouded. Here was James Sullivan, the leader of the Massachusetts' Republicans, standing as Attorney-General at one with the judges in condemning Ephraim. Sullivan was speaking:

"The human race is depraved, and man has become the prey of man. Wherever we turn our eyes, we discover the sad marks of a general apostasy. We see our world engaged in a contest against that truth and justice by which the great First Cause, who produced is pleased to govern it. We see mankind oppressing and committing depredations on each other. From these evils we fly to the arms of civil society for protection. Civil society must be obtained by laws, and laws, unless they are sanctioned by adequate penalties, are inefficacious and idle."

Adams winced when he heard Sullivan claim that the punishment of death alone would deter man from the crimes to which the depravity of his passions led him. The wily Attorney-General was alluding to the uncontrollable excesses of the French Revolutionists, whose guillotining of aristocrats and respected members of the Government provoked a hysterical fear in the ruling class of America. But Adams' expression changed to a sneer when Sullivan laid it down as without argument that the issue before the jury was not incest but rape. Ephraim's stupid lawyers made no objection, no move, no cry; they simply sat astounded by Sullivan's moralizing and incantation of the devil.

Betsy Wheeler was called to the witness stand. What a handsome young lady she was! Long black hair, high white brow, large black eyes and a full figure. Adams could hardly believe that she was thirteen.

She spoke clearly without hesitation, but, above all, her honesty was plain to see.

Sullivan coaxed the events of that fateful morning of June 8th out of her with deft questions. Sullivan's experience showed in his judgment during Betsy's examination. It was a masterful job and must have impressed the jurors.

Adams had not heard the story, and, as he listened to Betsy's testimony, which resembled a confession more than an accusation, he pictured the bickering and sudden violent interchange between Ephraim and his wife, the frustration of Ephraim as he left with his two children, the bend in the road at Partridgefield, the violent happening deep in the woods, the tears, the remorse, and the separation in their ways.

As she testified, Betsy's clear voice translated the fear she had felt. From the way Ephraim ordered her to lie on her back, threatening to kill her, he seemed to have been possessed with a sexual urge which severed him temporarily from his family, from his society, and actually, from his social self. For a few moments, he had become like an animal linked back through the millenniums to the savage beast, which dominated its weaker kind in the supreme exultation of power through the sexual act. Here was this unlettered, albeit eloquent, man in his forties always at the bottom in life, ever struggling, ever losing, able only to announce his manhood by negative action-- drunkenness, violence at home, announcing the separation of the children from the mother, and finally the rape! Adams gasped in admiration as it flashed upon him how brilliantly the Attorney-General was conducting the case. Sullivan had simply elicited "the facts," which set Adams to interpreting them, and which, Adams thought, must have affected the jurors with the same impressions.

Young Ephraim was called to the stand. The court warned that he must not tell a lie because the consequences would be many more times severe than telling a lie at home. Ephie's innocence and his serious look brought a refreshing good humor to the courtroom, which listened attentively to his clear-voiced responses. Obviously, he did not understand what had taken place; he said that his sister tearfully refused to accompany his father into the woods, and that when he offered to go in her place, his father told him to stay with the horse. Whereas Betsy had testified that she was afraid that Ephie had overheard her argument with their father before Ephraim clamped his hand over her mouth, now Ephie said that he had heard nothing.

But what struck Adams was Betsy's concern at keeping knowledge of the rape from Ephie. Despondent and despairing on the road back to Windsor, Betsy had the presence of mind to save Ephie from the shock of discovery. Adams was impressed by her intelligence, and he could no longer withhold his sympathy from this thirteen-year-old who had borne a youth of emotional stress and now disgrace. Adams looked over at Ephraim Wheeler and realized that his friend had another personality inside the man that he knew.

Judge Simeon Strong recessed the court for lunch. The Jury filed out, and the courtroom crowd began to break up. Adams sat for a while and reviewed the testimony in his head. Betsy's appearance made the strongest impression. She described the rape in a manner that there was no doubting her word. Yet she seemed to be telling the story as an obedient child would confess to her teacher; she seemed unaware that she was condemning her father to death. That was the tragedy! Adams thought. That was the mistake that would overtake them all one day.

Adams crossed the street to the tavern where much of the crowd had gone for lunch. He knew several people by sight, but none recognized him. He passed by the room where Sullivan and his legal aides were eating at table. There was a handful of others in the room. They were drinking and talking so that he passed among them unnoticed and ordered a glass of wine at the small bar behind. He settled onto a stool and listened keenly to the conversations in the room. From years of practice he was able to pick up a particular conversation in a crowded room and isolate others from it. The spasmodic talk between Sullivan and his aides attracted his attention.

"Who was it...said...we could lose?" a young lawyer said sarcastically.

"It's not over with yet," another retorted.

"You've nothing to fear, sir," the first lawyer said after taking a long drink of wine.

"No," Sullivan said. "The outcome of the trial was never in doubt; it is the politics of it that we have to fear, my friends."

"Politics!" said the first lawyer. "What possible danger can come from a common laborer?"

"And a convicted rapist?" added another.

"This is not the place to discuss its dangers," Sullivan said, setting down his knife and fork and looking casually around the room. "I want the trial to go no longer than one day. And," he said in a stage whisper, "we must convince the jury to bring in a quick decision."

"I think the judges are with us there, sir," said the first lawyer.

"Ssh!" Sullivan put his finger to his lips with a smile. "My rule of etiquette during a trial is to never mention the judges. Though you are right, my young friend. They don't seem to care much for Ephraim Wheeler."

Adams finished his wine and passed back through the tavern to the street. How could Ephraim be acquitted when the popular Attorney-General, who had just lost election to the Governorship by a small margin, was prosecuting him? Both judges and jurors would be inclined to accept his argument.

He went to the back of the courthouse, and, unobserved, looked through an open ground-floor window. There was Ephraim finishing his meal while his guard was still eating. By concentrating his look on Ephraim's face, he caught Ephraim's attention, and beckoned to the surprised prisoner to come to the window.

Ephraim looked admiringly at his well-dressed friend.

"You gotta get your lawyers to go after Betsy," Adams whispered. "Or you're finished."

"I'm finished anyway," Ephraim said glumly.

"Then start thinking of escape," Adams said. "I'll help."

The guard walked over to the window. "What are you doin'?" he demanded.

"Just a friend," Ephraim said.

"No talking with the prisoner," the guard said. "Get away or I'll have to arrest you."

"We'll be in touch." Adams touched his hat and moved away.

Ephraim had smiled easily, but in his eyes Adams had seen worry. Was it that Ephraim had expected his case not to come to trial, that his family would have relented and withdrawn? Surely he had seen that stronger forces than his family were arrayed against him and now controlled events.

Ephraim Wheeler returned to sit at his table and stared at his unfinished meal. He was naive when it came to politics. He stubbornly believed that because he was unimportant, everything that attached to him was unimportant. The first inkling of the true dimensions of the affair came to him as he watched the court admit jurors who were hostile to him and as he listened to his daughter tell her story. He saw then the likelihood that he would be condemned.

Hulbert opened the door and nodded to the guard who looked up from his meal. He came to sit beside Ephraim.

"I've spoken to Odel and a friend of yours, Michael Pepper," he said.

"Yes?" Ephraim looked puzzled.

"They are prepared to testify against Betsy."

Ephraim shook his head.

"I cannot in good conscience allow you to be convicted without resistance of some sort," Hulbert said angrily.

"Go after my wife," Ephraim said.

"But she's not in the courtroom; she means nothing to the jurors, as I told you!" Hulbert cried in exasperation. "Won't you tell me why Betsy, herself, Betsy, your daughter, is doing this? You swear you didn't touch her, then what happened?"

Ephraim shook his head. "I told you. My wife."

Hulbert stood up. "The court will resume shortly." He walked out the door. He was beginning to think that Ephraim committed the rape and deserved to die. Dewey had been of little help; the little dandy had given almost no time to the case.

"Well," Dewey said nonchalantly as Hulbert approached him in the hall. "Did our dear client change his tune?"

"No," Hulbert said glumly.

"He wants to die then," Dewey said sarcastically. "And we will be obliged to fish him out of the jaws of death with the brilliance of oratory."

"We need more than brilliance with this jury," Hulbert snorted.

"Yes, what a hostile group!" Dewey laughed as they walked back to the courtroom. "Half of them seem to hold a bias against our poor client. "

Hulbert saw from the corner of his eye a well-dressed man, whom he seemed to recognize, walking immediately behind them, but when he turned, the fellow stepped away behind a pillar. "You know how some in our Commonwealth still hate Shays' rebels." He stepped into the courtroom and all thoughts deserted him save his prepared speech in defense of Ephraim.

Hulbert remarked a change in the courtroom. It was a moment before he realized that Mrs. Wheeler sat beside Betsy at the prosecutor's table. His heart made a joyful jump. He stood up to speak. He stood near the jury box but turned at an angle so that he could look over at Harriette Wheeler whenever he wished to emphasize a point. But as he spoke and as he told of Harriette's attempts at manipulating her husband, of her desertion of him, of her obstinacy and refusal to understand him, he sensed that the jury was not seeing the humble-looking woman across from them in the light he was casting her. He condemned Harriette. He claimed that she had fabricated the rape in order to hurt Ephraim just as she had been trying to hurt him for years. She alone had examined

Betsy. There had been no doctor present. How could she be trusted? It was probable that she and her daughter were lying. They hated Ephraim so much, they were willing to see him hanged on a false charge.

Harriette sat with her hand on Betsy's arm to comfort her. There was pain in her eyes. Betsy looked bewildered by Hulbert's onslaught. Her innocence gave her a look of such vulnerability that Hulbert felt, even as he said the words, that he was damaging Ephraim's cause. Harriette with her black shawl and straight dignified features looked like the child's courageous guardian. He tried desperately to find some valid point of accusation, some way to penetrate the sheen of respectability that seemed to envelop them. He emphasized Ephraim's complaint that Magistrate Walker had refused his demand to have a jury examine Betsy. The court had only Harriette's word as proof that she was raped. But he saw by the faces of the jurors that they needed no other word than the mother's. Ephraim's demand seemed desperate indeed.

Abruptly turning back to his defense table, Hulbert called Michael Pepper as a witness. This tall, haggard-looking farmer was required to answer only one question. Was Betsy honest?

"Heard say she's not to be believed as well as some."

Hulbert called Isaac Odel whose serious mien and reputation as a hard-working farmer visibly impressed the jurors.

"She's not to be believed as well as some," Odel said meaningfully.

"You are her uncle, and she now lives under your roof?"

"Yes, sir."

"That will be all, Mr. Odel."

Sullivan leaped to his feet and recalled William Martin to the stand. Certainly his reputation matched Odel's, and, in the morning, the jurors had listened attentively to his description of Ephraim's use of a bayonet on his wife.

"I've heard nothing said against Betsy," he said, looking directly at the jury and stood down.

Dr. Wright, a rotund bustling man, testified in the same words, but in the reasonable-sounding tone of the professional man. He was followed by Robert Walker, whose methodical work as magistrate for the district had earned him deep respect. "I have heard nothing said against Betsy Wheeler," he said.

Hulbert knew that he had lost the case and blamed himself for panicking. After beginning by attacking the credibility of Harriette Wheeler, he should have stayed with it. By attacking Betsy at the last moment, he weakened his argument against Harriette. Moreover, he had built no argument against Betsy to support his charge that she was lying. Woefully, he looked at Daniel Dewey, who now stood to address the jury to try to save the case.

Dewey spoke with an intensity that surprised Hulbert. The little dandy was transformed into a fiery, sharp-thinking advocate of justice. All this so-called evidence was circumstantial, he was saying, the facts were hear-say, the descriptions could have been imagined. There were no witnesses, no testimony other than that given by a daughter under her mother's influence, and that mother with a reputation for carrying on a domestic war with the accused almost from the day they were married.

Gentle Adams sat forward in his seat at the back of the courtroom. For the first time, he saw a chance that Ephraim might go free. Dewey did not attack the opposition directly; he blamed the evidence, as if it had a life of its own separate from the actors of this drama, and, by innuendo, he began to ascribe certain motives to the accusers. The life of a man was too sacred to be thrown away when there was no solid evidence of a crime. He persistently reiterated his charge to the Jury that they would require evidence, clear, strong and conclusive.

The Attorney-General stood to address the jurors. The tall, handsome Sullivan, his silver hair brushed back from a broad brow reminiscent of a Roman senator, used his extraordinary charm. "How," he asked, "could the witnesses be false when their testimony rang so true? To be sure of a conviction, little Ephraim could have testified that he had followed his father and sister into the woods and witnessed the rape. But he was ignorant of it. Betsy feared that he had overheard their father threatening her, but the boy heard nothing. Falsehood, lies, and conspiracy were vicious charges to lay against a young girl who had been cruelly abused and who could look only to her community for protection. The bestial deed had to be punished if the community was to avoid its pernicious effects. Such a crime was clear evidence of the work of the devil amongst them."

Gentle Adams shut his ears to the remainder of Sullivan's argument, which he had heard many times in many guises. Sullivan's approach was superior to most because he added a sense of logic and a sort of legal confidence to his moral preaching. Already Adams could see Ephraim's conviction on the faces of the jurors. Ephraim had to die, not because he raped his daughter, but because his act undermined the security of the community.

Adams grudgingly admired the intelligence of the Attorney-General--grudgingly because although Sullivan was the leader of his political party, he held certain views which Adams resented. Sullivan was not really for the people. He was for the *status quo* but granted that ther should be some alleviation of the burden the people had to bear.

The court adjourned. It was eight in the evening. The sun was setting behind the hills as Adams stepped into the street. A September coolness seemed to drift down from the forests in the accompanying darkness. The judges gave the jury one hour to make a decision. If no decision was forthcoming, the court was to adjourn for the night. Adams watched the spectators go in groups to their houses. Sighing from weariness, he walked slowly to the tavern and listened to parts of conversations debating Wheeler's guilt in the night air. The man walking in front of him opened the door of the tavern, and, turning, held it for him. Adams recognized the man as Daniel Dewey.

"Liked your spirited defense," he said quickly.

Dewey, startled, smiled. "I thought no one was listening." He turned to go his own way.

Adams on a hunch made a sign with his thumb and index finger which Dewey caught with a look of surprise. Dewey returned the sign and, looking around to see that they were unobserved, he motioned for Adams to follow him.

Dewey led him downstairs to a small room with a private bar.

"We won't be disturbed," Dewey said, closing the door and locking it. "What can a brother mason do for you?"

"Nothing urgent," Adams said, amused at Dewey's conspiratorial air. "I don't want to take time from the accused."

Dewey shook his head sadly and going to the bar poured out two whiskies. "Wheeler is as good as dead, and no lawyer, as far as I know, has been able to help a dead man." He gave a whiskey to Adams, gestured to a chair, and slumped his short frame onto a chair across from it. "But here's hoping a miracle happens." He raised his glass and drank.

Adams rather liked the man. He took a drink and sat down. "Wheeler fought under my command on Shays' side."

"Ah, ha," Dewey laughed abruptly. "We should have had you for a juror. Most of them seem to have fought for the Commonwealth."

"You're absolutely right," Adams smiled. "The jurors won't need hard evidence to convict poor Ephraim. But what I have in mind is the possibility of clemency."

"Now you're bringing in politics, my dear Mr.--?"

"Adams."

Dewey cocked an eyebrow. 'The Radical? Aren't you supposed to be in the West Indies?"

"Supposed, yes," Adams grinned.

"But you're working with your nefarious Republican Party to upset us in the next election. You are clever! You've brought me into your secret and sealed my lips in the spirit of fraternity." Dewey took a long drink.

Adams was embarrassed but quickly subdued feelings of discomfort. "We have a common interest in saving Wheeler."

"Well," Dewey frowned. "I suppose you have a good reason. But how do you expect me to live with this secret and remain a good Federalist?"

Adams laughed. "As a lawyer, you know how to compromise. I'm sure you can overlook my existence after this evening."

Dewey nodded. "If you can risk your freedom to bargain for Wheeler's life, why can't I compromise?"

Adams looked at him with gratitude. "I can find ways to persuade the Attorney-General," he said, "but you must convince Governor Strong and his Council."

"Formidable tasks," Dewey smirked. "Your party leader conquers the devil and has Wheeler condemned to death; and then my party leader pardons Wheeler. That really will make us the devil's party."

"But if Sullivan takes a public stand supporting the Governor's decision..." Adams argued.

"He can't!" Dewey cut in. "He's been asking for the death penalty during the trial, how can he change? Unless he doesn't care for politics any longer--which I doubt." He jumped to his feet and began to pace. "We'll have to agree on a fundamental principle in all this."

"The principle," Adams snorted, "is that no man should be condemned to die because of a family dispute."

"Ah, well," Dewey stopped to stare at him. "You think there was no rape. I happen to think there was."

"There may have been," Adams corrected him, "but the principle has nothing to do with it."

"Oh, yes it does," Dewey replied sharply. "Rape relates to the violation of another man's property." Dewey snapped his fingers. "If a man rapes his own daughter, is he not violating his own property? Is it not permissible for a man to violate his own property?"

"You'd find that hard to argue," Adams said, "despite your forensic talents."

Dewey nodded in accepting the compliment. "It's not so much a matter of persuasion, because the Governor does not like to sign execution orders any more than you or I. It is a matter of what the public will accept. How can Wheeler, the devil, become Wheeler, the martyr? Only by taking the evil out of the rape."

"But first, Mr. Dewey, Ephraim will have to admit to it."

"That is the problem," Dewey conceded. "I wish we could reach him."

"He has a secret in his past," Adams said. "His love for a woman, Susanna Randal. She could be the key." He paused and pointed to the floor above. "I hear people moving out."

Dewey glanced at his pocket watch. "You're right. We'd better go back. You go first, Mr. Republican. By the way, how do we keep in touch?"

"By note in the Boston Lodge."

"Not the quickest route, surely."

'The best I can do," Adams said apologetically, and, stepping into the hallway, walked quickly for the courthouse.

When he sat down in the court, he noticed Dewey hastily approaching the table for the defense. Hulbert looked annoyed with him. Ephraim was sitting at the table and staring stonily into space. The jurors were filing into the jury box. The courtroom fell into a deep hush.

Judge Simeon Strong asked the jurors if they had come to a decision. Elijah Gates, the lead juror, stood to reply. His long gray beard and bushy eyebrows gave him the appearance of an Old Testament prophet about to pass judgment. "We find the prisoner guilty," he said and sat down.

There was silence in the courtroom. The verdict had come like an inevitable event. Not even Ephraim reacted emotionally. He looked at some of his old enemies on the jury impassionately. Then he looked over at his wife and Betsy, who sat with sad faces and averted their eyes from him.

Simeon Strong adjourned the court to Saturday morning for sentencing and banged the desk top with his gavel. Gentle Adams thought he detected a desire to be rid of the case in the judge's gesture. Be rid of it, bury it along with the guilty man. Bury the guilt with him. Cleanse the community. This was the unspoken motive in everyone's mind, he thought, as the spectators filed out of the courtroom. Adams sensed a mood of relief beginning to set in. Simeon Strong stood chatting with his fellow judges. Ephraim was shaking the hands of his lawyers. Appearing unconcerned, Ephraim walked with a police guard back to his cell.

Gentle Adams caught sight of Betsy Wheeler and her mother, shawls over their heads, retreating to a side door as if they were ladies in mourning. Staying behind in the well of the courtroom and gathering up his papers stood Daniel Dewey. As he turned to leave, he looked up at Adams, and their eyes met for an instant. They recognized in that look a feeling of complicity and commitment.

Adams stood up abruptly and walked quickly from the courtroom. It was late. He could not stay in town. There was a house on the road to Pittsfield where he figured he could stay. He took his horse from the barn behind the hotel and saddled it in the light from the stars. The tension he had felt during the trial seemed to drain from his body. He was beginning to feel hungry. He hoped that his intended host for the night would give him a midnight snack. He rubbed his heels against his horse's sides and set forth into the chill of the dark and forbidding mountain range alive with animals foraging in the night.

ELEVEN

Three hours later, Adams found a wagon trail turning off the main road and followed it through a wooded area to a farmhouse, faintly visible in the moonlight. He hitched his horse to a bar by the porch and walked to the side window where he beat out a tattoo with his nails on the pane. He waited and gazed over the clearing, which he could see, even in the dark, was unkempt. It pleased him because he could remark no sign of a man's hand tending the place, and there were flower beds near the house which he recognized as the work of a woman, the thought of whom began to rouse warm feelings in him.

He heard the front door open and a woman's voice call into the darkness. "Who is it?" The huskiness of it made him smile with anticipation.

"Molly Givens?" he said.

The woman was still as if the impact of her name had stunned her. "Is it you, Gentle?" she asked tentatively at last.

Adams walked quickly to the porch and smiled at the woman in her white nightgown. Her hair was grey now and her face a bit fuller. But she still was pretty.

"You!" she laughed. "If I was in my right mind, I would lock the door right away and leave you to grin out there in the dark."

"Just passing by, thought I'd look in," Adams said lightly and felt the happiness she had in seeing him.

"Five years ago you said the same thing, villain!" she said opening the door for him to enter.

He stood inside while she lit a lamp, and by the light of it he followed her to the kitchen. She set the lamp down and raised the wick so that the light flooded the room.

He remarked the full breasts that he loved and the slim round hips under the fabric of the nightgown.

"Let's have a look at you," she said. "Oh, aren't you looking fine!"

"You're beautiful!" he said.

She threw her head back in mock laughter. "Well, sit, and I'll give you grub. You bin riding long?"

"Since Lenox," he said, sitting at the kitchen table. He remarked the clean, neat look of the kitchen which contrasted sharply with the outside of the house.

"'Fraid you might have been with someone," he smiled.

"Oh, there've been men," she admitted as she took some meat from the larder and began slicing it. "But not at present. So you're welcome. But," she looked round at him with the mischievous smile he remembered so well, "even if I weren't alone, you'd get shelter here. You're always welcome in my home, Gentle. Though I'm a fool for saying so."

Adams looked down with slight embarrassment. He always felt guilty when he returned to the women he had loved, as if he had offended their love by his long absences. Yet the offense was unavoidable, he told himself. He took the mug of beer she handed him and smiled his thanks with his eyes. But in his look he betrayed his awareness of the fullness of her body and the knowledge that he would soon be enjoying it.

"Still like cheese?" Molly asked, "as much as you used to?"

"My tastes haven't changed," Adams said.

Molly gave him a flirtatious glance as she put a plate of cold meat, cheese, and dark bread on the table before him.

"Where have you been then?" she asked, sitting across from him.

"At sea, in the south, in jail," he said, swallowing the beer and handing her the mug to refill while hungrily regarding the plate.

"Politics as usual," Molly sneered and stood up to put the mug under the tap of the beer barrel in the corner. "You'll always be in trouble. I could see that when I tried to read the literature you left behind."

"There are those that think and those who don't," Adams said, chewing the meat. "Thinking can't help but bring one trouble. But not thinking can do the same." He took the mug from Molly and washed down a mouthful with a swallow from it. He ate in silence for a moment. "If society stops thinking," he said suddenly, "it can only act by blind instinct. That's when it destroys itself because its instinct is for self-preservation."

Molly looked at him uncomprehendingly.

He frowned. 'That's when it stops new ideas and, like a monster, begins to devour its members who get out of line."

Molly smiled wryly. "I know what you've been doing: You were at the trial in Lenox. What did they decide about the man who raped his daughter?"

"They'll hang him," Adams said sharply. "But they shouldn't."

"And why not?" Molly's voice rose in exasperation. "He broke the law, didn't he? What if he went free and did that horrible thing again?"

"By our code," Adams replied, "a woman can give a stranger a place in her bed for the night and expect not to be touched. Our people survive by absolute trust. Betsy Wheeler's story shocked them out of their senses. I could hear them thinking: if a man who grew up amongst us could violate his own daughter, how could we allow our women to trust strangers from now on? The very foundations of our society are undermined."

"You're a strange one," Molly looked at him doubtfully. "I ask a straight question and you give me a crooked answer."

Adams laughed. "You haven't changed, Molly Givens. You just won't see another point of view."

Molly bristled. "I hadn't noticed you changing yours!"

"Well," Adams swallowed the last of his beer, "Wheeler is an old friend. I think he was born a victim."

"And what are the rest of us?" Molly asked. "You, a hungry vagrant, and me, a poor widow?"

"Sounds like we were meant for each other," Adams smiled wickedly.

Molly stood and took away his plate and mug. "It was a mistake to let you in the house," she said, but not angrily. She put down the utensils on the sideboard and turned to find Adams standing beside her. "If I give you room in my bed, will you honor our code, as you call it?" She arched her eyebrows.

"Well," Adams said thoughtfully. He put one hand under her buttocks and cupped her left breast with the other. "I'm not a stranger."

Smiling she reached for the lamp and led him into the bedroom.

The world of betrayal and revenge slipped from Adams' consciousness as he lost himself in the excitement of Molly's love-making--but not before the thought of Ephraim enjoying his daughter's body crossed his mind, making him think of the blessed opiate Ephraim sought in the act of love.

TWELVE

It was Saturday morning, the second day after Ephraim's trial, when Betsy Wheeler suffered an attack of remorse so powerful that, for an hour after she awoke, she sobbed convulsively. Harriette sat on the bed beside her and could find no way to comfort her. Their landlady looked in sympathetically now and again and asked if there was anything she could do. All the women in the boarding house had seemed sympathetic. Now that Betsy had told her story in public as it were, she had dispelled the atmosphere of disbelief and suspicion that she had had to endure throughout the summer. But it was the sudden flood of sympathy that must have triggered some emotion deep within her and set her to crying.

Attorney-General Sullivan arranged for them to stay in Lenox until after the sentencing of Ephraim, which was to take place in mid-morning. Harriette had protested to him that the ordeal of testifying had worn them out and that they wanted to return to Cummington on Friday. She pleaded with him to allow them at least to be absent from the court for the sentencing. She explained that they could not endure it. Watching her daughter crying, she gave thanks that Sullivan had agreed to let them stay away. After all, was not their role to tell the truth? They had not come to watch her husband being punished. They had come to tell the truth. His punishment was none of their business.

Finally, in the warmth of her mother's embrace, Betsy stopped crying. She accepted some tea and nibbled on some toast, but she could not eat her breakfast. Ephraim had looked at her in the courtroom with an expression of hurt and sorrow. His look invaded her dreams in the night and haunted her in the day. She had begun to fear Harriette's constant admonition that she tell the truth. By telling the truth, she seemed to be going deeper into a maze rather than coming out of it. The truth was not freeing her but involving her more and more.

The revulsion she had felt for herself and her wickedness, which had been alleviated by her confession and Harriette's kindness, seemed to have been reborn when she testified in the courtroom. The recalling in detail of her cohabitation with her father in the woods convinced her of her worthlessness. She felt that she was marked for life by these few moments. Never again could she think of man without seeing her father. The evil in that thought overwhelmed her with self-hatred.

There was a light knock at the door. Harriette went to answer it and brushed at her fair hair as she walked. The lean face of Justice Robert Walker stared down at her.

"Ephie's eaten breakfast," Walker whispered. "He's playing behind the house. They're taking your husband to the court. I'd best be going there."

Harriette nodded and closed the door. She saw that Betsy had heard. The girl was staring as if in terror.

"Best get dressed," Harriette said.

Betsy slowly got out of bed and washed herself at the cabinet. She could not look at herself in the cabinet mirror.

"They may be kind to Daddy," Harriette said. "Mr. Sullivan told me they might keep him in jail only for a while, long enough to make him come to his senses."

Betsy made no reply. The silence between them seemed to speak for her. She got into her petticoat, and Harriette helped her with her dress.

"But Daddy's stubborn," Harriette continued. "He could've confessed and asked forgiveness. It's his fault that they convicted him. He's a fool!"

Betsy heard the angry resentment in her mother's voice rather than the words. The resentment had been there for many years, she thought. She could barely remember the time when it was not there.

"Do you feel sorry, Ma?"

Harriette finished buttoning the last clasp, gave her shoulder a pat, and moved away. "I don't know what I feel," Harriette sighed. "Best not to think of it."

"I don't want anything to happen to Daddy," Betsy blurted and ran to throw her arms about Harriette.

"We told the truth, dear," Harriette kissed her cheek. "That's all we can do. The rest is up to Providence."

The thought of Providence was consoling. Betsy thought of God and the angels sitting around in a circle and deciding goodness. It was she who had the evil in her. The men judging her father did not know, but God and the angels must know it. In her feeling of guilt, the memory of her father as a threatening bully had receded to be replaced by a kindly, gentle man who was solicitous of the children's welfare. Now that Betsy had been believed, her concern shifted from the object of telling the story truthfully. Her concern for Ephraim now over-rode other considerations. She began to think that whatever happened to

Ephraim would result from what she said. Ultimately, what she said was what happened, but, somehow, by saying it, she felt that she had taken on the guilt. Her anxiety about Ephraim increased as she sat trying to crotchet in the sitting room. The minutes dragged as she waited for news from the courthouse.

She heard a commotion in the street about eleven o'clock, and Harriette came into the room. She looked glum and pulled her shawl tightly about her shoulders.

"What's wrong?" Betsy asked.

"Mr. Sullivan's coming down the street with a party of men," Harriette said meaningfully.

Betsy tried to still her racing heart. She closed her eyes, breathed deeply, and asked God to spare Ephraim.

The landlady opened the door of the sitting room for James Sullivan, who, looking grave, entered alone. The sound of several people talking in the outer rooms was ushered in with him and clipped short when the door closed. Sullivan, scrupulously neat in the rich look of his broadcloth suit, lace ruffles, silk stockings, and polished shoes and buckles, stood in silence before the two women, who, both seated, looked at him expectantly.

"My news is not pleasant," he said finally.

Betsy gasped and bowed her head.

"As the prosecution we had to ask for the death penalty, and our request was granted by the court," Sullivan continued. "The Governor and his council must set the date for execution."

"But," Harriette murmured in protest, despite the stunned look on her face, "you said he might be imprisoned."

Sullivan nodded. "That was a distinct possibility, madam. But apparently the judges considered his offense a capital one. I am sorry." He looked at Betsy with pity, and, going to her, he patted her head affectionately. "Your courage throughout this sad business has been an inspiration to me and to my staff. You did well. You will always have my respect."

"Will Daddy hang?" Betsy asked fearfully.

Sullivan flinched at the terror he saw in her brown eyes, and he said kindly, "The Governor will decide if he dies. I hope he reduces his sentence...eventually grant him a pardon."

His words seemed to light flares of hope in the room. The word "pardon" seemed to dispel the gloom and bring an aspect of rationality to the problem. Harriette clasped her hands as she saw for the first time what she believed was Sullivan's strategy. Betsy took heart from her mother's smile of relief although she did not understand it.

"Pardon! Do you think Governor Strong will pardon Ephraim, sir?" Harriette asked.

"That is a distinct possibility," Sullivan said in his most kindly manner. "We must hope, and try our best. And you, young Betsy, must raise your head in pride. You told the truth. And through the truth alone there is salvation."

Tears came to Betsy's eyes, already red with crying, but she controlled herself and looked gratefully at Sullivan. He bowed slightly and left the room.

The women looked at each other in worry and confusion. Harriette stood up and went to the window. A crowd of people was joking and laughing in the street.

"Daddy's in God's hands," Harriette said. "Let us pray that God acts through Governor Strong."

Betsy felt suddenly very weak, very tired. She went into the bedroom and stretched out on the bed. She could not make up her mind if James Sullivan had come as a messenger from God or from the Devil. She feared the worst. She feared the Devil had been directing her life since Ephraim had taken her into the woods.

The Devil had forced her to tell her mother. He had taken advantage of her in a weak moment to make her blurt out the secret between her and Ephraim. She had been unable to conceal anything from her mother. Her mother's will was strong; it forced her to choose the easier path--tell and take the consequences. Mr. Sullivan and all those judges and men in court who hated her father, they were the consequences. It was her mother's resentment of Ephraim which, she sensed, was behind her, pushing her to testify. Sometimes she saw that resentment in the looks her mother gave her, and she felt a distance developing between them, as if Harriette blamed her for the rape and for the break-up of the family. But was not Harriette really wanting to be free of Ephraim? And did she not lack the courage to do it on her own? Betsy remembered thinking at the time she confessed the rape that she was giving her mother a reason for leaving Ephraim. It was just separation from Ephraim that Betsy wanted, not trials and execution. The Devil was in Harriette, directing her against both her husband and her daughter because of the evil between them, the betrayal of her family love, the sin that was as much in Betsy as in Ephraim. At the same time, she felt her mother's sympathy and understanding. Her mother was her source of strength, her one haven in the storm. These conflicting thoughts tore at Betsy's emotions. The storm, now that the ordeal of the trial was over, seemed to be intensifying rather than lessening. Betsy feared that Governor Strong was a more powerful Mr. Sullivan who would push her deeper into unhappiness and confusion.

"Oh Ma, Ma, Ma!" she cried remorsefully. "I'm frightened!"

Harriette came into the room and stared concernedly down at her. She saw her own fears reflected in her daughter. Unable to speak, she sat on the bed and put her hand sympathetically on Betsy's shoulder--a gesture that identified their unity more than words could have done.

THIRTEEN

Governor Caleb Strong sat at the head of the conference table and watched his councilor reading the report which he had had prepared for them. Strong was known as a wise old fox. He had been in politics for decades: first as a senator from Massachusetts, and then, as of the late seventeen hundreds, when he had tired of Washington politics, he became Governor of Massachusetts. His shift from Federal to State politics reflected the declining power of his Federalist Party. It also illustrated his preference for finding the political center and establishing himself with his attitude of moderation and reasonableness. In his annual speeches to the Commonwealth, he struck a moral tone with the equanimity of a country lawyer, which he had been at the start of his professional life.

The citizens responded to these civilized qualities at election time, but they also admired his ability to overcome personal hardship as an example to them all. When a student, Strong was stricken by smallpox and almost lost the sight of both eyes. His sisters read his law books to him. He passed the bar examinations with distinction. His secretaries still had to read to him, yet, as a man who thrived on conversation, Strong learned most of what he had to know through personal contact. Yes, it was the warmth of the man that the citizens of Massachusetts valued. The story was told of Caleb Strong's first inauguration as Governor. When his carriage was proceeding through the streets of Boston, Strong spotted the aged Samuel Adams watching from the doorway of his home. Strong, the Federalist, stepped out of the procession, and, walking up to Adams, took his hand in the most friendly manner, and, with a bow of deference, gave honor to the old Radical. It was generally believed that he sympathized with the ideals of the Radicals, who had freed the Commonwealth from England, but he considered them impractical. His critics, pointing to the harassment of Radical activity under Strong's Governorship, called him a hypocritical old fox.

"Well then, my dear friends, we have fixed the date for Wheeler's execution, have we?" Strong said in a mild manner with an undertone of humorous indulgence. "It shall be Thursday, February 20," he reiterated to the Council's secretary who sat writing beside him. "Do you have questions?"

There was silence. His councilors either kept their heads bowed pretending to read his report or stared at him dully. His eyes showed his amusement.

"Some of you gentlemen have made known your reservations about executing the man," Strong continued. "But our duty to provide an example to the community has guided us in this matter. Unlike our political opponents, we don't see 'the common man' as angel on earth." He smiled as his councilors responded with reserved laughter. "This man, Wheeler, from what I hear, has treated his family brutally. Therefore, he should die like a brute, I would say."

His councilors mumbled their approval.

From the political viewpoint, he smiled broadly, as if unable to keep back the joke any longer, "Mr. Sullivan has provided us with a remarkable show of Republican support, when he argued convincingly as prosecution in the case."

The councilors chuckled in appreciation of the savvy of the old man.

Strong adjourned the meeting. He stood leaning on his cane and chatted with several councilors about local problems. Suddenly jabbing his secretary lightly on the arm, he stepped away in a jovial mood and walked with the prim young man whispering into his ear, while he beamed greetings at legislators and members of their staffs whom he encountered in the corridors. Seeing Daniel Dewey waiting at the door to his office, he stopped abruptly, signed papers that his secretary held for him, and, with an expansive gesture in lieu of a greeting, waved Dewey into the Governor's office. His secretary glanced suspiciously at Dewey before hurrying away to set into motion the decisions of the Governor and his Council, including the date of Ephraim's hanging.

"I have a bad feeling," the Governor said, closing the door behind them, "you are about to ask me to do something that I cannot do."

The tall windows caught the September sun and suffused it throughout the book-lined office and over its large leather chairs, mahogany desks, and tables.

Dewey laughed and sank his short body into a leather chair. "You are in good humor, today, Governor."

"No, not particularly good, my dear young man." The Governor took some papers from a drawer in his desk and set them beside him as he sat down, as if to remind himself that they were the next order of business after Dewey. "My good nature misleads people to believe I am joking when I am not. In this case, I really mean what I say. Your client is to be hanged in February next."

"Then I have timed my visit well," Dewey smiled. "I am the first to have your ear after the official business has been done with."

The Governor frowned with irritation.

Dewey noticed it and altered his tone to convey a more serious purpose. "We can head off a lot of trouble by reducing the sentence."

Governor Strong slapped his hand on the arm of his chair. "My dear Dewey, rape is a heinous crime, but to rape one's own daughter is depravity." He glared. "The Statute books tell me what we must do. The people look to me to uphold the law. If the opposition wants to make hay out of it, we'll make mincemeat of them at the next election. What possessed you to try to change my mind?"

Dewey, taken aback by Strong's anger, stood up and said as affably as he could manage, "You know me well enough that I am not given to idle actions. I see that you are not prepared to discuss the matter, and I'll take no more of your time. Good-day, sir."

"Hold on," Strong said in a more temperate manner. "I'm glad to see you and welcome your good intentions, Daniel. I am busy, and," he looked apologetically at Dewey, "after all, we do have five months to arrange a pardon, if circumstances require it."

Dewey nodded. "Quite right, Governor. I'll leave it up to you to call on me when you may wish to discuss the subject." He moved toward the door.

"That's a good man," Strong said, and he began to peer at the papers on his desk in the sunlight. "Ask Jamieson to come in, will you?"

Dewey let himself out, and, seeing the prim-looking secretary look at him suspiciously from his desk near the door, he jerked his head back at the Governor's office. Jamieson picked up some letters from his desk and hurried to attend his master. Dewey was satisfied to have been the first to warn Strong and to leave the impression that he was informed on the matter although he had hoped to find the Governor more receptive. It appeared as if Strong were truly concerned about the morality of the issue, he mused, and would probably remain so as long as the general opinion favored Wheeler's execution. How long discussion of the case could be kept out of the Republican press depended upon the political authority of James Sullivan, who would not, of course, want to see his name coupled with the case in newspapers until public sentiment was clearly defined. Certainly the Federalist press would remain mute on the whole disgraceful episode. Dewey wished, with a sense of foreboding, that there had been some testimony other than that of Betsy Wheeler. As a lawyer, he felt uneasy; as the defending lawyer, he felt that he had been inadequate. That, he knew, was what Adams had divined so well, and why he had approached him rather than Hulbert. Adams was quite a remarkable man, he thought. When his colleagues considered him a dandy on the political right, Adams saw right away that what meant the most to Dewey was his professionalism. Moreover, Adams had to be taken seriously in the political short run. He could stir up the latent radicalism in the Commonwealth to the advantage of the Republicans. Intrigued by the challenge, Dewey cut across a corner of the Boston Common at an angle to bring him to his Club. He had no other business for the day. He hoped to hear some gossip from his legal friends, but the Club was practically empty. There was an envelope in his mail box, however. It had been mailed from Pittsfield.

He opened it and found a note from G.A.

> The way I see it, Wheeler's only hope is the woman Susanna Randal. Her rejecting him made his life miserable thereafter. If you could find her, she might help us to save him.

Dewey put down the note with a puzzled look. He remembered Wheeler's self-deprecating words which he would add quietly to his denunciation of his wife, "I don't pretend that I'm not passionate myself and been many times to blame." He could also be passionate in love, which, Wheeler told his lawyers, was how he had felt about Susanna Randal. Did he resent his wife because she could not become Susanna Randal? Wheeler blamed himself for the quarrels, but, at the same time, blamed Harriette for being at the bottom of them all. Poor woman! It was not her, but his love for Susanna at the bottom of them all. Or rather, Susanna's rejection of him. And perhaps that rejection was the underlying reason for Wheeler's rape of Betsy. Denied the woman he loved, would he not have transferred his passion to his child? A passion for which he had been "many times to blame." No, Dewey rejected the idea. His only real passion could have been Susanna. Obviously, through the years of their marriage, he mentioned Susanna to Harriette more in reproach than in sentimental musing. Could not Harriette have come to resent this Susanna and see her rejection in Wheeler's devotion to a lost love? Because of her sense of inadequacy, could she have believed too readily that Ephraim violated Betsy? Certainly she was using Betsy to rid herself of Ephraim.

Dewey began to pace the room. Damn Adams! he thought. The damned Radical had stirred him up. He had been inclined to agree with Hulbert that Wheeler was guilty but that he

97

should not hang. Now, he was not certain of Wheeler's guilt. But what sort of a monster would Harriette Wheeler be to send her husband to the gallows for something he did not do?

There was but one course to follow if he were to set his mind at rest. Susanna had lived at Saratoga, but that had been before Betsy was born, over thirteen years ago. He stuffed the papers back into the envelope and started out of the club with an alacrity that surprised an acquaintance who was entering. Dewey muttered an apology and strutted back to his office with an excitement that comes from having a sense of purpose. His partner could look after his legal work while he was absent, he thought. He would show Adams that he could be just as determined as any Radical to get at the roots of a problem.

FOURTEEN

Gentle Adams was spending his time in Pittsfield, contacting old friends and acquaintances who had been active in Shays' Rebellion, sounding them on their political views, and quietly organizing them into political cells by which they could work for the cause of Republicanism, and, in particular, for Colonel Larned at a by-election for representative to Congress.

Eventually his work would take him throughout the Commonwealth because, in order for the Republican Party to defeat the Federalists, all the disillusioned, the dispossessed, and all the politically dormant had to be galvanized into a potent left wing of the party. Adams relished the task. At last Jacobinism, as the Federalists called it, was being pulled out of the political wilderness.

It was just a few years ago that Thomas Jefferson and James Madison formed the opposition Republican Party, and already Jefferson was President of the nation. Federalism was in retreat, except in Massachusetts. Here the reactionary and conservative groups had swindled the farmers and artisans out of their share of the securities floated to pay for the Revolution and were collecting high rates of interest on them, which the farmers were being forced to pay. With such wealth it was no small wonder, Adams thought, that the Federalists consolidated their political power and oppressed the people greater than did the British in colonial times. But they could be defeated. And those who were moderate Federalists, which Dewey appeared to be, might be persuaded to join the Republican cause.

The men who were gathered in the back room of the tavern to hear Adams were in outward appearance no different from the farmers and artisans he had worked among for years. But there was a new spirit in them. A glint in their eyes, an unusual quickness of movement, a more animated tone of discussion, these were the differences he noted.

"No one," he began, and the assembly fell silent, "not one of us can afford to neglect the democratic process. Our noses have been pushed to the ground and soon, the way the bankers are treating us, they'll be under the ground. We'll have ourselves to blame if we don't make our chance with the Republican Party."

"To hell with the Party!" someone cried. "They'll do us in."

"Not if we get out the vote," Adams argued. "There's enough discontent in the Commonwealth to make Federalism a forgotten name. But we can do it only with the Republicans. They need us, and, Lord knows, we need them. Everyone here knows that it's no longer the farmers who are losing their farms. The small businessmen are losing their businesses. The Federalist base has been shrinking for years. If we don't hit them hard when they're falling, they'll be up again and hitting us even harder."

"That's all right," a tall farmer leaning against the wall spoke out, "but we can't trust Sullivan."

"You'll have to!" Adams cried. "He's known and he's got prestige. Look, if we put him in, he's going to have to listen to us."

"Exactly!" cried Meacham, reporter for the Pittsfield *Sun*, jumping excitedly to his feet and turning round to face the audience. "Sullivan is the only man who can match up to Governor Strong. If we dim Strong's star, Sullivan becomes Governor for certain." Meacham's brown hair, tussled on his young head, gave him the look of a harried young Radical, which many men in the room had been at one time.

"Dim his star!" someone laughed. "Do you mean, catch him in a scandal? He's clean as a whistle! What you talkin' about?"

"Never mind," Meacham said. "We've got the bloodhounds sniffing."

"We don't need scandal," Adams cut in and waved Meacham to sit down. "We just have to show the people that the Federalists have made them worse off than they were before the Revolution. Then we'll promise them credit, good paper money, and a real chance to get free of debt."

The men cheered.

"We'll get rid of the death penalty too. We'll get the hangmen out of office."

The men cheered again.

"So sign up. Get your literature at our table by the door," Adams said with a gesture between a wave and salute. "Just talk up what you read there, and I'll be round to see you all. Just a moment." He noticed Colonel Larned entering the door. "Do you want to say something, Sheriff?"

Some of the men clapped. Larned sparked a sense of excitement as he walked to the front. His straight bearing reminded them of his military achievement in the Revolutionary War, and his modest air told these men that he had always been one of them.

"My first run for the big office where we can do some real good. I need your help. Appreciate it."

Since Larned was known as a doer, not a talker, the men recognized that that was all he was going to say, and they cheered him. The assembly broke up, some of the men coming up to give Larned a pat on the back and shoulder. Adams went to the door to supervise the registration and talk with the men as they left. In the next few days he would come to their homes in the town and on the outlying farms. His dedication to the cause over years of danger and suffering made his name a watchword for resilience on the left throughout New England and the Middle States. These men could be sure that Adams was no Daniel Shays to lead them in a fruitless assault. He planned with care and moved only when he was certain.

When the men had left, just young Meacham and Colonel Larned remained behind to talk with Adams. They drank at a table and spoke in low voices.

"How do you see it shaping up round here?" the Colonel asked Adams.

"Good," Adams nodded. "People are criticizing the Government. And I mean criticizing, not just critical."

"And down East?"

"Almost as bad. Times are getting harder, and even in Boston they want easier credit."

"Which the Federalists won't give em," Meacham chipped in.

"We need an to catch their imagination," the Colonel said quietly, as if he were thinking of one.

"We could stir 'em up over Wheeler," Meacham suggested, "if Gentle would only let me report in the paper on it."

"Nope," Adams said. "Maybe some day, but you're playing with fire there." He turned to Larned. "What's being done for Ephraim?"

"Introducing a bill into the House this week takin' capital punishment out of the law as punishment," Larned said, and added wryly, "'cept for murder."

"Could it become law before February 20?" Adams asked.

CHOCOLATE

"Dunno," the Colonel frowned. "Depends on the pressure put on the Federalists."

"I wouldn't count on it," Meacham said.

"Where's Sullivan stand?" Adams asked.

"He favors the route through the legislature."

"Ha!" Meacham smirked, "count on that even less."

"Strong is in a predicament," Adams agreed, "since Sullivan made the crime out to be evil and Sullivan won the conviction. Strong can't look weaker than his opposition."

"That's the point," Larned smiled.

"But it's a man's life at stake," Adams said sharply. "I hope we're going to give Strong a way out."

"I hope so," Larned said.

"Politics," Meacham said with sarcasm. "Remember," Meacham said, "Strong commuted the death sentence on a fellow to life imprisonment about a year after he became Governor."

"Yep," the Colonel said. "And it was for rape. But that case was different. The woman was adult and no relation."

"Still," Meacham argued. "He set a precedent."

"We'll use it later, maybe," the Colonel said. "Right now I want an issue other than Wheeler."

"Can't find one as good as Wheeler," Meacham smiled. "We can hammer away at the land tax rates, but I think people are getting tired of reading that stuff."

"Try picking on the rich in Boston," Larned said, getting up. "They're getting richer when the people are hurting."

"That's good!" Meacham cried. "And Federalist tax policies are making it possible."

"Same as King George," Adams said. "Massachusetts has its own version of monarchy."

"Be sparin' with that word monarchy," Larned warned. "We may have to use it later to good purpose." He nodded and stepped away. "I'll be in touch, boys."

"Wait, Colonel!" Adams stood and walked after him.

Meacham took pencil and paper from his pocket and began composing an article as Adams accompanied Sheriff Larned out the door.

"Colonel, what are Wheeler's chances? Can you level with me?" Gentle asked.

Sheriff Larned studied Adams' concerned face and then shook his head slowly and turned away.

Adams watched the veteran soldier walk until he rounded a building out of sight. Only Larned would tell him the truth-- that Ephraim was just a political toy. He gritted his teeth. His friend was doomed, unless, he thought, unless he could pull a trick outside of the political process.

FIFTEEN

Daniel Dewey, in a week of riding westward, had traversed the Berkshire hills and entered New York State. Saratoga, he found, was pretty, especially now that the trees were turning yellow. The community was more prosperous than most, owing to the visitors to the springs who left a bit of their wealth behind. One of the town's streets was cobbled, and the hotel was commodious and comfortable. None of the residents knew of Susanna Randal, at least by her maiden name. Perhaps she had moved away right after she was married--gone to a big town like Troy or south-west to Pennsylvania. Dewey did not despair. He sat on the hotel porch and listened to conversations, he visited with the tradesmen of the town, he rode to the neighbouring villages and discreetly asked questions--seeking a sister, he said, who eloped with a man to these parts fifteen years ago. He began calling himself Bob Randal. After a week, he wondered if Ephraim Wheeler had been lying. Maybe there had been no Susanna Randal, or maybe he had never met her in Saratoga Springs. One morning, while reclining on a chair on the hotel porch and watching the traffic bustling in the main street, he flipped a coin. Heads! That meant he would go up river. Fetching his saddle-bags, he called for his horse, waited for it to be saddled and his bags to be placed over it, and fished some change from his pocket for the stable boy when he heard his assumed name called.

"Mr. Randal, sir!"

He turned round, but he could make out no one calling him.

"Mr. Randal!" The clerk from the hotel was calling out to an old gentleman, who was shuffling down the porch steps and who appeared to be hard of hearing. "Will you come back, sir!"

A gentleman, who was climbing the steps, touched Mr. Randal on the arm and directed his attention to the hotel clerk, who was now running across the porch in pursuit. The clerk held out a letter which the old man took with a puzzled look.

"You dropped it," cried the clerk, trying to conceal his irritation.

The old man smiled, stuffed it in his pocket, and continued to shuffle into the street.

Dewey asked the stable-boy to hitch his horse for the time being and followed the old man. Since the locals knew him as Randal, he wondered if he should use the coincidence of the similarity of name to meet him. But how and yet not appear forward? He followed old Mr. Randal into the general store and watched him at the tobacco counter. He stepped beside him and smiled at the store clerk who cried, "Hello, Mr. Randal."

Apparently the old man heard it, for he took a step sideways to get a good look at Dewey.

"I'll have the same brand as this gentlemen," Dewey said to the clerk, who was reaching on the back shelf for a tin.

"Wouldn't advise it," the old man smiled, "unless you're accustomed to it."

Dewey laughed and held out his hand. "I'm Bob Randal."

"Well," Mr. Randal said, gripping his hand in good humor, "I'm Martin Randal and pleased to meet you."

The clerk put down the two tins, and the men paid.

"Not often I meet someone of the same name," Mr. Randal said. "Are you from here?"

"No, Boston," Dewey said.

"Eh?" queried the old man.

"I'm from Boston," Dewey said loudly, and pocketed his tin of tobacco. "And you, sir?"

"Provincetown," Mr. Randal said as they walked together out of the store. "Just passing through. On my way to visit my daughter."

"Oh," Dewey said quickly, "where does she live?"

"Glen Falls, upriver a ways."

"I know," Dewey spoke louder now they were in the open air. "I'm just leaving for there."

"You are!" Mr. Randal grinned. "How long will you be there?"

"A few days," Dewey said.

"I'm coming tomorrow by stage," Mr. Randal said. "Why don't you take her address, and we can get together." He fumbled in his coat pockets and pulled out an envelope. "Thought I'd lost it," he said with relief. "Here's her address on the back."

Dewey read "Mrs. Susanna Bayberry, High Road, Glen Falls, N.Y." He could barely conceal his excitement. "Married, is she?" he asked.

"Widowed," Mr. Randal said sadly.

Dewey held out his hand when they reached the front of the hotel. "I'll be seeing you upriver then," he smiled.

The stable-boy, seeing him approach, brought out his horse, and, within minutes, Dewey was following the river road to Glen Falls.

The village, when he arrived in the late afternoon, stood in sharp contrast to sedate Saratoga Springs. This was a workingman's habitat. Loggers ran logs in the river, artisans were hammering and sawing in small huts by the riverbank where huge mill wheels were turned by the rapid current, and farming folk jammed the main street. The lone hotel needed repair but was reasonably clean. Dewey bathed and rested, ate dinner, and strolled down the main street in the evening. The lights from the cabins spread out over the rises back of the town, defining, as it were, the limits of the community.

He discovered the High Road running back of the village over the rises toward the west. Somewhere in the scattered dwellings along the road lay the house of Susanna Bayberry. Since it was very dark with only the light from several stars in the overcast sky to light his way, he decided to defer his quest till the morning. He was about to return to the hotel when he saw a young man hurrying out the high road, and he asked him where the widow lived.

"Right there!" came the sharp reply.

Dewey looked at the cabin set back about twenty yards from the road. There was a faint light from a side window. He stepped over the field and cautiously watched for signs of life at the windows. When he knocked on the door, he expected no reply because the place was deathly still. And for a moment there was no reply. He was about to turn away when the door opened, and a tall, blonde woman stood holding a lamp and staring at him.

"Susanna Bayberry?" he asked.

"What do you want?" Her voice was stern.

"Your father asked me to pay you a visit. But," he stepped back as if to go, "I may be disturbing you."

"Where'd you see my Dad?"

"Left him in Saratoga this morning. He'll be here tomorrow. My name's Bob Randal." He held out his hand.

She opened the door for him to enter. Her coolness seemed to evaporate, but she was still stern in manner, as if she mistrusted the outside world and was unwilling to make a friendly concession to it.

Dewey preceded her to the back kitchen where he watched her sit on a rocking chair and take up her knitting.

"Sit," she said.

He took a straight-backed chair that was against the wall, drew it near to her, and sat down. He smiled at her.

"Sort of lonely in a new town," he explained, "So I decided to seek you out my first evening."

"I'm home evenings," Susanna said.

"Things are quiet in this town, I imagine," Dewey said.

"No," she said. "I'm just quiet. My two kids are sleeping, and my husband died five years ago." She put her knitting aside suddenly as if she were forgetting herself. "I'm sorry. I only got tea to drink. Will you have some?"

Dewey accepted and watched her as she boiled the water. Her tall body was lithe and attractive. Dewey thought that she must have a lover.

"I'm surprised you haven't married again," he said.

"No interest in it," she said, leaning against the sink and regarding him as she waited for the water to boil.

"How do you feed your family?"

"I work in town. My Dad helps from time to time." She smiled for the first time, a slight, quick smile. "You're a curious one."

"Excuse me, bad Bostonian manners."

The water in the kettle began to boil, and she turned to make tea. The kitchen was rather bare but neatly kept, Dewey noticed. Susanna Bayberry had seen much better times. She must have represented quite a step up in the social scale for Ephraim Wheeler. He wondered why she had turned him down. From the looks of things Bayberry did not seem to have been much better off. She gave him a cup of tea and resumed her seat. Dewey sensed an awkwardness building between them since she had put an end to his idle queries. He decided to declare the purpose of his visit.

"Actually, I've come out this way looking for Susanna Randal, who once was engaged to a man called Ephraim Wheeler."

Susanna stared wide-eyed at him as she slowly put down her cup.

"Are you the Susanna Randal?" he asked.

She hesitated. "Why do you want to know?"

"He's in trouble, and I'm trying to help him."

She frowned. "I knew him. But that was many years ago. I can't see how I can help."

"Did he want to marry you?"

"I think he did," she said with some embarrassment. "You're not a lawyer, are you, Mr. Randal?"

He nodded. "Sorry if I'm pressing you."

"What's he done?" she demanded.

Dewey paused. "He's been sentenced to hang."

She caught her breath. "For murder?"

"Rape," he said.

She looked amazed. "I don't believe it. He couldn't be the Ephraim Wheeler I knew."

"Were you engaged in Massachusetts until he fell ill, and then you went away to Saratoga?"

"Did he tell you that?"

"And he found you in Saratoga, but you were ready to marry another man--probably Mr. Bayberry."

"That's right," she said firmly.

"Then Ephraim was telling the truth," Dewey said.

"Will that fact help him?" she asked quickly.

"Not alone," he smiled.

"Perhaps you'll come to dinner tomorrow evening when my Dad is here," she said. "I can tell you more about Ephraim then."

Dewey stood up and thanked her for the tea. He walked behind her to the door and sensed an attraction to the way her body moved. He held out his hand at the door on an impulse to feel her skin. They shook hands. The excitement and warmth in her hand stayed with him as he walked in the dark back to his hotel.

The next morning he asked the hotel proprietor about Susanna Bayberry. "Good woman," the man replied, as if that was the consensus of the town. "But her husband was no good. A drunkard. Drowned in the river."

Dewey felt too restless to spend his day in the village. He rode north to see the countryside. But he had been riding for no more than an hour when he chanced upon a gathering of two hundred people by the riverside. The autumnal sun glinted off the naked bodies of several men and women wading near the shore. An old man stood waist high in the water and touched the foreheads of each of the naked people in turn. Two men with him dunked the person thus anointed into the river water.

Dewey dismounted, sat on a grassy knoll, and watched the baptisms from afar. He admired people whose convictions sustained them to endure water as cold as the Hudson river's in October. With faces shining with the experience of having been touched by the Holy Spirit, they climbed the banks of the river and were immediately surrounded by friends who dried and dressed them.

In a half hour the baptisms were finished. The two assistants helped the old preacher to climb out of the water and escorted him to a lone tent pitched in the center of the gathering. As soon as the preacher and his assistants disappeared into the tent, the people began to bustle about unpacking parcels of food, lighting a camp fire, and chattering happily.

Dewey felt a tap on his shoulder, and, twisting round, looked up at a young farmer.

"Come join us, stranger," the farmer smiled. "We're simple folk; we'll make you good company."

Dewey responded to the warmth of the greeting, and, leading his horse, followed the farmer to the gathering. Someone took his horse, and others cheerfully accompanied him to the center of the encampment where people sat in a half-circle about the fire. The people, men and women of all ages, simply greeted him as he sat and seemed to hold back from starting a conversation with him. Minutes later, the preacher appeared from his tent and walked toward them. He was dressed in black. Dewey guessed he was in his seventies but looking hale and hearty. It was evident that the Baptists had wanted their preacher to be the first to converse with him.

The preacher smiled warmly and sat on the ground beside him. "Too bad you didn't come earlier, you could've joined these folks in the river."

Dewey laughed in surprise. "I'm not ready to see the Holy Spirit," he said, and he introduced himself, but this time using his real name. The Randal name which had served him well for the past days suddenly embarrassed him as an unworthy subterfuge among these religious people.

"Elder James is my name," the old man said, shaking his hand strongly.

Dewey considered him as strong as iron, which, of course, he would have to be to stand in the cold river for long stretches. Elder James turned away to speak to some of his flock, and Dewey watched the campers happily talking and eating. They had come from miles about to meet this itinerant preacher, and, most likely, most had never seen one another before.

"Where're you from, Mr. Dewey?" the Elder asked. When he heard Boston, he nodded approvingly. "I spent many years in Massachusetts. I ministered in Middleborough mostly."

"Baptists made a great many converts," Dewey said.

"Oh yes, in Middleborough 'specially," said the old man, his eyes sparkling. "It all began in the 1780's with Asa Hunt. People just loved to hear that man! What a preacher he was! He had fire, he had compassion, he had understanding, he had love, and he was no one's fool."

"Elder Hunt?" Dewey asked with a glimmer of recognition.

"He died young; the best always do," Elder James smiled. "I saw the last years of his ministry, and he was inspiring--a man blessed by the Holy Spirit. He taught me," he paused as if he were reliving a memory. "I wander the countryside now."

A woman handed them both plates with pieces of fish, corn, and bread. The preacher ate as if he were famished.

"Elder Hunt also had influence over a man I defended in court," Dewey said, remembering that Ephraim Wheeler had spoken glowingly of Hunt to his two legal defenders.

The old man looked at him quizzically. "Well, well, Mr. Dewey, so you're a lawyer. So you really are a sinner in our midst. Was the man a preacher?"

"Anything but," Dewey smiled. "He raped his daughter."

Elder James looked at him sharply. "A preacher can do that," he said. "Any man can do anything if he's driven to it. But I know the man you mean. It was in the papers up north where I was last month. Name's Ephraim."

"That's right," Dewey said in surprise. "Did you really know him?"

The Elder nodded, finished munching and swallowing, and said "Last saw him many years ago--before he married--woman in the Episcopalian faith."

Dewey, as an Episcopalian, winced at the deprecatory tone.

"Were you his leader?" Dewey asked hopefully.

"For a time after Asa Hunt died. But he was a wild-spirited young man. He wanted to feel free--maybe to make up for a constrained childhood."

"You know his life, then," Dewey said eagerly.

"What he told me," Elder James smiled. "But I lost trust in him when he changed his name."

Dewey frowned, puzzled. "Isn't his name Ephraim Wheeler?"

"He was Ephraim Haskins," Elder James said with a twinkle in his eye. "He helped two of his shipmates escape from jail in Providence. He had to change his name because the authorities were on the look-out for him. But I warned him not to. Once a man assumes an identity which is not his own, he lives under the shadow of his crime, which carries him into other criminal acts." He sighed. "So now he's going to be hanged."

Dewey could hardly believe his ears. "But what sort of man was he? Did you imagine that he could commit a violent act?"

Elder James shook his head slowly. "Poor fellow used to sink into depressions. He had so much violence done to him when a boy, it's not surprising to me that he's become violent in his turn."

"So you think he was capable of raping his daughter?" Dewey asked casually, although keenly interested in the old man's views.

"I think," said the preacher, looking him squarely in the eye, "you and I are capable of raping our daughters."

"He's guilty because he's human," Dewey smiled. "That doesn't persuade me he should be hanged."

"Mr. Dewey," the preacher cautioned, "I'm against all forms of execution. What I would ask you to do is to send him back to me because, you know, killing the body does not cure the soul."

Dewey was slightly repelled by the preacher's emphasis on the soul when it seemed to him that the saving of the body should be the paramount consideration.

The Baptists were gathering up their blankets and baskets as they prepared to go their different ways. Elder James swallowed a large piece of fish, wiped his fingers in his handkerchief, and stood up calling out to them. Everyone stood now to face him. Dewey quickly got to his feet and watched the preacher slowly move his arms in blessing upon them all. When he lowered his arms, there broke forth a great chattering and bustle. The Baptists cried out to one another, kissed, and waved as they set out for the solitude of their farms many miles distant.

"Well, well, city lawyer," Elder James said, taking Dewey by the hand. "The next time you're troubled, come see me. I've got a meeting to attend tonight and quite a bit of road to go."

Dewey watched the tough little man clamp his black hat on his head and brusquely stride ahead of a group of his followers across the fields. The boy who had taken Dewey's horse approached him with it. Dewey, finding a coin in his pocket, offered it to him, but the boy shook his head shyly and ran after the group following the preacher.

Cloud blotted out the sun, and the breeze felt cooler. Dewey, worried about rain, mounted and turned back toward Glen Falls. He was excited and pleased by his encounter with the preacher but also saddened by what he had learned because he would have to confront Susanna Randal with Ephraim's real name. It would be like reproaching her for not telling him.

SIXTEEN

Just before dark Dewey walked along the back road out of town to Susanna Randal's home. He thought of her so vividly as Ephraim Wheeler's fiancee that he could not remember her married name. He imagined the excitement Wheeler must have felt about her. Probably it was like the excitement he himself was experiencing then, he thought. He felt light-headed,and his blood seemed to race through his veins in a way he had not known for a long time. But as he approached the door of her cabin, he told himself that his investigation of Wheeler demanded that he calm down.

It was not the fact that Wheeler had changed his name that worried him; it was Susanna's concealment of that fact. Her action said something about Wheeler. And since it was Wheeler's real guilt or innocence he wanted to determine, he could not afford to be carried away into romantic fancy over the woman herself.

She opened the door to him. There was no trace of the frostiness in her manner of the night before.

"Go into the sitting room," she beamed. "He's been impatient for you to arrive."

Dewey was pleased at the pleasure that he saw in her eyes. Obviously her father meant a great deal to her. He waited until she closed the door behind him, and he took her hand. She was warm and sexually alive to him. For an instant he took in the full shape of her breasts, her hips, and long legs, and then, looking her straight in the eye, he said, "I was impatient to arrive here."

Laughing with embarrassment Susanna stepped by him. "Come, it's this way." She led him through a door off the hall into a long room with mats on the floor and wooden chairs and tables.

Mr. Randal sat in a rocking chair with his feet stretched toward a small fire in the hearth. He gesticulated excitedly for Dewey to pull up a chair beside him.

"Give us a spot of wine, my son," he said, pointing to a decanter of red wine and glasses on a sideboard. "You know, I've been thinking," he continued as Dewey poured the wine.

"I wont have any," Susanna said quickly. "Excuse me while I mind the kitchen."

"Oh, pity!" Dewey said.

"I shan't be long," she said or almost sang.

Dewey carried a glass of wine to Mr. Randal.

"I've been thinking," Randal said and took a sip of wine and said, toasting Dewey, "To your health," and he sipped it again. "My father had an older brother who lived somewhere along the Massachusetts coast. You couldn't be his grandson, could you?"

Startled, Dewey looked at him in surprise and then remembered that the old man was addressing him under his assumed name of Bob Randal.

"I don't know," Dewey said uncomfortably. "What was his name?"

"Alexander, I think"

"My grandfather was named Peter," Dewey said quickly. The falsehoods seemed to be growing one on the other. He could see himself creating a false family tree.

"Maybe his name was Peter, come to think of it," Randal said. "Was his wife Abigail?"

"No," Dewey shook his head vigorously. "There was no Abigail in my family. How was your trip today?"

"Fine, fine," said Randal, disappointed not to have discovered that they were relatives. "Whenever I come to see my daughter, the roads are like magic carpets bearing me swiftly along."

Dewey pictured the ruts and hollows along the roadways and laughed. "I understand what you mean."

Randal looked at him quickly with appreciation and then turned to gaze at the hearth. "It's when you're my age that you are glad you had a family," he said. "You look after the children growing up, and they look after you dying out. You take my word for it, Bob Randal, marriage has its compensations. You're not married, are you?"

"No, sir," Dewey said firmly. "How did you know?"

"There's an air of indifference about you, my dear fellow. Only bachelors develop it."

Dewey laughed. "Is that bad?"

"No, not too bad," Mr. Randal smiled, "but it's better to be involved in life. You know what I mean."

Dewey knew that Randal wanted him to be interested in his daughter, and the thought did not alarm him. Susanna came into the room and pulled up a straight-backed chair to sit close to them.

"Well, my daughter, its not often we have a Boston lawyer in these parts," Randal said. "He's apt to find us a bit rustic."

"The scenery is rustic," Dewey said quickly, "and I find the people warm and attractive."

"There!" cried the old man slapping his knee, "that's the polish I like to see on a young man! Won't find that among the lumberjacks out here."

Susanna blushed. "Oh Dad, please hush up."

Mr. Randal stopped smiling and looked embarrassedly at Dewey.

"I'm afraid," Dewey said, "many people in Boston would like to live as lumberjacks. Rustic life has undeniable charms." He stood up abruptly. "But I'm forgetting my good Boston manners," he smiled at Susanna. "Will you drink some wine now?"

"Please. Dinner will be ready soon," Susanna said. "I'm interested in Boston and the towns of Massachusetts. I haven't seen them for ten or fifteen years. Have they changed?"

"Immensely," Dewey said as he poured her a glass of wine. "A lot of new immigrants. We're getting the feeling of being a commonwealth. The sad sense of Britishness is disappearing."

They talked in this manner throughout the evening, Susanna and Dewey slowly finding out about each other, and the old man chipping into their conversation with observations and amusing anecdotes. Dewey liked the dinner, even said it was the best he had eaten since leaving home, and Susanna was becoming more animated, more confident. Her two children kept out of sight and appeared only to say an affectionate good-night to their grandfather before going to bed. Dewey admired Susanna's quiet efficiency. Altogether, he thought, it had been a long time since he had met a woman whom he found as attractive as Susanna.

Mr. Randal retired to take a cat-nap after dinner. Dewey and Susanna carried on their conversation in the chairs by the hearth, a conversation that moved effortlessly from subject to subject and brought the participants closer together than Dewey had thought possible within a single evening. But then Dewey remembered the reason for his visit, and, reluctantly, he directed their thoughts to Susanna's past and her relationship with Wheeler. She became stiffer, less open.

Dewey apologized. "I want to try to save his life. You might tell me something that, although not important to you, will have legal value in my eyes."

"I thought I had shut the door on that chapter of my life," Susanna said sadly. "It is painful to open it."

"Just tell me," Dewey said kindly. "Is he right when he says that you would not marry him because he spent all his money in the year he was ill?"

Susanna shook her head. "I may have let him think it, but that wasn't the reason."

"What then?" Dewey smiled and waited while she searched her thoughts.

"In the course of the year, I found I didn't love him," she said slowly. "I thought I did, but I think I had just felt sorry for him--him being an orphan and treated so bad."

"Was there something you didn't like about him?"

"Well, he used to drink because he was so frustrated with his life. He could be brutal. He threatened me when he was in his dark moods. But he never hit me," she added quickly. "I just found I didn't like him like that, and, gradually, I discovered I didn't love him."

"Did he call himself Haskins when you knew him?" Dewey asked casually.

Susanna looked startled. "How did you know that?"

"Lawyers get to find out things," he said whimsically. "When did he change his name?"

She made a grimace and looked at the floor. "I almost feel like I'm betraying him by telling this--but if you're trying to help him, maybe I should tell."

"I know some of it," Dewey said.

"Then, maybe you know I've been lying," she said mournfully.

Dewey concealed his surprise. "Maybe," he said.

"Well, Ephraim wasn't sick for a year. It's true he strained himself lifting something heavy, but for someof that time he was in jail. They say he'd gotten into a fight in a tavern, broke up furniture and property." Susanna looked as if she were confessing a personal guilt. "I went to visit him, but he seemed like a changed man. My friends didn't want me to start my life married to a man who had so many strikes against him. So I moved away before he was released. I didn't want him to find

117

me, and when he finally did, I was scared. He was determined to take me back with him--by force, if necessary." She laughed at the thought, now so safely stowed away in the past. "And he might have if the man I later married hadn't made him go away."

Dewey, alarmed by her story, stared at her in sympathy. "You poor girl. He must have been a monster. Just as they say he is."

"No," Susanna shook her head. "He's not a monster. He just feels deeply and acts strongly. There's nothing in the man that suggested to me he was a rapist. He was gentle when he wanted to be. I'm sure he's innocent."

Dewey looked at her in disbelief. His liking for her increased as he found her defense of Wheeler admirable. "After he tried to force you to go away with him, you think he's a good man?"

"I know he loved me," she said, tears coming to her eyes. She brushed her hand over them. "I can't say more. All l know is why he changed his name--to get a fresh start in life."

Dewey reached out to hold her hands. "I'm sorry I had to pry, but you've helped me understand. And your conviction that he is innocent has quite an influence on me. Because you have quite an influence on me."

Susanna smiled with understanding. "I hope you'll stay in town for a few days."

"I want to get to know you," he said, "but I must go back tomorrow. If I'm to save Ephraim, there's no time to lose."

Susanna looked disappointed.

"I may have to send for you. Will you come?" he asked.

She looked puzzled.

"I mean to help persuade the authorities to save Ephraim from execution," he added.

"Yes, I'll do whatever you think is necessary," she said sadly.

"We will see each other again." He stood up.

"Oh, where's Dad?" Susanna stepped into the next room and returned in an instant. "He's fast asleep, the poor dear. The travel must have tired him."

"Give him my regrets that I couldn't say good-bye," Dewey said, "and assure him I will see him again soon."

Their eyes met with meaning, and Susanna nodded. Dewey kissed her cheek, and, quickly donning his coat and hat, he departed from that warm hearth and that warm heart into the chill of the black night and the loneliness of the hotel room and his bachelorhood.

SEVENTEEN

After Dewey returned to Lenox, he met an ally for his cause to save Wheeler from the hangman--a young doctor. It happened as a result of Betsy Wheeler's unhappiness.

Harriette tried to comfort her, but Harriette felt as shunned by the townspeople as her daughter, the more so because she had to go among them daily to do the shopping for her brother's household. Isaac Odel barely tolerated her and treated Betsy with indifferent scorn. At meals, his dour face cast a constant reproach upon her for bringing public disgrace on the family. Without his shelter they would starve, but at times Harriette would have been willing to risk starvation if it were not for her concern and love for Betsy and the baby.

Isaac's wife spoke to them only when necessary and, in private, argued with her husband that they should be made to fend for themselves. Odel, regardless of his criticism, believed in the sacredness of the family and his duty to succor those of its members who needed it.

Betsy observed all these attitudes as if they were revelations coming one on top of the other. Within a few weeks, she aged so that her mind and emotions, like her well-formed body, developed beyond her nominal thirteen years. Above all, she learned distrust. She understood the hypocrisy of the Odels and the townspeople because they were confused. The duplicity of authority, however, dismayed and frightened her. Instead of helping her and her mother as they promised, Justice Walker and Attorney-General Sullivan had brought them to a state of ignominious despair. Her Daddy, regardless of how evil his crime was considered, was still her Daddy. And although he had threatened to put Ephie and her into service, he was committed to help them because he was their Daddy. Betsy thought of Mr. Sullivan as a betrayer of her trust.

The pain of her betrayal by the very people she had been taught to respect and her growing sense of guilt for testifying against Ephraim caused her to spend days at a time at her house duties without speaking, not even to Harriette. The more she pictured Ephraim in prison, the fainter became the recollection of her rape. But as she drifted into fond memories of her father, there came like a sharp arrow driven into her thoughts the scenes of whipping and beating and the violent arguments that her poor mother had to suffer at the hands of Ephraim. Then she would feel ill with the conflict of her emotions, and every sentiment of guilt over her father encountered a sense of shame and sympathy for her mother. At such moments, if Harriette were in the house, Betsy would go to her and work by her side, saying nothing but communicating a feeling of unity from which they both derived strength.

Harriette was in the house less frequently because she had to work. She found employment in the home of Mrs. Bryant, the wife of one of Cummington's two doctors and a woman quietly sympathetic to her ordeal. Harriette had been dismayed by Ephraim's death sentence, and, like Betsy, she felt betrayed by Sullivan. But as the weeks passed, she became hardened to Ephraim's plight. Her love for her children overcame her sense of obedience to her husband. The indifference for him, that she had long felt, hardened into an absolute divorce from all knowledge of him--from the moments of fun and affection, from the carnal acts--all were banned from her memory and her senses as if they had never happened. But she was sensitive to Betsy's concern for Ephraim. It was more on behalf of Betsy, rather than for any regard she may still have felt for her husband, that determined Harriette to stop the execution of Ephraim. But how? James Sullivan and the men around him gave her easy assurances without conviction. There was no one she could approach, which is why, one afternoon, when she was sewing in Mrs. Bryant's company, she broached the subject of Ephraim Wheeler.

"M'am," she began. "There's not a day goes by but I don't thank the Lord for your good Christian heart."

Mrs. Bryant, an active woman with a kind face and long dark hair, put down the garment she was crocheting, and looked sympathetically at Harriette. "You must be suffering a lot, Mrs. Wheeler. I wish there was more one could do."

"For myself, I want nothing more. Thanks to you I can keep my family alive. But what I am worried about--can I keep my family's spirit alive?"

"What do you mean?" Mrs. Bryant's face stretched in concern.

Harriette looked away from the warmth of the sitting room with its log fire and gazed out at the snow covering the landscape for as far as she could see. The cold outdoors had become equated in her mind to Ephraim's prison cell. "If Mr. Wheeler's hanged," she said, "my Betsy will think she killed him."

"Yes," Mrs. Bryant said. "I wondered about that."

"Bad as Mr. Wheeler is, I don't want him to hang," Harriette said. "I never want to see him again. I don't want him near my children, but I don't want his death on Betsy's conscience."

Mrs. Bryant nodded. "I agree, Betsy has suffered enough. But these things are in the hands of Providence, Mrs. Wheeler. The best we can do is to pray."

"Is there nothing you and your husband can do?" Harriette asked desperately. "You are people of consequence. They will listen to you."

Mrs. Bryant stood up, came over to Harriette, and put her arm comfortingly about her shoulders. "I'll speak to the doctor," she said. "Please don't worry about it. I'm sure it will work out in the end."

At the comforting tone of voice and the warmth of her embrace, Harriette suddenly broke into tears. She almost never cried, never allowed her emotions to get the better of her. But with this unexpected kindness from Mrs. Bryant, the first understanding she had been shown for a long time, she gave way and sobbed uncontrollably.

Mrs. Bryant, alarmed, tried to soothe her, but it was some moments before Harriette regained her composure.

"You poor, poor woman," Mrs. Bryant said. "Of course I'll do whatever I can. But you must not worry. Things will take care of themselves. And, Mrs. Wheeler, promise me you'll bring Betsy with you soon. I'm so looking forward to meeting her."

Harriette could scarcely believe that someone was inviting Betsy to enter her home.

"You're too kind," she said tearfully.

"Now, you've done enough work today," Mrs. Bryant smiled. "I'm sure your baby boy is waiting to see you with a love that any mother would be fortunate to have."

Harriette smiled appreciatively and quickly readied herself for the walk across the hard-packed snow.

As they said good-bye at the door, Mrs. Bryant said, "I'll discuss it with my husband. He'll know what to do."

The positive tone buoyed Harriette's spirit as she walked quickly down the slope from the old town on the hill to the Odel farmstead by the river. Darkness fell quickly so that, when she reached the river, she found her path only by the reflection of the snow. She was engrossed in her thoughts and did not see the dark figure on the snowy bank of the river. But when it moved, it caught her attention. Something about it alarmed her because it seemed to be a woman, and it was looking down at the river. Thinking that it might be Betsy, she approached it quietly from behind until she came within three feet of it in the darkness.

"Betsy," she said calmly.

The girl whirled round. "Ma!"

They looked at one another as the thought of Betsy's self-destruction passed between them. The only sound was the rippling river which broke free of the ice at that spot where there were rapids before submerging again under the ice. Harriette thought of Betsy carried into that icy prison, and, reaching out, took Betsy by the hand, and, together, they walked to Odel's house.

Dr. Peter Bryant had great difficulty adjusting to Cummington when he arrived in the community some years before. An older doctor, who was established there, resented a younger man, as if he were a threat, and spread rumors that cast doubt on Bryant's capabilities. When the young Bryant began to attract patients, the established doctor became openly unfriendly and accused him of overcharging for his services. Bryant, a sensitive man, determined to endure the unpleasantness, married a local girl and reared a son, a sickly boy, with whom he spent much time, introducing him to the beauties of nature and hardening his body against the sicknesses to which it was prone.

That evening, when Sarah Bryant told him of Harriette Wheeler's concern for the health of Betsy if Ephraim were hanged, Peter Bryant looked at the problem as a medical man. The saving of Ephraim Wheeler, he said, would not cure Betsy of guilt. His continued imprisonment would make her feel guilty. Even if he went free now, she would still feel guilty for accusing him. The real problem, he said, was in the carnal act, which she had committed. Somehow, she had to be brought to terms with the act in order to assuage her guilt.

Sarah Bryant thought for a moment before she replied. "Some day she may be able to do just that, but, for the moment, I understand Mrs. Wheeler's concern. If they hang her husband, they will destroy that young girl."

"'They' is the court," Bryant said with a grimace. "And it has decided."

"But you said you didn't think he should hang," Mrs. Bryant cried. "Doesn't the plight of this young girl give you cause to do something to stop it?"

Dr. Bryant looked with mystification at his wife. "My dear Sarah, what are you asking me to do?"

"Well," she said, "these people have no one to help them, no one who can understand their plight. All people do is go by the letter of the law, we know that. Why can't we who can understand them do something to help them?"

Bryant laughed suddenly and coming over to his wife bent down and kissed her cheek. "Why can't we indeed!"

Mrs. Bryant's face broke into a look of joy. "You will help her then? Oh Peter, you are a good man!"

"I can try," he said, "but it's going to take a lot of thinking before we make any moves. After all, the legal profession does not take advice from outsiders--unless there are a large number and well organized."

Sarah Bryant clasped his hand. "I can help you. I can talk to people we know in Cummington, Windsor, and other places."

"Be careful," the doctor warned. "Feelings run high for a hanging, and we can't afford to make enemies over a misunderstanding. No, Sarah, let me sleep on it tonight, and we'll talk again about it before we settle on a strategy."

"But now that we've started," she said excitedly, "I feel there's no time to lose. A man's life is in the balance."

"And if we make the wrong move, we could send him to the gallows for a certainty," he warned.

The doctor poked the blackened remains of the log fire so that they would smolder in the center of the hearth for the night. And then holding out his arm for his wife to come to him, he took her to bed.

Bryant had a fitful night. He woke up several times and lay thinking of the Wheelers. A man of compassion, he hated injustice. He could tolerate abuses to himself, but he would become enraged when they happened to others. If Sarah Bryant had not focused his attention on the Wheelers, of course, he would not have thought of them because his work as a doctor kept him busy with matters at hand.

He decided to go to the root of the problem: Ephraim Wheeler. He wanted to be able to judge the man for himself. He had to ride to Windsor in the morning when he could arrange the matter with Dr. Wright. The thought no sooner entered his head than he fell asleep.

The way from Cummington to Windsor was round-about over the hills, since the direct route through the valleys was made impassable by swampland. The heavy snow in the hills slowed the doctor's horse, particularly through the heavily wooded area at Partridgefield where huge drifts erased all signs of a roadway. Bryant had become accustomed to the hardships and almost relished the isolation because of the beauties of nature. He could not help reining in at places where the view of the white valleys and blue-ridged hills looked like a magic land. Or he would pause in the silence of the woods, broken occasionally by the sough of a breeze in the snow-filled firs. Understandably, his arrival in Windsor was later than it should have been.

The approach to the village up the slow rise of the hill ran past the farmhouse of William Martin where Bryant saw the tall, sturdy farmer sawing logs by the back door.

When he reached the summit, Bryant turned to a settlement to the north. There were three areas of settlement in the village: the one in the north, where Dr. Wright lived, was the richest. Dr. Wright's large wooden-framed house could have stood without shame in Lenox. Wright opened his front door when Bryant was still fifty yards from the house and bellowed for the stable boy, who came running, just as Bryant dismounted, and took the horse to the stable.

Wright greeted him warmly, helped him take off his coat, and handed his outer garment to the teen-aged maid who stood respectfully in attendance.

"I expected you well over an hour ago," Wright said. "I'm afraid a neighbour just dropped by; we'll have to discuss our medical business after he leaves."

"Sorry, my dear Wright," Bryant said. "Anyone I know?"

"By reputation," Wright smiled. "Justice Robert Walker." He opened the door to the sitting room and a warm hearth-fire.

The tall taciturn Walker stood, took his pipe from his mouth, and shook Bryant's hand.

"I've seen you about," Walker said respectfully.

They sat and talked about local news. Bryant took some letters from his pocket addressed to people in Windsor and put them on the table for Wright to deliver. Gradually Bryant directed their conversation to the Wheeler trial which the other two men seemed quite prepared to discuss, as if the subject had been on their minds.

The rotund Dr. Wright immediately began to declaim as if he again were testifying on the witness stand. "Despite all the sympathy I'm beginning to hear round about for that man, I have no time for him. He is a wife-beater, a drumhead, a no-good. Execution is the best thing for him. Don't you agree, Walker?"

Walker drew on his pipe before replying. His long slim fingers curved around the pipe bowl and along the stem. "He's guilty as charged," he said slowly, "that's certain."

Bryant looked at him sharply. "But do you think he should hang?"

Walker drew on his pipe again and blew the smoke to the side of his mouth. "No."

Dr. Wright reared back in surprise. "You arrested him! What do you mean by you don't think he should hang?"

Walker put his pipe down and looked offended by Wright's accusatory tone.

"I'm sorry, Justice," Wright looked flustered. "I'm excited because I'm disappointed. I expected a different answer from a man of the law."

Walker ignored him and looked at Bryant. "Incest is not a hanging offense."

Bryant nodded. "Why wasn't that argument raised by the defense?"

Walker smiled slightly, and, picking up his pipe, began to smoke again.

"Because to me," Wright said, sitting up as if testifying, "incest implies consent. This was rape."

Bryant shook his head. "But the defense would have done better if it had used the argument," he smiled. "Especially when Wheeler denied it was rape. What do you say, Justice? Did Betsy consent?"

Walker said: "Betsy may have been forced. But her rape was within the family. Consent is an argument to disprove rape, not incest."

The men fell silent as they thought over Walker's statement.

Bryant broke the silence. "I'd like to visit Ephraim Wheeler. Is that possible?" he asked Walker.

"Don't, Bryant," Wright warned. "You'll be getting involved in something that too many are involved in already."

Walker said: "I go to Lenox on business tomorrow."

"I'll go with you," Bryant said quickly.

"Well then," Wright slapped his knee, "that's that! I smell our mid-day meal! Let's go to it and talk about more pleasant things, shall we?" He stood up. "Oh Bryant, your room is the first at the head of the stairs. I'll show the Justice my new books from Albany while we wait for you."

Bryant hurried to his room and made his toilet. He was elated because he thought that Justice Walker regarded the Wheeler case in the same light he did.

They took a sleigh with eight horses over the hard-packed snow to Lenox. Besides Bryant and Walker, there were four other passengers who were minor officials in the county government. They passed the time by discussing the political situation. They all agreed that the Federalists were losing ground to the Republicans. If it were not for the widespread public respect for Governor Strong, the Federalists would be swept from power. Bryant voted Republican because he was sympathetic to the farmers and workingmen who had been saddled with high-taxes to pay off the public debt. Indirectly, he suffered from their poverty as they were unable to pay him for his services.

After Bryant found a room at a hotel, Walker, who was staying with relatives, took him to the law office of John W. Hulbert. In the months following Wheeler's trial, Hulbert did a lot of law work, even some court cases, but he seemed unable to put the Wheeler case behind him. News of the conviction had spread into other States, and Hulbert's defense was warmly debated. When Hulbert heard Walker introduce Dr. Bryant as interested in meeting Wheeler, he uttered a sigh of resignation.

"You're not the only one who wants to see him, doctor," Hulbert said. "The Court has stipulated that Wheeler cannot have visitors. It thinks that all this noise on behalf of the prisoner must be stopped."

"All this noise?" Bryant asked, looking puzzled.

"There's agitation been building up. Republicans appear to be behind it. They want another trial," Hulbert explained. "I could do no better at a second trial, I assure you."

"Some want his sentence commuted," Walker said.

"Governor Strong has decided against it. He can't go back on his decision," Hulbert replied. "If the case is a mess, it's Wheeler who is responsible. He still insists he's not guilty. How could I be expected to help a man as stubborn as that?"

"That's why I want to see him," Bryant said. "I may be able to bring him to reason."

Hulbert smiled. He had an unfortunate air of superiority which became offensive at certain moments. "Not possible, I'm afraid."

"Heard Dewey's in town," Walker said.

"Yes," Hulbert said coldly. "He's been here a week. And he's partly to blame for the agitation."

"He's Federalist," Walker said, as if to question Hulbert's assumption.

"I know, I know," Hulbert looked impatient. "But he's convinced that Wheeler shouldn't hang. Go see him if you like. He has more influence with the Court than I do."

Hulbert shook Bryant's hand limply and returned to his work. Bryant reflected on Wheeler's misfortune at being assigned such a lawyer, and he was curious to meet Daniel Dewey. Justice Walker understood his impatience. He took him directly to the tavern where Dewey spent the latter part of his mornings.

Dewey sat alone reading a newspaper from the light of the large bay window. He recognized Walker and seemed genuinely pleased to meet Bryant, particularly after Walker told him that Bryant was a Wheeler sympathizer.

"Ah, perhaps a new member for my group," Dewey said hopefully.

Bryant liked him immediately and was quite impressed with his charm.

"I return tomorrow morning," Walker said, as he left them to talk.

Bryant called a "thank you" after him. "The Justice really does stand for justice," he said to Dewey.

Dewey nodded. "Why, Dr. Bryant, are you interested in Wheeler?"

"I oppose executing him for his offense, and I want to save his family from having to bear the guilt of his death." Bryant paused. "I suppose that sounds rather unsympathetic to the man himself, but I hear he is not a person one can readily sympathize with."

Dewey looked pleased with Bryant's reply. "Seems to me you are loaded with sympathy. You may even find some for Wheeler when you discover that he's his own worst enemy."

"I suspected that," Bryant said. "I want to talk to him."

Dewey shook his head. "You can't. I'm his lawyer, and I spent a week getting permission to visit him. They are very, very concerned about contacts Wheeler has with outsiders, ever since a reporter from Pittsfield interviewed him."

Bryant could not help feeling disappointed. Even Dewey was discouraging him. "I wanted to talk to him as if he were my patient."

Dewey looked startled. "The idea just occurred to me. Why don't I take you with me when I visit this afternoon? You can be his doctor. He has had no doctor since he was in prison."

"I don't want to visit under false pretenses," Bryant protested, but his tone belied an interest in the suggestion.

"It's not false," Dewey laughed. "You really are too honest, Doctor. No, not false. He really does need a doctor. The cells are cold and damp. He may be quite ill. Moreover, it is the only way that you can see him."

"Agreed," Bryant said. He smiled, amused by the turn of events.

Dewey beckoned to the waiter and asked him to bring them lunch. "Whatever it is," he said to Bryant, "it's usually good. You know, our committee to commute Wheeler's sentence to imprisonment has become quite popular. We have numerous professional people, enlightened people like yourself, from both parties."

Bryant sensed a special significance in the phrase "professional people" as Dewey used it. Obviously, Dewey had formed a committee which by its very respectability would bring pressure on the Governor.

"How do the working people feel, the farmers and so on?" Bryant asked casually.

"They have their own means of protest," Dewey said disparagingly. "Those who support Wheeler are Republicans.

It's all politics with them. Let's say that Wheeler is a convenient cause to bring them to political power. They don't know what justice is, so how could they know how we think?"

Bryant was taken aback by Dewey's sweeping statement. He had forgotten Dewey's Federalist connection, and he wondered just how serious Dewey's committee was. Could it not also have been working for Federalism?

"Wouldn't you be stronger by joining forces?" he suggested.

"We think not," Dewey said decisively. "That group will make the Governor obstinate whereas we have the power of persuasion."

Bryant felt uncomfortable. How, he wondered, could a committee of the professional class divorce itself from a fundamental political issue? He said nothing of these thoughts to Dewey, however, and turning the conversation to Boston where he had attended medical school, he did not return to the subject of Wheeler until they were approaching the gaol.

"How often do you visit Wheeler?" Bryant asked.

"This is the second time since I came to Lenox last week," Dewey said. "And I had not been in Lenox since the trial. Hulbert has been seeing to his needs."

"Do you remark any change in him brought about by imprisonment?"

Dewey looked askance at Bryant. "Now he needs a doctor."

The gaol superintendent listened impassively as Dewey explained that Bryant came to give Wheeler a physical examination.

"On your word, Mr. Dewey, sir," he said, and stamped a pass for Bryant to accompany Dewey. "You know the way, sir."

Dewey nodded and led Bryant down a corridor to a large room, the threshold to which was blocked by a gate of iron bars. A heavy-set guard, perching on a stool and reading a newspaper inside the room, saw them at the entrance, quickly ran over to fit a key into the gate, and let them in.

"Your Wheeler's in a sulky mood today, sir," he said, and, grinning at Bryant, took his pass.

The dull light of winter fell through the high barred windows as Dewey led the way across the room and down one of the corridors leading off it, until they came to Wheeler's cell. The cell door was partially open. Dewey pushed it open wider with his finger tips, and it revealed Wheeler lying on his cot and pressing his face into his pillow as if in misery and frustration.

"Ephraim, I've brought a visitor," Dewey announced.

Wheeler looked up slowly, his deep-rimmed eyes impassively surveying Bryant.

"He's a doctor," Dewey continued. "I want him to take a look at you."

"I'm not sick," Ephraim said in mild protest.

"We won't know until Dr. Bryant looks at you," Dewey smiled. "I'll leave you two alone for a few minutes." He winked at Bryant and left the cell to talk with the guard.

"So you're Dr. Bryant," Ephraim said with interest as he swung his feet onto the floor and perched on the side of his cot. "I seen you in Cummington a couple a'times."

Bryant pulled up a wooden stool and sat facing Ephraim. "Take off your shirt, Ephraim, and we'll see if your lungs are healthy." He took a stethoscope from his black bag. "Your family seems well," he added. "Mrs. Wheeler does some work for us."

Ephraim paused in stripping his shirt from his arms as if the mention of his family had come like an unexpected blow. "Are they well?" he asked, taking off his shirt and throwing it on the bed. "And happy?"

Bryant could detect a slight resentment in his tone. "No, they are not happy. They want to see you saved from execution."

Ephraim smiled and shook his head in disbelief. "You watch out for Harriette, Doctor. She can lie better than any woman I know."

"Hold still, now," Bryant said, and, applying the stethoscope to Ephraim's chest, he listened and tapped about in several places, and, making Ephraim turn his back to him, he continued the process. "Open your mouth and stick out your tongue," he said. He saw that Wheeler was moderately healthy. Confinement and the poor prison diet had given him a sallow look. He sat back and began to probe Ephraim's mind as Ephraim put on his shirt.

"You don't believe that your daughter Betsy is very unhappy?" Bryant asked.

"Betsy?" Wheeler asked rhetorically. "I'd like to pretend I had no daughter."

"You've been feeling like that for a long time, long before the incident at Partridgefield," Bryant suggested. "Is that why you were going to put her out as a servant while you went off to sea?"

"I was doing the right thing," Ephraim said, a touch of anger springing to his eyes. "I didn't want her living with her mother and growing up with bad ideas."

"You were going to take the baby away from the mother," Bryant said. "Who was going to look after it?"

"I'd find somebody," Ephraim said.

"You were deprived of your parents at an early age. Don't you remember what it was like?"

"How'd you know that?" Ephraim demanded. "The newspaper?"

"That's the talk," Bryant said. "Your hard childhood has gained you a lot of sympathy, but it makes me ask how you could do the same to your own children."

"I was taking young Ephie with me to sea," Ephraim said defensively.

"You were taking the children away from their mother," Bryant said firmly, "because you wanted to hurt their mother as deeply as you possibly could."

Wheeler stared at the floor.

"Is that a reasonable surmise?" Bryant asked.

"Yes, sir," Ephraim said. "She hindered me at every opportunity, so I was getting even."

"Getting even because you couldn't make a living, always in debt, always having to board in another person's home, always visiting your frustrations on your wife so she had to have someone, her brother, or Mr. Martin to protect her from you. I've heard what people say."

"That's a lie," Ephraim cried. "She provoked me. She has a vicious tongue."

They were silent for a moment. Bryant saw that he had penetrated beneath Wheeler's surface, stirred up his emotions, and might now possibly get at the truth.

"When you were beaten by your master, didn't you want to get even with him?" Bryant asked.

"Of course I did," Wheeler said. "He humiliated me beyond measure, but there was nothing I could do. The law was on his side."

"But you did the same when the law was on your side," Bryant said accusingly.

Wheeler stared at him uncomprehendingly.

"You beat your wife in the same way. She had no recourse because the law would interfere only if you murdered her. So you beat her like your master beat you." Bryant stood up, stepped back and looked down at Wheeler, who was grasping at the implications of Bryant's meaning. "You used your family with the same cruelty you had been used. That's why you raped Betsy."

"I didn't," Wheeler groaned.

"You admit you took her into the woods," Bryant said angrily.

"To get avensroot to give to her mother because she was sick," Wheeler explained.

"Sick!" Bryant expostulated. "And you were beating her with a bayonet just a few hours earlier? No, my poor man, I am prepared to help you if you can tell the truth, but I am not going to help a man who lies to himself--such a man is dangerous to society." Bryant lowered his voice slightly and said sternly, "What did happen in the woods?"

Wheeler shook his head. "I don't want to talk about it."

"If you could, you might save your neck," Bryant warned.

"And you'd make our task easier," Dewey said, stepping into the cell.

Wheeler looked up in surprise and then turned away.

"For instance, telling us that your real name is Ephraim Haskins could have helped us."

Wheeler almost jumped up from the bed in surprise. He looked speechless.

"That you helped two prisoners escape would have been useful information," Dewey continued. "It would have explained your false name, your reluctance to talk about yourself, and given us an idea of your character, which I consider rather poor, but not poor enough to be hanged. But the resolution of all this lies solely with you. Do you want us to try to save you?"

"Yes," Wheeler said glumly.

"Then think about telling us the truth," Dewey said severely. The guard appeared behind him. "You'll have time to think because we have to go."

"Thank you, both of you, thank you," Wheeler said.

Dewey and Bryant followed the guard in silence to the prison gate, back along the corridor, and into the open air. Bryant felt as if he were being delivered from a pit of doom.

"Now," Dewey said when they were alone, "is he healthy?"

"In body, yes, but in spirit, no," Bryant said grimly.

"The shadow of the hangman would make anyone spiritually sick," Dewey joked. "But the point is, were you satisfied with the interview?"

"I'm satisfied that he is a disturbed man," Bryant said. "I don't think he is a rapist so much as a man who wants revenge."

"Ah!" Dewey said. "You have a point. But, and this is a very big but, he had desire for his daughter, asked her to lie with him earlier, when his wife was pregnant."

"But real desire does not incite brutality," Bryant argued. "His desire was play-acting so that he could humiliate his daughter. He has not only been lying to us, he is lying to himself."

"Really!" Dewey exclaimed appreciatively. "That is profound!"

"The mind is profound," Bryant said.

"Will you join our group then?" Dewey asked. "Some of us are meeting to discuss how we approach the Governor. We have to find a political way out of his hangman's stance. If we don't act soon, the Republican opposition will make it impossible for him to retract."

"I'm sorry," Bryant said. "I'm not ready yet. I want to give it serious thought."

Bryant thought he saw a trace of disappointment on Dewey's face, but they parted in good spirits. He continued on to his hotel all the while thinking of Wheeler on the gallows and of how he could prevent him from standing there.

EIGHTEEN

Wheeler was in a panic. He had kept calm until Dewey and the doctor left him; then he sat on the edge of his cot and trembled as in a convulsive fit. He fell on his back and clutched a blanket tightly about him. For years he had feared discovery of his real name, and now it had arrived. Now he was condemned for certain. There was no salvation for a man who lived as a fraud.

He wondered if Gentle Adams had betrayed him, but rejected the thought. Somehow Dewey had dug out the information and perhaps much more. Dewey pledged to save him, but he was a Federalist, and he had not defended him well at the trial. Could he trust Dewey? Dewey had announced his real name in the presence of a stranger, as if he did not care what Bryant thought of him. But Bryant had not seemed disturbed by the revelation. Bryant seemed interested in him as a man, not as Haskins or Wheeler. If he were to be saved, it would be from efforts by people like Dr. Bryant, he thought. But, at the moment, he seemed destined to hang.

He stopped shaking and tried to breathe easily. His past had been his secret, and, therefore, it had significance for him. But now that he had revealed much of it, it no longer felt a part of him. Now, even his dark secrets, his rescue of two friends from prison, his slaughter of British prisoners when he sailed as an American privateer, and his misadventures in France, all would become known and be divorced from him, as if Ephraim Haskins were a stranger. His past had become his enemy. It stood against him as surely as any of his judges.

He was turning these morbid thoughts over in his mind and catching glimpses of himself in many scenes from his past when he heard a racket at the door to the prison. A man was shouting angrily at the warden, the prison doors clanged shut, and there was silence, a kind of brooding silence that seemed to wait for another violent outbreak.

Wheeler, as much to shake off his lethargy as out of curiosity, got up, and strolled into the great room of the prison. With a shock, he saw Michael Pepper, his boyhood friend and witness at his trial, sprawled upon a bench by the stone wall. He had been beaten. Blood marks were on his face. Ephraim came swiftly to him.

"Michael!"

The tall, lean Pepper looked up grimly. "I've been breaking the peace. Good to see you, my friend."

Ephraim smiled. "Come with me, Michael." He excitedly led the stiff-walking farmer to his cell. "You can clean up here."

Pepper immediately poured water in the basin and washed himself. Ephraim sat waiting for him to finish, eager for contact with one of his own kind.

"Can anyone hear us?" Pepper asked suddenly.

Ephraim shook his head.

"Good." Pepper looked relaxed. He wiped his face and hands with Ephraim's towel. "Because I went through this so I could get to talk to you."

Ephraim was surprised.

"We've got a plan for your escape," Pepper said.

Ephraim's face registered sheer astonishment, which amused Pepper.

"I can't tell you who 'we' are, but all of them agree that you're going to hang unless you escape," Pepper said, grim-faced again.

"Is there no hope?" Ephraim asked sadly.

Pepper shook his head. "You hanged yourself by keeping silent at your trial."

Ephraim rubbed his hands in sudden anger. "The more I think of what that bitch did to me, the more I feel like killing her."

"You better forget your family, my friend," Pepper warned. "You get to another State and change your name again."

Ephraim nodded.

Pepper poured the blood-stained water into the floor drain. He put the basin back, and, straightening his shirt, he sat on the stool. He was an adventurous fellow, carefree, and independent in spirit. For years when Ephraim worked under the oppressive heel of the shoemaker, Michael Pepper was his closest friend, sometimes his only friend. It was Pepper's natural disrespect for authority which Ephraim admired so much. Many times when Ephraim sank into despondency, thoughts of the indomitable Michael stopped his descent and seemed to start his spirit on the long climb back to normalcy.

When Ephraim ran away to sea, he lost contact with Michael Pepper until he came across him established on a farm in Windsor fifteen years later. Pepper kept his secret. They never spoke of their life in the past, but Ephraim gathered that Pepper had fought in the rebellion under General Shays. They developed a trust in one another.

"You make it sound easy, Michael, changing my name and starting again," Ephraim said. "I don't think I can change my luck."

Pepper recognized the self-pity in Ephraim and ignored it. "I've been in touch with your aunt who lives in Cambridge, New York."

Ephraim gasped. "How'd you know her? I ain't seen her since I was seven years old."

"She remembers you," Pepper said. "She'll tide you over till you're ready to go West."

Ephraim shook his head bemusedly.

"It's a long road from here to there," Pepper said, "so you'll need help along the way. Off the main road, about three miles from here, you'll find a horse, saddled."

"When is this?" Ephraim asked ,surprised and pleased by this offer of help.

"Any time after six o'clock on New Year's Day," Pepper said, fishing in his pocket and drawing out a piece of paper. "I sketched this map for you, so you can recognize the place when you get there."

Ephraim took the paper and studied the markings.

"You ride through the night, and, when they look for you in the morning, you'll be safe in your aunt's home," Pepper said, his eyes dancing with delight.

"I hope so," Ephraim said doubtfully. "How do I get out of here?"

"The outside door will be unlocked. Here's the key for the inside door," Pepper handed him a long metal key.

Ephraim almost laughed. "It sounds easy."

"One thing. You'll find a warm coat and things right by the horse. You have to get to that horse without freezin'."

139

"I'll wear that thing." Ephraim nodded at the thick gray blanket on his bed. He put the key into his pocket. He suddenly felt euphoric. He had to sit down on his bed to keep from pacing excitedly about his cell.

"If anything goes wrong, I'll get word to ya," Pepper said.

"Just over three weeks to go then," Ephraim breathed the words as if he were sighing with relief and expectation.

"Then, Ephraim, my friend, start a new life. You've done it before. You can do it again."

"Can I?" Ephraim suddenly looked dubious. "I've not got luck, Michael. Nothing's ever gone right with me. I thought maybe my luck would change when I met Susanna. But I was wrong."

"Aw, things are different in the West. Here everybody meddles in your business. Things are too restricted, and the people love money too much," Pepper said.

"Where in the West?" Ephraim asked concernedly. "Do you mean in the Indian country? How'm I goin' to survive out there? I'm a sailor, not a hunter. No, Michael, if I make it out of here, I'm going back to the sea."

Pepper shrugged. "Suit yourself. Maybe it'll be better for you. But you can't sail out of New England 'cause you'll be caught sooner or later."

Ephraim smiled at Pepper's concern for him. "No, not from Massachusetts. I'm going to South America. I been to Brazil. There's a good livin' to be made down there."

"One thing's for sure--they'll never find you," Pepper said. "But what will you do about your family?"

"Good riddance," Ephraim said sharply. "Harriette can fend for herself."

"And the children?" Pepper asked, watching Ephraim closely.

Ephraim saw that Pepper was testing him. He changed his tone, sounding regretful. "Sorry about them, but what can I do? If I make money, I'll provide for them through Odel."

Pepper nodded as if satisfied with the answer.

They heard the clang of the inside gate.

"The guard will be looking for me," Pepper said and stood up. "I'd best not be seen with you. I'll spend the night in the other wing, and then they'll boot me out tomorrow morning. Good-bye, Ephraim. Don't despair."

Ephraim clasped Pepper's hand, and, too moved to speak, he expressed his gratitude through his eyes. A minute later he heard Pepper and the guard engage in angry conversation until their voices trailed out of earshot. He clasped his fingers about the key in his pocket as if to convince himself of the reality of the situation. Soon, he should be free. He would be rid of this death pall which prison had cast upon him. He was to be resurrected! But he sensed a foreboding which cast a shadow of another kind over his expectation. He could not define it. He knew only that it was a mistrust of himself, as if his freedom carried with it a danger. He shook off the feeling with a convulsive movement of his shoulders, and, pacing, the room, he thought of his escape and of the people he suspected were behind it. For their sakes, he had to make it a success.

NINETEEN

Peter Bryant, at home in Cummington, discussed Wheeler's crime with his wife, Sarah. They decided that he had been right to refuse to join with Daniel Dewey's group of gentry and professional people, whose motivation, they suspected, was more political than humane. The Bryants feared that Wheeler as an individual would become lost in Wheeler as a symbol of opposition to capital punishment.

"You know, Sarah dear," Bryant said as they sat in the early evening with their feet to the hearth fire, "I think I understand why Wheeler did not defend himself vigorously at his trial. He is a Baptist. There is a sense of fatalism in him. He's depending on the will of God."

"Too much, I'd say," she said emphatically.

"I think he believes that God will rescue him at the last moment, or, should I say, I think he believes in that possibility, but his disillusionment with life works against it."

"Did you remind him of his family?" she asked.

"He's philosophical about it. He still blames his wife for his predicament. I think, somehow, he has convinced himself that his intercourse with his daughter was consented to by her."

"How awful!"

"A man who has been constantly frustrated in demonstrating his manhood in society at large will employ a means of demonstrating it to those over whom he has control."

"That's why he raped his daughter?" Sarah asked astonished.

"Yes, I think so," Bryant said thoughtfully. "That's why he beat his wife, that's why he was planning to hire his children out, and that's why he planned to punish his wife so cruelly. All he had to go on was the violent treatment he received as a boy growing up."

"But, Peter dear, does that really excuse him for what he did?"

"I'm not excusing him," Bryant smiled. "I'm trying to differentiate him from a man who, as a rapist, will victimize women generally. I think Ephraim Wheeler is not a danger to society. But I think he is a danger to his family." Bryant stood up and began to pace the room with head bowed. "Sarah, I've been thinking a great deal about this and relying on my meeting with the man to set me right. I think Ephraim Wheeler can be cured. I do not think he should hang."

Sarah looked at him sympathetically. "But what can we do?"

"Once a man has been condemned to die, many, many forces take part in carrying out the sentence," Bryant said. "They all become so intertwined--religion, politics, personal, and social antagonisms--that it takes a lot of reasoning and probably luck to overcome them."

"But you are going to try?"

Bryant came to his wife, took her hands, and stared down at her. "We have no choice, do we?"

She shook her head, but doubt of their success seemed to be expressed in her eyes, and, sensing this, she avoided her husband's look.

"I'm going to visit the Wheeler family now," he said.

Bryant went to the vestibule and put on his outer garment. He and Sarah felt as if they were setting out on a mission. They clasped hands and said nothing as he prepared to step into the freezing cold.

He followed a narrow trail over the hard-packed snow down the hillside in the black night. The wind knocked the icicled branches in the trees together to sound like hollow warnings of some unseen presence. He came to Odel's house on the bank of the river owing to his knack of seeing better than most people in the dark, which was why he never carried lamps on his nightly visits to patients.

Isaac Odel opened the door to his knock. The stern farmer looked almost angry that anyone should be calling on that cold night, or, perhaps because he expected only trouble from his neighbours.

"Mr. Odel, may I come in?"

Odel lifted his lamp to get a better look at Bryant's face, and then, nodding in recognition, he stepped back to allow the doctor inside.

"There's no one sick here, doctor," Odel said.

Bryant had not seen Odel since the Wheeler incident. He remarked how the man had aged in a few months.

"It's a social visit," Bryant smiled. "I came to have a word with Mrs. Wheeler."

Odel's stolid expression seemed to crack with surprise. "Oh!" he paused. "I see. Well, she has a room in back where you'll find her, if you come this way."

Bryant remarked on the home-made furnishing, so common to farmhouses in this remote region where the wood belonged to everyone, and the sawmill served the community.

He followed Odel down a corridor past the open door to the sitting room where Mrs. Odel and her children sat by the fire and to a door at the end where he knocked.

There was the sound of movement from the room, and Harriette's voice said, "Isaac? Is it you?"

"Someone to see you," Odel shouted.

Bryant was struck by the isolation of the Wheelers from the Odel family. It was as if he were visiting a sick person.

Harriette opened the door cautiously. She had bundled a blanket about her.

"I'm sorry to disturb you," Bryant said.

"Oh doctor!" Harriette looked embarrassed. "You're welcome to come in, but the room's not tidy, and it's not very warm."

"I'll keep my coat on," Bryant smiled.

He stepped into a small room lit by half a dozen candles in a glass lamp on the lone table against one wall. Along the opposite wall was the bed. There were two chairs on either side of the table, in one of which sat Betsy, bundled up in heavy blankets. A book lay open on the table as if Harriette had been reading aloud to Betsy. Since the only heat in the room came from the candles, it was cold.

Betsy stood up and looked at Bryant uncertainly, as if she thought she was expected to go away, but, having nowhere to go, she was trapped.

"I wanted to talk to you and your daughter," Bryant said as Harriette closed the door. He took Betsy's hand and felt its coldness. "You are Betsy, aren't you?"

Betsy nodded.

"I've just seen your father and I wanted to tell you how he was," Bryant said.

"Please sit down, Dr. Bryant," Harriette said. "Betsy, sit on the bed, dear."

Betsy seemed too shocked to move. Although Bryant had tried to sound off-hand, his reference to Ephraim had a paralyzing effect on the young girl.

"Betsy," Harriette went to her and moved her by the shoulders, "just sit on the bed and listen."

Bryant waited for Harriette to sit on one of the chairs before he sat down. "I visited him in Lenox. He is well. He spoke of you. He seems to have a champion in Mr. Dewey."

"The lawyer," Harriette said, as if for Betsy's benefit.

Betsy sat back on the bed against the wall and stared at Bryant, as if she expected bad news.

"Mr. Dewey is organizing people to protest the sentence, have it reduced to imprisonment." Bryant looked down at the book open on the table beside him and saw that it was the Bible.

A soft cry came from a crib beside the bed startling Bryant who had not noticed the baby. Harriette went to the crib and fussed with the bedclothes.

Bryant smiled at Betsy. "You have a brother, don't you?" he asked gently.

Betsy nodded.

"Ephie is with the Odel children," Harriette said, returning to her chair.

"I see," Bryant nodded. He thought that Betsy was retreating too much into herself. "Do you help your mother look after the baby?" he asked.

Betsy nodded and stared at the top of the bed as if she wished to avoid further conversation.

"If it weren't for her," Harriette said. "I don't know what would become of my poor baby. I'm away all day."

"Some time," Bryant said, "when you come to us, bring the baby and Betsy."

"That would be nice," Harriette said, "wouldn't it, dear?"

"Yes," Betsy said unsmiling.

Bryant smiled at Betsy. "Good." Betsy's sullen agreement represented a successful beginning, he thought. In the days to come, she would respond to his invitation in her mind, and, before long, she might accept. He decided now to address mother and daughter together and bring Betsy into the conversation as an adult whose opinion he respected.

"I really came here tonight to tell you that I want to help Ephraim Wheeler," he paused to see the expression on Harriette's face, but there was no joy or great relief, simply interest. "I know that what he did was very wrong, but I agree with you that he should not die for it. Unfortunately, I don't hold out much hope for Mr. Dewey's method. I think we should try to work through the Attorney-General."

Harriette sighed, her breath becoming white in the cold of the room. "It's no use. Mr. Sullivan is set on execution. I shouldn't have told him as much as I did, I suppose."

"Was your husband as bad as all that?" Bryant asked, somewhat surprised.

"Yes," Harriette admitted. "He would have killed me sooner or later."

"But if you don't want him to die, surely Mr. Sullivan will follow your wish."

Harriette shook her head. "He says the Court's verdict must be respected," she said glumly. "To ask for clemency now would weaken our case and give fuel to those people who say we are lying. We have to stay united by the court decision, he says."

Bryant thought for a moment. "Then there is nothing you can do. But Mr. Sullivan can do something privately. I don't see why not; just so long as it does not become public knowledge."

"I think Mr. Sullivan fears that if Ephraim was released, he would try to harm us," Harriette said.

"Would he?" Bryant asked.

"Yes, if he could," Harriette nodded. "I think he hates me, and he'd want to punish Betsy."

Bryant had a momentary doubt. Perhaps he should not continue his crusade for Wheeler. Perhaps the man was a vicious criminal. But no, Bryant had faith in the power of nature. The elements that made Wheeler violent were balanced by elements that could make him gentle, unless he were insane, which Bryant knew he was not.

"But you do not want to see him hang?" he asked.

"No, no, a hundred times no," Harriette replied emphatically. "Betsy and I don't want to see him die. He's just a confused man. But we don't want to see him free either. Do we, darling?"

Betsy shook her head. She seemed to have made herself remote from the discussion, yet, at the same time, to be taking in every nuance, as if she were watching intently from afar.

"You'd feel guilty of his death?" Bryant asked Harriette.

"I don't know," Harriette said with dismay at not knowing her own feelings, "but Betsy might."

Betsy's eyes seemed to plead with Bryant as if the thought of her father's execution lay on her like a burden that she hoped that Bryant could alleviate.

"I don't want him to die," Bryant said. "I shall do what I can." He stood up to go. "You should know that your father does not hate you," he said to Betsy. "I don't think he will harm any of you if he were free. And you should not feel guilty. His crime against you was a violation of society. It is natural that society should punish him."

Betsy stared at him with only the slightest glimmer of gratefulness in her eyes.

"Thank you for coming to see us," Harriette said, following him out of the room. "You are very kind, doctor."

"I share your concern for Betsy," Bryant said and patted her affectionately on the arm. "I'll speak with the Attorney-General." He opened the front door and plunged into the snowy night.

He felt very cold. The damp cold of the room had penetrated to his bones, and, now in the colder outdoors, it seized him as if he were in a vice. He walked briskly to stir up his blood circulation and to reach the warmth of his home sooner. The isolation of Harriette and Betsy depressed him.

They were truly victims--innocent victims--first, victimized by their family protector, then, by the very society which proclaimed its duty was to protect them from abuse. How shallow were the deeds of the authorities, as if by putting a man to death and turning their backs on his family they had resolved the matter! It was his duty to show them how profound the matter really was. He would begin with the Attorney General.

TWENTY

Since six in the morning, through the chilling darkness of a day in December and through the sunless morning and afternoon to the bleak cold of the evening, Gentle Adams and his fellow workers in the Republican cause rode ceaselessly about Pittsfield and environs rallying the farmers and tradesmen to come to the voting booths in Pittsfield and make Sheriff Larned a U.S. Congressman. The by-election was made possible by the death of the incumbent, a Federalist, who had remained popular owing to his personal charm, and despite the vituperative attacks upon him by the Pittsfield *Sun*. The newspaper, by contrast, praised Larned as if he were going to right all wrongs and inspire the electorate to drive the Federalists from office in the State elections due the following May. By-elections did not usually incite great interest, and, particularly in this case, the Federalist opposition was token, there being no local Federalist politician with the admired personality and standing of the deceased. Larned, therefore, was expected to win, but Adams pushed himself and his crew to the fullest to get out the vote because he wanted such a lop-sided victory as to send fear up the spines of Governor Strong, his councilors, and his backers, the Essex Junto, the River Gods, and whoever else represented the greedy rich governing Massachusetts like a fiefdom. Adams found that with few exceptions the people believed in Wheeler's innocence. Wheeler, it appeared, was another poor laboring man caught in the merciless coils of Massachusetts' justice and strangled by the prejudice of the powerful, who resented his independent spirit. To survive, a laboring man had to be humble and accept the crushing burden of his life without complaint. The common people sensed the treachery of his wife when they learned that she had set their daughter to testify against him under the guidance of the Attorney-General. Although James Sullivan was the leader of the Republican Party in the State, they regarded him with suspicion because he was one of the Boston aristocracy, and, as the chief prosecutor of crime, he became the scourge of the lower classes. Moreover, any woman who brought the power of the State against a member of her own family was in league with the devil. To many, Ephraim Wheeler's version of the event seemed more credible than did Harriette's charge of the father raping his daughter. It was natural that Ephraim, after listening to his children tearfully plead with him, should relent and want to make peace with his wife as he had done hundreds of times. A poor man had only a poor choice of gifts, and avensroot being a favorite with his wife, he would send it back to her as a peace-offering. Attorney-General Sullivan, the judges, the prejudiced jurors, and Governor Strong would not understand the gesture, it was generally thought, because they knew nothing of the laboring man's life and had even less sympathy for its bleakness. And they argued further that, if Ephraim wanted to rape Betsy and put her out to service, he would not have returned her to her mother but kept her with him. But the idea of a father having sexual intercourse with his daughter was hard to believe, and, if by some aberration of God's Nature, it actually did take place, then the family rather than the court was the proper forum for its remedy. For such a crime to be publicly aired was an embarrassment to the citizens of the State, and, to some people's thinking, it was just one more charge that the ruling classes could use to intimidate and control their subjects.

So many tens of thousands struggled in debt without hope of relief just as Wheeler had. Many others were veterans of Shays' Rebellion and saw Wheeler as betrayed and disappointed by that ill-conducted protest as they were. Now he had become a victim of the River Gods like other hapless rebels, who, surviving the battlefield, were hanged for treason. The trials of Shays' rebels were still in the public memory. The dubious roles played by Simeon Strong and Caleb Strong, who were appointed to defend the rebels in the Berkshires, had cast these lawyers forever in the camp of the enemy. Adams told the voters that their only means of revenge on these powerful men was through voting Republican. His success surprised him. Hundreds came from the surrounding countryside to vote for Larned. The results, giving Larned the victory by a huge majority, were delivered to Larned and Adams in the back room of the offices of the Pittsfield *Sun* where they had spent the evening discussing their campaign for the forthcoming elections in the Spring.

"Well now, you see what this really means, don't you?" Adams said to Larned after they had taken several victory drinks from the bottle of bourbon whisky that the newspaper's publisher had left for them. "It means they want Ephraim Wheeler delivered from the hangman!"

Larned shook his head in wry amusement. "It means they want good government."

"Don't lose the human causes in the abstract ones, Colonel," Adams warned. "If we save Wheeler, we would be saving all the laboring men; we'd be giving hope to thousands and assuring electoral victory to Republicans for years to come."

"Not much I can do," Larned looked apologetic. "I'm still Sheriff."

"If all goes well, you won't have to do a thing," Adams said musingly.

"What does that mean?" Larned picked up his ears.

"Nothing to concern you," Adams said quickly and to throw Larned off the scent of his plans for Wheeler's escape he alluded to the importance of the citizens on Dewey's committee.

Larned scoffed. "The Governor's not going to change his mind for Dewey's friends. He's demonstratin' to the powers-that-be that he's in firm control of the lower orders. There's goin' to be no French Revolution in Massachusetts."

Adams smiled. "Trouble is, he's giving us cause."

"We're winning by the ballot box, so we'll forget all talk of revolution," Larned warned. "Besides, too many people like to believe Caleb Strong is a good man who'll commute Wheeler's sentence."

"Like God the Father," Adams said bitterly. "But Strong is no Christian God of forgiveness. He's Old Testament. How do you make out Sullivan, our illustrious leader?"

"Fair in judgment, hard-working, superior mind," Larned counted off his qualities. "Won't tolerate abuse of women and children."

"A question of sexual abuse seems to unbalance his judgment," Adams suggested.

Larned tilted his head as if weighing the implication. "Can't rightly say."

"Maybe he's showing the Essex Junto that he's as dependable as Strong when it comes to crushing the laboring classes," Adams said. "I look forward to the day when Republicans don't need a respectable upper-class gent as their leader."

"You've got him wrong, Gentle," the Colonel poured himself more bourbon. "He's a man of conscience."

"He don't know mercy," Adams said with finality.

They fell into silence, each man thinking of the future and the effect of Wheeler's death sentence on the rest of the Commonwealth.

"Well," Larned slapped his thigh and stood up. "You did a great job today, Gentle. Now we've got to do it again in May. Glad I got my foot in the door."

"You'll win for a full term," Adams assured him. "Just remember the importance of Ephraim Wheeler to the Republican cause."

"Like to think that they're votin' for me, not Wheeler," Larned replied. "Might be better for us if Wheeler hanged and was out of the way."

Adams watched him go with misgiving. As soon as a man became a politician, he thought, he started considering the angles rather than the people. He himself had played politics for the ideas, the possibilities, but never for the angles--which was why he had never run for elective office. He was now more certain than ever that Wheeler's only chance of escaping the hangman was to run for it.

TWENTY-ONE

Sullivan, pacing his office, lost his temper. He had just read a letter from Dr. Peter Bryant, a man he had heard of vaguely as a prescriber of natural remedies for illnesses and a believer in the curative powers of nature. He appealed for Sullivan's help in commuting Wheeler's sentence. The doctor's tone of moral righteousness and attitude of reasonableness put the Attorney-General into a foul mood for his meeting with Governor Strong. He stomped angrily out of his office and glared menacingly at whomsoever he encountered on the streets until he reached the Government building.

Jamieson, the Governor's secretary, seeing his mood, called upon a source of quiet, respectful charm that he used on occasion with Governor Strong. It worked with Sullivan who liked the flattering attention of a clever young man. After a few moments of animated gossiping with the well-informed Jamieson, Sullivan was smiling and could remark with amusement the scowl of Judge Simeon Strong as he approached them. Sullivan learned that the Judge had been summoned as well. No doubt their discussion was to include Ephraim Wheeler. But such was Jamieson's good effect on Sullivan that he looked forward to expressing his views on the subject, especially as he knew they coincided with the Judge's. The Governor's doors opened and, on the threshold, stood Caleb Strong blinking myopically at them with a broad smile.

When they were seated on a sofa and chair in the Governor's office, Jamieson poured them cups of coffee which he placed on the coffee table between them and quietly departed.

Caleb Strong complained of the draughts in the Government building and told Sullivan with a roguish look that should Sullivan ever become Governor, Caleb would show him where all the winter draughts were to be avoided.

Sullivan replied that he would be just as grateful if Caleb imparted his skill in avoiding political draughts.

"Ah," Caleb Strong poked his finger whimsically at Sullivan, "you have brought us right to the point of our meeting. It is *your* skills that I am calling upon. You know, of course, that I am referring to the Ephraim Wheeler case."

"Yes, Governor," Sullivan said, "we suspected you might be suffering from that particular political cold wind."

"It was you two as prosecutor and judge who put me in it," Caleb said with a smile and added in a suddenly serious tone. "I would like you to get me out of it."

Judge Simeon Strong raised his bushy eyebrows in feigned surprise. "Not possible, Caleb. The poor man is going to hang. Some people don't like it. But that's too bad. Wheeler must serve as an example. We have passed sentence on all child molestation."

The Governor regarded his cousin disagreeably. "You have passed sentence on a man, a poor, illiterate laborer. It is the man who will hang, not child molestation, as you put it. No, no, Simeon, I need a better reply." He regarded Simeon's brooding black eyes and scornful facial expression as suitable for a hangman but unwelcome in a judge.

"Judge Strong is right," Sullivan said. "I am for clearing away hypocrisy and secrecy in our social institutions, as you know. Child molestation must be punished, not only as a crime but vigorously, to assure our womenfolk that the courts will support them when they reveal the truth. In this case, the girl might not have complained if her family was not to be broken up and her security undermined."

"An interesting point," Caleb mused. "She and her mother might have kept her violation a secret within the family if they were not threatened with immediate separation. Wheeler's mistake was to insist on splitting up his family. Otherwise he would be a free man today, and, perhaps, continuing to rape his daughter."

"But," Caleb raised his hand to prevent interruption, "his family must be suffering now. How must Betsy feel to know that her testimony has brought about her father's death?"

"By coincidence," Sullivan smiled, "I just received a letter which expresses those sentiments." He pulled Bryant's letter from his pocket and offered it to Strong. "You may want to read it."

Governor Strong nodded and put it on his desk.

"The court does not deal with eventualities; it deals with events, actualities," Simeon Strong argued, his deep voice harsh with irritation.

"It's not the official position of my Party," Sullivan said quickly. "And I shall see that it will not be."

"Good." The Judge allowed the slightest flicker of a smile to pass over his stern features. "You see, Caleb, we stand by our decision, and we demand that you carry it out quickly. Once Wheeler is dead, all protest will die away."

"I wish," the Governor mumbled. He sipped his coffee and fell into a reverie. He regarded the fire in the hearth. "Mr. Sullivan! Will you be with me when the deputation for the commutation of Wheeler's sentence calls at the State House?"

"Respectfully, I decline," Sullivan said.

"You see, Simeon," the Governor glared at his cousin, "you know nothing about politics. Our Federalist Party will be seen to hang Wheeler. We are the party of monarchy simply because we are unable to show mercy. Our friend, the Attorney-General, takes no responsibility for the hanging, yet insists that we do it because it's the law. And now you, who are determined that the sentence be upheld in the face of criticism, you conspire with him against me." Caleb Strong, agitated, sprang from his chair, and strode about the room.

Judge Strong blanched, and, reaching out in a placating gesture, he spoke soothingly. "My dear Caleb, Sullivan and I cannot change our position. You are the politician. You choose your course of action."

The Governor stopped pacing and looked sharply at both of them. "I have a proposal. Not a nice one. In order to nip in the bud this so-called movement for Wheeler, we shall accuse its leader of dishonesty in his practice of the law."

Sullivan frowned. 'Without basis in fact?"

"His partners can be persuaded to bring charges against him," the Governor said off-handedly. "We need only discredit him temporarily until the sentence on Wheeler has been carried out."

Judge Strong shook his head. "This concerns you two. Since you obviously do not intend it to reach the trial stage, I won't pass judgment."

"I shall regard it as a maneuver by the Federalist leader to discipline one of his own party," Sullivan smiled genially. "So long as it's within reason."

"I can count on you both then?" Caleb Strong glared at his cousin

"For the peace of the Commonwealth," the Judge said sarcastically and stood up. "Good-day, cousin."

"When you have decided on the charge," Sullivan said, pulling himself up stiffly and delicately smoothing his cravat, "I'll send over one of my legal department." He turned and walked after the Judge out of the room.

Strong followed them to the door. "Jamieson!" he cried sharply and strode back to sit at his desk.

Jamieson stood calmly in the doorway.

"See that I am not disturbed in the next half hour, if you please," Strong said, and watched Jamieson nod and close the door.

Strong picked up Bryant's letter in a distracted manner and began to read it. The writer's sincerity impressed him. Here was no political activist, no self-righteous critic.

> My concern for Wheeler's life stems from my
> concern for his family, in particular for Betsy
> who shows the strains of guilt for having been
> the cause of her father's impending execution.
> Already voices in the community accuse Betsy
> and her mother of lying in order to bring about
> Wheeler's death.

Governor Strong folded the letter and put it in a drawer of his desk. How he wished he could have the freedom to be this man, to be able to live by good conscience, even to allow a thought or two to be governed by conscience. But a Governor had no such luxury. It was not concern for Betsy Wheeler or consideration for the goodness of a few men like Dr. Bryant which motivated a Governor, Strong smiled wistfully to himself, it was all those others who quickly formed an opinion or its opposite and threatened the civic peace with their disharmony. Strong thought of Sullivan receiving the letter and the sour response he must have given it. No, there was little room for decency in politics, and, Strong thought, he was being weak by recognizing decency when he saw it. But wait, perhaps there was an idea in Bryant's letter which might give him a way out. Suppose Betsy and her mother could be found to have lied. Suppose they had plotted to have Wheeler put in prison. Suppose Wheeler's claim that his wife hated him could be proven.

Squinting, his face close to the table so that he could see the scribbles he made on his notepad, Governor Strong drew up a possible scenario and tested the plausibility of each assumption as he made it.

Should sympathy for Wheeler grow to the point where his execution became politically unwise, then would the gossip condemning his wife and daughter become useful for staying the execution. He was in a quandary? Was it not his reputation for compassion that accounted for his repeated election to the Governorship? He knew that he was expected to show sympathy for Wheeler. His party, however, was fighting in the Assembly for its survival over the issue of retaining capital punishment. Poor Wheeler! he sighed. If any man were doomed to suffer the consequences of his actions, surely it was he!

TWENTY-TWO

Ephraim sat brooding in a corner of the common room of the Lenox gaol. He watched his fellow inmates talking among themselves. They were thieves and debtors. Some shunned him, others pitied him. Ephraim gave them the impression that he expected to be released. He boasted that Dewey's committee for clemency had growing influence among the legislators, despite warnings from Adams that Dewey was opposed by most Federalists and scorned by Republicans because his committee would not confront the root of the problem--Federalism itself.

Ephraim, however, deeply hurt by his family's rejection of him, grasped at Dewey's plans as a drowning man grasps at straws. He was amazed that professional men from Massachusetts should sign a petition to Caleb Strong to save his life. They cared more for him than did his own family who seemed to have forgotten him entirely.

His lonely months of imprisonment drove him to examine his crime. His impulse to take Betsy into the woods, he thought, was unexpected. Harriette was the real object of his anger. Her disobedience forced him to turn on Betsy. Harriette, as his wife, was bound by law to obey him. His frustration at the hands of Martin and Justice Walker led him to take the children away and prove that he commanded the household. He began to tremble as he trembled that moment he forced Betsy into the woods and satisfied the urge which had nagged him from when he first noticed her womanly shape. The idea came into his mind like a thief entering a house.

Her submission restored his confidence. Their union broke his bond to Harriette and assured him of his command over the family. For a brief moment he expected to develop the respect that was owing to him, but Harriette's betrayal and malicious use of Betsy against him reaffirmed his belief that he could never be loved. He cursed himself for his mistakes. Was his life not miserable enough without this catastrophe?

The jailer approached him with a letter. Prisoners watched because it was the first time Ephraim had received mail. Hiding his surprise, Ephraim casually pocketed the letter and sauntered back to his cell as if he intended to read it in private. He fingered the envelope and looked at the scrawl on its front with impatience. He had seen enough writing to recognize a woman's hand. The thought of contact with a woman again sent him hurtling back to his love for Susanna.

The happiness of their days together, the pain of their separation, the desperate search he made for her, and the shock and disappointment of her rejection of him swept over him in flashing images, slices of memory, and spasms of regret. Thoughts of Betsy began to compete with his mental pictures of the past. Horrified, Ephraim rejected them as if they were unclean, as if they travestied his love for Susanna. He sought the purity of his memory, a time of open love and the joy of innocence. This moment from the past breaking within him like a shaft of glorious sunlight represented the reason for his life, he thought. Beside it, all else was meaningless. Only his moments with Susanna had given his life a value. Her rejection of him was owing to some mistake he had made, a mistake he was destined to make by the very make-up of his luckless being.

Ephraim plunged into self-pity, and, as the shadow of the gallows fell across his memories, tears came to his eyes for the first time in many years. At that moment Daniel Dewey entered his cell. Dewey was disconcerted by his own thoughts and did not notice Wheeler's sadness at first. Only after he sat on the cell stool did he see the wetness about Wheeler's eyes and his downcast expression.

"You look the way I feel," Dewey joked. "Cheer up, Ephraim. This time it's your turn to give us some hope."

"I hope you're not bringin' bad news," Ephraim said glumly and slowly rose to a sitting position on his bed. "I'm dependin' on you."

Dewey looked sadly at him. "I know, my friend, believe me. I want to help you with all my heart. But we've had a setback." He paused to give Ephraim time to prepare for his news. "Mr. Hulbert just paid me a visit. He doesn't like my group of Wheeler sympathizers, and he told me that the Governor doesn't like it."

"And so, Mr. Dewey, what does that mean?" Ephraim looked puzzled.

"It means that the demonstration before the State House on your behalf must be called off," Dewey said. "Mr. Hulbert and the people he represents could not have persuaded me to desist with intellectual argument, my poor Wheeler, but they have loosed an argument that is all too effective. It seems that my law firm in Boston is charging me with theft of funds. Defalcation, the legal term is. I shall be imprisoned until my innocence can be proven. I have been forewarned to allow me to avoid arrest."

Ephraim looked at him with astonishment. He had always assumed that men of Dewey's rank were immune from injustice.

Dewey looked away. "I am sorry. I had no idea that the Governor would play politics as dirty as this, but then I should have known better. He will live to regret it, of course, because it betrays his weakness which will become ever more apparent in future."

"That's bad news," Ephraim said. "What will you do, Mr. Dewey?"

"Leave Massachusetts and fight this charge through my friends in Boston," Dewey said angrily. "By George, it shows how insecure the Governor's men really are! It tells us, as well, how determined they are to have their way with you."

Ephraim nodded. "I expect the worst. Don't worry. I'm prepared." He thought of his escape. He had to follow the plan. Hopes for clemency were foolish.

"Don't give up hope, whatever you do," Dewey said firmly. He rose to go. "I'll work for your welfare from wherever I am."

"Mr. Dewey," Ephraim said, pulling the envelope from his pocket. "Could you read this to me before you go? If I'm not holdin' you up."

Dewey smiled and taking the envelope saw that the postmark was Glen Falls. He opened the letter with curiosity and noted with surprise that it was from Susanna Bayberry, which he told Ephraim immediately.

The surprise and pleasure on Ephraim's face alarmed Dewey. He read the letter through while Ephraim waited expectantly.

"She says," Dewey reported, "that she's upset by your imprisonment and offers to help you in any way."

"But how did she know?" Ephraim exclaimed.

"She heard talk," Dewey lied. He did not reveal that she wrote that his lawyer had informed her.

"She remembers me!" Ephraim cried with astonishment.

"Well," Dewey said, putting the letter back into its envelope, "she's in Glen Falls, New York, so she can't help much. Of course, we could ask her to write to the Governor."

"No," Ephraim said. "That can't help. It's enough that she thought of me."

Dewey handed the envelope back to him. "She sounds like a good woman. Now, I have to leave, Wheeler. Don't despair." He stepped from the cell.

"God speed, Mr. Dewey," Ephraim called after him and clasped the letter to his heart. He tried to think again of the Susanna he had known and struck away the interfering images of Betsy. Her letter had given him a good reason to make sure that his escape was a success.

TWENTY-THREE

The Christmas week passed quickly. There was a snow storm on the second to last day of December 1805. It ended finally late in the evening and left a crisply clean white blanket over the mountains and valleys of the Berkshires, as if to suggest that the New Year was beginning with a clean slate.

Daniel Dewey was ensconced in a hotel in Glen Falls, New York, and was reading Meacham's report on the delegation to the Governor on behalf of Wheeler in the Pittsfield *Sun* which had reached him by stage coach the day before. Meacham had stoked the fires of resentment in his article and just fell short of accusing Governor Strong of ruling by divine right.

The other actors in our drama stayed in their homes with their families and passed the week-end by reading, playing card games, feasting, and, in one or two cases, gazing out over the reaches of snow as if looking for a spectre of hope on the horizon.

Ephraim Wheeler paced his cell impatient for the hour to arrive. Ever since Michael Pepper had outlined his escape plan and given him the key, Ephraim had thought constantly of his escape, the difficulties he would be likely to encounter, and how he would overcome them. Being by nature impetuous, he had to repress every impulse to use the key and walk away. By the time New Year's Day arrived, he had disciplined himself more than at any time in his life. But now that the day was upon him, he was nervous. The great snowfall was unexpected. He would have difficulty making his way through it. Since few people went outside, he would be more noticeable than usual.

As the day darkened at the window high on his prison wall, Wheeler began to feel depressed. Should he be successful and reach his aunt's home in Cambridge, he would have to leave for the West where the life was hard and danger from Indians was expected, or for Canada where he would disappear into the wilderness as Pepper had suggested. He loved the gentle Berkshires and the easy independence of the people. They were his real home, his only real sense of security. In all his wanderings at sea he thought of the Berkshires, the clean smell of the woods in summer, and the solid look of the blue-tipped hills in the first days of frost. The place was a part of him. If he had to live away from it, he knew that he would have to return eventually. But if he did not face up to the verdict against him, he might never be able to return. He was not convinced that Pepper and Adams, and whoever else was involved in his escape, were right that he had no chance for clemency. But he was doing as they asked because they were educated and probably knew what was best for him. All the educated, the lawyers, the merchants, and the farmers who could read and write, seemed to form a mysterious world of signs and symbols. They saw everything differently; it was as if they had some rule of conduct that only they knew, and which guided them in everything they did. They were a powerful world, and they governed all the other worlds with an arrogance that was taken for granted. Ephraim was only happy in his world of the unlettered, when aboard ship, or in a tavern, or with his family on the farm where he could not be disturbed by the educated. He found happiness, too, in the world of natural things; there he would never even think of the educated world, except on the occasion when he would encounter hunting groups of the educated tyrannizing the countryside.

Ephraim had learned to mistrust the educated because they seemed to favor only themselves in a way that he found disgusting and greedy. He learned to fear them because of their self-centered manner of thinking. They claimed to be logical, but they were simply opinionated to the point of being blind to the consequences of their actions. It was as if education had cut in half the perception of life that man inherits at birth and condemned the educated to live in one-half while controlling the whole. The unlettered, like him, became victims of the educated because they lacked the single-minded drive and the knowledge of the symbols to express themselves.

Thus, when Gentle Adams and Michael Pepper, who belonged to the educated, advised him on how to escape the clutches of the educated, he believed them even when his own judgment counseled otherwise. He found both men unusual because they could belong to the educated and the unlettered at the same time. Adams was the only man to make Ephraim wish sometimes that he had been educated.

The gaoler, a short, mean-spirited man, opened his cell door and slapped a plate of food onto his table. Then with a sour look around the cell, he retreated and pulled a food wagon onto the next cell. The evening meal was served at 5.30 or shortly thereafter. The cell doors were left open for the prisoners to throw the remains into a bin in the common room outside and leave their trays for the gaoler to collect. Meanwhile, the gaoler ate his meal in his quarters and returned to lock the cells for the night at 6.30.

Ephraim ate his meal hurriedly, folded one blanket from his bed about his pillow to make it appear that a man was asleep, wrapped his other blanket over his arm, took his tray and emptied the remains into the bin. The gaoler, having finished serving the prisoners who were in their cells, had just retired to his own quarters. On New Year's day, there was but this one gaoler on duty. Without hesitating, Ephraim walked quickly to the barred gate of the common room, unlocked it with his key, and closed it softly behind him. He stepped down the long dark corridor to the front entrance of the prison and passed out into the street cast in darkness. The drifts of snow gave off a dull glow by which he found his way through the deserted streets, up the hill, and onto the road leading north. No one appeared from the houses he passed. He watched the dimly-lit windows for signs of life but could see no person move inside the houses. All of them were dining or resting from the celebrations of the night before. The cold wind knifed through the blanket, with which he enshrouded himself, and pushed him as if to hurry him towards the house of Molly Givens. One good thing, he thought, the wind would carry the snow over the tracings of his footsteps.

He struggled to get through the snow drifts, sometimes plunging up to his knees. He became aware that his confinement had weakened him. His legs felt as if they would give way and topple him onto the road, at which times he would lean against a tree and wait until his breathing became regular again. His slow progress began to worry him. Fear caused him to summon the energy to push forward at a pace more rapidly than he could have attained normally. Visions of a posse riding out of the darkness flashed through his mind whenever he was tempted to rest. Finally, he knew not how long, he came to a bend in the road with a lane at a tangent to it which he recognized from Pepper's sketch.

He hurried along the lane to the house, which was dark in front. He went to the back and made out the form of a horse standing beside a shed. It was saddled. He felt provisions in the saddle bag. As he inspected the saddle he became aware that his fingers were stiff with cold. If he continued, they would be frostbitten. He doubted he could hold the reins properly. Looking back at the house, he noticed there was a light in one of the windows--very low and flickering. He approached and looked in through the glass to see a woman reclining on pillows on the floor beside a fire in the hearth. She was reading by candlelight. He hesitated, aware that he should not involve her in his escape more than was necessary, but he could not escape with his hands in their present condition, he reasoned. He tapped at the window. The woman, Molly Givens, started at the sound, looked at him, and swiftly went to the back door. She was waiting with the door open when he reached it. Saying nothing, she beckoned him in and led him to the hearth.

"You poor man," she said, watching him shiver with the sudden warmth and hold his hands out to catch the heat from the fire. "I'll be right back."

She disappeared into the front of the house for a moment. Ephraim had time only to look around the room, see the figurines made from metal and glass, the oil paintings on the walls, and sense the touch of refinement in the room before Molly reappeared with a heavy winter cape and a pair of fur gloves.

"The cape hasn't been used for years," she said. "My late husband wore it in the Indian Wars. It'll keep you warm."

Ephraim nodded his thanks and motioned to take them and leave.

"No! Put them on the table," she said. "I'm not sending you away just yet. Sit!"

She went into the kitchen while Ephraim put the clothes on the table and sat obediently. A thought of a posse surrounding the house came to him then, but it faded immediately and seemed less important. Molly reappeared with a large mug of hot coffee and a plate of bread and cheese. Ephraim took the cup, cradled it in his hands, and felt its warmth course through his body.

"When Gentle planned this he didn't imagine a storm as bad as this one," she said. "Do you think you can reach New York State by morning?"

"It'll be easier with a horse," he smiled.

She watched him drink the coffee, take a bite of cheese, and follow it with more coffee.

"There's lots of folks on your side," she said. "You mean a lot to people who've been trying for years to be heard by the Government."

Ephraim paused from sipping his coffee and looked uncomprehendingly at her.

"The unrest is getting stronger," she continued. "General Shays was defeated on the field of battle but not in the people's hearts. They see you as a victim of the Government like they are."

Ephraim laughed sarcastically. "I'm a victim of my wife."

Molly frowned. "I understand how you can hate her for what she's done, but don't forget it's the Federalists who want to hang you."

"I can't forget that," Ephraim said seriously. "I wish there were some other way than escaping. I already changed my name once. I know what it's like living with the fear of being found out." He swallowed the rest of his coffee. "But that's my problem." He stood up, put on the cape, flexed his fingers and put on the fur gloves. "Say, that makes a difference all right. I think I can make it now."

Molly preceded him to the door. "The horse is a good one."

"Yes, m'am," Ephraim said as he stepped into the cold. "I thankyee much." He reached out and shook her hand.

Molly stood in the doorway until he mounted and wheeled the horse round towards the main road. In an instant he had disappeared into the blackness. Rubbing the chill from her arms, Molly returned to her reading by the hearth and thought that many people would rejoice in Wheeler's escape.

Wheeler made his way to Pittsfield with difficulty. His horse knew the route, picked its way uncannily in the dark around large drifts, but their speed was less than half what it would have been if the road had been clear. It was still dark in the early morning as he rode through the town. No one was about. He headed due west for the village of New Lebanon on the New York border--still many miles to go through the snow. But he figured the gaoler would not notice that he had escaped until six when he brought the breakfast. He had a good head start. He would soon be safe, he reasoned, that is, if no one recognized him on the route.

TWENTY-FOUR

Dewey had been at Glen Falls for almost a week. He was restless with the inactivity and the uncertainty. His only satisfaction was his reacquaintance with Susanna Bayberry, whom he had visited four times, the last being on New Year's Eve. As they grew closer in friendship, he became more uncomfortable with his assumed name, Bob Randall. On New Year's eve, when they spent the evening in Susanna's home, he sensed their attraction for one another--in their voices, in their glances, when their hands touched accidentally--but it was muted by his sense of dishonesty and possibly by her reluctance to become romantically attached to a cousin.

The situation between them became more intense each time he saw her. He had thought of running away from it, but she entered his mind at such moments, and, like a Syren, lured him to remain in Glen Falls where he could be close to her.

The lines of her body and the soft look of her skin were beginning to preoccupy him. After a restless night, he rose to an early breakfast on the second day after New Year's day, spent a couple of hours in trying to read and pacing his room, until the morning had advanced to the point when Susanna would be at work in the tobacconist and confectionery shop behind the main street. He left the hotel with a rising sense of relief at being on his way to see her.

The snow was piled high in the street, but the walkways had been cleared. The bustle of business on the main street, the women in colorful shawls, and the men shouting at horses and helpers in colorful language seemed to encourage Dewey's anticipation. He strode in high spirits into a side street that led to Susanna's shop. The dark clouds were rapidly drifting out of the sky to reveal a rich blue. He had made up his mind to buy tobacco, and if Susanna were not busy, to chat with her. Just a few minutes with her would hold him until he could see her in the evening.

The door bell tinkled as he pushed into the shop. A young girl stood behind the counter. Dewey asked for pipe tobacco and, not seeing Susanna, casually asked about her. He expected she was in the back of the shop, but the young girl informed him that she was not working. He frowned questioningly, and she added that Susanna was ill.

Dewey retreated from the shop as if he had been caught by an unexpected blow. He stood in the snow wondering if he should invade her privacy, but, being unable to restrain himself, he decided to call on her. At a brisk walk he reached her door in ten minutes and knocked. He saw the curtain in the front window move as if someone had been looking at him. He began to feel uneasy, foolish, as if he were causing an awkward situation. The door opened, and Susanna stood before him. She looked uneasy, slightly embarrassed.

"I heard you were ill," Dewey said awkwardly.

She shook her head. "I was thinking of getting in touch with you," she said grimly. "Something has happened. Come in."

Dewey detected her agitation as she closed the door hurriedly behind him and led him back to the kitchen. "He came to my door early this morning," she said as she stepped aside to allow Dewey to see the man sitting at the kitchen table.

"Well, for God's sake!" Ephraim Wheeler sang out cheerfully, "I never thought I'd meet you here!"

Dewey gasped with surprise. "Did you escape?"

"I'm escaping," Ephraim said, delighted with the shock he had caused. "My old girl friend is giving me a helping hand."

Dewey could not prevent the slight smile that curled his lips. "How did you find her?"

"Don't you remember? You read me her letter," he smiled, turning to Susanna. "He's my lawyer."

Susanna nodded. "He came here asking about you."

"To see if I was telling the truth? All lawyers are suspicious," Ephraim laughed. "Funny thing is, they say you can't trust a lawyer."

"Susanna," Dewey said, "may I speak to you alone?"

She nodded and said to Ephraim, "Help yourself to coffee." She led Dewey to the front room.

"I don't know how to say this," Dewey said. "I was trying to find a way to tell you. Now that Ephraim is here, you'll have to know. My name is not Bob Randall; I'm not your cousin. I'm Daniel Dewey."

She looked at him uncomprehendingly.

"I called myself Randall so I could get to see you."

She laughed. "Was it that difficult to see me?"

"Problem is," he said. "I have to keep the name Bob Randall. There's a State posse looking for me."

She gasped and looked at him in wonder.

"The powers in Boston object to what I was doing for Wheeler," he said and gave a short laugh. "They must be thinking that I helped him escape."

Susanna's look of amazement gave way to laughter. "Think of it! I have two wanted men in my house!"

"It's dangerous for you," Dewey said seriously. "You can be accused of harboring criminals."

She pushed the thought away with her hand. "I've been accused of worse things."

"I'm more or less safe out of Massachusetts, but Ephraim, being convicted of a capital crime, is safe nowhere. Massachusetts can easily get permission from the New York authorities to have him arrested and extradited back there."

"What are we going to do with him?" she asked. "Do I still call you Bob?" She smiled with her eyes.

Dewey thought she looked pleased that he was not her cousin. "I rather like the name," he said whimsically. "It sounds more sporting than Daniel."

They went back to the kitchen to find Wheeler washing his hands at the sink. "I feel good," he said. "I shaved off two day's growth of beard when I got here, and Susanna's given me the best breakfast I've had in almost a year."

"Do you think the authorities know which direction you went in?" Dewey asked.

"I don't think so, Mr. Dewey. I've kept out of sight pretty well. I'm supposed to go to Cambridge where my aunt lives."

"That's due east of here!" Dewey cried. "Why didn't you go directly there?"

Ephraim ducked his head in embarrassment. "I had it in my mind to see Susanna first."

Dewey pursed his lips. "I understand. She's worth the risk." He saw Susanna shake her head with amusement. "By the way, I go by the name of Randall here."

Wheeler looked quizzically at both of them. "Are they after you?"

"Not like they're after you," Susanna said. "You look very tired. You can sleep in the spare room upstairs and give your horse rest at the same time."

"That's really nice of you, Susanna," Wheeler said with a sincerity that Dewey noted as unusual for him "The biggest mistake of my life was not marrying you."

Susanna blushed and glanced apprehensively at Dewey. "That's all far in the past. It's your future which has to concern you, Ephraim. Go on up now, and we'll think of how we can help you on your way."

Wheeler sensed Susanna's partiality for Dewey with a twinge of disappointment. Suddenly feeling his great tiredness, he stifled a yawn, waved feebly, and walked slowly along the hallway and up the stairs.

"What do we do now?" Susanna asked.

"I'll take a look at his horse." Dewey went out the back door and approached the most tired-looking horse he had seen. It was not tethered. It looked too tired to move. He stepped into the shed and returned with a bucket of oats, which he placed in front of the animal's hanging head. While it sniffed at the food and began to eat it, Dewey unbuckled the saddle and carried it into the shed. Then carrying the bucket of oats in one hand and holding the reins in the other, he carefully guided the tottering horse into the shed and left it to feed.

Susanna had finished washing the breakfast dishes when he returned.

"Ephraim will have to take my horse. His won't go any further."

Susanna looked at him admiringly. "You are kind!" She came to him and held his hand. "And I'm glad we're not cousins."

Dewey impulsively threw his arms about her. She returned his pressure, and it was a long moment before they broke away to look at one another in happy amazement.

"I'll get my horse," Dewey said.

She nodded and pressed his hand in hers.

Dewey, a sworn bachelor, could not help feeling that he had just taken a big step into an entanglement. His first thoughts were on the dangers of romance: the emotional commitment, the imprisoning charms of marriage. But his attraction for Susanna pushed these thoughts away, and he dreamt of her thoughtfulness, her personal charm, the way her eyes smiled at him as if challenging and seducing him at the same time. He was almost reeling with the sudden expression of his innermost and subconscious feelings, which surfaced during their long embrace, when he approached the hotel stable and froze in his tracks. There, his back turned to him, stood Sheriff Larned talking earnestly to one of the stable hands. If the sheriff had turned round at that moment, he would have looked squarely at his prey, caught as if paralyzed in a trap. But Larned was too interested in the reply of the stable hand, a large, well-meaning man with a speech impediment, which obliged his listener to pay particular attention to understand what he was saying. Dewey, recovering his composure, wheeled, and walked determinedly toward the hotel. He glanced behind him only when he had reached the porch and was about to open the door. He had not been observed. Larned was still conversing with the stable hand.

Swallowing with relief, Dewey stepped into the front sitting room, picked up the newspaper from the rack, and sat where he could observe the stable through the window. Who was Larned after? he wondered. Wheeler or himself? He began to fear that it was himself, and that Larned was asking around the town if a man of Dewey's description had been seen. Dewey knew of Larned's remarkable record in tracking down criminals. Larned had learned to scout the enemy in the Revolutionary War and honed his skills in the service of the law for the past thirty years. Dewey's heart sank as he thought of being pursued by this man for the remainder of his life--and just when he had fallen in love. But he had to be sure. He stayed still when Larned began walking toward the hotel. The sheriff's sharp eyes seemed to search the building as if he were divining where its secrets lay. Dewey raised his newspaper to cover the bottom half of his face should Larned, by some exceptional feat, be able to see through the light curtain in the hotel window.

As Larned entered the door, Dewey moved in his chair in order to keep his paper as a screen should Larned look in from the hallway. There were three other gentlemen in the room, two of them talking, the other reading. Larned glanced in as he went to the front desk. Dewey heard him ring the bell and the tenor voice of the registration clerk coming from the back.

"I'm a sheriff from Massachusetts," Larned announced.

Dewey could not see, but imagined that Larned was holding out some identification. His tall lithe body, lean face, and long thin mustache were better identification of his profession than a badge, Dewey thought.

The clerk's tone became reverent. "We are ready with any help you may need, sir."

"Looking for a man." Larned's calm, laconic voice seemed to place the hotel under arrest. "Below medium height. Well-dressed gentleman, Boston accent."

"Well, I don't know," the clerk said nervously. "Can't think for the moment."

The other men in the room stopped talking and listened.

"Let's see the register," Larned commanded.

"Yes, sir," the clerk said promptly. "What name you looking for?"

"The man we want is Dewey," Larned said quietly; the words winged like arrows into Dewey's heart. "But he could be here under another name."

Dewey stood up, calmly put the newspaper on the rack, and went out the side door of the sitting room onto the porch. He climbed the outside staircase to the second floor and swiftly walked down the corridor to his room, in which he found the maid making his bed. He greeted her nonchalantly, and, going to the bureau, gathered up his shaver and toiletries, which he put into a small case. Then, taking his pajamas from the maid who was folding them, he explained that he wanted to take them to be washed.

"We can do that for you, sir," the maid, a bright-eyed girl, said eagerly.

"I have a friend who will do it," Dewey said sharply, giving the impression he would be saving money.

"As you wish, sir," the girl said and left the room.

Dewey folded his pajamas, which he had had to purchase when he arrived in Glen Falls along with his toilet case and a small overnight bag, into which he stuffed them together with his few other belongings. The corridor was clear. He locked his door and quickly descended the outside staircase. He imagined that Larned was still talking to the registration clerk, but he could not risk going to the stable for his horse lest Larned come out the front of the hotel and see him. He climbed over a snow bank to reach the street behind the hotel and hurried to Susanna's house. He sensed the fear in his body, as if it were a symptom of an illness. Having always been on the side of the law, he was not psychologically prepared to run from it.

When he knocked at Susanna's back door, he thought his knock sounded frantic. He gritted his teeth, breathed deeply, and forced himself to be calm. Susanna opened the door to him as if she were welcoming her romantic prince.

"I haven't brought my horse," Dewey said when he stepped inside. "The fact is I have to leave town myself."

"Why?" Susanna cried in surprise and disappointment.

"There's a sheriff here looking for me."

"Oh no!" Susanna looked frightened. "Does he know you're here?"

"He's on the track of Robert Randall, Esquire," Dewey smiled grimly. "Until he gets a look at Randall, there'll be doubt in his mind. He'll be hanging around my hotel."

"You can stay here," she cried.

"No, I'm not our real worry," he said. "Sheriff Larned can't arrest me outside Massachusetts; he can only harass me or get the New York authorities to arrest me for false representation. It's Wheeler we've got to worry about. Larned may run into him and drag him back to gaol."

"Do you think he's after Ephraim too?" Susanna asked, recovering from her initial shock.

"He probably hasn't got word of his escape, but the news will be in tomorrow's papers," Dewey said, sinking into a chair at the kitchen table. He looked appreciatively at her. "I'm sorry to add to your worries." He could barely admit it, but he wanted to get Wheeler out of her life.

She laughed and tossed her head, her long brown hair falling about her shoulders. "I'm not worried. The sheriff's not after me."

"You could be charged with complicity by sheltering escaped criminals--which is why I can't stay." Dewey motioned to get up, but Susanna pushed him back with her strong arms.

"Stay and think," she said. "We know more than our opponent. We have the advantage."

"We have a day's head start," he said. "I have to get my horse right now. Larned will be nosing about the town, asking questions, putting two and two together." He stood up and went to the door.

"Wait!" Susanna said and coming up to him kissed him on the lips. "Take care."

"I'll be all right," he said sadly. "If I'm not back in half an hour, you'd best throw my bag into the garbage." He pointed at his overnight case on the floor.

"What an awful thing to say!" she frowned.

He stepped into the cold, and, keeping a sharp lookout for Larned as he walked through the streets, he entered the hotel stable by the back door. The stable hands were busy with the stage coach, which had just arrived and required fresh horses. He located his horse in the stalls, took his saddle from a hook on the wall, quickly fastened it onto his horse's back, and discreetly led his horse out the back door. Now he could be arrested for horse thieving, he thought. There was no one about who saw him mount and ride his horse in a canter in a round-about way to Susanna's home.

He left his horse in the shed beside Wheeler's horse, which was beginning to look revived. Another twenty hours' rest and Wheeler's horse would be ready. Wheeler, himself, would need about another five hours, he figured. He saw Susanna at the window, made an okay sign, and mouthed, "I'll be back."

She nodded and pulled the curtain.

He decided to eat lunch in a tavern, which he had been frequenting, and listen to what the townspeople were saying about the sheriff from Massachusetts. He intended to track the sheriff rather than let the sheriff track him.

TWENTY-FIVE

The news of Wheeler's escape caused consternation in the Odel household in Cummington. Harriette expected Ephraim to break raging through the door. Her fear infected the other members of the household, in particular Betsy, who expected that her father would kill her. Isaac Odel tried to reason with the two, near-hysterical women, but even he was worried that he would be called upon to prevent bloodshed. The Odel members of the household wanted no part of what they knew would be an ugly scene. The quarrels they had witnessed between husband and wife over the years would seem like childish spats compared to the fury they imagined that Ephraim was capable of visiting upon them all now. They remonstrated with Odel to remove the Wheelers from the house until Odel in exasperation sent young Ephie over the snow to the Bryant's to ask if they would take in the Wheelers temporarily. The Bryants assented. Thus the Wheelers with their few belongings made their way over the hillside to the Bryant house. Sarah Bryant made them comfortable and, through her cheerfulness, restored a calm to their frightened souls.

The shock to Harriette, however, brought a severe reaction the following day. Throughout the ordeal of the trial and the hostility she encountered, Harriette maintained a determined, almost stoic, resolve to free her family from Ephraim's influence. As long as Ephraim was in prison, she felt justified in bearing witness against him, as if the court decision blessed her with moral rectitude. But now that he was on the loose, the supporting framework of the Attorney-General and the law no longer sustained her. Ephraim might appear at any time and subject her and the children to frightful punishment to which the law had been indifferent in the past.

Inconsolable, breaking into crying jags lasting for hours, Harriette clung to her bed. Dr. Bryant gave her sedatives and warned everyone to stay away from her as she had to weather her depression by herself. Harriette's disillusionment was at the root of her problem. For years she had told herself that Ephraim loved her despite his cruelty to her. Their struggle to feed their children kept her close to him. And whenever they separated, she knew they would come together again and that she would believe his promises to stop drinking and abusing her. This time her illusions were shattered. She had kept herself from admitting to the deep psychological effect of her disillusionment simply by concentrating on affirming his violation of their daughter. She clung to her disgust for his act and her love for Betsy as a raft by which she isolated herself from criticism and stayed above the swirling waters of guilt, self-doubt, and self-recrimination. His escape seemed to have upset her raft and left her to drown.

Paradoxically, as Harriette became irrational and dependent, Betsy grew emotionally stronger. Over the months since their first encounter, Betsy and Dr. Peter Bryant had established a rapport. It had been at first an uneasy, somewhat mistrustful, then acceptable and welcoming, and, finally, a completely trusting relationship. The doctor had used his love and great knowledge of nature to interest Betsy in the world about her once again. She began to truly understand the wild creatures and the roles they play in the evolving changes of the seasons. Gradually, she began to understand human relations from the viewpoint of nature. The Bryants restored her confidence. Sarah Bryant, on occasion, left her baby, William, in Betsy's care when she was caring for her mother's baby at the same time. Betsy began to look to Dr. Bryant as the source of wisdom.

After dinner when Betsy sat reading with Bryant in the sitting room and while Ephie was with Sarah in the kitchen, Betsy asked if they could discuss something she had been thinking about for some time.

Bryant put away his newspaper and leaned forward to listen. "About your father?" he asked.

She looked down and nodded.

"He may be well on his way to a new life in Canada," he said.

"He's not coming here?" she asked with surprise.

"No, no," Bryant smiled. "He doesn't want to be caught."

She looked relieved. "Do you think he'll get away free?"

"Everyone thinks he will," Bryant said. "But there's no need to be afraid of him, Betsy. You may never see him again."

She seemed to consider this prospect for a moment and then said: "I want him to be pardoned."

"I know how you feel, Betsy," Bryant said. He sensed that the guilt he had almost persuaded her to purge from her mind had flared up with the escape of Wheeler as if it were a disease. "But the Government will not change its mind."

"If I spoke to Governor Strong," she said determinedly, "he'd listen to me."

"What would you say to persuade him?"

"I'd say I was as much to blame as my father."

"Is that true?"

Betsy paused, blushed and nodded.

"Do you mean he did not rape you?"

She looked guiltily at Bryant. "I knowed what he was going to do when we went into the woods that day."

"How did you know?"

"Because he tried a couple of times before. Remember, I told that in court. So I knowed. And I didn't resist him at first."

"Why didn't you resist?" Bryant asked. "Were you afraid of him?"

She shook her head vigorously. "I didn't fear him. I was afraid of what we was going to do."

"Do you mean, my dear girl, that you think your father thought that you were consenting to have intercourse with him?"

Betsy nodded, staring at the floor.

"And there was no violence? He did not seize you by the throat? Did he threaten to strike your head with a rock?"

"Oh yes, yes, he did those things. But that was after. I mean, he forced me on the ground. I didn't want to, but I could have run away, maybe. It was after that he said he'd knock my brains out if I told."

Bryant's sympathy for Betsy at the moment was the strongest in all the weeks he had been talking with her. "Dear Betsy, you are a brave girl to tell me this, but you must not take blame for that which you are blameless."

"But I knew what he was goin' to do," she moaned.

Bryant held out his arms to her, and she flung herself into them.

"There, there, my dear girl," he said softly. "Sometimes things get blown out of proportion. Human beings tend to make evil out of many things. If they observed the ways of nature more, they would not be so quick to judge the motives of their fellow human beings."

"I shouldn't have told Ma," Betsy said, tears streaming down her cheeks.

"Indeed, you should have," Bryant said comfortingly. "You needed her help."

"But somehow the story came out wrong. I mean my Daddy got all the blame. I mean, he's in prison, or I mean, was in prison."

"That's right, was in prison," Bryant said firmly. "Let's not talk on this subject for the time being. Think of your father in Canada and forget what you might or might not have done. We've gone by all that. We'll talk again about it, all right?"

She nodded, smiling. "Thank you, Dr. Bryant."

They heard the others coming from the back of the house, and Betsy quickly pulled away, picked up her newspaper, and pretended to be reading it.

Bryant was troubled by the impications of Betsy's confession, if that was what it was. How one interpreted the facts meant everything. It appeared that the court had its own viewpoint before Wheeler's trial had begun, and Wheeler was tried under the influence of that interpretation. Who had been the first to blame Wheeler? Betsy, or Harriette? Could Betsy, out of guilt for what she had done, have blamed her father to win sympathy from her mother? And had Harriette, out of desperation to keep her family together, encouraged Betsy to put all the blame on Wheeler? Or had she been too overwrought to consider the consequences of her action? Or perhaps both mother and daughter had been manipulated by the Attorney-General, who, it was obvious, had his distinct views on original sin and guilt. Was incest too horrible for the Attorney-General to contemplate? Had he charged Wheeler with rape so that he might hang him for the darker sin of incest, which he could not admit took place? Incest was not a capital crime. Wheeler could well be a victim of Attorney-General Sullivan's inexplicable taboos.

The others were sitting with him now, and he left off his thinking to join them in the pleasantries of conversation.

TWENTY-SIX

Wheeler woke up in the late afternoon. Startled by his surroundings, he remembered quickly. Refreshed, he washed his hands and face, put on his shoes, and went downstairs to find Susanna sewing in the sitting room.

"Was the bed comfortable?" Susanna asked.

"Too comfortable," Ephraim stretched his arms. "I didn't plan to sleep so long." He sat in an armchair. "Your house is neat and pretty."

"Thank you, Ephraim."

"'Course, far as I know, I might be dreaming. Being with you like this is too good to be real."

Susanna laughed, pleased. "It's real. It's the circumstances which are unreal."

"Hope I don't wake up in jail," Ephraim sighed. He was on his best behaviour with Susanna; in fact, he had to force himself to overcome a sense of reticence, even shyness. "If I'd have married you, my life would've been different. For one thing, no one would be trying to hang me."

Susanna felt his despair and said sympathetically. "We can't tell what our life would have been like, Ephraim."

"I guess I needed a woman who would have taken me up in the world. My wife, Harriette, she dragged me down."

Susanna was taken aback. "You shouldn't hate her."

Ephraim smiled slightly. "I shouldn't but I do. She's the cause of my troubles."

"How is that?" Susanna sounded compassionate, but she was curious.

"She wants me dead, doesn't she?" he said flatly, as if that fact were reason enough. "She got our Betsy to tell lies about me in court. She always went against me in everythin' I did." The corners of his mouth fell as he looked at Susanna.

"Are you really innocent, Ephraim--really, truly, honestly innocent of that awful charge?" she asked, looking him straight in the eyes.

"Do you think I'm not?" he replied, alarmed. "Do you think I could rape my own daughter?"

"Well," she swallowed hard, "if you didn't, your wife must be a horrible person. How could any woman send her husband to the gallows and use the reputation of her own daughter to do it? Ephraim, she must be a monster!"

"That's what I've been trying to tell everyone, but no one believes me." He gave Susanna a pitiful look. "You believe me, don't you?"

She paused, surveying him with troubled eyes. "I want to believe you, Ephraim. But, could you not have done that awful thing in a moment of anger, when you were not yourself, and then forgotten? People forget things that they don't want to remember."

"Not me!" Ephraim shook his head. "No, my sweet Susanna, I love Betsy, and I would do nothing to harm her. My children are all that I have in this world. I need love, Susanna. I need a woman to love me."

She looked at him with great sympathy. "Poor Ephraim! You have been through a terrible ordeal--convicted of a crime you did not do and imprisoned for months."

"Susanna," he said Softly. "I love you still. I have always loved you. I have dreamt of you many times throughout the years. I know, I just know my life would've been better if we'd have married."

"That's all past now," she said firmly, withdrawing slightly.

"But there'll be a future for me if you can," he paused awkwardly, "return my love." He looked at the floor. "It's the worst time to ask you to marry me, but if I escape and set up a homestead somewhere, will you come to me?"

Susanna put her hand to her chest, uncertain how to respond.

"I'll treat you good, Susanna," Ephraim added reassuringly. "I need you." He took her hand in both of his and tried to draw her to him, but she recoiled.

"Too sudden," she said sharply. "Please, Ephraim, I've got to think." She withdrew her hand and thought she saw an expression of sudden anger in his eyes. "You have to get away, cheat the hangman--then we can think about it." She felt very uncomfortable and wished Dewey would return.

Ephraim, seeing that he was frightening her, smiled quickly and sat back in his chair. "Sorry, I been too tense. I just been thinkin' of you all the time in prison and guess I got too eager. All I wanted is just to see you again."

Susanna relaxed at seeing him smile. "That's a compliment, sir."

He frowned and gave her a desperate look. "I don't know what I'm goin' to do. I don't know if my life is worth it. Better I should hang, I guess."

"Don't, Ephraim," Susanna said sharply. "Don't get down on yourself. Go far away and make a different life." She smiled encouragingly. "And cheer up. Think how lucky you are to have friends who can help you make the change."

Ephraim tried to smile back at her. "I'm in debt to you, Susanna. I'll never forget your kindness to me."

There was a knock at the back door.

"That's Mr. Dewey," she said, starting eagerly to answer it.

Ephraim's face clouded as if the interruption were unwelcome. He sank back in his chair as he listened to their voices. Susanna sounded excited and happy. Ephraim felt a twinge of jealousy despite his remorse.

Dewey strode quickly into the room. "Wheeler, I have news. The afternoon stage just arrived bringing stories of your escape from Lenox prison. Everyone's talking about it."

Ephraim stood up. "I've got to go"'

"It's all right," Dewey said. "It's just getting dark now. Susanna's fixing you something to eat."

"Were there any lawmen on the stage?" Ephraim asked.

"No, just ordinary passengers who had heard people talking down the line. But you've got to watch out for Sheriff Larned."

"I know him," Ephraim said, impressed.

Susanna called, and they went to the kitchen. She had meat and bread on a plate and a mug of ale. Ephraim sat and began to eat.

Dewey, sitting opposite him, watched him eat for a few moments and then remarked: "Larned's smart, but I don't suppose he knows you have an aunt in New York State."

"I hope not!" Ephraim said between mouthfuls.

"There's no indication from what people are saying that they know which way you went," Dewey added.

"You should give yourself a disguise when you reach your aunt's house," Susanna suggested. "Grow a beard and mustache and speak with a southern accent."

Dewey laughed. "That's what I was thinking of doing!"

Susanna laughed with him.

Ephraim stood up, swallowed the rest of his ale, and seized his cape and gloves which were hanging behind him. "Much obliged again," he said, and he took Susanna's hand and kissed it.

She blushed. "Remember what we said about a new life."

Nodding, Ephraim stepped outside and looked up at a clear, star-lit sky. Dewey accompanied him to the shed.

"I'm giving you my horse. She's fresh. Take your saddle."

Dewey led his horse out of the shed into the night light. Wheeler brought out his saddle and put it on the animal. They shook hands, and Dewey stepped back to watch Wheeler mount and ride into the street.

Wheeler turned in his saddle. "Which way's north?"

Dewey pointed with his arm outstretched, and Wheeler turned to gallop in that direction. The night got darker as Dewey stood there listening to the sound of his horse's hoofs fade into the distance.

He went back to Susanna who was waiting in the kitchen. They embraced without saying a word, and they kissed and pressed one another. Dewey began to take off her blouse.

"Wait, Mr. Dewey," she said, and, picking up the lone candle from the kitchen table, led him through the dark house to her room upstairs.

"Where are your children?" he asked.

"They're spending the night at a friend's house," she said.

He smiled to himself. If this were a trap, he thought, it was one he was going to enjoy thoroughly.

They undressed quickly and fell into each other's arms in the bed. He quickly surveyed her beautiful form, blew out the candle, and made love as only a sexually famished bachelor can.

TWENTY-SEVEN

Attorney-General Sullivan, in response to the Governor's summons, hurried through the bleak, wet early morning to the Massachusetts State House. This was a Boston winter thaw, and very nasty, he thought, as he avoided stepping into the wet snow. Jamieson, looking even leaner than usual, welcomed him with his customary smile.

"Go right in," he said with a flourish of his hand. "The Governor is waiting."

Sullivan found Governor Strong holding a cup close to his face and pouring tea into it. The man's poor sight was symbolic of the trouble they were in, he thought. Strong lacked a broad vision.

"There you are, Sullivan!" Strong cried. "Your breakfast is ready for you. Did you bring the report?"

"Morning, Governor." Sullivan sat and fished a document from his bag. "I put the finishing touches to it last night."

Strong seized it and, leaning to catch the window light, began to peruse it. "Help yourself to tea or coffee."

Sullivan ate his breakfast silently as Strong carefully scanned each page of the report. He finished eating and was drinking his second cup of coffee when Strong put the report on the table.

"Looks as if we blundered by seeking Dewey's arrest," Strong said with a questioning look.

"It was Wheeler's escape which drew attention to it," Sullivan grimaced. "The Government appears to be repressing dissent."

"Well, well, well," Strong said, looking disturbed, "I suppose I lost my temper. I should have remembered that Dewey has followers in the liberal wing of the Federalist Party. But can't you, as leader of the Republican Party, persuade your own Republicans to stop the invective and let the whole issue die?"

"If I did that, I wouldn't be leader very long," Sullivan said sharply. "As it is, I'm suspect for my part in Wheeler's trial."

"We're in a weak position. The description of the unrest throughout the Commonwealth, which that report of yours paints so vividly," Strong picked up the report and dropped it on the table for emphasis, "makes me wonder if we can't find a way to reprieve Wheeler's sentence."

"We cannot!" Sullivan shook his head vigorously. "The Government will look foolish. We'll lose the people's confidence."

"We wouldn't want to witness that," Strong agreed. "But there is an action that would be more damaging to us than a commutation of Wheeler's sentence of death." He looked askance at Sullivan, and, seeing his puzzled expression, he leaned forward to whisper: "Picture Colonel Larned leading Dewey into Boston bound, gagged, and tied to his horse as a prisoner of the State."

"I don't want to picture that," Sullivan shuddered.

"Shall we call Larned off," Strong suggested.

"I would if I could," Sullivan said glumly. "But I don't know where he is."

"Good Lord!" Strong closed his eyes in exasperation. "It's like having the sword of Damocles over one's head."

"You can issue a statement to the effect that you have made an inquiry into the affair of the defalcation of funds, and it is clear that no blame should be attached to Daniel Dewey, Esquire, against whom all charges as a consequence are dropped. Disciplinary action will be taken against certain members of the Governor's staff."

"Up to the word 'disciplinary' I agree with you," Strong said. "But I cannot afford to embarrass, nay, insult my staff."

"All right, then, we avoid attaching guilt to anyone," Sullivan frowned. "Though people might wonder what the fuss was about in the first place."

"Our enemies will be so glad that Dewey has been let off, they won't question any further. Besides, the newspapers are not the kind of medium for imputing motive," Strong said. "The statement, of course, will need your signature as Attorney-General, with mine."

Sullivan caught the Governor's sly look and nodded with appreciation for the touch of a master politician.

"One other point before we discuss Wheeler," Strong tapped the table. "Who are the two men reported to have been working secretly with Dewey?"

"Members of my party--trouble-makers," Sullivan said, suddenly angry. "The journalist is named Meacham. He delights in making me out to be a Federalist."

Strong laughed.

"The other one is a mysterious figure. I haven't been able to identify him other than he seems to be known to a dissident element."

"You'll have to watch out for them. And please, Mr. Attorney-General, call Colonel Larned off the hunt."

"I'll find him soon," Sullivan said.

"By exonerating Dewey, I think we'll be relieving the pressure on us over Wheeler, at least for a while?" Strong said, as if asking for Sullivan's opinion.

"Nevertheless, we have to catch Wheeler," Sullivan said, consulting his papers. "I've alerted our men in all corners of our state, and I've given our neighbors a complete description."

"He seems to have vanished," Strong said, "which he could not have done without help. I'm worried about the sort of opposition it's stirring up. It's the same rabble which we thought we'd put an end to years ago."

"That is why we must find Wheeler and hang him," Sullivan said.

"I almost wish he would not appear again," Strong said wistfully. "Sentencing him to death was a mistake politically. I can see that now."

"But if we aren't severe with his class of person, we shall lose control over them. I know what I'm saying, Governor." Sullivan stood up and paced the room. "Don't ever commute his sentence, because, if you do, we are all lost."

"You sound too dramatic, Mr. Sullivan," Strong said impatiently. "Moreover, I shall make my own decisions. The manner of your advice is such that I wonder if it is offered out of good reason or bad emotion. Certainly there is sufficient of your self-interest in it to make me wonder if it is in my interest to follow it. Now, I shall have the legislative council approve the statement on Dewey when I meet with it this afternoon. Hence, I shall send it to you for signing. As for Wheeler, keep me posted on all the latest information, regardless how insignificant. Good-day, sir."

"Good-day, Governor." Sullivan bowed his head slightly with respect, grabbed his bag from off the chair on which he had set it, and walked swiftly from the room.

Sullivan growled at the genial Jamieson and began to work up a temper as he strode back to his office. He stepped into wet snow, and puddles of ice and mud, which exacerbated his anger. As thoughts of Governor Strong and the day when the Federalists would be defeated at the polls stormed about in his head, he stamped the wet off his shoes at his office door and took a letter from the hand of his clerk. Shaking off his coat, he opened the envelope as he went into his office and glanced at the message before sitting.

"Have located Dewey under name of R. Randall in this town. Can have him arrested for impersonation. Please advise. Larned, Hotel Glen Falls, New York.

Sullivan tossed the letter onto his desk. His hope was that Dewey could stay out of Larned's clutches long enough for the statement of the Government's lifting of charges against Dewey to reach Larned. Sullivan groaned and sank his large bulk into a chair. Everything was going wrong! Larned could have been used for tracking down Wheeler.

TWENTY-EIGHT

Ephraim thought that he had concealed his emotions well from Susanna. Those few hours in her house, in her presence, had been the happiest he had known for many years. She was the first person to whom he felt that he could talk about his trouble. She was capable of understanding him. Those moments together had brought him close to her again. But Dewey's arrival had ended the closeness. Dewey's presence made him remember his real situation--that she had rejected him years ago and had not changed her mind. He reflected bitterly on the fact that he was unlettered whereas Dewey belonged to the educated. His depression came over him again, his head began to ache, and he thought of doing away with himself.

He followed the road north running alongside the river, which he heard but could not see in the darkness. The forest echoed the sounds of night life, the hoot of the owl, the howl of the wolf, and the cries of smaller animals hunting and being hunted.

He rode for hours. The night was bitterly cold. Despite the warmth he had worked up in the act of riding, the air seemed to cut into him, until, feeling frozen throughout his body, he determined to take refuge at camp fire which blazed in a large clearing on the bank of the river. He walked his horse cautiously toward the encampment, which, he could see by the flickering light from the fire, comprised a score or more of human forms stretched out asleep on the ground and a male figure standing and tending the flames

These could be a robber band who might murder him to steal his horse, or a group of wanderers who preferred the nomadic life and discouraged intercourse with strangers. Ephraim dismounted, and, as he led his horse toward the fire, he saw the standing figure stoop to pick up what looked like a rifle and advance toward him. He stopped to allow the man, who had his rifle pointed at his chest, to walk close to him.

"I need shelter," Ephraim said.

The man motioned for him to walk ahead of him. Ephraim tethered his horse to a tree and stepped up to feel the heat from the flames. The guard seemed to relax and lowered his rifle. Ephraim felt the pleasurable warmth course through his body. He stared into the center of the flames as if to absorb whatever energy they threw his way. He sensed the encampment was not hostile. The guard was simply being cautious; he approached Ephraim, tapped him on the shoulder, and motioned to blankets laid out on the hard-packed snow.

"No," Ephraim said, "I'll sit." He sat on the ground and drew up his legs. The contrast of the cold on his back and the heat on his front made him distinctly uncomfortable, so he stood, and, walking over to where the guide was gathering firewood from a pile of branches, he helped carry it to the fire. He wanted to discover who was this band, but the guard discouraged conversation, perhaps out of concern that their voices might awaken the sleepers, perhaps out of a natural reticence. Sitting down by the blankets and staring once again at the fire, Ephraim drew a blanket about his shoulders to shield his back from the cold. Within minutes he began to doze, and, when he next opened his eyes, he saw the morning light and the campers, men and women, preparing breakfast by the fire.

A young woman approached him with a cup of hot coffee steaming in the cold air and a piece of bread which she gave to him with a smile. He drank and watched the campers gather into groups of three and four talking quietly and eating breakfast around the fire. He had finished eating his bread and was drinking the last of his coffee when an older man, wrapped up in a cape with a hood over his head, came to him and sat down beside him on the blanket which he had thrown over the snow.

"Do you think, Ephraim Wheeler," the man said hoarsely, "that God sent you to me in your trouble?"

Ephraim, startled, looked into the man's broad and kindly face. The glint of humor in the man's eyes caused a flash of recognition to strike Ephraim like a thunderbolt and recreate the scene of baptism by the river shore.

"Elder James!" he gasped.

"You remember me," the Elder nodded his head appreciatively.

Ephraim seized his hand and, bending, kissed the back of it.

"Ephraim, Ephraim," said the Elder, "you have wandered far from us these many years."

Ephraim hung his head in shame and avoided looking directly at Elder James.

"You forgot the message of our Saviour," Elder James chided him gently. "You put yourself above Him and above your fellow man. But He will forgive you if you are prepared to ask His forgiveness."

"Yes," Ephraim said dejectedly. "I want to be forgiven."

"Then stay with us, my son. Rest here, camp here with us for a day. We are moving southward tomorrow, and I know you wish to go to the north. But we shall talk throughout the day, and we can commune with our Lord."

Ephraim nodded. "I want to," he said gratefully. He felt as if a burden were falling off his back, a burden that he had not been conscious of carrying. "I don't feel afraid any longer. I think I am ready to return to our Lord. I wish I'd never left," he groaned. "I should have spent my life moving about the country with you like these people," he nodded at the campers.

James patted his hand. "No one spends a lifetime with me. But you might have come back to see me from time to time."

"I regret it," Ephraim said, and tears sprang to his eyes. "I regret my life and don't want to go on living. I was cursed from birth."

"Everyone has a place in God's plan," the Elder said sympathetically. "Don't blame yourself. Come back to Jesus and you will live again."

Ephraim impulsively embraced Elder James, and, overcome with emotion, turned his head away and stared at the ground.

"Try, Ephraim, try to speak to God," the Elder said encouragingly. "Come. Bow your head with me and think of God and try to speak with Him. I shall be with you to plead for your forgiveness."

Ephraim nodded, and, kneeling on the blanket as Elder James did, he bowed his head and tried to remember how he felt in the early days when he was introduced to the Saviour for the first time. But he was aware only of a torrent of emotions cyclining in his heart and mind. When he tried to will himself into a state of calm, he felt inert as if encased in a vacuum that defeated all attempt to make contact with divinity.

"Never mind, my son," Elder James said softly. "We shall try later, after you have been with us for awhile. God has not forsaken you."

Ephraim got to his feet slowly, his muscles aching from being unaccustomed to the strain upon them, and looked hopefully at Elder James. "I can remember listening to you read the Bible. Will you read it to me today?"

"We shall read it together at our prayer meeting in mid-morning, and you shall sit beside me," Elder James smiled as if he had been given a wonderful gift. "Meanwhile, I shall introduce you to my flock, and you can help us make provision for another night here in the open air."

"But why sleep out of doors in this cold weather?" Ephraim asked. "Can't you find rooms in the towns?"

Elder James laughed. "We are used to it, my son. The elements have become a part of us. Besides, unlike rooms in town, camping in the open air is free. As long as we have a good fire and heavy blankets, we are content even in the coldest weather. Last night was mild. Listen!" He paused and cocked his head. "Do you hear the river? If it were really very cold, the water would be frozen still." The wrinkles on the old man's face turned up in good humor.

Ephraim, recognizing the Elder's pride in his ability to brave the cold, smiled with him. He remembered how early the Baptists had accepted him into their group when he was a wild young man, and how they had made him feel one of them, and made him content within himself for a while. Now, as Elder James introduced him to this group, he felt their warmth and kindness once more. The hard and bitter years which had etched the sharpness and the pain into his face seemed to be instantly erased as he shook their hands and received the embrace of some of them. One of their own had returned to the fold, Elder James said, which was a time for them all to rejoice.

The men were forming themselves into a hunting party to look for rabbit, wood grouse, and, by good fortune, deer. Ephraim took the rifle held out to him and set out in line formation to penetrate the forest. As they walked over the hardened snow, with only the faint sound of their boots breaking the stillness, Ephraim reflected on the strange succession of events which had brought him to God's threshold so to speak. Only the complete success of his escape, wherein he left no trace, made it possible for him to dally with these folk. As it was, he was somewhat concerned that a posse might be on his trail. No escapee can be confident that he is safe from arrest. He thought also of his aunt awaiting his arrival in Cambridge, a woman he vaguely remembered from his childhood. At first he could not comprehend why the woman would offer to help him, but as he met with kindness after kindness along his route, he understood gradually that her concern was for a human being whose link by birth to her called upon her to step forward to save him from death. A shot rang out, jarring him into the present. A pheasant beat its wings in the bushes ahead of him as it rose. He fired and hit it. The men around him were firing as the thickets bloomed with birds, which floated away in low-flying retreat into the woods. Laughing, the men stooped to claim their prizes. Ephraim picked up the bird he had killed and prepared to continue into the forest, when the leader of the party, a young bearded fellow, called: "Enough. Let's go back."

Ephraim was surprised. Whenever he went hunting, he spent hours looking for kill after kill; it was part of the fun. But these people killed only for their immediate needs. He sensed a self-discipline in the group that in some inexplicable way gave him a feeling of responsibility. There was great strength here, great powers of moderation and balanced judgment. Ephraim cursed himself suddenly for abandoning this way of life as a young man to pursue adventure in the pathways of the world. One of the men was speaking pleasantly to him about the feast they would have that evening, and Ephraim responded, savouring his acceptance once more into the world of just and honest men.

Later that morning as the whole of the group huddled close together near the fire and listened to Elder James read the scriptures, Sheriff Larned riding by on the road a few hundred yards away stopped to watch them. At dawn he had inquired after Robert Randall at the hotel and discovered that he had not been there that night. Then he learned that Randall's horse had been taken, first noticed to be missing the evening before. A farmer coming into town from the northern road and stopping at the hotel stable volunteered that he had seen a stranger galloping north after dark. Larned quickly set off in pursuit because he was certain that Randall had been Dewey.

As he sat on his mount and surveyed the Baptists with their blankets about their shoulders, he felt disinclined to disturb their prayer meeting. He was sure that the fleeing Dewey would not stop with the Baptists. Dewey was the type of man who could not endure religious exercises. But, because his training had taught him to be thorough, Larned rode over the snow toward the Baptists to get a closer view of their faces. He halted about fifty yards from them, and certain that Dewey was not among them, he spurred his horse away and continued northward.

Ephraim did not see Larned until he looked up at him sitting astride his horse a short distance away. Larned seemed to look directly into his face, but apparently without recognizing him. Fear kept him motionless as he watched Larned ride away. His eyes followed him until he disappeared from view, but his body remained as if petrified. Gradually Elder James's voice restored him to the calm of the group, and the thought crossed his mind that the Good Lord was watching over him.

TWENTY-NINE

Susanna and Dewey awoke in one another's arms, took their pleasure and, braving the cold morning air after such a night of bliss, faced the reality of work, and, in the case of Dewey, surveillance. Susanna had no time to make breakfast. Dewey dressed rapidly with her and accompanied her to the small store where she had to spend the day.

"I can make you breakfast in the back," she suggested to Dewey. "We've plenty to eat."

"Thanks," Dewey shook his head and kissed her brow. "I'll go to my tavern and see what my pursuer has been up to."

In the tavern Dewey learned that Sheriff Larned had ridden north at dawn after some stranger. At first he feared that Larned had discovered Wheeler, but, after conversing with the men at the bar, he was relieved to find that Larned was after someone who had been staying at the hotel. Dewey took a seat at the window table, away from the crowd of men and the smell of chewing tobacco, where he could eat his ham and eggs in thoughtful solitude. His body was still tingling with pleasure. It seemed to have developed a bubble of energy about it as if it were at the center of a magnetic field. Every movement was effortless, every casual thought carried him back to Susanna's nakedness, every interruption of his dreaming by the actual world about him was brutal. In this mood, he happened to gaze out the window and see the morning stage arrive with newspapers from Pittsfield and elsewhere. He called the bar boy, gave him some coins, and told him to fetch the Pittsfield *Sun* and any Boston paper. In a moment the boy was back with two newspapers which Dewey plunged into like a man hungry for newsprint. The *Sun* was full of Ephraim Wheeler's escape and "miraculous" disappearance, but the unexpected was in a small box on the fourth page: Governor Strong and his Commission of Enquiry have dropped all charges against Daniel Dewey. The Boston paper reversed the importance of the news. Dewey's exculpation from blame in the Boston "misunderstanding" (it was no longer called a "theft") was on the first page, whereas Wheeler's escape was on the fourth.

Dewey was impressed. The political heat must have been mounting against the Government. It was the right moment for his return to Boston. He walked with enthusiasm directly back to Susanna's store as he tossed ideas about in his head. He tried not to show his happiness at being free again lest Susanna misinterpret it to mean that he was glad to be leaving Glen Falls, but he could not contain himself. His face beamed as he looked across the counter at her.

"What's happened?" she cried.

He showed her the front page of the Boston paper.

"Daniel, I'm happy for you," she laughed with relief after glancing through the article. "And to think it was all a 'misunderstanding'."

"I'll accept that," Dewey smiled. "The word, in fact, is in my favor, because it implies faulty thinking on the Government's part. I can extend this to its treatment of Ephraim--a misunderstanding of the true facts of the case."

"Does this mean you'll be going back now?" she asked.

He nodded and watched for tell-tale signs of disappointment on her face, but there were none. "We'll eat lunch together, we'll make plans. And then I'll take the horse that Wheeler left."

"What sort of plans?" Susanna asked cautiously.

"About how you'll be coming to Boston," he said. "About how we'll set up house there."

She smiled broadly. "Are you proposing to me, Mr. Dewey?"

"I propose we marry when we are in Boston," he said, grinning.

"That's sweet of you, Daniel. But I want to be sure before I leave all I have in this town." She looked around at the store. "This might not seem much to you, but I spent years building it up. The folks in town give me respect. Would I get the same respect in a snooty place like Boston? The people there would look down on me as a savage from the backwoods. And don't say they wouldn't. Remember, I lived east once upon a time."

Dewey narrowed his eyes with determination. "As Mrs. Dewey, they'd show you respect, plenty of respect."

"We'll talk about it at lunch, my darling," she smiled. "Right now I've got some customers."

Dewey felt the word of endearment like a tender caress.

"At the hotel at noon," he said, and, sending her a kiss with his eyes, he walked back to the main street to settle his accounts.

Ephraim Wheeler, unwitting catalyst to Dewey's romance, at that moment was undergoing a different experience. Throughout the day Wheeler talked with Elder James about his troubles and then with other members of the group. They read passages from the Bible together. They prayed. Ephraim began to understand that the incident with Betsy sprang from his need for love, of which he had been deprived because of the frustrations and mistrust of others, which he had brought upon himself. If he had been living in the way of Christ, he would have seen the harm he was doing to himself and to Betsy. He took a walk by the river before dark and thought his life through. He felt that this day had given him a new perspective; it had taught him that he could have lived a very different life, an exemplary life, if he had made just a little more effort to understand and adjust to others. His mistakes were glaringly, hurtfully obvious. He winced and groaned to himself as he pictured the times when, with a little wisdom, thoughtfulness, or even awareness, he could have brought success out of disaster. But, at the same time, he sensed that his real self could not have been different than it was. The state of goodness he found himself in at this moment could not have been sustained throughout his life. Too many emotions, too many curiosities, too many enjoyments of the flesh and the rest lay within him ready to be coaxed to the surface and direct his actions. The thought depressed him somewhat as one in euphoria is made to recognize reality in all its starkness. Death by hanging was his stark reality. He returned to the campfire, threw his blankets over some pine boughs, which kept him above the wet snow, which was beginning to melt by his proximity to the fire, and fell asleep without a word to anyone.

The next morning he was the first to rise. He helped himself to a cup of coffee, and stepped over to kneel beside the reclining Elder James, who was awake and watching him.

"The trouble is deep in you," the Elder said sympathetically. "I grieve and pray for you, my son."

"You have given me one of my happiest days," Ephraim said, tears springing to his eyes, and he clasped the old man's hand. "Whatever happens to me, I've learned from you. And I feel that Jesus goes with me now."

Elder James broke into a beaming smile. "That pleases me, Ephraim. That pleases me."

Ephraim bent down and kissed the Elder on the forehead. Then wiping away his tears with his arm, he went to retrieve his horse. The night guard had saddled it and was leading it toward him.

"God speed," the man whispered and reached out to shake his hand firmly.

Ephraim felt the honesty in that hand clasp, in the man's straight look, as if the night guard was sending him away morally reinforced, which would sustain him from now on.

For some time, Ephraim rode east as if in a dream. Scenes of prayer and communal feeling kept flashing through his mind so that it was mid-morning before he began to take note of the roadside, before the trees and the rocks took on their accustomed clear contours, and the wind and the snow began to impress their coolness upon him. He was taking the road going east and southward to Cambridge; his flight had taken him in a circle, but the effort and the risk had been worth it, he thought, to see Susanna once more. His stop-over with the Baptists had cost him valuable time, but, again, the experience meant a great deal to him. He spurred his horse to a canter and began to consider the dangers that might lie ahead. He rode through several villages without stopping, but, by the early afternoon, hunger was gnawing at his stomach, and a glass of ale began to dominate his thinking. He figured he could be in Cambridge by nightfall after which others would hide him and safely guide him north over the Canadian border. If he could keep on, he thought, he need fear the hangman's noose no longer.

But his horse began to tire. It needed to stop and feed to be assured of carrying him the remainder of the way. He turned aside at an Inn near a small town and left his horse in the care of a stable boy to be fed. He went as discretely as he could into the tavern and sat at a corner table. Regardless how quietly he behaved, as a stranger, he was noted by the handful of men standing at the bar. There was a sudden ceasing of talk, a few murmurs, the departure of a couple of men, and the shy smile of the girl approaching to wait on him.

He ordered food that was ready to be served: soup, meat and potatoes. Gentle Adams had left funds in his saddlebag that provided for his wants along the way, but this was the first time he bought anything. The others in the tavern had resumed their conversations, but he was aware they were watching him, as if they had been warned to look out for a stranger. He ate hurriedly because he feared that Sheriff Larned had traveled this route and had been asking questions and sowing suspicion. He drank his ale slowly, deliberately, and considered taking the next road northward rather than continue on to Cambridge. But actually he had no choice but to call at his Aunt's home. She would have his escape route marked out for him, the safe houses where he was to take shelter, the method he was to use for crossing the border, and where he was to stay in Upper Canada. He could not continue without that help. He would have to risk coming across Larned, who, he guessed, would have given up the pursuit of Dewey and be on his way back to Massachusetts. Perhaps he had passed through Cambridge by this time and was far to the south. Wheeler took comfort from this thought, and, paying his bill and avoiding the curious looks of the men at the bar, he collected his horse, which also had eaten hurriedly, and galloped toward Cambridge, which he hoped to reach within three hours.

Meanwhile Colonel Larned was riding the same road to Cambridge but at a slow, thoughtful pace. Ephraim's surmise that he had given up the pursuit of Dewey was correct. Larned had stayed the previous night at the very inn where Ephraim had eaten his mid-day meal. There he had seen the Pittsfield *Sun*, which told him that the Government was no longer after Dewey and that Wheeler had escaped. With his long experience at hunting fleeing prisoners, Larned knew that Wheeler would follow the most direct route north through Massachusetts, swing over through New York State, and pass through Cambridge toward Canada. It was for this reason he was heading for Cambridge, but he was in no hurry because he knew that Wheeler by this time would be far north of Cambridge. Larned wanted to discover if he had passed through the town, and if he had, then Larned would take the stagecoach day and night to the Canadian border where he would find the best opportunity for heading off Wheeler.

It was late in the afternoon. There were a few snow flakes tossed about in that state of nature when it is too cold to snow. Larned halted his horse by the side of the road, dismounted, and led it a few yards into the woods. He found a fallen log, and, pulling down his trousers, sat over it. There was a very slight chance that anyone would be passing along the road, but Larned was a modest man and took every precaution to answer nature's call in the most private way possible. He sat watching the road but invisible to anyone who happened to be passing. It was while he was in this state that he observed a horseman in a great hurry galloping from the direction he had come. With an amazement that rendered him motionless, he recognized the worried features and mane of dark hair of Ephraim Wheeler. The rider was by him in an instant. The Colonel, quite unable to move in pursuit and unwilling to shout and expose himself, struggled to regain his equilibrium. Seizing snow and dead leaves from the forest floor, he wiped himself, girded his trousers firmly about his waist, untethered his horse, and rode in rapid pursuit. They were only a couple of miles out of Cambridge. Wheeler looked like a black speck in the road ahead of him. The Colonel had no hope of catching him before he reached the town, and presently the black speck he was pursuing became enmeshed with other black specks. Farmers were driving their carts and wagons out of town at this hour in order to reach their farms before nightfall. By the time Larned came up to them, they cluttered the road. He had to slow his horse to a walk and wend his way through them. Wheeler was not in sight.

The sheriff could not conceive of a reason for Wheeler coming to Cambridge from the north-west rather than the south-east, unless he had lost his way, which seemed highly improbable. The main street bustled with activity. Larned halted at the railing outside the main hotel, dismounted, tethered his horse, all the while watching both sides of the street, and took a stroll by the shop fronts. Of one thing he was certain: Wheeler would not be riding further south; this certainty led to another: within a short time Wheeler would be riding north.

Meanwhile Ephraim had galloped into town and followed the rough map that Gentle Adams had left in his saddlebags. His aunt's house lay in the east end of the town, two-storied, and with a long front verandah. He arrived at it as if by instinct, left his horse at the side, and found the back door opening as he approached. A tall slim lady in her sixties stood regarding him curiously.

"Mr. Ephraim Wheeler?" she asked.

"Yes, m'am," he said respectfully.

"I'm your Aunt Ida. You're late! Come in." She stepped aside to allow him to get by and closed the door. "What made you so late?"

"I went to see an old girl friend," he admitted.

She reared back in surprise and then laughed. "I suppose old girl friends come before old aunts. Go into my dining room. You can help me eat the dinner I prepared for us. And you can wash up in there." She pointed to a bathroom at the side of the hallway.

"Thank you, Aunt Ida," Ephraim said as he followed her directions. He liked her immediately. And he could tell she liked him.

There was precious little time to get to know her. As they ate, they talked about the escape route, and she gave him the rough sketches indicating the safe houses on the route to Canada.

"Mr. Adams said you can't read," she said.

"Never learned," Ephraim said defensively.

"I'm not criticizing you, my dear boy," she said sympathetically. "I'm unhappy that I couldn't have done something for you children when your mother died. The fact is, I was in my teens, working as a servant. I had no money and no means. But I regret it. And I should have tried to contact you earlier, but I didn't know where you were, or even that you were alive, until I read about you in the newspapers."

"Don't blame yourself," Ephraim said. "I guess what happened was meant to be. I'm ready to forget the past and live only for the future. I want to make a new start and maybe I'll learn to read."

"That's the spirit!" the old lady cried. "I'm glad we met and really glad I can help you get away from that ridiculous hanging court in Massachusetts. I've always considered those people mentally ill on the subject of man and woman. There's something evil, dark, satanic in their thinking. Stems from their puritan forebears, I think."

Ephraim smiled broadly. She lightened his heart.

"But we'd better think of your safety," she said quickly. "You're more than a day behind the schedule we planned on. Now, it's up to you. You can stay the night here, or you can take the fresh horse I have for you out back and leave now."

"I'll leave now," he said and stood up.

"Good," she said. "The sooner you reach Canada, the better."

"I'll come back some day, Aunt Ida. I want to go West, make my fortune, then I'll come back East here and see you."

She laughed. "We'll be waiting for you, Ephraim."

He went out the back door, took his horse to the barn in back of her house, put his saddle onto the horse which his aunt had waiting for him, and led it to the back of the house where his aunt stood wrapped in a cloak. It was night. Candlelight glowed from the windows of neighboring houses.

"You may kiss me," she said.

He clasped her shoulders in his hands and kissed her cheek. "You don't know how much your help means to me," he said, choking back the tearful emotion in his throat.

She patted the side of his head. "Just get the hell away from this country," she said. "And come back see me some day."

He rode away with an immense sense of confidence in himself. His aunt had given him a new spirit that was extra to the spiritual blessing of the Baptists, something connected with his deepest emotions, something to do with his identity, with the blood relationship. It was the first time he had met one of his relations in many years, he mused. He felt almost rejuvenated. He wanted to live now more than he ever had.

He took the route he had come to town upon. There were still people in the streets, but no one paid him attention. The night was turning bitterly cold. He pulled his gloves from the inside pocket of his cape and put them on as he guided his horse toward the road heading directly north. The houses grew scarce and then disappeared altogether. There was a half-moon rising in the sky; its light caught the hard-packed snow of the road making visible the sides of the road right up to the trees which stood darkly on either side. There was silence, no wind. The road made a bend before him; it turned round a copse of trees which reminded him with a start of the copse at Partridgefield into which he had taken Betsy. He shook his head as if in a spasm to drive the scene out of his mind, and spurred his horse from a walk to a canter to leave the copse behind him. Just as he rounded the bend, a rider detached himself from the side of the woods, as if he were a shadow of the night, and without a word rode up alongside him.

Ephraim could not make out the face of the stranger until he was as close as five yards when he saw the mustache, the lean face, and the piercing eyes of Sheriff Larned. He was about to spur his horse in a paroxysm of fear, when Larned said, "Don't!" and he saw the rifle aimed at him.

Ephraim halted. An overwhelming feeling of loss took hold of him, rendering him incapable of action.

Larned took a short rope from his saddle horn and quickly tied Wheeler's wrists together behind his back. He seized the reins of Wheeler's horse, turned the horse round, and led it back toward Cambridge.

THIRTY

The Sheriff did not stop over in Cambridge but continued through the still night with his prisoner in tow until the road, swinging eastward, took them over the New York border to an inn in Williamstown, Massachusetts. They arrived just before dawn. The gloom and despair which circulated in Wheeler's head during that long silent ride may well be imagined. Sheriff Larned was not jubilant; in fact, he was rather depressed. He knew that many people would celebrate Wheeler's escape from the hangman, in particular his own political constituency in Pittsfield. Although considered to be a man of steel because of his war record and efficiency as sheriff, he could not overcome his dissatisfaction with himself for having apprehended Wheeler.

They were the first to eat breakfast in the inn. A boy was dispatched to fetch the local sheriff, who, when he arrived, acted like a bumptious bully and roughly shoved Wheeler ahead of him to the local gaol.

"Five hours rest," Larned called after them. He planned to take Wheeler down by stage to Lenox. He warned the clerk who took him to his room to wake him on time.

News of Wheeler's arrest was all over the town within minutes. A runner for the Pittsfield *Sun* who lived in the town rode at a gallop to Pittsfield with the news and a description of Wheeler as he was brought in.

Gentle Adams had just finished his breakfast when he heard the news. He raced over to the *Sun*'s office and seized one of the first copies to come off the press. The defeated-looking Wheeler, head-bowed, and shivering with cold, had been captured by the veteran Sheriff Larned! Adams could not take in what he was reading so shocking was it to his system. In a rage he threw the newspaper on the floor and stormed out of the office down the street to the Republican Party headquarters. He was beside himself with intermittent anger and pity for Wheeler. He complained bitterly to the few men who were there that Larned was a short-sighted, bureaucratic fool, who not only was condemning a good man to die but had condemned his political future and perhaps that of the Republican Party. What could they do? Could anything be salvaged or should they wash their hands of it all and leave the field to the Federalists?

The men around him, as disappointed as he, advised caution, to do nothing until they could get the story from Larned. Adams nodded in agreement, left the office, saddled his horse and rode for Molly Givens' home. He did not want to be in Pittsfield when Larned arrived as he feared he might do something violent to him.

By the time he had ridden the many miles in the bleak cold to Molly's home, his temper had cooled, and he was able to consider the disaster with his customary calm. Molly was surprised to see him and more surprised at the news.

"There's no danger to any of us," Gentle said. "Ephraim won't implicate anyone. I'm positive of that."

Molly laughed suddenly.

Adams smiled. "It's laughable when you think of it. Damn! it's so funny it hurts me."

"Don't get discouraged." She put her arms around his neck and kissed him. "We can plan another escape."

"He's got just over a month," Adams said dejectedly.

"That's time enough," Molly said, her eyes twinkling into his.

Adams let his hands go over her full round breasts and down to her waist. It would be so good to lie with her, he thought, and, as if by instinct, they moved together to her bedroom. In a moment he forgot his disappointment in the beauty and the pleasures of making love to Molly.

The news of Wheeler's capture spread across Massachusetts by the time Wheeler was reincarcerated in the Lenox gaol. The Legislature in Boston instructed the prison system to speed up the construction of a new prison which had been on the planning books for some time. Meanwhile a bill to repeal the death penalty, which had been making its way slowly through the legislature, received an impetus from the Republicans. Although there seemed to be a majority in favor, it looked doubtful to observers--that is, the editorial writers-- that it would become law before February 20, the date set for Wheeler's execution.

Justice Walker and the noted men who led the petitioners to the State House to demand clemency for Wheeler, all were disheartened by the news of his recapture. Only a few blamed Sheriff Larned, because it was generally recognized that he was doing his duty, for which he was widely respected. The most disappointed of all was Betsy Wheeler. She locked herself away from everyone, including her mother, for two days, and then, early in the morning, before anyone was up, she went to Dr. Bryant's bedroom door and knocked.

Sarah Bryant answered the door and looked alarmed at the sallow look and tortured expression of Betsy's face.

"I want to go to Boston," Betsy demanded.

"My poor girl!" Sarah said and reached out to caress her cheeks, but Betsy brushed her hands away.

"I want Dr. Bryant to take me to Boston," she demanded.

"I'll take you to Boston," Bryant's voice answered from the bed in which he was propping himself up by one elbow, "if you go to the kitchen and fix our breakfast."

Betsy, with an expression of relief that she quickly subdued, turned away and went down to the kitchen.

"Do you have time?" Sarah asked her husband with concern.

"I have time for nothing else," he said. "If there's an emergency while I'm gone, our local rival will be only too glad to step in."

Sarah grimaced and thought of the disparaging tongue of the town's other doctor. "Her wanting to go to the Governor may be just a reaction. It may be wrong to humor her."

"It would be wrong not to!" Peter Bryant said as he addressed the cold water in the wash basin and sponged himself. "I've been promising to see some Government official on the matter for months. I think now is the time."

Sarah let out a long sigh and went to her baby's crib to see how well he was sleeping. The boy was sickly, but Peter had told her not to worry. Nature provided a healthy remedy, he said, and she felt confident that he was right, just as she felt confident about all his decisions.

Betsy had the breakfast ready when they came to the table. Dr. Bryant had worked wonders with her, Sarah thought. From a frightened girl, who had retreated into herself like a snail into its shell, he had brought her out and given her confidence. A sense of guilt for what happened still stayed with her, but it was no longer crippling. Harriette Wheeler, recovering from her breakdown, had never admitted guilt, and became as a result rather sharp and peremptory in dealing with people. But Dr. Bryant had helped her to see her difficulties with Ephraim as connected with their struggle for survival rather than as solely personal. She confided to Sarah that she had begun to see the viewpoints of the people who condemned her: they suspected her of lying about the incident because they regarded the family unit as intrinsically divine and could not accept the idea of incest.

Harriette joined them for breakfast. She was worried about Betsy's journey to Boston. "Don't make a fool of yourself," she warned her. "They are busy men and don't have time to listen to nonsense."

"Yeah," said young Ephie, who sat at the table and smiled at Betsy. "You'll get us all in trouble."

Betsy ignored him. "I think it's right to do," she said to Bryant.

"Right or wrong," Bryant said, "we'll do it. Come along, Ephie, we'll hitch up the wagon."

Sarah and Harriette quickly prepared a basket lunch while Betsy cleared the table.

"When they return from Boston," Harriette said. "We'll move back to the Odels. You've been kind to have us for so long."

"We understand how difficult it's been for you, Harriette. We want you to know you're always welcome here."

Bryant shouted from outside the house, and they rushed to finish packing the lunch. Betsy carried it onto the wagon and sat beside the doctor. They waved and set off for Boston.

"I hope they'll be all right," Harriette said worriedly, watching the carriage disappear into the distance. "It'll take them at least two days."

"Dr. Bryant will make everything turn out all right," Sarah smiled reassuringly. "I expect his visit to the Governor will help your husband, Ephraim, more than we can imagine."

THIRTY-ONE

The morning after delivering Wheeler to the Lenox gaoler, Colonel Larned was writing a report of the capture to Attorney-General Sullivan, and was too engrossed in trying to explain why Wheeler had not gone directly through Cambridge to notice that a man stood quietly waiting directly before the table on which he was writing. He looked up to think and saw the grim face of Gentle Adams.

"Think you'll get a medal for what you've done?" Adams asked sarcastically. "Sullivan is going to be pleased with his dutiful sheriff."

Larned blanched and sat straighter. "You don't think I should have closed my eyes and pretended I didn't see him?"

Adams frowned. "Did you catch him by chance, then? Not by tracking him?"

"Right," Larned said sharply. "But don't misunderstand. If I'd been told to track him, I would have. I go by the law, and there's nothing wrong with that."

"Do you mean to tell me that there's nothing wrong with bringing Ephraim back to certain death just to oblige the capitalists in Boston?" Adams looked angrier as if he were about to leap on the sheriff. "Are you Republican or aren't you?"

"That's got nothing to do with it!" Larned said, his voice rising in defense. "The State decides whether he hangs or not. My job is to make sure he's locked up till the State decides. I'm just doing my job."

Adams shook his head with exasperation. "You have a blind spot, Colonel. Do you want to see Ephraim die?"

"No!" Larned cried. "I want to get him out of there the right way."

"And how is that?"

"Through Governor Strong. He's politician enough to know that an awful lot of people want Ephraim free. I'm working my opinion into this report to the Attorney-General."

"Sullivan's not going to be listening to you?" Adams said scornfully. "He's more pig-headed than you are."

"You may be right," Larned nodded.

"Whereas you just destroyed yourself politically in my opinion. You betrayed those Republicans who respected you for your criticism of the Federalists. Maybe you'll pick up some votes from the hanging lobby." Adams rubbed his chin. "You've put us in mess!"

"Look, Gentle." Larned stood up and paced away from his desk in thought. "Tell them the truth about me. I'm dedicated to obeying the law, but, at the same time, I'd give my right arm to see Wheeler free. I think the folks will understand."

Adams shook his head as if the situation were hopeless. "I've got no choice but to make them understand. If you don't win, Colonel, our Party's going to be set back a decade. And if Sullivan does win, and he looks like Mr. Republican, no one will be able to tell the difference between Republicans and Federalists."

"We don't want that, do we?" Larned smiled.

"Listen, Colonel, you get out, talk to the people, explain that you are conscientious about doing your public duty, but say that Wheeler ought to be free."

"All right, Gentle. Can you arrange for it?"

"Better than that!" Adams said, raising his arm as if catching an idea. "Meacham's coming back from Jersey. He'll be here tomorrow. Give him an interview. Tell him that Wheeler is a model prisoner. You hated to put him back in prison. He's no danger to anyone."

"I'll do that," Larned nodded. "I apologize to you and my supporters if I've upset you and put you to a lot of trouble."

Adams looked him in the eye. "I hope you'll have the opportunity to apologize to Ephraim Wheeler for the same thing." He moved to the door. "And tell that bastard Sullivan to pay attention to the wishes of his own party."

Larned played with his mustache for a minute after Adams had gone; he thought of Adams' persuasive underground influence in the State and his importance to Larned's candidacy for Congress; he could not help feeling a twinge of guilt because it was not solely out of duty that he brought back Wheeler: he was proving once again his capabilities as sheriff, and, of course, it put him in a good light as far as the Attorney-General and party leader was concerned. He sat down and returned to writing his report to Sullivan.

Meanwhile Gentle Adams walked down the main street of Lenox to the gaol. His anger had turned to exasperation. He felt that the fates were against him. Like a Greek hero he was doomed. Certainly Wheeler was doomed, and Adams had identified himself closely with him. Wheeler's capture had deflated the movement for clemency. Pessimism, a side-rider with Fate, governed all discussion of the Wheeler case. He noticed that the entrance to the gaol was stricter. He had two checkpoints to pass through rather than the one guard at the gate. The old gaoler was still on the job, although he looked chastened. He had enough composure left, however, to ask

211

Adams with a twinkle in his eye if he were visiting or staying for a term.

Ephraim appeared to be cheerful, but Adams perceived that he was concealing his despondency. They joked about the homing bird, flying out of the cage and finding nowhere better to live. Then, sitting at the small wooden table in the cell, and lowering their voices, they spoke of the escape, and Ephraim's round-about flight to Susanna in Glen Falls. Adams brought his hand to his forehead as if to say Wheeler had no brains, but he checked himself when he remembered the man's emotional state. He understood why the visit to his young love had been necessary for him.

"They've questioned you about how you got out, of course?" Adams asked.

"I didn't answer them," Ephraim said.

Adams nodded. "We'll try again soon as we can figure a way."

"I don't want to bring you trouble," Ephraim said.

"No trouble. We'll use the same escape route except next time I'm riding with you to make sure you go in a straight line."

Ephraim laughed.

"Your escape caught people's attention. We were making the most of it to show up the Government," Adams said. "Can't go at it too strong or we'll make 'em tired of the subject. We got our men out talkin' it up casual-like."

"I don't know why you're doing all this for me," Ephraim said, looking down to conceal his emotion. "I appreciate it."

"Everybody's got his motive, Ephraim. But the first one, far as I'm concerned, is our friendship, which goes back to the rebellion." Adams stood up. "They're watching us. Remember to look out for the next attempt. It'll take a couple of weeks to set up."

They shook hands. Wheeler watched Adams walk to the gate and turn and wave as he left. He didn't want to tell Adams that he was loath to try another escape. He was too despondent to even think of expending the effort. His only hope realistically was for a change of heart of the Governor and his Council. He thought of Betsy and the crime he stood condemned for, and he pressed his face against the stone of the prison wall.

Betsy and Dr. Bryant arrived in Boston and checked into a hotel. It was when they were walking to the State House for a meeting with Governor Strong the following morning that they encountered Daniel Dewey. They recognized each other at the same instant, and, standing at the side of the walk, they exchanged their news. Dewey was looking exultant. Wherever he went people clapped him on the shoulder, cried greetings to him, and made the thumbs-up sign. He had been working to get together the "responsible" men of the community, the merchants and the professional people. But he was surprised and very pleased by Betsy's mission.

"He's a slippery old eel, Miss Wheeler," Dewey said. "Pin him down to a definite promise before you leave."

"I'll try," she smiled nervously.

"You'll stay in my house of course," Dewey said to Bryant. "I'll send a man to your hotel for your luggage. Here's my address." He handed Bryant his card. "I won't hear no!" He smiled. "Good luck with that old eel, Miss Wheeler."

The encounter with Dewey cheered them. It was as if his breezy good-will had given them an emotional lift. He made everything seem possible. Bryant squeezed Betsy's hand as they climbed the steps of the State House. She was practically shaking with anticipation.

Secretary Jamieson met them with a broad, ingratiating smile, and asked them to be seated on the red sofa before his desk. He returned to his desk and scribbled some letters for several minutes until the doors to the Governor's office opened and emitted a delegation of merchants, who were laughing and chatting amiably as they left the august presence of the Governor.

Strong stood by the door and peered over at Jamieson. "Who's next?" he asked.

"Ah, Governor Strong," said Jamieson, beckoning to Betsy and Bryant to walk forward to the Governor, "the petitioners in the Wheeler case."

"Dr. Bryant!" Strong exclaimed, "how good of you to come all this way from Cummington. And to bring Miss Wheeler. I'm charmed to make your acquaintance, Miss Wheeler. Please come in and be seated."

They went into his office and sat in two chairs before the Governor's desk while Strong spoke privately with Jamieson. Then closing the doors behind him, Strong strode happily to his desk, sat down, brought some papers close to his face to read something, sat back and said pleasantly, "I've heard of your treatment with natural herbs, Doctor. You are the marvel of Massachusetts."

"Thank you for the compliment, Governor. I've simply been trying to keep Indian lore within the scope of our general knowledge."

"I wish there were more men like you in Massachusetts," the Governor said wistfully. "So many of us reject another culture because it's foreign. Very few of us seem to be able to adapt."

"Indian ways cannot be rejected," Bryant said. "They form the basis of this land, and we take them over whether we are aware of it or not."

"The old story of the conquered undermining the conquerors," the Governor smiled.

"Not undermining," Bryant said. "It's more like underpinning as a sub-structure."

"Ah well, I see I am speaking to a man of science and getting beyond my depth. Perhaps Miss Wheeler and I are on the same plane of communication." Strong turned to Betsy with a smile. "How do you like Boston, my dear girl?"

Betsy, who had been frightened speechless when they met the Governor, had been relaxed by his cheerful banter and was startled to hear her own voice. "It's pretty. I like the big buildings."

"They do impress one, don't they," the Governor laughed. "I've grown so used to them, I forget how pretty they are. But, forgive me, you've come to see me for a particular reason."

"It's about my Daddy," Betsy said.

"Ah yes," Strong said, looking slightly uncomfortable. "You want me to commute his sentence, I suppose?" He looked at Dr. Bryant.

"I don't believe in the death penalty," Bryant said firmly, "and in this case in particular the very conception of killing a man for what he did is abhorrent to me."

"Ah, my dear Doctor, we are not the law. We must live by the law and the judgment of our peers, that is to say, the finding of the jury in the Wheeler case."

"There is room for humane intervention in every human matter," Bryant said firmly. "This is a case which cries out for compassion."

"But it appears that the majority of the citizens of Massachusetts want to see the penalty carried out," Strong said sadly.

"But as their leader, is it not your duty to show them their mistake?" Bryant argued.

"It was a heinous crime," Strong bristled. "I cannot see that their judgment was a mistake."

"But it wasn't Daddy's fault!" Betsy cried.

Strong looked curiously at her.

"It was my fault," she added.

"How so?" Strong asked.

"I knew he was after me that way, but I didn't do anything about it," she said tearfully. "I should have told Ma, but I was too scared. If I'd have known it was so bad, I'd have told her the first time he tried. But I didn't know all this would happen."

"Hmmm," Strong looked sternly at her. "You're saying that if you had known he could hang for it, you would have stopped him, or you wouldn't have told anyone?"

Betsy wiped away her tears with a handkerchief. "I wouldn't have told," she said.

"Hmmm," Strong regarded her thoughtfully. "You would have stopped him if you could?"

"Yes," Betsy admitted, "but I didn't understand it then the way I do now. It's different now."

Strong turned a puzzled look on Bryant.

"She means," the doctor said, "that she did what her father asked her because she was taught to obey her father and mother. She sensed she shouldn't do it, and she felt guilty afterwards. That is why she told her mother. She was afraid that Ephraim Wheeler was going to take her away with him, and he was going to use her the same way."

"Then, your father was an evil man," Strong said to Betsy. "You told the truth in court, did you not?"

"Yes," Betsy said shyly.

"Then, it was up to society to judge your father. You have done nothing wrong," Strong said sympathetically. "Children, when they are abused by their parents, do not speak out sometimes because they think they share the guilt for the crime that their parents do. But, thank God, you did speak out, and your mother did the right thing."

Betsy burst into tears and sobbed into her hands.

"There, there, my child," Strong quickly stepped to her side and patted her shoulder. "You did your duty and stopped a terrible thing from happening again."

"I don't want my Daddy to die," she said sobbing.

"We'll see what we can do," Strong assured her. "Don't worry about him. His fate is in the hands of God. Whatever we do, my child, whatever happens to us is all planned ahead of time by the Almighty. We move at His bidding and we die at His calling. Leave your father's fate in the hands of God. Thank you for coming this long way to Boston to see me. I'll do whatever I can to save your father." He stepped to his desk, picked up a large bronze bell, and rang it, startling Betsy. "My secretary will talk with you." Jamieson opened the door and

216

stepped in. "Tell him, my dear girl, exactly what we should do for your father." He took her by the hand and led her to Jamieson who came forward to escort her from the room.

"Quite a scene," Strong said with relief when the door closed. "She is very unhappy."

"I think that if Ephraim Wheeler is hanged, she may never be the same again," Bryant said.

"Is it as bad as that?" Strong asked, regaining his desk and sitting. "I think time is a great healer, Doctor. Some day she'll see it all as a bad dream."

"I disagree," Bryant said firmly. "I have done all I could think of to disabuse her of the conviction that she is to blame for her father's raping her. But once such a thought enters a young, sensitive mind, it cannot be dislodged."

"Hmmm," Strong squirmed uncomfortably. "Your bringing her to see me showed me a new dimension to the problem. I wish she could talk to the legislative council, but I would be accused of using her to manipulate them, quite aside from the fact that she could not undergo the ordeal."

"If she has touched you, Governor, is it not enough?" Bryant said, a note of passion creeping into his voice. "Does not this child's love for her father speak to you over and above the heads of those who want him to die?"

"Please, Dr. Bryant, please," Strong raised his hands placatingly. "I have enough pressures as it is. I'm glad you brought her, glad we met. I see the problem in its human dimension, which we who try to govern this body politic do not meet with often." He smiled, stood up, and extended his hand.

Bryant stood and shook his hand warmly. "I am certain we could have found no better person to put our trust in. Thank you for seeing us and for your kindness."

"Not at all, and, by the way, Doctor, if you have a remedy for poor eyesight, send it along will you."

"Will do," Bryant smiled and departed the room. He thought that Governor Strong had been moved by Betsy's plight, but he wondered if the Governor would care enough to challenge the opinion of his political supporters. Since he had come to Boston, Bryant had heard that Wheeler's attempted escape had condemned him further in the eyes of the men in power, who wanted him to hang. The power structure wanted to make an example of Wheeler. How much of this family rape or incest was taking place and going unreported? people were asking. Was this just an aberration or a symptom of a wide-spread affliction? The suspicious minds of the clergy tended to the latter mode of thought. Bryant had gleaned as much from the innuendoes in the sermons he had heard in Cummington, and his conversations with Bostonians had confirmed his opinion. On the other hand, the people generally wanted to disbelieve the accusation. Nothing like it could ever happen in Massachusetts, they said. The mother and daughter had made it up to destroy the father. It was as if the disgrace was too great for the people to accept.

Jamieson was finishing copying down what Betsy was telling him and stood up as Bryant approached. "The Governor will study this, young lady," he said to Betsy, and bowing slightly, wished them a safe journey back to Cummington.

Scarcely had Betsy and Bryant left when he took the piece of paper upon which he had written Betsy's wishes and rushed into Strong's office. "Governor, why in Heaven's name humiliate me with the task of taking down the silly words of that little girl?"

"My dear Jamieson," Strong said placatingly. "I had to humor her. You did me a great service."

"Well, I hope you aren't going to take this seriously." Jamieson placed the paper on Strong's desk. "We're too far down the road to think of turning back."

Strong nodded. "However, I'd hate to damage the victim of the crime more than she has been. She has suffered, Jamieson, and Dr. Bryant warns us that Wheeler's death could cause her irreparable hurt."

"You are Governor of this State," Jamieson reminded him. "You cannot act on the behest of a thirteen-year old girl. You must think of all of the people."

"Yes, yes, Jamieson, I get your point. Leave me now, I have other business to attend to, if you don't mind."

Jamieson bowed slightly and left the office, offended by encountering the Governor's resistance. He sat at his desk and scratched a note to Attorney-General Sullivan warning him of the danger which could arise as a result of Betsy Wheeler's interview with the Governor.

THIRTY-TWO

That evening Dewey entertained Betsy and Peter Bryant at dinner. Betsy had never been in a house with servants. She stayed quiet and observed every movement of the maids who served them dinner and Dewey's tactful manner of directing them. Her trip to Boston had been like a voyage in fairyland, she thought. Everything she saw was unexpected, novel, and exciting.

Dewey and Bryant were analyzing the mood of the country. Shays' Rebellion was still in the minds of most people, Dewey said; its memory was unsettling to the average citizen whose inclination was to suppress any challenge to authority.

"Possibly," Bryant said, "but could his bad luck not be because he is poor? If it weren't for you and your political concerns, Daniel, his case would attract no attention. Our powerful men could have written him off without compunction."

"I like to think," Dewey replied, "that that wouldn't happen in our liberated society, but I'm afraid you're right. And how is our Miss Wheeler? Have you had enough to eat? Would you like more dessert?"

"I'm fine, Mr. Dewey," Betsy smiled and looked at Bryant. "Daddy said people didn't like him because he was independent."

"How is that?" Bryant asked. "He worked for other people."

"For a while, maybe," Betsy explained. "But he never stuck to one plan for long. And he liked to go to sea. He used to tell Ephie and me about his adventures on ships, in foreign countries and places like that."

"Would you say he was a good father to you?" Dewey asked.

Betsy nodded. "Last year things went wrong, though. After the baby came, things weren't like they used to be. Daddy said he had a lot of trouble, and he used to fight a lot with Mama. We lived separate from him. Mama said we were going from bad to worse."

"They couldn't be worse," Dewey confirmed.

"Oh! I wish the Governor would save Daddy!" she said suddenly.

"Keep your fingers crossed," Bryant said encouragingly.

The knocker on the front door sent a heavy thudding through the front of the house.

"Sounds like an impatient visitor," Dewey remarked and swallowed the last of his coffee as the others quickly finished eating.

"Attorney-General Sullivan to see you, sir," announced Dewey's butler from the threshold of the room.

"Show him to the sitting-room," Dewey said. "We'll be there presently."

"Just the man I've been wanting to meet," Bryant chuckled. "What brings him here at this hour?"

"You and Miss Wheeler, I assume," Dewey said, "unless he has another warrant for my arrest."

They laughed, and Betsy smiled broadly for the first time.

"He'll be fishing for hints as to what Governor Strong told us," Bryant warned Betsy. "We have to be careful what we say. You need not stay, my dear. You've had a very tiring day."

"I don't want to see him," Betsy said suddenly as if remembering an unhappy incident.

"Just pay your respects," Dewey said cheerfully. "Well, are we ready?"

Dewey, walking beside Betsy, led them into the sitting-room, lit by a large fireplace and several candelabras. John Sullivan at six foot five and heavy-set stood in the center of the room like a Titan bringing a message from the gods.

"Good to see you again," Dewey said, advancing and putting his hand into Sullivan's great paw. "You know Miss Wheeler, and this is Dr. Bryant from Cummington."

Sullivan shook their hands. "How is your mother?" he asked Betsy. "She didn't come with you?"

"She had to mind the baby," Betsy said.

"Give her my regards," Sullivan said. "If there is anything I can do for you, you should let me know."

"You could stop them from hanging my Daddy," Betsy said angrily.

Sullivan blushed. "Well, Miss Wheeler, the court listened to your story and decided on the appropriate penalty. There is nothing we can do, I'm afraid."

"But it wasn't right, and you know it," she said accusingly.

"You told the truth, did you not?" Sullivan smiled. "If you have changed your story you should inform me."

Betsy burst into tears, and Bryant put his arm about her shoulders and comforted her.

"She's very tired," Dewey explained. "Have a good long sleep," he said to Betsy.

Betsy curtsied to Sullivan, and, smiling her thanks through her tears to Bryant, left them without another word.

"I'm sorry if I brought that on," Sullivan cleared his throat.

Dewey waved his hand slightly as if to pass it off. "Please sit down, Mr. Attorney-General. Would you like some coffee?" He turned to the butler who stood waiting by the door. "Coffees for us all--demi-tasse, please."

Sullivan settled into a large chair and gave Dr. Bryant a winning smile. "Your correspondence with me has been helpful. I've seen the Wheeler situation from another viewpoint, thanks to you. Unfortunately, the whole matter is out of my hands."

Bryant perched forward on his chair. "Just a simple statement from you would work wonders."

"Ah!" Sullivan raised his hand with a smile. "I've had my say in court; I can't go back on it now. Too late. Moreover, Wheeler's penalty still strikes me as just. He is a dishonored and mistrusted man. It would be better for him to be dead sooner than later. I think the Governor holds the same opinion."

The sense of a *fait accompli* fell over the room. Sullivan had come to discourage them from acting, Dewey thought, and he was experienced in his task. He recognized the lawyer's courtroom tactics of persuasion.

"I believe the Governor has changed his mind," Dewey argued "We expected you to do so as well, especially after that group assembled at the State House."

"Morality cannot be changed by petitioners," Sullivan said sternly. "I won't say more as I've not come here to quarrel. I wanted to meet Dr. Bryant and tell him the legal difficulties of mitigating the decision in the Wheeler case."

Dewey smiled wanly and concealed his pique at Sullivan's peremptory tone. "Regarding the legal viewpoint," Dewey said pleasantly, "had I known at the time of the trial what I know now, we would have conducted a much stronger defense."

"That's all water over the bridge now, Daniel," Sullivan said.

"We would have questioned Miss Wheeler closely," Dewey continued, "and ascertained that she did not report the first two advances by her father to her mother. Thus, at the time of the third advance, the one at issue, we could have shown complicity in the act. Only after the act was there a sense of guilt followed by Miss Wheeler's confession."

"I am sorry, Daniel," Sullivan frowned with irritation. "I don't propose to retry the case in your living-room or anywhere else for that matter." He smiled at Bryant. "Now, Doctor, the apparatus of the State has been set in motion in the Wheeler case The issue has passed through all the legal stages fairly, and there has been unanimous agreement that Wheeler must be executed according to the law on our statute books. As the prosecutor, it is my duty to see that the court's judgment is fulfilled. Do you understand my position?"

"I understand, sir, that you oppose my plea for clemency," Bryant said calmly, "because you feel that it is undermining the legal system of the State by calling attention to its inadequacy in this case."

"Well said, Doctor," Sullivan colored slightly.

"However, I am not the Attorney-General and am not as concerned as you are over the legal system," Bryant continued. "I am a medical doctor and concerned about human lives. I think Wheeler should be allowed to live. I am opposed to the excuse given for hanging him, law or no law. If our laws are to reflect the great moral law set by the Almighty, it is my belief that Ephraim Wheeler be brought back in line with our moral principles rather than be killed by a vengeful and thoughtless State machinery." Bryant's voice rose with the anger beginning to build under his words.

"And in addition," Dewey said, catching Bryant's anger in his own voice, "Wheeler is a victim of our politics. Our ruling class, my dear Sullivan, is still shooting prisoners after defeating the Rebellion."

"Preposterous!" Sullivan shouted, suddenly angry in his turn, "What poppycock! The man raped his daughter. This evil must be punished!"

"Evil!" Dewey exclaimed. "That's an abstract term conveniently applied to the enemy. And the enemy in your case is the underclass."

Sullivan stared at Dewey as if he were mad. "It's the company you've been keeping which has addled your brains."

"You know," Dewey said, "as long as you remain at the head of the Republican cause in this State, my Federalist Party has a chance to stay in power for some years yet."

"I see that I've been pretty well insulted," Sullivan said, standing up and reaching for his cape and gloves. "But before I leave, I want to tell you, Daniel, that I've arranged for the arrest of one of your companions." He paused and looked sharply at Dewey.

"Another mistake, no doubt," Dewey said indifferently.

"He goes by the name of Gentle Adams, and he uses other names. He's a seditious character."

"That's his great evil again," Dewey said to Bryant who stood next to him. "All his palaver about freedom of thought and the great Republican Party comes down to the imprisonment of those whose opinions differ from his."

Sullivan smiled with difficulty and reached out to shake Peter Bryant's hand. "I'm sorry we couldn't have met under more pleasant circumstances, but perhaps I'll stop by one day when I'm in Cummington."

"I should like that," Bryant said warmly. "I do hope you will reconsider your opinion on Ephraim Wheeler. Beneath his rough exterior and his obvious faults, he is a good man."

Sullivan swallowed hard. He respected Bryant's reputation and recognized the integrity of the man. He disliked having to oppose him. It made him uncomfortable. "It's Governor Strong's decision. I'm sure your presence in Boston has had an influence."

"I think it has," Bryant nodded significantly. "But I considered my intended meeting with you to be of the most importance. As counsel for Mrs. Wheeler, you, like myself, have the welfare of the Wheeler family foremost in mind.

That is why I am so pleased that you came by this evening. I have a great deal to talk over with you." Bryant looked at Dewey.

"Please stay, James," Dewey said quickly. "I'll leave you two gentlemen, as I believe I am the discordant element. Moreover, the coffee is here if you care to help yourself."

A butler entered the room and set down a tray of coffee cups and coffee jug on the table before them.

Sullivan, suddenly restored to good humor, smiled at the departing Dewey. "The thought of your absence has already brought harmony." He cocked an eyebrow at Bryant. "May I pour you a cup?"

Bryant watched the Attorney-General pour two cups of coffee and add sugar and cream while he reflected on the man whose opinion he had to win over. Sullivan was the best-dressed man in Massachusetts and just as meticulous in his law practice. He was an outdoorsman. He used to ride for miles everyday as a circuit judge while he thought through his decisions. In the evenings he wrote histories and treatises. He founded the Historical Society of Massachusetts whose trustees had recently turned on him for his refusal to lead the Government into war with the French for interfering with their trade. He was a man of high principle with the will-power to overcome accident and disease crippling to a lesser man. Brother to one of the nation's great military leaders, he was a modest person with concern for the disadvantaged and a charming way with children, though he was said to be a disciplinarian with his own. Here was a good man, very close to his heart. Surely he could find the right words to persuade him to save Wheeler's life.

Taking his cup and sitting to face Sullivan, Bryant opened the discussion with a reference to Harriette Wheeler's depression. Sullivan was concerned. "With rest," Bryant continued, "she'll recover. The hard part is to forget the past. She considers her life with Ephraim all that she has. I am afraid that his execution will have a devastating effect upon her as well as on the boy and girl."

Sullivan nodded appreciatively. "Her love for her children, and in particular her baby, will carry her through. I am like a surgeon, Dr. Bryant. I will cut away the offending part whereas you will try a curative, is that not so?"

"An agreeable metaphor," Bryant smiled.

"Betsy will suffer when her father is hanged," Sullivan continued, "but not as much or as continually if he were imprisoned for life. Cut him out of their lives, I say, and he will soon be forgotten. The State will take the responsibility and the guilt for his death. Tell the family that I am to blame, if that helps."

"And what about Wheeler?" Bryant asked. "Must a single act against our social mores be punished without an opportunity for redemption?"

"In this case," Sullivan cried, "his crime is so easy and so tempting to commit. Our penalty for it must be death to accord with our sense of outrage at a man's betrayal of his duties of guardianship. Society, if it is anything, is the sum of our responsibilities to protect and care for one another. Once that principle is violated, there is chaos, my dear doctor, and you and I know, as professional men, that caring with integrity must be the motive for our actions and the guiding light of human endeavor for the well-being of our communities."

Bryant had to agree and felt that Sullivan was arguing him into a corner. "Order based on individual responsibility and observance of morals rather than on force--yes, you are right, Mr. Sullivan, but by executing Wheeler, are you not coercing the community with force?"

Sullivan reflected a moment. His eyes appeared to look into the distance before they scrutinized the doctor once again. "In this case the force reflects the will of the people. It is the means by which the community corrects any trespassing upon its moral obligations."

"Yet, in this case," Bryant warned, "the majority of the community has given no thought to the execution, and, of those who have, the majority believe Betsy was lying and that Ephraim should be pardoned. They are mistaken, but by your reasoning they are the conscious element by which the State must take its guidance."

Sullivan chuckled. "We don't know the true thought of the majority; it has elected officials, such as myself, to do its thinking because it does not have the facts and cannot come to a consensus of agreement on everyday issues."

Bryant nodded grimly. "It boils down to your decision."

"Based on the law," Sullivan added, "which is the will of the people."

"Without mercy?"

"Without mercy in this case," Sullivan said finally. "Wheeler is a roughneck. He has no redeeming qualities. His death will be healthy for his family and the Commonwealth." He saw a hopeless look come over Bryant's face. "Death on the personal level is always tragic. But I was elected to act on a higher and impersonal level. I am sorry that I can not grant your wish, my dear doctor. I am truly very sorry."

Bryant sighed. "We are in different businesses, Attorney-General. I am a healer, not just of men's bodies but of men's souls in the old Greek sense."

"But you must admit that Nature destroys as much as it heals," Sullivan smiled as he rose to leave. "That is how I see the Wheeler case. From the beginning it was propelled by natural passions, starting long before the rape, and ends with Nature's solution to all things."

Bryant thought, but did not say, that Sullivan was forfeiting the human role in nature. Dewey stepped into the room just then as Sullivan and Bryant warmly shook hands with an obvious respect for one another.

"I'll find my way out, Daniel," Sullivan said moving stiffly toward the door.

"No, you won't, James," Dewey said, following him and handing him his hat which he had forgotten. "At least let me show you the way out since you won't accept my guidance in other ways."

Bryant heard Sullivan reply in a pleasant tone but his words were indistinct. The butler arrived with another tray of coffee, set it on the table, and went way. Dewey reappeared and poured coffee for Bryant and himself.

"Of course, he came to tell me about Adams," Dewey said. "And he wanted to get a good look at you. He's a wily fella. Not to be trusted."

"Is Adams so important?" Bryant asked, sipping his coffee.

"He's the backbone of our movement for Wheeler's clemency," Dewey smiled. "With him out of the way, we're going to carry more of the burden."

"But how?" Bryant asked. "All I can think of doing is to warn our rulers of the consequences."

"They don't listen to warnings," Dewey laughed. "Oh no, they listen only to political persuasion. And that's my department."

"We'll be heading for Cummington early in the morning," Bryant said. "What can I do?"

"Take every opportunity to tell people what you told Governor Strong. The word will travel." Dewey went over to the fire and gave the logs a poke. "I'll have to come up with a strategy."

In the meantime, the same thought in a different context was going through the mind of Susanna in Glen Falls, New York. She had received a passionate letter from Dewey. She re-read it at intervals, trying to divine if there was love behind the passion. He asked her to come immediately to Boston. But should she drop everything and run? Wasn't she too old for such romantic behaviour? Were her two children less important than Daniel Dewey? What would he think of her if she left them for him on the spur of the moment? He didn't mention them in the letter. But if he wanted her, he would have to take them! If she demurred for the present, would she risk losing him? Really, it all amounted to how much she loved him. Her mind picked constantly at the problem all day as she waited rather absent-mindedly on her customers. By bed-time as she tucked in her children and kissed their foreheads, she reckoned they needed a father. She went down to the kitchen and scribbled a note to Dewey that she and her "young ones" would take the stage to Boston on the weekend.

THIRTY-THREE

By this time Gentle Adams saw that Wheeler's capture had taken the steam out of the movement for a commutation of his sentence. People had been encouraged by his escape but resigned when he was returned. Perhaps it was God's will that he be hanged, they thought. Adams cursed the religious blight over the State which he regarded as inhibiting thought and action. He was speaking on the subject with Mallard Meacham in Pittsfield. In Meacham, he could not have found a stronger critic of religion, too strong for Adam's taste, and he deftly steered the conversation back to the Wheeler case.

"Your piece on the Sheriff was good," Gentle said. "It made him out to be a reluctant hero."

"I wasn't exaggerating," Meacham replied. "He really was unhappy that it was Wheeler he caught."

"Exaggerated or not," Gentle smiled, "it brought our people to believe in him again. There's nothing like the power of the press."

"The press is all right," Meacham shrugged. "But the real power is in the writing. You're like everyone else; you think power is abstract; it isn't, it's individual. Every line in that newspaper is written by a man with a unique mind and a unique set of experiences. No, Gentle, the power of the press is really the power of expression of a number of men with the talent to reach other people. Without them there is no press."

"What are you driving at?" Adams frowned.

Meacham shifted restlessly in his chair. "I had a run-in with the editor. I think we should go after Strong and Sullivan as monarchists who'd hang every poor man from the nearest tree if they could. But my editor says that because Sullivan is a Republican, we can't do that. All right, I said, let's go after Strong. No, he's the Governor, it would be disrespectful. So, Gentle, there's your power of the press for you--tongue-tied."

"There's a kind of apathy out there," Adams said. "I've talked to many of the same farmers we've met during the year, and they've decided to leave the whole Wheeler affair up to the good judgment of the Governor."

"Damn it!" Meacham said, jumping to his feet and walking about. "Ephraim's as good as dead unless we do something!"

"We cant start a revolution," Adams said, amused at his friend's alarm. "But maybe you can do something. I heard from the grapevine that Betsy Wheeler went with Dr. Bryant to Boston to see Governor Strong. There must be a good story in that."

"Good Lord! Why didn't you tell me this before? Where are they now?"

"They'll probably be leaving Boston soon," Adams said, catching some of Meacham's excitement. "You could meet them in Cummington."

"That's right! I will! But," he paused and looked seriously at Adams, "even if I do get a good story that raises sympathy for Wheeler, I don't think it'll save him now. You'd better think of getting a rescue party together. Time's getting short."

"That's too risky," Adams shook his head. "Some men would get shot if we tried to storm the jail. Besides, we'd lose whatever sympathy there is for Wheeler. No, Mallard, there's no go there. It's up to you and the power of the press."

Meacham left him with a sour look.

Adams turned his thoughts to the election coming up in May. So far Governor Strong had kept his balance well. He gave the appearance of firmness and resolution, yet, at the same time, he was regarded as compassionate, such that there had spread a belief among Republicans that he would reprieve Wheeler at the last moment. Adams tried to discourage the sentiment wherever he found it, but it was like trying to cast doubt on the existence of God: despite all the good reasons for Strong's doing nothing, there remained the hope, based on faith in the goodness of human nature, that he would act in the final instance.

The next morning as Betsy and Peter Bryant left Boston for Cummington, Mallard Meacham left Lenox for Cummington. Meacham intended to interview people along his route to get a sense of the public's opinion on Wheeler. He went by stage and got off at the towns along the way, staying over for the next coach if he found the place interesting. It was a slow way to travel, but he knew Betsy Wheeler was not due back for another two or three days. At the close of the third day, he arrived at Windsor, and, standing at the crossroads perched on the hill overlooking the route west to Pittsfield and east to Cummington, he slung his bag over his shoulder, took a deep breath of the fresh cold mountain air, and asked a passer-by for the way to Michael Pepper's farm.

He was shivering from the bitter cold when he knocked at the door of Pepper's farmhouse. One of Pepper's sons opened the door and took him to the warm kitchen where the family was gathered.

Pepper's questioning look gave way to a smiling welcome at the mention of Gentle Adams. Pepper took Meacham's outer garments while his wife prepared some food. The family gathered round him and watched as Meacham ate. It was a scene that Meacham had repeated often in his travels about Massachusetts. He held the center of attention and directed the conversation whichever way he wished.

"So Windsor is mostly sympathetic to Ephraim," he concluded after listening patiently to Michael and his sons.

"That sort of stuff goes on around here," Pepper's eldest son said with a grin and brushed his tousled brown hair back from his forehead. "I know of some girls who've had trouble with their dads."

"Hush!" Mrs. Pepper said sharply. "That's not true!"

"Yes, it is, Ma," said another son. "We heard about it at school. It's talked about."

"Probably it doesn't happen as often as it is talked about," Pepper said, "but the boys are right. Some people think Ephraim's being set up as an example to the others. But, it won't do any good. That sort of thing happens, and there's no way that hanging one man for it is going to stop it."

"What do you think?" Meacham asked Mrs. Pepper, who was squirming uncomfortably.

"As for it happening around here, maybe it does, but no more than in other towns," she said defensively. "I don't think Ephraim should suffer. If anyone's at fault, it's Harriette. She shouldn't have reported it."

"She wouldn't have if he wasn't going to take away her family from her," Pepper said. "That's what it's all about, if you ask me."

"You mean a quarrel between husband and wife," Meacham said.

"Yep, I think he was paying her back for leaving him alone all winter long."

"God! That's ridiculous!" Meacham said. "While our men of State see it as rape, his neighbors consider it a family quarrel."

"And while you're chewing that over," Mrs. Pepper said, her plump face brightening with another thought, "there's that special relationship between Harriette and William Martin that folks have been talking about."

"Martin was just sharing the house with them, wasn't he?" Meacham asked. "He was a good friend of Harriette's who could protect her from Wheeler's rages."

"Folks say there was more to it than that," she rolled her eyes at her husband.

"Maybe there was, maybe there wasn't," Michael Pepper said. "All I know is that Ephraim couldn't have told about it if it were true. He kept his problems to himself and tried to solve them on his own."

"That other woman who testified at the trial," Meacham said, "wouldn't she know?"

"Eunice Hart," Pepper smiled. "She up and left for the coast months ago. Nobody knows where she is."

"She wouldn't say, anyway," Mrs. Pepper added. "With Mrs. Martin dead, she'd let the past bury the past."

"But if we could show there was a relationship," Meacham cried excitedly, "we could show a conspiracy to get rid of Ephraim Wheeler."

"No," Michael Pepper shook his head. "It's nothing but speculation. The only ones who know are Harriette Wheeler and William Martin, and they're not going to talk."

"But it is possible that Harriette Wheeler took advantage of Ephraim's thing with Betsy to get rid of him and open a way to be with Martin, whose wife was dying."

"Possible," Pepper agreed, "but we'll never know."

"It makes me even more determined to get Ephraim out of jail," Meacham gritted his teeth. "I wish I could write all this in my newspaper."

"No use stirring people up more than they are already," Michael Pepper said, interlocking the fingers of his large hands and clamping them over his knee. "They can't do nothing. Only makes them more unhappy."

"Gentle's going to spring Ephraim again soon," Meacham said suddenly. "He asked me to tell you."

"He may not be able to," Pepper said flatly. "My neighbor told me this morning that Justice Walker and a couple of men rode to Pittsfield yesterday to pick Gentle up on orders from Boston."

Meacham let out a whistle. "He's not in Pittsfield now. They might not find him. He's out doing the farmer's circuit and building up Colonel Larned's image as a down-to-earth Republican."

"For Ephraim's sake," Michael Pepper said, "I hope they don't find him."

They sat talking until it was time to retire. Pepper agreed to take him to his neighbor's house in the morning before he departed for Cummington. Meacham spent a restless night worrying over Gentle Adams and wishing there were some way to warn him of his danger.

THIRTY-FOUR

Justice Robert Walker sat straight and stiff in his saddle. He had a good idea whom he was looking for: the strongly-built, tough-looking, and mysterious figure whom he had seen talking with Sheriff Larned. The order to arrest him smelled of politics and of a kind which Walker disdained. Attorney-General Sullivan, he thought, pursued his goals as a State administrator as zealously as he prosecuted "the accused" in court. Walker was a stern disciplinarian, but he was not a manipulator. He disliked it when he was used as an instrument to affect a change that in turn influenced other changes to bring about a result that somehow perverted the true nature of the problem. But he was the Justice of the Peace, and, mistrustful of his mission, he did as he was bidden, all the while wondering why Sheriff Larned had not been sent on it.

He learnt in Pittsfield that Adams had left for Lenox. Immediately he and his men, who were as taciturn as he, set out for the County Seat. They stayed at a farmhouse on the route for the night. At breakfast the next morning, their host said he would ride a ways with them as he was going to a meeting about fifteen miles away.

They paid the farmer's wife and rode in softly falling snowflakes.

"Political meeting?" Walker asked, breaking the silence.

The farmer, cheerful and open in countenance, was glad to be given the chance to air his views.

"You bet. I'm Republican Jeffersonian. Folks in our State are too conservative. The best man we got is Sheriff Larned. He'll represent us right. He's the only honest man in politics."

"I like him," the Justice said.

"The Federalists are a hanging bunch. Look what they're doing to that poor fellow Wheeler."

"Raped his daughter," the Justice commented as the farmer caught his breath. "Deserves to die."

The farmer reared back in his saddle and looked askance at Walker.

"Say something wrong?" Walker asked.

"You listen to this fellow I'm going to hear, and you'll change your tune. If you like Larned, this fellow is a Larned man. And he's a good speaker, one of the best."

Walker thought for a moment. He knew the fellow was going to be Gentle Adams; his instinct told him. He felt like ignoring the invitation and proceeding to Lenox, but he turned in his saddle to his two companions following behind them. "We'll accompany this gentleman to his meeting."

The men nodded. Walker fell silent. The farmer continued to talk politics but, finding Walker unresponsive, he soon lapsed into silence. They turned down a side road, the ruts of which were packed hard with snow and ice, and rode for a couple of hours.

"That's the place!" the farmer pointed to a barn across the snowy fields where numbers of men were gathering and to which riders could be seen coming from other directions.

When they reached the barn, Justice Walker and his men left their horses in the care of men whose responsibility was to tether them. He calculated at a glance that there were over two hundred men in the barn, which was set up with chairs facing a podium on a permanent basis. The farmer, seeing friends in the front row, left them. Walker instructed his men to sit at the back near the door. He walked to the back and center, found a chair, and set it behind the last row where he was obscured by the men in front of him. The seating was quickly filled, and the chatter of the men subsided as the farmer, who seemed to own the property, called for silence.

Aside from a wood stove at the front, it was the men's body heat which kept the place warmer than the outdoors.

The farmer welcomed them all in the name of Republicanism and the future, to which they responded with a roar. He introduced Gentle Adams, who detached himself from the men seated in the front, mounted the podium, and struck an aggressive pose, his fists cocked and his chin tucked into his neck.

"We're in a fighting frame of mind," he shouted. "Almost February, four months to the big day."

From the cheers and shouts of encouragement, Walker recognized Adams' immense popularity with these people. He could not expect to arrest him under such circumstances without facing violent opposition.

"Well, folks, things haven't changed since I was here last. Land taxes are still goin' up. Rents are goin' up. And they hate printin' paper money in Boston. (Laughter). Meantime the rich are gettin' richer. They grabbed the public securities meant for us who earned them, and now our taxes pay off the debt which they hold at eight percent interest. They want us to fight the French because the French Republic is interferin' with their trade with the English monarchy. The Federalists have forgot that it's the French who are our friends. (Cheers). The only bright spot since those days is the advance of the Republican Party in this country. (Loud cheers). I wish Tom Jefferson would come pay us a visit, but it's a long ride from Washington, D.C. The next best thing is for us to send Colonel Larned to

Washington. (Cheers). He's tough enough to make the trip. If he can find an escapee when no one else has the slightest idea where he is, I'd say he's a determined man. (Silence). He didn't want to catch Wheeler, but when he was told to do it, he did. That's the kind of politician we need in Washington. A man who will do what we tell him whether he likes it or not. (Cheers). But havin' a good link to old Tom in Washington ain't goin' to help in Massachusetts unless we loosen the grip that the Federalists got here on the election. We gotta send old Strong packin'. Since he can't see the door, we have to take him to it (laughter) and give him a shove! (Cheers).And send the Essex Junto with him!"

Justice Walker looked round him at the enthusiastic crowd becoming gradually more excited as Adams became more intense in his criticism of the Federalists. His arrest of Adams would make him the most unpopular man in the Berkshires, he thought. Moreover, Walker intended to support the Republicans. This Wheeler affair had decided him to vote against Federalism. The thought of his arrest of Wheeler lay like a hurt inside him. He would regret it to the end of his days. And now the Attorney-General was leading him to another excess of keeping order. By imprisoning Adams at this time before the election, he would open himself to charges of undermining the election. He began to perspire as he thought of the anger he would bring upon himself, and, of course, unlike Larned, he could not say that he was following an order. As Justice of the Peace he was the law. Adams had broken it by his shady and nefarious past and had to be called to judgment, but why not after the election? His connection with Wheeler was merely conjectural. Why risk the good name of the law on the vague supposition that Adams could help Wheeler escape? But reason as he could against arresting Adams, he knew that it had to be done.

Adams in his talk to the farmers strayed from general politics to local concerns, which he appeared to know well. Walker observed men nod to each other at various points

Adams was making. The crowd admired him. And when he introduced with fulsome praise certain farmers in the audience, he brought the crowd to its feet as it applauded and shouted. Walker took that moment to stride quickly across the back of the barn and signal with a motion of the eyes for his men to follow him outside.

They walked along the rows of tethered horses, untied the reins of their horses from the wooden bars, which had been set up to run in long rows across the field, and nodded good-bye to the young man who had tethered them and was watching them with interest.

"Don't like the politics?" the young man asked.

"I'm a Larned man," Walker smiled slightly. "Don't need to know more." He paused as if he had just thought of what he was about to ask. "Where does Gentle Adams speak next?"

"Out towards Richmond," was the answer. "Tomorrow morning."

Justice Walker touched his hat, and he and his men mounted and rode silently out to the cart road where Walker led them to the west in the direction of Richmond village.

One of the men cleared his throat. His voice rasped when he spoke. "I knew that man 'bout ten years ago. Went by the name of Raspail. He's good with a gun."

"We'll be careful," Walker said.

The snow had stopped falling. The land looked crisply white and beautiful. Walker turned over in his mind the ways he could capture Adams--ambush, confrontation, trickery--they all seemed unsafe. The man impressed him with his intelligence. It was hard to capture an intelligent man.

THIRTY-FIVE

When Mallard Meacham reached Cummington, he just had to ask the first townsperson he met to discover where Betsy was staying. Sarah Bryant answered his knock.

"I've come to talk to Mrs. Wheeler and her daughter," he said as if he were on official business.

"Are you from the Governor?" Sarah asked in surprise.

"I'm a reporter for the Pittsfield newspaper," he explained.

"Oh, well, come in," she said flustered. "I don't know whether they'll see you, but I'll ask."

She left Meacham in the sitting room and found Harriette Wheeler in the kitchen.

"I don't know if it's wise," Harriette said doubtfully when she learned that a reporter wanted to speak with her. "Possibly Betsy would want to."

"I'll get her while you talk to him," Sarah said, quickly putting the coffee pot on the stove.

Harriette, smoothing her dress, went uneasily into the sitting room with Sarah, who, after introducing her to Meacham, went upstairs.

"The papers have been at fault for not giving more attention to your husband's case," Meacham said. "We want to make up for that now."

Harriette frowned at him. "I don't understand."

"We take the view that the people run the affairs of this State, and, if they are not properly informed, they cannot see that justice is done. In your husband's case, I think the Government is doing an injustice in the name of the people."

Harriette nodded. She liked this young man who was so patient in his explanation.

"Allow me to ask, do you think your husband should be executed?"

Harriette was taken aback. "No, I don't want him to be." She paused. "Rough as he was to me and bad as he was, I don't want to see him hanged."

Meacham jotted her words onto a pad of paper he took from his pocket. "But you want to see him punished?"

"He has to be punished," she said.

"When you informed the authorities of his crime, were you aware of the penalty?"

"Yes," she admitted, "but it wasn't until the trial when I heard Mr. Sullivan ask for capital punishment that I thought it could happen."

"Did you think that your family would be disgraced?" he asked, watching her closely.

"I thought of it," she admitted, "but I needed help. I couldn't do anything else. Mr. Martin couldn't help me; only Justice Walker could do that."

"In a fight between Ephraim Wheeler and Mr. Martin earlier in the morning, the Justice intervened and fined both of them a shilling," Meacham said. "What did you think he would do when you told him about the rape?"

"I guessed he would lock Ephraim away for a while, at least, until we could arrange to live separately again." Tears came to her eyes.

Meacham felt a surge of sympathy for her. She had been called the villain in the case, but she was a victim. She bore the responsibility for everything, but she had had no control over the events, really, no say in the direction they took her and her family.

Betsy entered the room at that moment. Her full figure and pretty face impressed Meacham. He wondered, as he was introduced to her, what had made her vulnerable. It was when she spoke that he saw the slight hesitation in her manner, the insecurity in her glancing eyes, and her natural openness ,which the unscrupulous of this world never failed to exploit when they found it.

Betsy spoke briefly of meeting Governor Strong and staying with Daniel Dewey.

"Did the Governor give you any hope that he'd change his mind?" Meacham asked.

"Yes, he did," Betsy said. "I think he'll save Daddy."

Meacham looked impressed. "Did you see the Attorney-General?"

"Yes, I did."

"Did he say that he'd save your father's life?"

"No," Betsy looked down. "I don't think he will try."

"It's not up to him anyway," Meacham smiled. "You're a courageous girl. I hope all you want comes true."

She smiled at him as if a rainbow had broken through the darkest clouds.

Sarah Bryant came in with a tray of coffee for them all. "You will stay the night, of course, Mr. Meacham."

"I'd like to, m'am," he said, "but I've got to get back to Windsor by tonight to hear the new preacher."

"Who is that?"

"Samuel Shepard. Do you know the famous Episcopalian from England? He's been in Boston for a year, and he's touring these parts for a while. My editor asked me to hear him. I've no choice but to catch the stage leaving within the hour."

"Oh!" Sarah looked disappointed. "You'll miss Peter."

"Give the Doctor my regards and regrets," he said. "I have another question for Miss Wheeler," he smiled winningly at Betsy. "If Ephraim Wheeler is hanged, what will you do?"

Betsy froze at the question. It was as if she had suddenly cut off all contact with her surroundings. She shook her head.

"I'm sorry," Meacham looked guiltily at the other women. "I should be off." He stood. "Thank you all for your hospitality."

Sarah saw him to the door. "Be kind to them in what you write," she said.

He said fiercely. "Sullivan and his ilk are destroying them." He turned away, walked quickly over the snow into the street, waved to Sarah in her little house on the hill, and pondered how he could thwart the Governor's obvious intention to hang Wheeler.

Left alone momentarily with Meacham's last question ringing in their heads, Harriette and Betsy looked at one another in panic. What would they do if Ephraim was hanged? A stranger had posed the question. It was as if the outside world had intervened into their private hopes and fears with a fatal suggestion that neither of them had been willing to contemplate. Until now they had wrestled with the question of whether he would hang and convinced themselves that he would not. At the last moment God would intervene through Governor Strong, Harriette told Betsy. But Meacham brought a worldly wisdom in an objective reportorial way to shatter their illusions. The fears that they had wished away returned suddenly, subtly, importunately, and because of the innocuousness of Meacham's question, powerfully. Until this point Harriette stuck resolutely to her desire to see Ephraim punished. His violation of Betsy was the unforgivable crime--a betrayal to which both she and Betsy could cling as justification for their prosecution of Ephraim. Throughout the months, however, his crime seemed less important than the memories of their love and their sharing through their devastating hardships and disappointments, yet it remained foremost, supported as it was by officialdom. Suddenly, the personality of the man and the sense of his belonging to her seized her emotions. All her anger and resentment fled before the unrelenting remorse that tore at her soul. She saw Betsy staring at her in consternation and wonder, and, rather than let Mrs. Bryant catch her in such an emotional state, she fled the room.

Betsy sensed her mother's despair and, shocked by the transformation, just saved herself in time from tumbling into a similar fit of remorse. She retained sufficient composure to apologize to the returning Mrs. Bryant for her mother's sudden indisposition and asked to take a cup of coffee to her. Sarah, seeing at once the ill-effect of the reporter's visit, quickly poured a cup and handed it to her with a smile of sympathy. Sarah blamed herself for allowing Meacham to speak to the Wheelers and worried what the doctor would say when he returned from his rounds.

Betsy found her mother lying on her bed with her hands clasped tightly over her face. She put the coffee cup on the table at the head and sat beside her, watching her and waiting for her to speak. Until now, the ordeal had been Betsy's, the pain had been Betsy's, and Betsy had been the victim. Yet, in one instant, Betsy saw that her mother was the true victim. With her mother's bravery behind her, Betsy had condemned Ephraim, but it was really her mother's condemnation of her father that he had expressed. She, herself, had merely told what happened in the woods and prayed that Ephraim would not hurt her, and the people would not shame her. Now Harriette was feeling the pain far more intensely than Betsy had. Harriette felt the guilt and the shame. Harriette groaned with remorse. Harriette no longer sustained the fiction that Ephraim alone had committed the crime and that Betsy alone had been raped. Harriette sensed that she was involved in the crime just as much as if she had been the perpetrator or the victim because Ephraim was a part of her concupiscence against which he had rebelled.

"Don't Ma," Betsy said softly and gently tried to pull her mother's hands away from her face. "Don't be afraid. Daddy's not going to hang."

"Daddy and me were fools," Harriette said in a moan. She put her hands on the bed and pushed herself to a sitting position, leaning against the headboard. "We were too stubborn. I didn't know I was drivin' him so far away from me-- so far that he'd pick on you." She threw her arms about Betsy and held her tightly against her. "I can't let him be hanged!"

"But Ma," Betsy whispered, gently disengaging herself from her mother's arms. "We can't do nothin' about it."

243

"We can, you know," Harriette said, looking meaningfully into Betsy's eyes. "We can say we made up the whole story."

Betsy felt as if her insides had collapsed. She stared speechless at Harriette.

"You won't be blamed," Harriette said quickly. "I'll say I made you testify to keep Daddy from taking away my children."

"But Ma, that's lyin'," Betsy protested. She pictured the Attorney-General's face on hearing that she had lied, and she shivered.

Harriette nodded and said grimly. "But they won't believe us. Not now. Not after everything. My poor husband! Oh Lord, save him! Save us, oh Lord, save us!" She stared at the ceiling in anguish.

"Do you still love Daddy?" Betsy asked, her voice shaking with the experience of her mother's agony.

"No!" Harriette said. "I don't want to." She smoothed Betsy's hair back from her face and remembered the scene when she handed this baby girl to Ephraim who stood grinning with happiness at the side of her bed. "But I failed him."

Betsy felt sorrier for her mother than she had when she thought of the fights and the beatings.

"I wish he didn't hate me so," Harriette said. "I gave him cause, I suppose." She lowered her head. "Pray for Daddy, Betsy, pray with all your might for God to move the Governor's heart to mercy for Daddy. Pray that his friends can help him. 'Cause if he don't escape, I don't know what we're going to do."

Betsy seized her mother's hands in both of hers, and, with heads bowed, they prayed, Betsy for her father, and Harriette for forgiveness for sending her husband to execution.

THIRTY-SIX

Near the Massachusetts-New York border, Justice Robert Walker and his two companions came in sight of the farmhouse where Gentle Adams was to address a congregation of farmers the next morning. Walker figured that Adams would be sleeping at the farm over night, hence he would be riding the road to the farmhouse sometime before dark, which would be in about three hours.

"What do you think?" he asked his men. "Where do we make the arrest?"

"Where he can't make a run for it," the first man said.

Walker looked at the expanse of white fields about them and frowned. "At the farmhouse then?" He looked over at the tall wooden house and the barn sitting deep in a field behind it. "Too great a risk of hurting other people," he said.

"He's a good shot," the second man said.

"You mentioned that before," Walker smiled grimly. "Seems to me, we've got to ambush him."

"How many men will be with him, though?" the first man said.

"Just the young fella who was tending the horses, I reckon," Walker said. "Well, let's dismount, give our horses a feed, and then one of you go up the trail a ways, and get in the woods out of sight till they pass you. Wait till you hear me challenge him before you show yourself." He turned to the second man. "And you keep out of sight on this end till you hear my voice."

The men nodded, dismounted, and taking oats from their saddle bags began to feed their horses. Walker surveyed the beauty of the countryside in its pristine silence. He regarded man as the ugly taint upon it all. Soon he would be upsetting the perfect equilibrium of nature by the unnatural act of arresting a man and possibly shooting and killing him, or being killed in his turn. He looked at his companions who were experienced in this sort of work. Actually their cast of mind

245

made them more criminal than was Adams, he thought. They could work for a brigand chief as easily as for a Justice of the Peace. Adams, on the contrary, had some ideals and expected to realize them through his political work. Adams was savvy and could be ruthless no doubt, but his spirit was of the sort that could blend with the countryside as if it belonged, whereas these other men clashed with it. He fed his horse some oats from his hand and stroked the animal's neck as he thought how faithfully it served him; but then, it had no choice, just as he had no choice but to confront Adams in the name of the law.

"Let's take our places, then," he said.

"If I see them coming," the first man said, starting back along the trail, "I'll give a caw, like this." He imitated the call of a crow perfectly.

Walker moved down the trail with the second man to a cluster of trees and bushes on the side, their black branches thrown up like a veil, and the evergreen shielding them.

An hour later, as the sun sat on the rim of the horizon, Adams with only one companion, as Walker had surmised, rode towards the spot. His companion was the son of a local politician. He volunteered to help Adams with any small jobs and keep him company on these barn-storming tours. They were making a preliminary run of the area. When the weather became milder, they would escort Colonel Larned over the same route. The crowds would be bigger to hear the Colonel, but, most important, the Republican message would have had time to sink into the farmers' thoughts.

"Did you hear that?" Adams asked suddenly.

"What?" His companion slowed his horse to keep beside Adams. "Do you mean that crow?"

"Yes," Adams said, scanning the sky. "I've never heard a crow caw like that when it wasn't in flight."

"Could have been flying low in the woods. We just couldn't see it."

"You may be right," Gentle smiled. "There's our destination." He pointed at the farmhouse in the distance. "The woman there is a good cook if I remember right."

"You're right," the young man nodded.

They passed the spot where the first man was concealed. As Adams laughed at an incident he remembered from his speech that day and was about to relate it to his companion, he saw a horse and rider appear in the trail ahead of them as if by magic.

"Where did he come from?" he asked.

"Don't know."

"Careful. You ride behind me and to the side. Quick now."

The young man reined in his horse and followed a length behind and to the side. Adams strained to make out the features of the man in the darkening day. He recognized Justice Walker when they were three lengths away and reined in his horse. He relaxed his hand on his short rifle which he kept in his saddle.

"At last I know you're not intending to rob us," he said.

Walker brought his horse up directly in front of him. "Sorry, Mr. Adams, but the Government has asked me to detain you."

"Do you have a warrant with you?" Adams asked. He saw a horse and rider appear in the trail behind Walker.

Walker handed him a copy of the warrant which Adams read through quickly. Adams spoke to his companion and noticed a horse and rider was in the road behind them.

"They want me for my sins of the past," he smiled. "You will ride ahead and tell our friends that I'm going to have to go to Lenox."

"I'll stay with you, Gentle," the young man said concernedly.

"Do as I say," Adams said sharply. "You give the speech tomorrow. You know what I've been saying."

The young man nodded and rode down the trail past Walker and past the man with the gun on his arm in the trail behind him.

"Wait!" Adams said when Walker started to move close to him to tie his arms. "I want to make sure he gets clear." He watched the young man for a few seconds until he was far out of reach and then handed the warrant back to Walker.

As Walker reached for the paper, Adams slipped his rifle out of the saddle holster and put its muzzle into Walker's stomach. "Keep your hands down," he whispered, and, keeping his rifle against Walker, he maneuvered his horse round to head in the same direction. "Forward," he said.

The sun had dropped behind the horizon; its rays lit up the cold gray sky, but the light was too indistinct for Walker's men to see that Walker was the one under arrest. Adams led Walker toward the first man who sat waiting up the trail with his gun at the ready, and he passed by him so that Walker was between them.

"Don't try to be clever," Adams warned the man, who looked in surprise at the rifle pointed at the Justice's midsection.

Adams spurred his horse and commanded Walker to make his mount keep pace with him. "Hands up now," he said. He glanced back to see the two men on their horses conferring excitedly. He figured that he had a few seconds of advantage owing to the surprise. He took the gun away from the Justice's body lest it go off accidentally and rode slightly behind him.

Walker said nothing, but gritted his teeth, and rode swiftly with his hands over his head. They dashed back along the trail in this manner, the two men following at a distance, for five minutes. Then, as darkness fell, Adams shouted for Walker to rein in.

"Dismount! Quickly!" he cried, and taking the reins of Walker's horse, he spurred his own horse barely leaving Walker time to get his foot out of the stirrup.

As he sped forward with Walker's horse in tow, he glanced back and was able to make out the shapes of the horsemen approaching the dim figure of Walker standing in the center of the trail. Adams straightened up in the saddle and smiled to himself in satisfaction. He heard the report of a gun and felt a pain in his left shoulder. His left arm went numb, but he held onto the reins, and, leaning forward over his horse's head, made himself a smaller target for other shots. He allowed his horse its head, and just clung on with his knees, and held firmly to the reins of Walker's horse with his right hand.

He rode on an on, indifferent to time, watching only for tell-tale turnings in the road, which let him know where he was and how far he had to go. Pain throbbed along his arm, but he willed it away.

Finally, he came into the main road running from Pittsfield to Lenox about three miles from Molly Given's house. He turned, thinking of Molly, keeping her face in his mind like a beacon. He passed two or three other riders in the darkness but so quickly that he could not be sure of the number. He looked round when he turned into Molly's lane. No one was near-by. When he rode into Molly's yard, he slid off his horse and relinquished the reins of Walker's horse. Both horses and he hung their heads in exhaustion. He walked awkwardly to the door, knocked, and seized the door frame to steady himself. He heard the door being opened and saw Molly worriedly standing in front of him. He fell to his knees in a sudden weakness and threw himself across the threshold as he lost consciousness.

THIRTY-SEVEN

Meacham arrived in Windsor in time to hear the Reverend Samuel Shepard, a tall, rakishly thin, dynamic man, whose voice could cut the air like a razor and the next minute sing in dulcet tones. But the content was not new to Meacham. He spoke in the fashion of the school which declared that God had pre-planned the direction taken by every hair on one's head. The Government was clever to bring this preacher from England at the moment, Meacham thought, because he supported the status quo and advised everyone to be happy with their lot because it was pre-ordained. In other words, Wheeler was to hang because God decided he was born to hang. It was the kind of message the Federalists welcomed.

Meacham's editor rejected his article on the Wheeler family as too controversial. "Can't risk stirring up people's sentiments. The Governor's looking for an excuse to close us down as it is. Sorry, Mallard. It's well written."

Meacham was sorry for the Wheelers. It could have been their last chance to be understood, to get some real justice. But he was too experienced as a reporter to argue with his editor. The man had considered both sides of the question, put them in the scales, and made his decision. As consolation, he wrote a scathing article criticizing the attempt of the Federalist Government in the person of Justice Walker to arrest the popular Republican barn-stormer, Gentle Adams. Meacham claimed that the Federalists wanted to silence Adams' effective criticism of them before the May elections.

In the meantime, Walker and his men found refuge for the night in a farmer's barn. The farmer gave them blankets to keep out the cold, and they slept in the hay. The search for Adams would begin the moment they reached Lenox, Walker promised.

Molly Givens took out the bullet from Adams' shoulder and cleaned the wound. She had tended the wounded at the time of Shays' Rebellion and never forgot her surgical skills. General

Shays wrote to her once in a while from his exile in New York. She had looked after him during a serious illness, and he never forgot her tender ministrations, which, he said, were as spiritually healing as they were physically. Molly hid Adams in a small room under the stairs, the door to which was not visible. She put the horses in her barn and stashed the saddles in a bin, which she then covered up with paraphernalia. She was determined that Adams was not to be found.

Walker became the subject of local satire. He was confronted also by an angry Colonel Larned, who, learning that Walker received his order from Sullivan, began to plan a subtle attack on Sullivan in his campaign speeches. What was the use of supporting a party in the cause of liberalism? he asked, if its leader used every means to impose his conservative views? As an editorial in the Pittsfield *Sun* remarked, the Republican Party of Massachusetts was in trouble.

Wheeler's family, the Bryants, and even the taciturn Isaac Odel felt hopeful that Governor Strong would commute Ephraim's sentence to some years in prison. As the days went by and the calendar moved toward the fateful February 20, there was an undercurrent of expectation that Wheeler would be saved from execution at the last minute. It would be a lesson he would never forget, some people said. Others still considered that he was innocent, and that the rape charge had been trumped up by his vindictive wife and simple-minded daughter.

Dewey and his liberal friends tried again to approach the Government on Wheeler's behalf, but the Governor was "too busy with the problems of State."

Dewey provided a couple of rooms in his home for Susanna and her children when they arrived from Glen Falls, and he declared their engagement immediately. He introduced Susanna to his society, an operation that took much time, planning, and foresight. His immediate family came first, and that had to be done in bits and pieces, sometimes in single interviews, where he had to leave Susanna alone with a

251

relative for them to get to know each other, so essential if they were to help bring her into the society. It must be remembered that Susanna came from a lower class; it could be only through a united front of the Dewey family that she could find acceptance. Otherwise, social sharpshooters could wound her and cause Daniel all manner of complications in his married life. Dewey, therefore, had less time for the Wheeler case than he had planned. It was a few days before February 20 that, like Adams, he realized that something drastic had to be done if Wheeler was to be saved. Whereas Adams' thoughts turned to helping Wheeler escape from prison, Dewey considered that a concentrated assault on Attorney- General Sullivan to change his position would prove to be Wheeler's lone chance for survival.

Dewey wrote a critical article on the Attorney-General's prosecution of the case in which he claimed that Sullivan had misinformed the Wheelers about the severity of the penalty that could be given Ephraim Wheeler. But the Federalist newspapers refused to print it lest it cause divisions in the Federalist camp before the elections. The Republican editors rejected it because Sullivan was their political leader and had to be supported right or wrong. Dewey then contacted John W. Hulbert, who had long ceased to be concerned about Wheeler, and insisted that they argue for a new trial on the ground that they had not time to prepare adequately for Wheeler's defense. "You must admit," Dewey wrote to Hulbert in Lenox, "that we allowed Sullivan to parade his witnesses without questioning them. We allowed Wheeler to be convicted under the general assumption that he was guilty. We allowed a father to be sent to his death on the word of his thirteen-year old daughter."

Hulbert in his reply believed that such an argument could not be sustained; at the very most it could delay execution by a few weeks, and that was unwise considering the resentment smoldering under the surface in parts of the population.

Dewey read between the lines. Hulbert was not concerned about the fate of a common laborer. He was concerned, however, about maintaining control within the State, and he was thinking about the upcoming elections. There was, therefore, only one thing to do: Dewey would humble himself before Sullivan and plead for Wheeler's life. It was with this object that he met Sullivan in his office on Tuesday morning two days before the proposed execution.

Sullivan welcomed him with a strong handshake and a solicitous frown. "You look ill, Daniel. Not been sleeping well?"

"You know what I'm worried over," Dewey said grimly. "I'll come to the point. I'm prepared to join your party, swing my influence behind your election as Governor, and I have quite a following as you are aware; I'll support the Republican political cause despite my misgivings of its true intentions towards the people, if you do one thing."

Sullivan opened his eyes wide and stared in a mixture of disbelief and humor at Dewey. "And what could I in my humble position do to merit such a generous offer?"

"Declare publicly that Wheeler's sentence should be commuted to imprisonment," Dewey said with an intensity that surprised Sullivan.

Sullivan sat back in his chair and stroked his chin to give him time to think. "You are really convinced we are hanging an innocent man, aren't you?"

Dewey nodded.

"Let me tell you why he cannot be helped. There is an air of revolution in our land. Violent uprising lies just under the surface. We've witnessed one very bloody revolution. We won it, and we're not going to lose it to anyone else." Sullivan's dark eyes flashed with anger. "The French gave the world a lesson in the savagery which a people can wreak on its rulers. Incessant internal conflict, thousands upon thousands butchered, and then Napoleon leading the whole murderous crew into the rest of Europe where they pillaged and burned. Yes, I am

253

Republican, but I know that the survival of my party depends upon our complete and utter divorce from Jacobinism. Our people are frightened, and well might they be, with mysterious characters like your friend, Adams, on the loose. My duty as Attorney-General is to protect our citizens from the murderous forces of Jacobinism We will not tolerate it. We will maintain the law and use the full power that it gives us to punish its transgressors. That is why, my friend, Ephraim Wheeler must hang."

"But he is not leading a revolution!" Dewey protested.

"He was in Shays' Rebellion. That was enough to hang him in the eyes of our jury," Sullivan said quickly. "And I have absolute faith in our jury. I have to demonstrate my faith in it if I want our democratic way to survive the test which your Jacobinical friends are putting it to."

"Wait just there!" Dewey raised his hand placatingly. "Those so-called Jacobins form a strong segment of your political party. You cannot expect to win an election without them. This Wheeler affair is not a central issue in the question of law and order. By giving in on it, you will be consolidating the strength of your party and winning more support for you personally."

"Oh!" Sullivan groaned with impatience. "Don't try to reason with me along political lines, Daniel. You are a political naïf." He stood up, put his hands in his coat pockets, and strode away from his desk. "I don't care about this election in May. I am planning to win the one after this. I've considered this very carefully. I can hold my party together from a viewpoint which you would consider monarchical, shades of George III," he smiled suddenly, "but which is the only way for us to win in the future. Our left wing, for all its protesting, has nowhere else to go. After Wheeler is executed, he will be forgotten within a month. That's the political reality, my dear Dan. That you cannot understand because you're too concerned about the welfare of the individual. As far as I'm concerned, Wheeler raped his daughter, the court in the name of the people will hang him, and Caleb Strong has to abide by the decision because, like the rest of us, he has to keep the Jacobins in check. As for your offer to trade parties, I don't need you or your influence. I shall win the election after this one simply because we are drifting into Republicanism."

"You are going to let Wheeler die because you want to control the drift," Dewey said sarcastically.

"Right you are," Sullivan replied sharply. "We cannot afford to risk the chaos which comes from allowing the radicals to stir up trouble."

There was a pause as Dewey sought some countervailing argument.

"Don't waste your breath, Daniel." Sullivan stepped toward him with his hand outstretched. "Enjoy married life, settle down and add to the reputation of our profession. I like your fiancee by the way."

Dewey stood up to shake his hand, and, mumbling his thanks, allowed himself to be escorted to the hall and to part amicably with his last hope for Wheeler's reprieve.

He walked disconsolately along the streets of Boston. He was depressed by his inadequacies to affect any change whatsoever. The thought occurred to him that he was being made to suffer now because he had failed to take seriously his responsibility as a lawyer for Wheeler's defense. But Lord! what a change in him over the intervening months! He was a very different man from the dilettante who seconded Hulbert's indifferent attitude during the trial, he thought. But that being said, there was nothing he could do, other than to feel very sorry for Ephraim Wheeler.

He wondered what Gentle Adams might be planning. Surely, he thought, this ingenious man was devising some way to rescue Wheeler.

Actually, at that very moment, Michael Pepper was riding into Lenox from Windsor. Adams' cryptic note had directed him to consult with Meacham about "freeing their pet." The "incapacity of G.A." kept him from "looking after the animal." Pepper waited over two hours at the tavern near the Court

House before Meacham came in to have his mid-day meal. The reporter saw him immediately, brushed his hand through his tousled hair, casually picked up a newspaper, and slid into the chair across the table from Pepper.

"Can you tell Wheeler tonight about our plans?" Pepper asked.

"What plans?" Meacham looked incredulous.

"I figure the only way we could rescue him is when he's left the prison to go to the Church on his way to the gallows." Pepper paused to see if Meacham was in accord.

Meacham shook his head. "He'll be in irons. He can't ride a horse carrying all that lead weight. And he'll be closely guarded. But you're right. That would be the best time to set him free."

Pepper looked at him in dismay. "Are you saying he can't be rescued?"

Meacham's resigned expression revealed his thought. The idea behind Wheeler, the idea of man's right not to be executed at the whim or prejudice of those in power, this idea had been motivating the Radical Republicans. The idea was still strong, but it was no longer associated strongly with Wheeler. Somehow Wheeler's fate had become bound up with Governor Strong's judgment of him. Republicans were trusting that Strong would show mercy to the poor man. "Nobody's going to risk his life for Wheeler."

The lean, raw-boned Pepper listened as if he were hearing his own death knell. "If only Gentle were here," he sighed. "He'd think of something."

"No, he wouldn't," Meacham said sadly. "There comes a time when you know you're beat, and you pick up your things ready to do battle another day." He signaled the bar girl for two beers. "Stay here for the execution," he said to Pepper, nodding his head with the significance of his meaning. "And you'll store up enough bitterness to make sure you're in the next fight."

"I've bitterness enough now," Pepper said between his teeth. "I never thought I'd be waiting for a reprieve from a Federalist Governor!"

"Strong could surprise us," Meacham said as he thought of the august figure, whose love of pomp and ceremony led him to have a guard of mounted boys dressed in gold braid to accompany him on State functions. "Somehow he might find mercy in his heart for a poor laborer."

THIRTY-EIGHT

Wheeler tried to avoid thinking of the rope on his neck and the sharp crack across his windpipe as he fell through the trap door. He prayed to God to move Governor Strong to commute his sentence, to soften men's hearts, but his pleas to the Almighty seemed feeble, as if undermined by the powerful intuition he had of his death. The day seemed interminable. Early in the morning he was able to fall asleep and won some hours of relief from the fearful end drawing close upon him.

The gaoler brought him a large breakfast with jam for his bread, which was unusual.

"It's the 20th at last," Ephraim said to him.

"Is there anything you want done?" the gaoler asked gently.

"What do you do for other men like me?" Ephraim asked, more out of curiosity than a wish for some favor.

"Only had one man who was hanged," the gaoler said, taken aback. "Some years past now. He gave me a letter for his wife."

Wheeler, turning pale, shook his head and said nothing.

Wheeler forced himself to eat. He relished the jam and, for an instant, fancied he was breakfasting in his own home preparatory to doing his chores on the farm. He grasped at other memories from his childhood, from his days at sea, with his friends, with Harriette--happy moments, all jumbled in no order, which he clung to as long as his mind would hold them. Time now began to move too quickly. At ten o'clock, the prison chaplain, Reverend Ayer, from the Congregational Church, entered his cell. Wheeler reminisced about his happy thoughts with him until Ayer, noting that time was slipping by, asked him to kneel in prayer.

Ephraim could no longer concentrate on the words the minister spoke. He sank his consciousness in the mood set by the man's calm and sonorous voice. They sat in silence for a few minutes, and then, just before eleven, the Reverend Ayer left the cell. Wheeler remained alone, waiting to be called to his death.

As if he were the angel of death, Sheriff Larned appeared before him. Larned's expression was conciliatory. The long mustache and stern lines of his face, which had made Wheeler quake at other times, now looked softened and kindly. He held out his arm as if he were to take Wheeler by the hand. But he was gesturing to his deputies behind him, who entered bearing a black wooden coffin, which they set down in the center of the cell.

"You'll sit on it, if you please, Wheeler," Larned commanded.

Ephraim carefully lifted his leg over the lid and straddled it. The deputies carried leg irons and chains into the cell.

"Can you bring your legs together as if you were squatting," Larned ordered.

Ephraim did as he was told. The deputies went methodically about their business of strapping the irons onto his ankles, linking the chains around his arms and wrist, and then securing them to the sides of the coffin where metal clasps had been fitted to receive them.

"Make yourself as comfortable as possible, Wheeler," the sheriff advised him. "You'll be sitting like that for some time."

Larned stood back, pulled out a pocket watch, and motioned to several deputies to pick up the coffin with Wheeler balanced on top of it. "Eleven," he said sharply. "The rest follow in formation behind the coffin. Go!"

Larned led them out of the cell, through the prison common room, where Ephraim caught sight of the gaoler and his family watching with fearful fascination, and heard cries of "God Speed" and "Take Courage" from some of his fellow prisoners, who watched through their cell doors. In the courtyard, the militia was drawn up. The cavalry rode in advance and on either side of the coffin. The infantry was drawn up in marching formation. Larned led his group of deputies bearing the coffin to a point in advance of the infantry. A small band in the midst of the infantry struck up a slow dirge, and the whole moved into the street and turned west toward Gallows Hill.

The sides of the streets were lined with people, who stood in a ghastly silence staring at Wheeler, who clung as best he could to the top of his coffin. The solemn procession turned away from West Street, which was the route to the Gallows, and followed a side road leading to the Meeting House, about which it seemed thousands of people were gathered.

Ephraim gazed in wonder at such crowds. He was amazed that he could be the focus of so much attention. The silence of the crowd and the somber music cast a spell over the scene that transformed it to a spiritual experience.

Every seat in the Meeting House was taken. People stood along the walls. A sea of faces turned to watch Wheeler being carried behind Colonel Larned down the center isle. The military band, which remained outside with the militia, continued to play until Wheeler was set down before the platform at the front of the hall, when a man at the door signaled it to cease.

The sudden silence was spell-binding. Wheeler almost forgot that he was to be executed. He looked about to see what would happen next.

A tall, thin, rake-like figure in black glided from a side door into the pulpit. His blue eyes gleaming down at the prisoner, his long gray hair hanging in thick curly bands about his shoulders, the Reverend Samuel Shepard stretched out his arms as if they were an eagle's talons and he were about to make a strike.

"Probationers, placed here on earth," his voice crackled as if the divine fury within him were breaking out of his body to thunder down at his listeners, "we are all bound to another state of existence." His voice hardened. "To a world of light and joy," he cast his eyes at the ceiling, "or to the regions of darkness and woe," he glanced down at Wheeler. "Which of these is to be our destiny is determined by our character. In our hearts, we carry our title either to eternal glory, or infinite wretchedness. Read we our hearts, then," he called out, as if challenging the almost one thousand persons who could hear his voice both inside the Meeting Hall and standing by the open windows outside in the snow, "and we read what is to befall us, beyond the grave. The dying man," he looked down at Wheeler, "needs not inspiration to inform him to what world he is hastening; for, he may read the decree of the Eternal God written on his own heart!"

Michael Pepper and Mallard Meacham stood listening at the back of the Meeting Hall. Whereas Pepper was thinking how the deputies might have been overpowered, and Wheeler hustled out the back door of the Meeting Hall and away in a carriage before the militia out front were alerted, Meacham was listening to Shepard's words to detect signs of leniency or forgiveness toward the prisoner. If Governor Strong intended to commute Wheeler's sentence to life imprisonment, the Reverend Shepard would be told of it beforehand in order to fashion his sermon accordingly.

"Called as we are this day," Shepard intoned, looking to the back of the Hall, "to attend the execution of an unhappy man, under sentence of death by the laws of his country, our minds should be filled with awe. Viewing him, also, as standing on the borders of the eternal world, and, according to his own concessions, conscious that he is 'in the gall of bitterness, and in the bond of iniquity,' we should listen, as if to hear him explain, 'Lord, save me.' This is the language of one in imminent danger, and is recorded in the Gospel according to Matthew XIV, Chapter and Part of the 30th verse--'AND--HE CRIED, SAYING LORD, SAVE ME.'"

Meacham dropped his chin on his chest. There was no hope for Wheeler. Shepard's message to the hopeful was that only God could save Wheeler now. He heard Shepard rail on about discharging debts to God for a sin that no good works can atone for.

Elsewhere in the Hall sat Justice Walker, bored with the minister's rhetoric and impatient for the hanging to be over with. He yearned to be free of the whole affair and return to the quiet of his judicial fiefdom in Windsor, content in the likelihood that no incident as serious as this one would ever occur in his territory again within his lifetime.

Colonel Larned stood at ease, and, looking back at his men, signified that they were to do so as well. He felt sorry for Wheeler who would be perched uncomfortably on his coffin for three hours. In a way, he regretted having to hang him. The whole business was wrong to his way of thinking. But the State had to be served, the decorum had to be preserved, and he took comfort from the fact that he was an important member of the procession, the leader, as it were, of orderliness and discipline.

"See him, when about to enter 'the valley of the shadow of death!'" Shepard continued. "He looks back on his past unhappy life with an aching heart, and forward into eternity without a ray of comfort!"

Larned, in company with others listening, began to dream about life gone by and possible sins.

"Clouds and darkness involve him, and the joys of immortality, bear not on his beknighted soul."

Although Ephraim could not understand the exact meaning of the words, he realized that the Reverend was speaking about him. He looked at his legs cramped into iron bands and beginning to pain him. The gloom of the assembly depressed him now. He hung his head and tried to keep his composure, tried to rest his back, which had to strain to support the chains that bound him to his coffin. He stopped listening to the words, and tried to think of the past. Harriette's face, laughing in the early years of their marriage, came into his mind. He was overcome with sadness at the way his life had worked itself out. It all seemed useless, a foolish exercise or experiment or whatever it was. Just foolish, of no consequence.

He caught sight of John W. Hulbert sitting to the right of his coffin. The lawyer was listening enraptured by the sermon. Ephraim bore him no resentment, even if he did represent that large group of people who had made life difficult for him wherever he went and who was sending him to the next world. They would be following him, he thought.

"Let us who are enabled to maintain a good reputation in the community behold the man!" Shepard cried.

Hulbert looked at Wheeler.

"And make the interesting inquiry 'who maketh us to differ?' And let them be thankful for any restraints which are laid upon the evil propensities of the human heart; for without the restraining grace of God, what is there to be found in the heart of man, naturally, as a security against the commission of those crimes, which would put our friends and enemies to an eternal blush?"

Ephraim recognized the language as meant for the educated like Hulbert. He was shut out from it as he had always been. He knew too that the long peroration must be coming to an end because speeches always concluded soon after they addressed the educated.

"Let all who have a heart to pray, behold the man! and carry him this moment, in the arms of their faith and prayer to the throne of grace--lay him down at the feet of the divine sovereignty--and ask that his sins may be done away by divine mercy." Recognizing the concluding tone, Wheeler straightened himself, and, despite the shoots of pain in his legs, held his head high, staring ahead, seeing nothing. "And his pardon be sealed in Heaven, before he goes hence to be here no more!"

Shepard's voice cracked. He raised his arms as if supplicating God. "Let the painful scene before us...but...I can say no more...." There were tears on the faces of some listeners. "Silent tears, and that anguish of soul excited in view of the multiplied miseries of man which sin hath procured..." there were groans of remorse from several in the large crowd, "must speak the rest." Shepard lowered his arms and let his head drop onto his chest.

Wheeler took a deep breath of relief. He felt as if he were witnessing someone else's execution.

A stranger, obviously a gentleman, rather handsome, smiled at him, and asked if he still hoped for a reprieve from the Governor.

"Yes, because when I was in France, I, on one occasion, had to be saved from death by friends at the last moment," Wheeler said.

His coffin, on which he was still perched, was lifted up by the deputy sheriffs. Colonel Larned took the lead out of the Meeting Hall, and Wheeler had time only to nod good-bye to the stranger before he was carried away.

The crowd outside was immense--in the thousands. As the group carrying Wheeler on his black coffin stepped out, the sun broke free of the clouds and lit up the green and yellow coats of the cavalry and infantrymen, who were standing in formation, ready to receive the prisoner once more. Some people looked skyward with happy exclamations as if the sun augured good tidings. The gloom of the long service seemed to have dissipated, but there remained the terrible, awesome silence, as the people quietly followed the procession with its mournful music back to West Street and up to Gallows Hill.

Meacham, following in its wake with Pepper, listened to the occasional whispering in the crowd, and learned that a great many people hoped, some even expected, that Governor

Strong was going to intervene somehow. None of the Government officials from Boston was present. Dewey, who hated executions, did not come, and the Bryants, who opposed capital punishment, stayed away. Peter Bryant spent the hours after noontime talking with Betsy, who, as if by clairvoyance, sensed her father's slow and painful ride to the gallows at that time.

Gallows Hill was a hillock on the side of the steep hill that one climbed to leave Lenox for the West country. There had been a few hangings there over the years. The crowd lined the hillside from the gallows down to the foot of the hill. Meacham spoke to the militia commander, who informed him that the official count was five thousand persons, but he believed there were many more. Meacham was amazed at the orderliness of the people and unnerved by their stillness. They stared as one, waiting for the drama to unfold, tense with expectation.

Wheeler could no longer avoid thinking of his death. His aside to the stranger about his escape from death in France was wishful thinking about the present and a bit of bravado. With the gallows in sight, its long rope and platform over a steep drop in the hill looming before him, he suddenly lost all hope. Meacham reached his side at that moment. Wheeler recognized the tousle-headed reporter who had once interviewed him in prison, walking alongside his casket.

"Holding up all right?" Meacham asked.

Ephraim smiled sarcastically. "They're holding me up all right. I'm getting sick of this."

"Do you still claim you didn't rape your daughter?" Meacham raised his eyebrows as if to indicate that this was his last chance to tell the truth.

"Whatever went between me and Betsy," Wheeler said, "was agreed on."

Meacham glanced at Sheriff Larned, who had heard the exchange and who looked round from where he was marching in front of the casket in alarm.

"She consented?" Meacham asked.

Wheeler, clenching his teeth, looked away and refused to answer. Larned gestured to Meacham to get back into the crowd following the procession.

With each measured step toward the gallows, Larned disliked his role in this spectacle less and less. He disliked the impression he was giving that he was Wheeler's nemesis, escorting him to the gallows, making sure that there were no deviations on Wheeler's road to perdition. He took his watch from his pocket; it was now after one-thirty; the sermon had lasted over two hours; the procession ought to deposit Wheeler in the shed beside the gallows by two. He heaved a sigh. Everything was going smoothly.

Just before two, they reached the crest of Gallows Hill. Wheeler was taken off his coffin. His legs were freed and his chains were removed. He was led into the waiting shed by two green-coated guards.

The dark and damp shed with its one small window suddenly brought home to Wheeler the fact that he would soon be dead. For the past three hours, while he had been on exhibit, he had kept his composure, but now he dropped his head in his hands in despair. He saw his life as a total mess, a waste, a mixture of embarrassments and stupidities. He remembered scenes that he had never thought of and faces that he had forgotten. He thought of Harriette and the love they had had at one time. Betsy and young Ephraim as children ran across his mind. This whole crazy, unexpected happening seemed a result of the great mix-up, nay, disorder in his life. Had he not worked hard? Had he not provided somehow? What went wrong? Why did it happen to him? The sensation of intercourse with Betsy crept like a furry beast over his flesh, but his mind refused to picture the sacrilege. How did he allow it to happen? He stood up and gazed sullenly out the little window at the thousands of spectators solemnly standing below the gallows. He could see the bands of people hurrying in the distance toward them as if they feared to be late. The picture of his shipmates rescuing him from the hangman in a small French town came back to him. He began to yearn for those same faces, gleeful and excited, to appear before him now. A guard, a tall muscular man, took him by one arm, and motioned for him to return to sit on the bench between him and his militia companion, an older man who feigned indifference to the proceedings.

Meanwhile Sheriff Larned conducted local officials and their wives to chairs set up on a platform placed near the gallows and facing the hanging rope from the side. Larned was impressed by the solemnity and disciplined behavior of the crowd. What did this stillness and concentrated awe portend? he wondered. Was it a disbelief amongst the people that what was actually happening could be taking place? A man hanged for raping his daughter! No better example, he thought, could be provided of the power of authority to direct people's lives. They seemed suspended in a mood of expectancy and passivity. The horror and shame that Wheeler had brought upon them by his act no longer seemed important, or even remembered.

The sympathy Larned had once felt for Wheeler, but had effectively suppressed, now came over him again, and he had to turn aside to pause, looking down as if subduing an impulse to call off the whole affair, to declare Wheeler a free man, and to break this spell, which held the spectators bound helpless to the will of the men who feared "the evil" in the State. That so-called "evil" was French republicanism, which he admired. He knew that in the end, Wheeler had to die because the Old World had been shattered by the events of the French Revolution. Republicans like Gentle Adams had heard the message from across the water and were preparing to bring in the new order for Massachusetts. Yes, he thought, that was why he felt sorry for Wheeler. But Wheeler was just another victim to the cause. He would be taking his place with the graves of those who fell in Shays' Rebellion, and who fell in those small outbreaks of resistance that were quickly and easily quelled by the militarized State, which waited and watched for disaffection in after years. With an effort, he moved away to direct his deputies in the seating of other local dignitaries, in the inspecting of the hanging apparatus, an in the mingling in the crowd to watch for any sign of a last-minute attempt at rescue.

The Reverend Ayer, a kindly young man with a sorrowful face and a patient disposition, entered the shed. He asked the militiamen to leave him alone with the prisoner. The tall guard was unwilling to move, but the older guard with a motion of impatience told him to come outside.

When they had gone, the Reverend asked Wheeler if he had anything to confess. "You must not go into eternity with the burden of untruth on your soul."

Wheeler looked apprehensively at him, and then, his words bursting forth in an emotional appeal, he cried: "Believe me, oh God, believe me, I never, never thought of raping Betsy. It never occurred to me, never, never! I couldn't do that to my own daughter! I couldn't do it to anyone!" Tears came into his eyes with the frustration and the helplessness of his position.

"Is that your last word on the subject?" Ayer asked, his brown eyes looking hurt by the pain Wheeler was revealing for the first time.

Wheeler nodded, and, with his arm, wiped the tears streaming down his cheeks. "I forgive my wife, I forgive Betsy, I forgive them for everything. They're not to blame. There's no blame attaching to them. Will you tell them that?" He choked, paused, and cleared his throat. "Please tell all those people that I forgive my wife and daughter."

"Yes, I will," Ayer said, moved by Wheeler's display of emotion. "Shall we pray."

Wheeler knelt beside the bench, and the Reverend knelt beside him. Together they said the Lord's Prayer.

"We'll pray silently for a moment," Ayer suggested.

Ephraim could think of nothing more to say, his mind swirled with images of people, and he felt ill to his stomach. After a moment, he stood up, and, as the Reverend stood beside him, he thanked him. For Ephraim, time had stopped. He seemed to be trapped in a gray area, as if he were already in eternity. The minister left him, and his guards returned to sit on either side of him.

Sheriff Larned spoke with the hangman, who had stepped unobserved from a group of men standing at the back of the gallows. He wore a black hood. Larned knew him yet was taken aback at the fierce anonymity that the mask gave him. The man's long, strong arms, his barrel chest, and thick legs gave him the impression of a huge insect come forth to grapple with its prey.

"Have you gone over the equipment thoroughly?" he asked sternly.

"Yes, sir, thoroughly."

"There will be no problems?"

"No problems, sir. He'll be dead in seconds."

Larned looked down at the trap door and thought of the swift fall through it. He gazed out over the multitude congregated in a dense mass on the slopes of the hill below, to the sides of the gallows, and some on the hill above. The sun was bright now. The mood was tense. He glanced at the officials, sitting composedly on their chairs and waiting patiently for the appearance of the prisoner. Taking out his watch, he saw that it was five minutes to three. He went into the shed and asked Wheeler to walk with him onto the gallows.

Wheeler was slightly weak in the knees when he stood but recovered quickly, and, refusing the help of the guards, he walked out of the shed door. He stepped with Larned to the center of the gallows platform. The noose of the rope shivered in a slight breeze that blew coldly upon the face, reminding everyone that, despite the thawing snow, it was still winter.

Wheeler looked abashed at the officials, dressed in fine clothes, who stared in curiosity at his every movement. The hush of the immense crowd, which was watching him as if it were one great eye, sent an inexplicable fright through him. He turned to the Reverend Ayer, who had come onto the platform to stand beside him, and said to him in a choking voice: "Tell them I am innocent of the charge against me."

There was a murmuring in the crowd that sounded like a hive of bees. Wheeler spoke to Ayer again. The minister bent his ear close to Wheeler to hear him, so strained had Wheeler's voice become.

"He wants me to tell you," Ayer shouted. "He wants me to tell you." Again he had to swallow away the emotion that came to his throat. "That he has been wrongfully accused."

The murmur of the crowd began to rise again, this time in a wave of sound that began with those standing close-by and continuing to the foot of the hill in the distance.

Wheeler seized the Reverend's arm and said something to him that he had to repeat because the minister had not heard. Ayer took his arm away from Wheeler's grasp and held his hand as if questioning him.

Ayer turned again to the multitude which seemed to strain in expectation. "He forgives his accusers and all the world," Ayer cried out tearfully. Then fearing that his emotion had prevented his voice from carrying, he cried again, "He forgives his accusers and all the world. He is prepared to die."

Such an announcement, made beside the hanging rope and the hangman, could only sound pathetic. Larned sensed the pity rising in the crowd. He reached for a paper in his inside coat pocket and stepped to the front of the platform. There were cries of delight, cheers, a sudden expression of happy relief, as for a brief instant the solemnity of the crowd dissolved in hopeful expectancy. Everyone thought that Larned was about to read a message from Governor Strong commuting the sentence to imprisonment.

Wheeler felt the expression of joy and gazed in wonder at Larned, scarcely hoping that it was a reprieve. He glanced at the crowd near the gallows and caught Michael Pepper's eye. Michael, smiling at him, raised his hands, clasped strongly above his head. Wheeler smiled sadly in reply.

Larned, clearing his throat and putting the best face he could on his predicament, read from the paper to Wheeler: "In the name of the people of the Commonwealth of Massachusetts, the Governor and the Legislative Council, according to the laws of the State, hereby condemn Ephraim Wheeler of the town of Windsor, found guilty of the crime of rape, to be hanged by the neck until he is dead."

A few groans greeted the Death Warrant, and a glumness fell over the crowd, which began to prepare itself for the event.

Ephraim's shoulders sank slightly, but he picked up his head as Larned finished reading the warrant. There was not a sound, not even the noises of birds, or the wind in the trees, as the hangman led Wheeler under the noose and placed the rope firmly around his neck.

The Reverend Ayer and Colonel Larned moved to the side of the platform. The Colonel glanced at his watch. It was sharp on three and he nodded at the hangman. Wheeler stood as if abruptly miniaturized in this great scene of hill and sky and the horde of silent people. Then he was gone. The spectators stayed motionless watching the dangling body, its neck broken, until Sheriff Larned stepped forward to instruct his deputies to bring forth the coffin.

Some people began to move then, but the bulk remained to watch a doctor examine the body, which the hangman lowered to the ground, and to see the deputies deposit the body in the long black coffin.

The cavalry and the infantry formed themselves at the foot of the hill as the people made way for them. The band struck up a sprightly march. Relief broke over the crowd, which began to chatter and laugh. The deputies carried the coffin to a central place among the infantry, and, led by the cavalry, the procession marched in a rather disorderly and happy fashion back into town. Sheriff Larned did not walk with it. He went over to the local officials and walked with the leaders of Lenox in deep conversation back to their houses and to an entertainment to be attended by certain selected guests.

The deputies carried the coffin in the midst of the cavalry and infantry back through town, past the gaol, and on to the burial ground.

A grave had been dug but was not yet finished. The military and the several hundreds, which were still in attendance, stayed back while the deputies put the coffin beside the open grave. The Reverend Ayer, looking pale and chastened from his last moments with Wheeler, came forward to say a prayer. His voice carried clearly, as there was very little wind and the people had fallen almost as quiet as they were at the gallows.

Meacham and Pepper stayed for a while after the military, the deputies, and the curious had left. The sun glanced off the top of the black coffin giving it a glistening sheen. Two gravediggers approached, took up their spades, and jumped into the grave to continue their work.

"It's sad," Michael Pepper said. "I knew him a long time, and he wasn't a bad sort. It's very sad."

"It's a goddamn shame!" Meacham cried angrily. "What good does it do anyone? Just a lot of harm. His family is going to suffer, if it survives."

"Harriette Wheeler will be all right," Pepper said. "She's tough. Trouble is, now that Wheeler is dead, the talk against her could get worse."

"Right," Meacham agreed. "It should be against the Government. I'll write a short piece for my paper describing the hanging, and I'll tack on a strong criticism of our benevolent Governor Strong." He gave Pepper a sarcastic smile. "Come on, let's have a drink. Ephraim Wheeler can be left alone now."

Meacham's caustic reportage in the Pittsfield *Sun* brought furious retorts from Federalist newspapers, whose editors defended Governor Strong and his decision not to commute Wheeler's sentence. The weeks of Spring passed quickly to the election day of May 28, 1806. As the Governor, the legislative body, and a large audience met to hear the traditional sermon in the State House before the results were announced, it was whispered about that Governor Strong had been re-elected.

The Reverend Samuel Shepard preached the sermon and arranged the wording to reflect the Governor's re-election with praise for his wise and considerate manner of governing. The Reverend, in the course of his sermon, however, did allude in a veiled way to the threat from the opposition, to which the case of Ephraim Wheeler gave substance. "As public conflagrations do not always begin in public edifices, but are caused more frequently by some lamp, neglected in a private house; so, in the administration of states, it does not always happen that the flame of sedition arises from political dissensions, which, running through a long chain of connections, at length affect the whole body of the people."

Caleb Strong took the Governor's chair once more and gave his State Message, but he was there on sufferance only. The people withheld their approval of Sullivan, as he suspected they would, because he had prosecuted Wheeler. The Republicans gained strength within the Commonwealth, but Colonel Larned did not hold his Congressional seat. The voters may have forgiven him for capturing Wheeler, but the picture of his conducting Wheeler to the gallows in his role of County Sheriff remained in the public memory to condemn him at the polls.

The following year, May 1807, the people relented and elected James Sullivan to the Governorship, but his great energy deserted him within months, and he died before the close of his term.

Judge Simeon Strong died two months before Wheeler was hanged and could not take part with his fellow judges and other members of the Essex Junto in defeating all efforts to legislate an end to capital punishment.

Gentle Adams, when he recovered from his shoulder wound, went with Molly Givens, under the protection of Sheriff

Larned, out of the State, and eventually settled in Barbados. Fifteen years later Molly and Gentle returned with wealth to settle in Boston. In the meantime, Caleb Strong and the Federalists returned to the Governorship for several years before they relinquished power once and for all to the liberal parties.

Daniel Dewey married Susanna in June 1806. When Strong returned as Governor after the death of Sullivan, Dewey was appointed to Governor Strong's slightly liberalized Council, and later he became a U. S. Congressman. John Hulbert also became a Congressman.

The Wheelers did not fare so well. Betsy went into shock when she heard of her father's execution. She would not talk for weeks. Dr. Bryant tried to bring her out of her shell without success. She was thought by the townspeople of Cummington to be "simple," and, in after years in stories told of the event, she was blamed for her father's conviction because her "simple" mind had been easily led to make up the charge of rape by her vindictive mother. Harriette Wheeler took the brunt of the criticism. She could not shop in town without encountering the hostility of her neighbors and rudeness from the shopkeepers. That summer of 1806, in deference to the future of her children, especially young Ephie and the baby, she prevailed upon her brother to sell his farm and take the family westward. Odel left no forwarding address, and not even the Bryants knew what happened to the Wheelers.

Dr. Peter Bryant tended to the sick in Cummington and neighboring towns with an ever-growing reputation for his medical powers. He taught his sickly son to strengthen his body by exercising with the elements of nature. Perhaps the Doctor's understanding that his physic for the body was also a spirit for the soul led his son, William Cullen Bryant, to become one of the world's great nature poets.

Mallard Meacham, the reporter, printed a small pamphlet about the life and trial of Ephraim Wheeler for the edification of posterity. He tried to paint an objective picture of the man, but, in after years, he realized that Wheeler's character could never have been reformed. Like all men, he had been made up of contradictions, but his one constant trait was his self-delusion.

The next execution in Massachusetts was in 1813, and it was for the same offense, when a colored man raped his daughter. The following execution took place in 1819 and was also for the same offense: rape of a girl by her father. Both these executions took place on Gallows Hill in Lenox and drew an immense multitude of spectators.

finis

After the American Revolution, the United States had one political party, the Federalists. By the time of this story, 1805, Thomas Jefferson and James Madison had founded the Republican Party, which was the antecedent of the Democratic Party of the twentieth century. The Republican Party had won the Federal election, but the Federalists were still in power in the more conservative Commonwealth of Massachusetts. Shays' Rebellion (1787) was an uprising of the farmers and artisans of Western Massachusetts against the ruling classes, who had impoverished the farmers with high taxation to pay for the huge war debt after the Revolution. Taxes and the reimposition of private debts, suspended during the War, reduced multitudes to beggary. Veterans called for another revolution when they had to pay in coin which was not available because the imbalance of trade against the American States had drained Massachusetts of its currency and the legislature refused to issue paper money. As a result of the many legal actions and land foreclosures the lawyers grew richer. The name "River Gods" was given to the ruling classes in Massachusetts because they lived near the Connecticut and Housatonic Rivers.

The story of Ephraim Wheeler comes from a rare pamphlet of twenty-three pages printed in 1806. It was brought to my attention in New York by a friend representing a client who wished to sell it to the Research Libraries. She suggested that I write a novel on its theme because of its relevance to our day.

D.R.B.

SOURCES

PRIMARY

WHEELER, Ephraim (1762-1806). *Narrative of the Life of Ephraim Wheeler Who Was executed at Lenox February 20, 1806. For a rape on the body of his daughter penned from his mouth and signed by him, the evening before his execution.* Stockbridge, Printed by H. Willard, March 1806.

WHEELER, Ephraim, defendant. *Report of the trial of Ephraim Wheeler, for a rape committed on the body of Betsy Wheeler, his daughter, a girl of thirteen years of age. Before the Supreme Judicial Court, holden at Lenox, within and for the county of Berkshire, on the second Tuesday of September, 1805.* Pub... according to act of Congress. Stockbridge, H. Willard, 1805.

SHEPARD, Samuel (1772-1846). *A sermon delivered at Lenox (Massachusetts) February 20, 1806; being the day of execution of Ephraim Wheeler, pursuant to his sentence, for a rape committed on his daughter, Betsy Wheeler.* Published at the request of his hearers. 2nd Stockbridge edition; Stockbridge, Printed by H. Willard, April 1806.

SHEPARD, Samuel. *Election Sermon, May 28, 1806.* Stockbridge, 1806.

"Legislative History of Capital Punishment in Massachusetts," *Mass. House Document 2575 (1959),* p.98-110.

Sarah Bryant of Cummington, "Diary, June 1794-May 1819." *Harpers Magazine,* September 1894, p.633ff.

Pittsfield *Sun,* 1805-1807.

SECONDARY

Historical.

Bidwell, Barnabas. *Address to the People of Massachusetts, February, 1805.* [n.p.] 1805.

Birdsall, Richard D, "The Reverend Thomas Allen: Jeffersonian Calvinist," *New England Quarterly,* v.30, (June 1957).

Davis, Thomas L., "Aristocrats and Jacobins in Country Towns: Party Formation in Berkshire County (1715-1816)," Ph.D.. Diss., Boston University, 1975.

Hale, Richard, "The American Revolution in Western Massachusetts," *New England Historical and Genealogical Register,* v.129, (October 1975).

Strong, Caleb. *Patriotism and Piety; the Speeches of his Excellency Caleb Strong, Esq....from 1800 to 1807.* Newburyport, Printed by Edmund M. Blunt, 1808.

Sullivan, James. *An impartial review of the causes and principles of the French revolution.* Boston; Benjamin Edes, 1798.

Taylor, Robert, *Western Massachusetts in the Revolution,* "Chapter VII, Shays' Rebellion." Providence, R.I.; Brown Univ. Press, 1954.

Vaughan, Alden, "The Horrid and Unnatural Rebellion of Daniel Shays," *American Heritage,* v.17, (1966).

Wood, David H. *Lenox, Massachusetts, Shire Town.* Published by the Town, 1969.

Psychology

Hobson, William Frederick, Cheryl Boland, and Diane Jamieson, "Dangerous Sexual Offenders," *Medical Aspects of Human Sexuality,* v.19, no.2, (February 1985).

Pelletier, Guy and Lee C. Handy, "Family Dysfunction and the Psychological Impact of Child Sexual Abuse," *Canadian Journal of Psychiatry,* v.31, (June 1986).

BOOKS BY DAVID BEASLEY IN PRINT ELSEWHERE

The Canadian Don Quixote; The Life and Works of
Major John Richardson, Canada's First Novelist
(Erin, Ont: Porcupine's Quill) $6.95 (C) "Definitve
work"; "Not only a good read but the fulfillment of
'an aching void'." *Brick;* "very useful" *Globe & Mail*

How To Use A Research Library (New York City;
Oxford Univ. Press) $9.95(U.S.). "Communicates well
the excitement of doing research," *Library Journal.*

The Suppression of the Automobile; Skulduggery at
the Crossroads (Westport, CT, Greenwood Press)
"Railroad interests did all they could to prevent the
development of the automobile in the 1830s" *Journal
of Economic Literature* "Excellent...superbly spun
story...thorough research," *SAH Journal.*

EDITOR
MAJOR JOHN RICHARDSON: SHORT STORIES (PENTICTON,
B.C.; THEYTUS BOOKS) (THEY DEAL LARGELY WITH THE AMERICAN
INDIAN. MAJOR RICHARDSON WAS RECOGNIZED AS THE BEST
WRITER OF INDIAN TALES--CANADIAN CONSULATE GENERAL, NEW
YORK CITY) $5.95(U.S.), $6.95 (CAN)